BLOOD

TIES

Books by Kelly Clayton

The Jack Le Claire Mystery series

Blood In The Sand (2015)

Blood Ties (2016)

BLOOD TIES

KELLY CLAYTON

Published by Stanfred Publishing 2016

ISBN: 978-0-9934830-2-8

Book design: Dean Fetzer, www.gunboss.com
Cover design: Kit Foster Design, www.kitfosterdesign.com

For Drena and Clem,
Mum and Dad Number Two

Thank you for everything

Prologue

Jersey, Channel Islands

Scott Hamlyn knew three things to be absolute truths: he was not the most prepossessing of men, his one talent was the law and his entire future happiness – and that of those he loved – depended upon what happened this evening.

His stomach lurched as he crept through the gardens. He had skirted the main house, as directed, and followed the line of the high wall to where it opened onto a courtyard in front of a large granite building, the style in keeping with the ancient manor.

He looked back across the lawns. Lights blazed from the bank of ground-floor windows, and there was a constant thrum of noise from the party. He quickly patted the bulge in his inside jacket pocket. It was all going to be fine. It had to be – her future depended on his next actions.

His back against the brick, he inched around to the doorway. He felt like a fool but couldn't risk being seen – he wanted no backlash from tonight. He didn't need any rumours to spoil the future. His hand fumbled in the darkness until it connected with the door handle; he pushed down on the thick metal, and as the door swung inwards, he instantly recoiled from the blast of balmy heat.

The only light in the huge space came from the spotlights embedded in the sides and bottom of the swimming pool, which turned the sparkling water a glittering turquoise. There was a noise to his right, the slap of shoes on tiles, and he spun round. He tried to school his features, but he knew the initial shock of surprise would have been plain on his face.

"I wasn't expecting you." He cursed the tremor in his voice, but he was anxious, and it was already going wrong.

The harsh laugh echoed through the pool house. "I'm sure you weren't, but it's me you have to deal with tonight."

"I don't understand." Scott shook his head, trying to rid himself of his jumbled thoughts. "Did you send me the message? You're DarkRider1?"

A bow was made that mocked the situation. "That's me, at your service."

Scott couldn't get his mind to work as thoughts jumped and jarred. "Why here? The place is overrun tonight with the party going on."

"Indeed, and therefore the perfect place to throw shade on our discussions. Plus, I knew you could get in unnoticed."

Scott swallowed and cleared his throat. "Okay, fine. I don't get all the cloak-and-dagger stuff. And I certainly don't understand why you're doing this."

The words were snarled. "All that fancy education, those brains, and yet the simplest concepts are beyond you. My message said it all – 'I know everything'. Wow, what a scandal if that dirty little titbit gets out. You need to be careful what you leave lying around." The words were punctuated with a snigger. "That's the problem with secrets; as soon as more than one person knows, they won't stay hidden forever."

"Why are you doing this? What do you get out of my misery?"

"What I get out of it is down to you."

"Jesus, I don't even recognise you like this. All you're going to do is hurt someone who doesn't deserve it."

"Oh, it's deserved all right."

Scott tried to dampen his rising panic, to no avail. He hated the unsteadiness in his voice and detested the words he had to speak. "Don't do this, please. Don't ruin all our lives on a whim."

"By tomorrow night, the island will eagerly be digesting all the salacious details unless you walk away."

"Please don't do this. You know I can't do that." He tugged at his collar; the bow tie was digging into his throat, and he gasped in some air to clear the suffocating feeling.

"And we both know, dear Scott, that you've got another little time bomb ticking away. What if that came out as well? The family would be completely ruined. I told you; it's time for you to make some decisions. Walk away from one and you protect the other. Consider what's important to you."

"We can work this out. Look…"

He reached into his pocket and stopped in shock as hurried footsteps preceded the quick hands that rammed against him. He took a moment to steady himself. There was no softness in the familiar voice. "Easy! What have you got in your pocket? Don't be stupid."

Sweat was pouring off his brow as he stumbled over his words. "You don't understand. Look…"

He withdrew his hand and held the white envelope in the air, but a violent shove pushed him backward. His leather-soled dress shoes were slickened by the moist heat of the pool tiles, and he struggled to keep his footing. His feet slipped and slid, his arms windmilled. His attacker stood back, no emotion showing. No movement to assist.

The envelope tumbled to the floor, and its contents poured out. Wads of money scattered on the tiles, tumbling into the pool and floating on the surface.

He saw familiar features shift, settle into a feral grin as lips pulled back and teeth were bared. He realised the moment the decision was made, but he wasn't expecting the punch to his stomach, wasn't prepared. He crashed to the floor. The last thing he heard was a sickening thud; the last he saw was a well-known, grinning face.

CHAPTER ONE

The party was in full flow. Over three hundred people were crammed into the manor's main entertainment space. The original eighteenth-century ballroom and vast hallway were now modernised with gleaming checkerboard floors, huge abstract candelabra flickering with imitation flames and recessed lighting that cast a flattering glow.

Dinner-suited men and beautifully gowned women mingled, catching up with friends, meeting new contacts and eyeing up the next conquest. The room reeked of money, and the filthy lucre was the reason most people were here tonight. The manor's new owner, Aidan Gillespie, was a self-made man, and rumour had it that he had made a lot.

DCI Jack Le Claire of the States of Jersey Police hated parties. He disliked feeling trussed up in a bow tie and constricting wing-collar shirt, and he abhorred meaningless social chitchat as people attempted to show off their wealth and make political friends. Most of all, Le Claire detested being trooped on parade as his father's supposedly tame little policeman. Philip Le Claire was well-known in the island, had even been a Senator in the Jersey parliament for a while and continued to make money from a plethora of business interests. Le Claire hadn't seen his father in the hours since they had arrived. No doubt he was schmoozing with the great and the mighty – certainly the rich.

"Jack, for the love of God, put a smile on your face and stop grimacing. Aidan Gillespie has done us the courtesy of inviting us here this evening to celebrate the manor's renovation; you have a glass of Dom Perignon in your hand and a beautiful woman on your arm. It isn't a torture to be here."

His mother's voice was tinged with habitual exasperation, and Le Claire sheepishly admitted to himself that, as he was here, he may as well stop complaining and just enjoy the evening. "You are, as usual, absolutely right." He turned to his date. "Sorry, Sasha, I'll buck up. It is our first public outing after all."

His wife rolled her eyes and lightly punched his arm, her gaze warm and eyes playful. "Jack, if anyone asks, just introduce me properly – that way we won't get twenty questions."

"So I should just say you're my estranged wife who has finally, reluctantly, agreed to go on a date with me?"

Sasha's smile was wide and her eyes crinkled at the corners as she laughed; a throaty, sexy sound that caught the attention of more than one man around them. Le Claire felt possessiveness rise as he looked at Sasha – properly looked at her – and saw her through the eyes of others. Her shiny dark hair was swept back on one side by jewelled combs and fell over the other shoulder in a sweep of chestnut-brown curls. She wore more makeup than usual, eyes lined in party kohl, her full mouth emphasised by pinkish lipstick. Her dress was a Grecian affair, draped over one shoulder with an ornate clasp; the pale pink silk hugged and caressed her body. His wife might be devoted to yoga, but it hadn't diminished her gentle curves, only enhanced them with taut, toned skin.

"You don't have to tell the whole truth, Jack! Stop being a policeman just for tonight."

His mother's voice broke across their conversation. "Jack, Sasha, you remember Caro Armstrong?"

Le Claire didn't have a clue who the coiffed and primped middle-aged blonde was, but he could play the social game when pushed. "Of course, how are you?"

"I was just saying to your mother that she better be careful with her help. My girl seemed like a dream. Well behaved, intelligent – you know these girls, Polish, Romanian, whatever, come to Jersey to better their English, and they are happy to work as au pairs and suchlike. Well, Katrina seemed to enjoy looking after my two kids, her bedroom was more like a studio apartment and she had every evening and most weekends off. So I couldn't believe what she did. I just couldn't."

It took Le Claire a moment to realise that Caro Armstrong had stopped talking and that all three women were looking expectantly at him. He stepped up to the mark. "What did she do?"

A vicious look wiped any attractiveness from her face. "She skipped out on me. Went away with a boyfriend for the weekend and never came back. She even left some of her junk, and I've had to pack it up."

His mother's voice oozed sympathy. "Poor you. I've heard of this happening before. They either find jobs in London or the boyfriend is a local chap with housing qualifications and a good job. They just run off to their new life without even working notice."

"You must be careful, Elizabeth, in case that girl of yours runs off. You don't want the same thing to happen to you."

Le Claire clutched his champagne glass a little tighter. Jersey had long been a melting pot, with many of the residents having originally relocated from somewhere else. Yet people like Caro Armstrong still had their petty prejudices and easily cast racial slurs.

His mother's eyes sharpened, and there was frost in her voice. "Ana isn't an au pair. She is Philip's PA and a fabulous help to me. She has relatives in the island and isn't the sort to go running off. She's a reliable girl. She is here this evening doing some waitressing."

Le Claire frowned. "Why on earth is Ana doing that?"

His mother sighed and fixed him with a sharp glance. "I swear that you never, ever listen to me, Jack. I told you at Sunday lunch last week. Aidan Gillespie had a meeting with your father and happened to mention he was having issues in getting trained staff for the party. Ana overheard and offered to help. Waitressing helped her pay for university, and young people can always do with a little more cash. It was lovely of her to give up her Saturday to help. Aidan was pleased."

A twinge of memory floated just out of Le Claire's grasp. Maybe she had said something. He had argued with his father over lunch and had probably zoned out when his mother had started talking to fill the awkward silence.

Sasha placed a hand on Le Claire's arm, and he could feel the fire of her touch all the way to his groin. They had never had any issue sexually; it was in every other way that the distance had grown between them.

"Let's mingle, shall we?" She smiled at his mother and her friend. "Please excuse us."

As they walked off, Sasha slipped her soft hand into his and leaned in closer. "Thought I better get you away before you exploded. Let's leave them to their small-minded comments."

He squeezed her hand, thankful that they were slowly getting back to a normal relationship.

Ana's feet were aching, and wispy tendrils of hair were falling into her eyes from what had started as a neat bun. She tugged at the neckline of her plain black dress, pulling the fabric away from her hot skin. The air was heavy and humid from the remnants of the day's heat and the crush of bodies. She checked her watch and saw that it was just coming up to 10:00 p.m. She wasn't sorry that she'd agreed to help Mr Gillespie, but she hadn't waitressed in a while, and she'd forgotten how tiring it was. That's what happened when you spent your life sitting at a desk. She'd be finished by midnight, so she only had two more hours to get through.

"Hey, you, it's Ana, isn't it?"

She turned quickly and bumped into the harassed-looking catering manager. The woman had a frantic look in her eye, and Ana could imagine what she was thinking. If she got this night right for Aidan Gillespie, he'd give her more work, and the island's elite wouldn't want to miss out on the latest best thing. She'd be inundated with work, or at least that's what she had said earlier in the evening when she had warned the serving staff to make sure their effort levels were at 110% and that anyone, anyone, who ruined this for her would be bad-mouthed and blacklisted. Ana had wondered how you'd blacklist a waitress in an island overflowing with restaurants and where those with money had to have their parties catered and staff were scarce. Look how she'd been dragged into tonight's event.

"Ana, are you listening to me? We've nearly run out of San Pellegrino in the house, and Mr Gillespie won't allow any other sparkling water. Be a dear and run down to the pool house for me. There's loads of Pellegrino in the big fridge as you go in the door. Bring back a dozen bottles, and we can get more later."

Ana sighed but kept it inside. It wasn't that far, but it wasn't that close either. She pasted a smile on her face. "Sure, I'll go now."

She slipped out the door and followed the path leading through the gardens. The party sounds grew faint as she hurried in the direction of the pool house; the only sound her ballet slippers as they slip-slapped against the tiles. Small lanterns lit the way, throwing hazy shapes amongst the shadows. As she neared the glass doors, fluorescent light beamed toward her. The pool was lit and cast a watery glow, shafts of light flickering across the walkway. She pushed down the handle that opened the door, and a blast of heat hit her like a tidal wave, rendering her breathless for a moment. She stepped in and closed the door behind her. The muggy heat was cloying, and she was already covered in a sheen of perspiration. Her dress was starting to stick to her, and she ran a hand around her neckline, pulling the top from her body, letting air circulate. She'd better hurry. She opened the tall glass-fronted fridge and pulled out bottle after bottle of ice-cold water, counting them as she went. A neat dozen and she was done. She had brought a couple of plastic bottle bags with her and quickly filled them.

As she turned to leave, she glanced at the pool. How the other half lived indeed. And to think she had thought her Jersey relatives wealthy. The water glistened, gentle undulations sending shafts of light across the walls and over the ceiling. There was a dark shadow in the far end of the pool. She walked toward it, drawn. The nearer she got, the clearer the shape became, the shadows coalescing into a recognisable form.

She screamed, an involuntary expression of horror. A body, large and male, floated in the shallow end of the pool. "Oh Christ." Her voice was weak, and she heard it crack as she felt a surge of panic. The body was moving with the gentle waves and bumped against the steps, the water slapping over the edge of the pool. The sound galvanised her into action, and she jumped into the shallow end. The water was hot and lapped around her waist. She waded in the direction of the body and, reaching out, tried to lift the head, cupping her hands under the man's chin. He was floating on his back, but the head was turned away from her, lolling on one side. Her wading through the water caused a slight swell, and the movement caused the body to tilt and float to one side. The head turned in her direction.

Ana looked straight into a dead man's face. Recognition made her brain stutter, the images taken by her eyes stopped and started and her thought process faltered as she tried to make sense of what she saw. She opened her mouth and screamed again. One thought ran through her mind on a loop. This couldn't be true. It couldn't be him – not him, it just couldn't.

CHAPTER TWO

Le Claire was on his third glass of champagne and starting to enjoy himself. The lights had dimmed, and the subtle background music had given way to more energetic notes. The bank of doors that led onto the wide terrace had been fully opened, and the silky breeze was a welcome relief from the overheated room. The air was heavy with night-scented stock, the dark purple blooms weaving and trailing around and over the edges of their containers.

Sasha was by his side, her face flushed from dancing and, perhaps, the champagne. Her look was coquettish and flirtatious, and he felt closer to her tonight than he had in a long time. It had only been a few weeks since they'd put their pending divorce on hold, and they had been tiptoeing around each other, neither seemingly able to recapture what they once had or move forward to create a new reality. In many ways, it felt as if they were still separated – except they were now talking to each other rather than shouting. The interaction was tentative, discussing their days and even the weather, debating the latest snippets from the local news but never venturing deeper, never touching on what had driven them apart, kept them separated and led them to the brink of divorce.

Tonight was different. He held out his hand, reached for Sasha's. "Come on, let's get some fresh air." He pulled her through the open doors and onto the virtually deserted terrace.

Her smile widened. "Are you trying to lead me astray? And with your parents here."

He recognised the wicked gleam in her eye and felt his body react. He shook his head and grinned. "Hey, I'm a representative of the law. I can't be caught in a compromising situation, can I?"

Her smile softened. Her gaze was direct as she spoke. "Then let's go somewhere else. Come home with me, Jack. Stay with me tonight. It's about time, don't you think?"

His pulse quickened, and he reached out for her. Pulling her closer, he held her tight and whispered, "Come on, we'll call a cab and just tell Mum and Dad we're leaving."

A commotion in the gardens below caught his attention. Someone was running through the grounds, and they were shouting. A group of people farther down the terrace were leaning over the balcony. One man had descended the stairs and started running toward the figure. It was a woman.

Instincts kicking in, Le Claire moved away from Sasha and followed the man onto the lawn. The woman collapsed in a heap, and just as Le Claire ran up, he heard the man ask, "What's wrong? What do you want?"

The woman's eyes looked past the man and locked on to Le Claire's. She pointed. "Him, I need him."

The light from the nearest outdoor light was feeble, but he recognised her voice with its faint accent, and even in the dark, her features slowly became clearer. "Ana, what has happened?"

"My cousin, it's my cousin. It's Scott." Her voice ended on a sob.

"What about your cousin? Where is he?"

He knelt down beside her, gesturing for the other man to move to the side. Ana was kneeling on the grass, her shoulders slumped, her eyes wild. He reached out and gently touched her arm. She stared up at him, pointed to the high wall that enclosed the grassy area. He could just make out an arched opening in the dim light. "The pool house. He's in the water. I think…I think he's dead."

"Jack, what's going on?"

He looked up and saw Sasha beside him, her eyes wide as she recognised the figure on the ground. "Take Ana inside for me, will you? I won't be long." He looked up at the house. "We passed a small sitting room when we first arrived tonight. It's just off the main hallway. Take Ana there and wait for me."

It took him mere minutes to jog in the direction pointed out. The swimming pool complex was easy to find, the fluorescent light shone through the glass entrance and called like a beacon. Once inside, he ignored the heat, although he felt his shirt stick to him. He looked directly at the pool and walked round to the far end as his instincts and training kicked in. The body lay face-up in the shallows. The torso was out of the water, lying awkwardly across the topmost steps. He approached the figure, followed procedure and checked for sign of life. Checked again, to be sure, but there was no pulse. The man, Scott, as Ana had called him, was dead. He'd call it in, secure the scene and wait for the officers and CSI to show up. They'd determine cause of death and work out the story behind this man's last hours, but swimming pools, parties and alcohol rarely mixed without mishap.

Le Claire catalogued the scene in his mind in preparation for the notes he'd dictate into his phone. As was his usual discipline, he focussed on the deceased; the rest of the scene could wait. However, his attention was caught by movement in the water. He sat back on his haunches as he realised what he was looking at. A £50 note was bobbing on the surface. He looked closer, saw another and another. Peering into the depths of the pool, he saw dark shadows, distorted by the depth of the water. Was it more money?

His nerves tingled; he had a dead body and what seemed to be a huge amount of cash floating in the pool. He pulled his phone from his pocket. He didn't think this would be a case for the duty team. He searched in his phone for the saved number he needed.

# #

Detective Sergeant Emily Dewar had been looking forward to her Friday night ritual. Her shift had finished at 9:00 p.m., and she was exhausted. The white wine was chilled, the takeaway guy had just delivered her chicken curry and she had changed out of her uniform into loose sweatpants and baggy T-shirt. She would be sharing her evening with several favourite TV programmes she had recorded earlier in the week.

She could almost taste the curry and fried rice just from the smell. She poured a generous glass of wine, savoured the aroma. She'd been waiting for this all week and raised the glass to her lips. The ringing of the telephone gave her a jolt, and wine slopped over the rim of the glass, dripping onto her hand. "Damn."

She saw the caller ID, and all thoughts of a quiet night in disappeared as she quickly answered. "Le Claire, what's up? I thought you were off gallivanting tonight?"

Her boss's voice was clipped. "I was. I'm at Honfleur Manor. Get here immediately; we'll need the CSI team as well, so call Vanguard and tell him to put down whoever he is dating tonight and get to the manor. There's been an incident."

"A death?"

"Isn't it always? A suspected drowning in the swimming pool."

She knew there was more to this. "Why not call the duty team?"

"Money and dead bodies always make me wonder. I'll explain when you get here. Hurry up."

As the phone went dead, she looked longingly at her full glass of wine and, with a sigh, poured it back into the bottle. Maybe tomorrow night.

CHAPTER THREE

Dewar arrived just as Le Claire had finished briefing the CSI team. He held a couple of plastic packages and threw one toward her. "The guys have just set up. Here you go, new outfit for you."

Dewar rolled her eyes but kept any quip to herself as she unrolled the baggy plastic cover-ups. They suited up in the standard protective issue, slipping on covers for hands and boots. Although their own fingerprints and DNA were on file for elimination purposes, they couldn't risk contaminating the scene with random evidence. Le Claire could feel sweat on the back of his neck, and Dewar was starting to glow. Gillespie obviously liked his pool house to be kept at Caribbean temperatures. The plastic clothing wasn't helping.

Le Claire briefly updated her. "The person who found the body knew me and that I was here this evening. She came to find me. Young Hunter arrived minutes before you. Thanks for calling him in. I sent him to the main house to inform the owner that there has been an incident."

The door opened behind them, and in walked the final team member Le Claire had been waiting for. "Viera, how come you always get the weekend duties?"

Dr David Viera smiled, his white teeth in contrast to his swarthy skin, his dark hair a riot of curls. "I think it's called getting stuffed 'cos you're single, childless and probably thought to be friendless as well."

Le Claire took the words for the irony they were. Viera was a young and energetic local GP, and he had signed up for the Force Medical Examiner programme – which meant he got paid a retainer in return for being put on the call register. Le Claire knew he often volunteered to be first on call over the weekends so that married men and fathers could enjoy their family time. Most call-outs were natural causes or accidents, but Le Claire suspected that wasn't the case this time; at the very least he didn't think it would be straightforward.

"I have a hunch that we may not be looking at an accident. I checked for sign of life, but it was negative."

Once Viera was suited up, the three walked past a makeshift barrier made of chairs that acted as a scene demarcation line. The body lay at the far end of the building, to the side of the pool itself. Le Claire and Dewar stood back whilst Viera got on with his job. He hunched down and, following protocol, double-checked for a pulse. His hands, encased in protective gloves, inspected the head, checking inside the mouth and pulling the eyelids back. He turned the head over. "Christ, that's nasty." The gash on the back of the head was about two inches long.

"He was found in the water?"

"Yes, I moved the body out of the pool to keep it from floating around."

"What was the position of the body when you first saw it?"

"Floating by the top steps."

"Face-up or down?"

"Face-up. Why? Ah." Le Claire knew he had answered his own question, and Viera quickly agreed with him.

"Yep, you've got it."

Dewar's voice cut across them. "What? What are you talking about?"

Le Claire gestured toward Viera. "You explain."

"A body in water, where drowning is the cause of death, will usually float facedown. Not always, but most of the time. We therefore need to check whether he was moved."

"Which would mean someone else was here?"

"Yes, and that is where it gets challenging. It is very difficult to prove anything other than an accident."

Le Claire frowned. "In what way?"

"You have to discount any skeletal facial injuries, damage to the neck or larynx. They can naturally occur as the body fights for survival. If a person goes into the water alive and gets into difficulties, then one of the key stages before unconsciousness is struggle. In around one in ten drowning fatalities, the autopsy will reveal bruised and ruptured muscles to the shoulders, chest and neck."

Dewar's tone was dry. "Thanks for the medical lesson; let us hope that this was a tragic case of misadventure, then."

Le Claire pointed at the pool. "But then there is the money." He picked up a long-handled net from the rack of pool equipment and used it to skim the surface of the water. Lifting it high, he pulled it out and laid the now full net on the tiles. It was packed with £50 notes. Viera let out a long, low whistle. Dewar turned and voiced their thoughts. "Okay, not conclusive that we're looking at anything other than an accident, but strange indeed."

One of the CSI team removed himself from his colleagues and approached Le Claire.

"I'm Buchanan. We've split the area into squares and have swept for evidence. What I'd like to do now is work my way around the scene and check for latent stains. Do you mind if we put the lights out for a moment? It won't take long. We'll cover half the area and then do the remainder when the body has been taken out."

"No problem, we'll wait for you to finish."

They moved to the wall by the entrance. Buchanan and a colleague used handheld sprays to cover the area in a fine film. Any cleaned-up stains, such as blood, left a trace behind. Hidden traces, undetected by the naked eye, that were only visible under blue light when the area had been sprayed with fluorescence. The lights went out. Buchanan used a blue light scanner as he covered the room, inch by inch. Suddenly, he stopped, re-scanned an area, knelt down to look closer and called out, "You better see this."

Le Claire pushed away from the wall and, squatting down, saw what had drawn the technicians' attention. The blue light had revealed a long stain that stretched all the way across the tiles to the edge of the pool.

Le Claire's eyes locked on to Viera's. "Seems a clear trail. Looks like the body was dragged to the pool, lying on its back. The blood would be from the wound at the back of the head. I don't believe this death was an accident."

Viera reached for his phone. "I'll need to get a Home Office pathologist across from the UK. I better call it in."

Le Claire was in agreement. "I'll contact the chief. We'll need a Major Incident Room set up."

Dewar asked, "Shall I get on and identify the victim?"

Le Claire shook his head. "No need. He was known to the person who found him, so let's talk to her first."

Le Claire beckoned for Dewar to follow him. "Let's go and speak to the host as well; there's nothing we can do for this chap now. But first we need to close this party down and find out more about the deceased and what he was doing here."

# #

Le Claire paused outside the closed door. He gave it a quick knock and was relieved when it opened a crack and Sasha peered out.

"How's Ana's cousin?" Her voice was soft and low. He shook his head, and she stood back and motioned for him to enter. He heard her greet Dewar, and then she spoke to him, "Jack, I'll leave you to it. I'll be outside if you need me. I'll make sure you're not disturbed."

The door shut with a metallic click, and Le Claire considered the weeping figure huddled on the sofa. Ana was a pretty girl. She must be twenty-four or so but looked about eighteen to him. She was a wreck tonight. Her long fair hair was escaping from some sort of updo. She was pale, and her tears had made her mascara and liner run, turning her into a smudged mess. Her blue eyes were dull and vacant, her lips bloodless.

She stared at Le Claire, seemingly unseeing for a moment, and then jumped to her feet. "How is he, how is Scott?" Her voice was anxious, and her eyes even more so. He did what he had to, spoke the familiar words, without hesitation or pause. "I'm sorry to let you know that your cousin is dead, Ana."

"No. No, that can't be true. We're having dinner tomorrow night. He can't be."

She let out an anguished sob, her breath hitching. She was trying to control herself, but, as he knew, that often made it worse.

"I have to ask, did you touch Scott? Did you turn him over?"

"I didn't turn him over, but I did pull him clear of the water a bit."

Yet more corroboration that this was no accident. "Thank you. I need to know about Scott. What was his surname, and did you know he was coming here this evening?"

"Hamlyn, his name is Scott Hamlyn. He knew I was working at this party tonight. I told him, but he never mentioned that he was going to be here. I spoke to him yesterday when we organised meeting for dinner tomorrow night."

"You say he's your cousin. Was he Polish?"

"No, he's as Jersey as they come. My mum's originally from the island. Scott's mother, Sarah, is my aunt. She is my late mother's sister."

A piece clicked into place. The few times he met Ana, he had wondered where she had learned English; her accent was only slightly discernible, and she used colloquialisms with ease. Mystery solved.

"Was Scott married?"

"No, he has a girlfriend though. I've only met her a couple of times. We were meant to be having dinner tomorrow night. Scott is really into her."

He noticed how she shifted from present to past tense when she spoke of her cousin. It would take time for her to accept that he was gone.

"I'll have to notify Scott's parents. Would you like to come with us? It may give your aunt some comfort."

Ana's brittle laugh struck a discordant note. "My aunt wouldn't be comforted by my presence; the exact opposite, in fact."

"The two of you don't get on?"

She shrugged. "I don't know how it started, but my mum and aunt became estranged. There had been no communication between them in years. My mum met my dad when she was at university in England. They lived in London, and I was born there, but they moved back to Poland when I was tiny."

"How did you come to the island? You've worked for my father for about six months, haven't you?"

"About that. I went to university in London and then went home. My parents died in a car crash several years ago. It seemed too much of a coincidence when my best friend from school said she was moving to Jersey. I came with her. I'd hoped to get to know my mother's family better, but I only see Scott."

There was bad blood in this family, and Le Claire didn't need to bring more trouble to the deceased's mother. "We will be classing Scott's death as suspicious until we know more. Can I ask you to keep all of this quiet until I speak to his parents?"

Ana's eyes were wet with unshed tears, her expression solemn. "For sure. My aunt will see bogeymen in corners once she knows I found Scott."

"Stay here, we'll get someone to take you home."

CHAPTER FOUR

Aidan Gillespie looked dazed. He was a well-built man in his late forties; of average height, he had a carefully styled shock of salt-and-pepper hair. His skin was lightly tanned, which made his bright blue eyes even more striking. Le Claire had only met Gillespie this evening, but he had already formed an impression of him as a fastidious man from his neatly manicured nails to the expensive cut of his dinner suit. A man whose face was now flushed, his bow tie askew and his suit jacket wrinkled as he sat slumped in one of the winged armchairs that flanked his desk. His voice was hoarse. "The young officer you sent to speak to me said there had been an incident – a death. Who was it? What happened?"

"A Mr Scott Hamlyn was found dead in the pool house."

Gillespie jerked upright, his attention sharp and focussed on Le Claire. "What was he doing here?"

"You hadn't invited him?"

"I barely knew him." He looked behind him. "Danny, what's going on?"

A man moved out of the shadowed corner of the room. He was a younger, trimmer version of Aidan Gillespie, who introduced him. "This is my brother, Danny. Fetch Ben, he dealt with the guest list."

Danny Gillespie quickly left the room.

Le Claire carried on. "So you didn't know Mr Hamlyn's name was on your guest list? That seems unusual – I mean that someone could be invited to your party and you don't know who by."

"I have people who deal with these things. One of them will be here in a moment."

Danny Gillespie returned, followed by another man, who was probably in his late twenties. He was tall and well built; fair hair was left a little long and framed an undoubtedly handsome face; his jaw was stubbled, and vivid blue eyes matched those of Aidan Gillespie. Le Claire could almost hear Dewar's thoughts. She stood slightly behind him. He couldn't see her, but he imagined she'd be standing straighter and sucking in her stomach.

The newcomer seemed puzzled as he looked around the room. "Aidan. What can I do for you?"

"Detective, Sergeant, this is my cousin, Ben. He looks after things for me."

"Some things, I do most of it." Danny Gillespie's voice was defensive.

Aidan Gillespie was dismissive of his brother's protestations. "Sure, sure, of course you do. Ben, there's been an accident. Scott Hamlyn has drowned in the pool. How the hell did he get in here?"

"Scott? Christ, that's insane." He shook his head and roughly raked his fingers through his hair. "Crazy. I mean, he definitely wasn't on the guest list when we prepared it. Look." He opened up a small tablet and, with a few swift swipes, said, "Here's the list." His finger flicked upward as he scrolled. He stopped and looked again. "He isn't on the list. How the hell did he get past security?"

Aidan Gillespie's words were spat out. "That's what I'd like to know."

Ben raised his hands in supplication. "His name wasn't on the list, Aidan. Security would not just have waved him in."

"Who did, then? Who?" Aidan Gillespie had turned a dark shade of purple.

The cousin's voice was soothing. "Take it easy. He must've sneaked in somehow."

Aidan Gillespie slumped into his chair. "It bloody well sounds like it, doesn't it? Now he's dead, and my party is ruined."

Le Claire ignored the self-pity. "How did you know Scott Hamlyn?"

"He did some minor legal work for me. I have no idea what he was doing here." His eyes were pleading. "Can we keep this quiet until the party finishes? I mean, there are some very important people here; your father amongst them."

Le Claire heard Dewar gasp next to him. He didn't blame her, for it was a pretty blatant comment.

He felt anger rise, automatically dampened it and held his emotions in check. That was the problem with the rich; they all acted like they were owed favours. Not in his world.

"Several squad cars have arrived, and I've secured the area, which is being taken apart by the Crime Scene Investigators. We would like your guests to stay here until we have finished our preliminary investigations. We'll take down their names, addresses and contact details and also whether they saw anything unusual this evening and if they left the main house since the party started. We'll also do general checking on whether they knew the deceased and what their movements were during the evening."

Aidan Gillespie briefly closed his eyes. "Don't you think that's a bit of overkill? Some of the most prominent people in the island are here tonight; I don't want them badgered."

"I'm afraid it's what the investigation demands."

There was a long pause until Aidan Gillespie finally nodded in acceptance. "Yes, of course, Detective." The man clearly understood that the evening's events had transformed his party guest from Jack to DCI Le Claire. "My people will give you all the cooperation you need. Ben will go with you and see to it."

"Thank you, my colleague and I are on our way to inform the family. We have to do this quickly; otherwise the evening's events will be on Facebook and Twitter before we know it."

Gillespie winced at his words. Le Claire guessed he was realising the enormity of the situation. His party would be remembered, but for all the wrong reasons. Anyone who was thought to be anyone had been invited, and almost all had attended, no doubt mainly out of curiosity as to what this self-made man had done to one of the island's most important historical manors. Now these guests were being questioned by the police and bundled unceremoniously on their way.

#

As the police exited the room, followed by Ben, Aidan Gillespie caught his brother's eyes and flicked a gaze to the open doorway. Danny picked up on the unspoken order and closed the door tight.

Danny was younger by twenty years – the offspring of his father's second marriage. He figured his father had put it about a bit, and he probably had other siblings, but Danny was the only legitimate one and, in many ways, was more like a son to him than a brother. Danny's upbringing had been very different from his own. A few years ago, Gillespie had put him in sole charge of the entertainment division.

He turned to his brother. "We could have contained this if that stupid cow hadn't screamed like a banshee and run straight for Le Claire Jr, who happens to be a bloody Detective Chief Inspector with the local police. Now the place is swarming with coppers."

Danny laid a hand on his brother's arm. "Take it easy. It can't be helped."

Gillespie brushed him away and rose and paced the room, hands behind his back and frown on his face. "Do you know how much effort it has taken to start to be accepted here? These people aren't just interested in money – they want style and something else. What they don't want is their champagne guzzling to be interrupted by a dead body turning up and then to be interrogated by the local plod. It's all messed up."

He could hear the petulance in his voice and hated himself for it. He walked to the antique sideboard that took up most of the far wall. The top was covered in decanters, bottles and crystal glasses. He poured them each a generous measure of malt whisky, handed one to his brother and downed his in one. The fiery liquid burned his throat, and he relished the physical discomfort as the alcohol eased his fractious thoughts.

"You get this cleared up, Danny – you hear me?"

The Hamlyns lived in the picturesque seaside village of St Aubin. Their pink-washed three-storey home sat above the bay in a terrace of similar properties. The neat front garden was lit by multi-coloured solar lamps. The door was opened by a slightly crumpled looking man in his fifties; he was tall with a narrow frame and stooped a little. Le Claire had checked his watch before ringing the doorbell. It was just gone 11:30 p.m. When he'd worked in the Met, a Londoner's response to a late night visitor was to open their doors a crack, peering past the security chain. Here in Jersey, it was normal for a person to fling the door wide open and ask with a smile, "Can I help you?"

The man's cheerfulness made a difficult job unbearable. Le Claire flashed his badge. "Mr Charles Hamlyn?" He continued at the man's nod. "I'm DCI Le Claire, and this is DS Dewar. May we have a word?"

Surprise crossed his face, but he motioned them through the long narrow hallway into a pretty kitchen at the back of the house. The kettle was boiling, and a woman busied herself with the makings of a late night pot of tea. Scott Hamlyn's mother presumably; her hair was a carefully highlighted caramel-blonde bob, cut to frame her face and highlight her cheekbones. Le Claire could immediately see traces of Ana in her features.

"Darling, it's the police. Detectives, this is my wife, Sarah."

Sarah Hamlyn's face was a polite mask. "How may we help you?"

Le Claire was quick and direct – always the best way. "I am sorry to inform you that your son, Scott Hamlyn, has been found dead. I am very sorry for your loss." He knew they were meaningless platitudes in the first sharp hit of shock.

As so often happened at these times, Le Claire saw the same range of clashing emotions vie for supremacy as the Hamlyns tried to understand what was being said. Incomprehension gave way to disbelief. Charles Hamlyn was the first to speak. "What? That's absurd. You've made a mistake."

Before either Le Claire or Dewar could comment, his wife interjected; her voice was strong. "I'm going to call Scott right now, right this minute. Where's the phone, Charles? Where is it?" Her voice was rising in panic.

She rummaged through the magazines sprawled over the kitchen table, and they spilled onto the floor, revealing a telephone handset. She dialled a number from memory. Her face was white as she listened to the ringtone. "He'll just be a second. He always answers when he sees it's me. No matter what he's doing. Scott's our only child, and we're very close. So he'll answer. He always does." Her brittle smile faltered as the phone kept ringing. In the silent room, they could hear the distant click of an answerphone.

Dewar reached out and carefully took the phone from Sarah Hamlyn, set it down and led her toward a squashed and well-loved looking sofa. She moved mechanically, unresisting as Dewar placed a hand on her shoulder and gently pressed her to sit.

Recognition and understanding aged her in front of their eyes. "Oh dear Lord, no, is it true?"

"I'm afraid so, Mrs Hamlyn."

"What happened?"

"Scott was found in the swimming pool at a private home. We'll be treating it as a suspicious death until we know all the facts. It was Aidan Gillespie's place."

He didn't need to explain further. Everyone in Jersey had heard of the multi-millionaire who had just completed a costly refurbishment of the manor. They'd be hearing it again soon, when news of the death became public knowledge.

Charles Hamlyn's eyes were bleak. "Are you positive it was Scott?"

"Yes, he was found by his cousin, Ana."

Sarah Hamlyn had been resting her head in her hands, but she sat bolt upright at these words. "Ana? What does she have to do with this?"

"She was waitressing and was sent out to fetch some supplies from the pool house. She found Mr Hamlyn and then came to find me."

Charles Hamlyn said, "Ana knows you?"

"Yes, she works for my father."

"Ah, of course, you're Philip Le Claire's son. You're young to be a Detective Chief Inspector."

Le Claire didn't even bother to grit his teeth. It was just a throwaway comment. The usual sly insinuation wasn't there, that nepotism had got him his job and, at just turned thirty, he had a rank that usually went to a more seasoned policeman. Little did they know that their suppositions couldn't be farther from the truth. A man who had just been told his child was dead could be afforded some leeway. Charles Hamlyn's little colour had all but disappeared, leaving his face an ashen mask of grief as tears filled his eyes. Sarah Hamlyn's voice was tired, resigned. "Never mind the detective's age, Charles."

She asked Le Claire, "Can we see Scott?"

Le Claire said, "Of course. We will need you to complete the formal identification. We'll collect you in the morning. Now we'll stay here until the Family Liaison Officer arrives. We'll just give them a call."

Sarah Hamlyn's voice was sharp. "No, don't do that. We don't need anyone." Her eyes beseeched him. "Please just leave us alone, please."

He nodded, and with that left them standing alone in their kitchen, a couple whose future would be irrevocably shaped by this night's events.

CHAPTER FIVE

Ana had woken as the first tendrils of dawn crept through the slatted blinds, shafts of light beating back the dark for another day. For one tiny second, one infinitesimal moment, she was cocooned in the blissful twilight world between sleep and awake. And then her stomach lurched, her eyes flew open and she remembered. Scott. Christ. She lay flat on her back, staring at the stain on the ceiling, but not seeing it. Thank heavens Jack Le Claire had been there. She had run straight for him and not felt any of her usual nervousness when she was around him. For one, he was police; Ana had felt as if his perceptive eyes were analysing her the few times they had spoken. It made her feel guilty, even when she knew she hadn't done anything. She had always been a little shy and gauche around him. He was a handsome man with neatly trimmed dark hair and eyes that she imagined could draw you in, should he wish it. He was also well over six feet and towered over most people. He had been professional and focussed last night, but he had shown a softness that Ana had more than appreciated.

She sighed out loud. She'd have to phone her aunt later. No matter the harsh words that Sarah had fired at Ana, she was still her aunt, her blood. She checked the time on her phone and saw the reminder flash up. She dragged herself out of bed and pulled on jeans and a T-shirt, slipping her feet into sandals. She grabbed her backpack and was out of the door in five minutes. She had an appointment, and she had to keep it, otherwise Irena's possessions would be in the rubbish bin.

She figured she was nearly at her destination and pulled the crumpled piece of paper from her pocket again and peered at the address. Irena had once told her it was the large detached house at the end of the cul-de-sac, number seven. Her friend had complained there were children's brightly coloured plastic toys to be found lying in the manicured front garden and drive. Ana found the place straightaway and made her way past the predicted jumble of toys.

The doorbell was answered by a man who Ana assumed was David Adamson. He looked harassed, his brown curling hair was a little mussed, his clothes were rumpled and he hadn't shaved recently – however, that didn't mean he was unattractive, and Ana blushed a little that her thoughts might show on her face.

"Yes, can I help you?"

"Mr Adamson, I am Ana Zielinska, Irena's friend. We spoke on the phone?"

"Of course, come on in."

As she followed him into the house, Ana noticed that a tea towel was thrown over his shoulder, and he had a sauce-stained apron tied around his waist. Irena had said the wife was away a lot, and most of the household chores fell to her husband. That had been a wonder to Ana. Her dad had been her hero, but his culinary expertise had started and finished with a thick stew made of anything and everything.

They entered a large kitchen/diner, where modern appliances and sleek cupboards were softened by a family wall planner and cartoon drawings stuck to the American-sized fridge door.

Ana asked, "Have you heard from Irena?"

David Adamson ran his fingers through his hair. "Ana, I am sorry, but as I told you on the phone, she has just skipped out. She's taken her passport and most of her clothes. I'm sorry your friend didn't tell you she was leaving, but she's let us both down. My wife works abroad for several weeks at a time, and I relied on Irena to look after the kids. Now I'm stuck here when I should be running my business. I'm glad you turned up. My wife packed up all of Irena's belongings in an old suitcase. As I said on the phone, I was under strict, and I mean strict instructions to dump everything. The bin men come tomorrow, and this lot would have gone out with the trash. Beth, my wife, would have gone crazy if it was still here when she came home."

He sounded anxious, and Ana could guess who ruled this household. He pointed to a suitcase by the door, and her heart sank. Then she realised it could be rolled on wheels.

She hefted her rucksack higher on her shoulder and, pulling the case, made for the door. "Thank you, but will you please call me if you hear from Irena? Tell her I just need to know if she's okay." She pulled a neatly folded piece of paper from her pocket. "This is my number and address. I wrote it down in case you need to contact me."

She opened the front door, and David Adamson's voice drifted down the hall. "Do you need a job, Ana? I could do with some help around here." At that, she could hear small voices shrieking from the back garden. "Daddy, Daddy, come here now!"

Ana was shaking her head before the words were out. "No thanks. I work as a PA. Afraid I wouldn't be good at the kids and cooking thing."

David Adamson nodded, and Ana could feel his eyes on her as she walked down the path, and headed for the bus that would take her home, if you could call it that. Ana had one room and shared a bathroom with three other girls. She had use of the kitchen and a TV that didn't always work. Nor did the lock on her bedroom door. Her parents hadn't left her much, and they hadn't planned to die in a car crash. She was alone and standing on her own two feet, or trying to.

The broken lock forced her to carry her valuables with her, and the weight of the rucksack made the straps dig into her shoulders.

She waited at the bus stop, people-watching to distract her from thinking about Scott. Even ordinary people looked better here, the women with well-tended hair and subtle makeup.

She ran a hand over her own hair and considered having it cut; it was light brown, straight and long, flowing halfway down her back. Irena often teased her and said she looked like a little girl. At just turned twenty-five, Ana had often wished she was more like her older and infinitely more outgoing friend. Irena's white-blonde crop contrasted with the dazzling blue of her eyes, and sharp cheekbones accentuated her pixie features. Where was she? Ana was battling between a sliver of fear that something bad had happened to Irena and a sense of disappointment that her friend had just left her without a backward glance. Now she had lost her cousin, her only real family in this island, and felt more bereft than ever.

She could see the bus in the distance. She needed to buck up, get home and see what, if any, comfort she could offer her aunt and uncle.

# #

Le Claire had gone to bed after 2:00 a.m. and was at his desk by seven. He had spoken to the chief the previous evening and been appointed the Senior Investigating Officer. His first job was to get the right resources in place to manage the investigation. It was now mid-morning, the Major Incident Room was being set up in the largest conference facility they had and he had chosen the team to work with him. The majority of them were out on the road carrying out interviews, having been allocated names of the partygoers and serving staff from the night before.

Another team was looking into Scott Hamlyn's life. Le Claire had put DI Bryce Masters in charge of the sub-team. Le Claire might not like the smug Masters, who, with his gleaming smile, sleek black hair and handsome looks, was a walking advert for the police, but he knew Masters had a nose for digging around in the debris of a person's life – even if he couldn't stand the man, he had to give him credit where it was due.

"Sir? I mean Le Claire…" He turned as Dewar walked into his office. "Masters is digging into Hamlyn's financials, and Hunter is reviewing his social media sites whilst we're running a hit on the police national database."

"Thanks, Dewar. That only leaves one thing to do, and I better be the one to carry out that task. Let's go and collect Scott Hamlyn's parents."

# #

Viera was waiting for them. Le Claire had called and asked if he would meet them at the morgue. The young doctor had a pleasant manner and was, to his disadvantage, a calming force in such circumstances. Sarah and Charles Hamlyn hadn't said much on the way into town. They'd sat in the back of the car, a seat breadth between them, as each had stared out of their respective windows, seemingly lost in their own private and, apparently, separate grief.

The morgue was an antiseptic, cold-tiled and cheerless space. It had a function, and it did its job. Hamlyn's body had been moved into the viewing area. From the way they parents held themselves as they stood in that ice-cold and unnatural place, Le Claire knew they were holding their breath, hoping against hope that it wasn't their son that lay beneath the hospital-issue sheet. At Le Claire's nod, Viera exposed the head.

"Oh dear Lord – no, no – this is so much worse than I expected. It's him, it's him." Sarah Hamlyn's anguished sobs echoed against the walls. Her husband reached out and pulled her into a comforting embrace, his arms holding her tight. From the slight stiffness of her body before she sank against husband, Le Claire wondered if it had been a very long time since the Hamlyns had touched each other.

Charles Hamlyn's eyes met Le Claire's. His voice was broken. "That's Scott. That's our son."

"Thank you. Come this way, please. We'll get you some refreshments and then take you home."

With an economy of movement and a competent air, Dewar had them swiftly settled into one of the small interview rooms and fulfilled the requested orders with Styrofoam cups of tea and coffee.

Sarah Hamlyn cupped hers in both hands. She sipped and sighed. "Somehow, at a time like this, tea is so soothing."

Dewar replied with a rare smile. "Tea is my go-to medicine for many ailments, physical or of the mind or heart."

Le Claire saw Sarah Hamlyn shoot a sad smile in Dewar's direction. The dour Scot amazed him sometimes; beneath her brash nature beat a poetic heart, although he had to admit it was seldom seen.

Charles Hamlyn said, "I'll put the undertakers on notice. When can they collect Scott?"

Le Claire cleared his throat. There were matters they needed to discuss. "I'm afraid we can't release the body at the moment. Not until the Home Office pathologist arrives in the island and carries out the autopsy. We also need to tie up some loose ends."

Charles Hamlyn's eyes sharpened. "Last night you said you had to treat Scott's death as suspicious until you knew more. Have you found out anything?"

"Scott's body was discovered in the swimming pool at Honfleur Manor. Several indicators at the scene were inconsistent with accidental drowning. A detailed autopsy will be required before the body can be released. Scott also had a deep gash on his head."

Sarah Hamlyn's voice was shaking. "Are you saying someone killed Scott?"

"We just need to be sure that any anomalies are cleared up and discarded from our investigation."

Charles Hamlyn's voice was strident. "Ridiculous! You're putting us through this for nothing, nothing at all. No one would have had any reason to harm Scott."

His wife's voice was weary. "Charles, we don't know that. Not after the last few months. In truth, we didn't know him any longer."

Le Claire's interest was caught. Not-so-happy family, then. "Had Scott, or his circumstances, changed recently?"

Sarah Hamlyn looked at her husband; she appeared to be weighing up her words. "My son never gave us a moment's trouble. He was one of the youngest advocates ever to qualify in Jersey. He lived for his work and came for dinner every Friday and Sunday and once during the week. Scott wasn't one for going out much. He had some old school friends that he occasionally met up with. He didn't make friends easy, as he could be a little shy and quiet."

Charles Hamlyn cut in. "Sarah, you always saw him through a mother's rose-tinted glasses." He sighed, leaned forward and rested his arms on the table. "Scott was my child, and I loved him dearly. However, he could be arrogant and standoffish; some of that was driven by shyness, yes, but he also got irritated by people who weren't up to his intellectual standards." He sighed, ran a hand across his brow. "I'm sorry. I just wanted you to know the truth."

His wife's tone was shrill. "Truth? You want us to tell the truth?" Anger reverberated through her words. "Fine. Scott changed, Detective. I half thought he might be taking drugs or something. That's what happens when you run with a fast crowd. It's that girl's fault."

Charles Hamlyn snarled, "Stop it! He was just happy."

Le Claire had to bring this back on track. "Mrs Hamlyn, you mentioned a female. Who do you mean?"

Sarah Hamlyn sighed. "It gives me no pleasure to say this but Scott became foolish over a woman. Her name is Laura Brown – a little bird of a name for a whopping predator."

Dewar asked, "Predator? I take it you had concerns about Miss Brown's involvement in your son's life?"

Sarah Hamlyn's snort filled the air. "Oh indeed. I have met Laura Brown once – just once – and that was enough for me. I know that type. Scott was an okay-looking chap, but he earned a great deal of money, and that has its own allure. Laura Brown swooped in and flattered him, and now my son is dead. Nothing bad ever happened in his life until he met her – and then it all went wrong. That woman has no morals." Her voice ended with a sob that cut the air.

Dewar pulled out her notepad. "Where can we find Miss Brown?"

"She lives in London, but I don't have any contact details for her. However, Scott had declined Sunday lunch with us today as he said she was coming to visit. I think he gave her a key, so I assume she's at the flat. I'll give you the address. It's in St Clement."

Sarah Hamlyn looked him over. "You might be young, but you caught that vicious killer a while back, didn't you? I read about it in the *Evening Post*. I want to know who did this to my son. I'm putting my trust in you."

"We'll do our best. Please wait here and I'll send someone in to take you home."

He headed out to the car, Dewar close behind him, and said, "We better go see this Laura Brown."

"Mrs Hamlyn certainly didn't like her."

"Scott Hamlyn was hardly a kid. I wonder if there was tension between him and the parents; certainly the mother at least."

Dewar headed east as he stared out the window. His mind was busy with thoughts of uninvited guests and how Scott Hamlyn's life had ended in a rich man's swimming pool.

CHAPTER SIX

Dewar pulled the car into the visitor parking in front of the imposing granite apartment block. The high, arched balconies were softened by the mass of wisteria that wound its way over the facia. Wide, deep steps ran up to intricate wrought-iron gates. They were unlocked, and the pair entered a large courtyard that lay between the road-front and seafront-facing buildings. Le Claire pointed to the seaside block. "That's the one we want. I had a friend whose parents lived in a neighbouring flat."

"And yet again I see how the other half lives. It's enough to give a girl an inferiority complex."

From what she had commented on in the months they had been working together, Le Claire figured that she either had socialist leanings or a huge chip on her shoulder. Neither was his concern or issue, but he was still glad that she didn't know just how well-heeled his own parents were. Guilt made him sharper than called for. "These are nice places, but let's just get on with our jobs, shall we?"

The main doors to the apartment block lay open, wedged in place with a cheese-shaped piece of wood. Le Claire raised a mental eyebrow at the sloppy security. They made their way up in the lift, and at his sharp knock, the apartment door was opened by a stunningly beautiful woman. She was taller than average, slender but with impressive curves. Her eyes were a sharp, brilliant blue, showcased in a heart-shaped face. Her shoulder-length hair was an expensive, smooth fall of caramel tones and blonde highlights. Le Claire's eyes widened a little, and he saw the trace of a smile flash across the woman's face – she was no doubt used to inspiring that reaction in those who met her, and he flushed as he cursed his lack of control.

He flashed his police card. "Are you Miss Laura Brown?"

She looked surprised and a little wary, but this was swiftly covered with a polite smile. "Yes, I am. How may I help you?"

"It would be better if we spoke inside."

Laura Brown hesitated for just a moment, a slice of a second, and then nodded and beckoned them in. They passed through a long hallway that led to a wide, spacious lounge decorated in classic yellow and pale blue, mirroring the view. One entire wall was made of glass, which overlooked the sandy beach. The tide was out, and the foreshore gave way to a rocky seabed with formations that resembled a lunarscape. Dewar gasped, and Le Claire couldn't blame her.

Laura Brown just looked at them, didn't say a word, which was a little unusual, as most people with nothing to hide were usually vocal and demanding about the police turning up at their door.

"Miss Brown, would you please confirm your relationship with Scott Hamlyn?"

Now she looked puzzled. "Scott is my boyfriend. I'm sorry, but what's it got to do with you?"

Le Claire took on the job of life changer and soul destroyer. "I am sorry to tell you that Mr Hamlyn was found dead last night."

Laura Brown's face was a blank, devoid of any discernible emotion. "I'm sorry. I don't understand what you mean."

Le Claire had encountered this numerous times before, the refusal of the brain to accept what the ears were hearing. "Mr Hamlyn was found dead in a private swimming pool."

"No, no, no. You've made a mistake. Let's phone Scott. He'll just have gone to the shops for the papers or something. I'll call him."

Dewar stepped forward. "Sit down, please." She gently led an unresisting Laura Brown to one of the long sofas. Her Scots burr was soothing and calming: "I am very sorry, but Mr Hamlyn has been identified by his parents. There is no doubt that it's him."

"Oh Christ – no – I just can't believe this. No, this can't be true." She shook her head as she spoke, a violent motion, as if she tried to dislodge their words. She closed her eyes, crossed her arms and wrapped them tight around herself as she rocked back and forth, a pained wail accompanying her tears. They let her be. After a moment, her eyes opened, and he was taken aback by the force of her watery blue gaze. She took a few gasping breaths.

"Tell me what happened."

"Mr Hamlyn was found in the swimming pool complex of a private house where a large party was taking place. Where did he say he was going last night?"

"He didn't. I wasn't due to arrive until this morning. I'd only just got here when you came to the door. I can't take this in. He can't be dead, he can't. What was he doing at this house? Where is it?"

"In St Ouen, a Honfleur Manor. Do you know it?"

It seemed to him that her face was carefully blank. "No, I can't imagine why Scott would have been there."

Dewar asked, "Can we call someone to stay with you?"

"No, I'll be fine. There isn't anyone."

Le Claire said, "What about Mr Hamlyn's parents?"

Laura Brown's laughter was sharp and devoid of mirth. "I'll find no support there. Sarah Hamlyn can't stand me. Hates that Scott loves me – oh God, it's *loved* now – he loved me. We were talking about getting married. This is all so surreal."

"May I ask where you met Mr Hamlyn?"

"We met at a party, about six months ago."

Le Claire considered his next question but knew he had to ask it. "Miss Brown, was Mr Hamlyn in the habit of using large amounts of cash?"

She looked surprised. "Not really. Although he did prefer cash when he went on holiday or came to see me in London. Said he felt vulnerable if he only had a cashline card on him when he was out of the island. He used his Amex for day to day stuff; he was obsessed with spending enough to get a British Airways companion voucher so we could fly first class to the Maldives. We're going there later in the year." Her face crumpled, and her eyes filled with tears, which she held back with loud, hitching sobs.

"Thank you, Miss Brown. I'm afraid I am going to have to ask you to stay on the island for a few days until we've completed our investigations. We must treat Mr Hamlyn's death as suspicious until we know all the facts."

"Of course, I understand."

They left Laura Brown sitting in a room bathed in sunlight, her head in her hands and, no doubt, her immediate future in ruins.

# #

Le Claire was slouched on Sasha's sofa; head thrown back, eyes closed and empty wineglass in hand. He'd left work, picked up dinner from a beachfront cafe and driven to Sasha's place.

He could hear her busy movements as she loaded the dishwasher. He should offer to help, but he was exhausted, which dampened any feelings of guilt. The couch gave way as Sasha sat next to him. He opened his eyes, and she was half-turned toward him, a look of concern on her face.

"You look tired. Why don't you go and have a lie down in the bedroom. I'll wake you later."

He smiled, a teasing note in his voice. "If I end up in your bed, I won't be sleeping, or at least not straightaway."

"You're far too shattered for that. Rough day?"

"Yes, I took the parents to identify the body this morning. Then I had to tell his girlfriend. Not good."

"It's all over the news. They've released the name, Scott Hamlyn."

He grimaced. "We've got to be quick at announcing things like this; otherwise social media users fill the air with misconceptions and half-truths."

"My mum knows his parents. Not well, but they have some friends in common."

"What's the gossip?"

She bristled, as he knew she would. "Not gossip! Mind you. Mum says Mrs Hamlyn is a bit intense."

"In what way?"

"She chairs a women's movement. You know, the one that had a big demonstration in the Royal Square a couple of months back."

He sat up straight. "As I recall, a group of about fifty women congregated outside the parliament building to protest against legal highs. A couple of them even got arrested for throwing eggs at the Senators as they came out. Some of the uniforms got splattered as well."

Sasha's lips pursed. "I can't believe you arrested them."

"It wasn't me, and it was only to give them a fright. What's the group called again?"

"MAI, pronounced *May*. Mothers Against Immorality."

He couldn't help his scepticism. "I wonder what their manifesto is."

"Very funny. Mum got dragged into going to one of their meetings once. She said it was one huge moan-fest about how dissolute the younger generation is today, how easy drugs are to obtain and how rubbish the police are. Sorry."

"No offence taken. They seem pretty innocuous."

"Mum says the conversation took an uncomfortable turn. They were talking about a mutual acquaintance, and they were trashing this woman. Her daughter moved in with the boyfriend and had a kid without getting married. Seemingly, the ladies were disgusted. Mum left after that. She couldn't stand their old-fashioned thinking. She said Sarah Hamlyn was one of the most vocal."

"It amazes me that people like that even exist."

He thought of Sarah Hamlyn, and he could envisage her as some morality crusader. He knew she hadn't approved of her son's girlfriend. How deep-rooted did that run?

Sasha's voice broke into his musing. "How tired are you, Jack?"

He yawned, stretching weary arms over his head until he felt his aching shoulders pop. "Shattered."

"That is a shame." She was looking up at him from beneath lowered lids.

He shifted. "Why do you ask?"

"Well, seems to me you made promises on Saturday night. Don't for one minute think I'm upset you didn't come back here. You have a job to do, and it's interfered with more plans than I can recall."

Her lips were parted, and her eyes darkened as she continued. "But you're here now. Pity you're tired."

He smiled; felt an adrenalin rush as energy and anticipation poured through his veins. He stood, pulled her to her feet, his grin getting wider. "I'm never that tired, love. Come here; I guess I'm staying the night."

Laura had walked for hours through the country lanes. She'd had to get out of the apartment and escape her own thoughts. Her life had been settled; she'd been content and opened herself up to Scott in a way she hadn't dared for a long time, if ever. Now she was adrift again.

She closed the apartment door behind her, kicked off her trainers and leaned back against the wall. The apartment was quiet and the air heavy as the last rays of sun, blinding in their dying intensity, poured through the wall of glass that overlooked the beach. She crossed the room and, unlocking the security latch, pulled the glass slider wide open. The sea breeze floated in, cooling the room and caressing her bare arms. The flashing message light on the phone caught her attention. She pushed the replay button once; she wanted the new message, not the twenty-six old ones. Scott never bothered deleting the damned things, and it hadn't been her place to do so. She listened to the automated tones that had invited the caller to leave a message. The line had been connected, but no one spoke. She shivered, but not from the breeze. The recorded silence, with its electronic tone, was unsettling. She'd had a call like that before she had gone out.

The rest of the evening stretched ahead of her. The only company she had were memories. Scott had been out of his depth when they first met. He'd been standing alone at the party, sipping champagne, isolated and with an arrogant lift of his chin. She'd been about to turn away when something made her look closer. She'd taken in the guarded, protective stance, arms crossed in front of him as if to ward off the other guests. He was shy. In the time they had been together, she had seen through his facade to the insecurities that were usually hidden from view. It made her love him all the more.

She had to do something productive, anything to banish her thoughts for just a little while. She should catch up on some emails, stare aimlessly at Facebook and take vicarious pleasure from other people exposing their lives in minute detail.

Her laptop was in her carry-on luggage, and she took it out and set it up on the dining table. She tried to fire it up, but nothing was happening. She held the power button down, pressed it another couple of times. Nothing; the battery must be low. She trudged to the bedroom and rummaged through her case. Everything she expected to be there was except her laptop power cable. That put paid to her plans to lose herself in social media for a few hours. Then she remembered. Scott had changed the password on his laptop a few weeks ago and had asked her to write it down in the book he kept to record everything like that. She'd always said it was a bad idea; now she hurried to get it. She could use his laptop.

She rarely went into the study, but the sight that met her stopped her in her tracks. Scott wasn't tidy; his working papers and personal mail were usually scattered across his desk, spilling over his laptop, which was permanently plugged in. It was hard to tell that the large desk was a fine rosewood antique. However, this was something different. There was a cleared space along one side of the desk. It looked like someone had simply swept the bundles of documents and mail to the floor, where they now lay in an untidy pile, and there was an empty space in the middle of the desk where his laptop should have been.

CHAPTER SEVEN

Ana wearily crawled out of bed just past sunrise. She had lain awake all
night, tossing and turning as she thought of Scott or, more to the
point, tried not to think of her cousin, but it hadn't worked. She'd
given up on sleep as the sun rose, quickly showered in the shared
bathroom and dressed in a plain, dark sundress. It was Monday, and
she'd be working from Philip Le Claire's home office. She'd called and
left a couple of messages for her aunt, but there had been no response.
Part of her thought that was typical; the other couldn't imagine what
the woman was going through as she mourned her only son.

Without thinking, she followed her usual routine, grabbing a coffee
and pain au chocolat from the little bakery near the bus station.

She hopped off the bus in the middle of the countryside and
turned into a private lane surrounded by fields and bordered by
hedges. Ahead were the tall gates with the sign that proclaimed this
the entrance to La Belle Haven. She entered the key code in the
numbered panel, and with the faintest of metallic whirrs, the tall
gates swung open, revealing a long drive that ended in a bend to
the right. There were a mass of plants, flowers and trees crammed
into the overflowing borders that were wide enough to have small
shingled walkways scattered through them.

She walked around the side of the large house and, with a quick
knock, entered through the kitchen door and greeted her boss's
wife. "Morning."

Elizabeth turned, a look of surprise on her carefully made-up
face, her silvery bob swinging back into place. "Ana, what are you
doing here? Didn't you get my text message?"

"Yes, I did, and it was kind of Philip to say I should have the day
off, but I think I'll feel better having something to keep me
occupied."

Elizabeth frowned. "Well, it's up to you, but see how it goes."

#

The morning brought rain, that light, incessant drizzle that often affects coastal areas. The smell of damp jackets and raincoats hung in the air as Le Claire entered the incident room. He'd slept the night through with Sasha by his side, and the past hadn't come crawling into his dreams. He'd woken refreshed and happy. Then he had driven home to shower and change, as if they were a couple who were dating and not one that had been married for years.

He looked around the room with an appraising eye. Everything had been set up as he had requested the day before. Several banks of desks with high-speed monitors and fast Internet connections jostled for space with high-tech printers. One wall was dominated by a massive white board. Pairs of desks lay waiting for the detectives who had been seconded to the team.

Several of the workstations were occupied, and Le Claire approached a young constable. "Hunter, how are you doing?"

Hunter coloured, jumped up, sent the papers flying off his desk and bent down – even pinker now – to pick them up. Le Claire just resisted raising his eyes heavenward. The boy was naive and clumsy, but he was a computer whizz, so Le Claire had tasked him with finding out all he could about Scott Hamlyn's online profile and what that told him about the man himself.

"Leave the papers, Hunter; just tell me what you've found."

Hunter stood up quickly, a mass of papers lying at his feet. "The victim did not appear to have any of the usual social media profiles; no Facebook, Twitter, WhatsApp or Instagram." Le Claire was getting a tick under his eye just thinking about the rise of social media – he just didn't get it. If you wanted to catch up with someone, then telephone or meet them for a drink. Or was he in the minority? Even his mother had a Facebook account.

"So nothing there."

"He did have a large online gaming presence. You know, war games and suchlike."

Le Claire didn't know what to say. Scott Hamlyn was a lawyer and a professional, not some spotty fifteen-year-old. "So he played games online."

"Yes, Ranger94, his tag, had some pretty decent scores. He must've spent a long time playing these games. Often the regular users exchange messages online and build up friendships."

"See what you can find out. We need to look at every angle, but I find it hard to believe that one of his Internet war buddies was also at the party and decided to kill him – then again, stranger things have happened. Know the victim, know the killer. The stronger a picture we build of Scott Hamlyn, the closer we'll be to knowing who murdered him."

Le Claire turned at the thump of regulation police shoes across the carpet tiles. He only knew one person whose presence was announced in such a way, and he turned to greet Dewar. Her face was round with a chin that displayed determination or a stubborn streak. He had seen both. She'd removed her uniform jacket, and he noticed the sinewy muscles in her slim arms. She wasn't a skinny girl but nor was she carrying extra weight – she'd been doing some training recently, and he was glad. Le Claire hated to see good officers let themselves go, which happened all too often in an island where food and drink played such a large part of social life.

"Dewar, have you ever played personal console games?"

"Like Xbox or PlayStation? Sure, as a kid I loved *Tomb Raider*. I used to spend hours pretending I was Lara Croft."

Even Le Claire knew that Lara Croft was the pneumatically built female adventurer who always seemed to have a rifle slung across her back and a hunting knife strapped to her thigh. It cheered him to think of the criminals who came Dewar's way if she was in a Lara Croft mood. "It seems our victim liked to play soldiers online. I wonder what that says about him."

"On its own, not much; I mean, loads of our guys play."

"They do? Who? No, don't tell me, I don't want to know. But I guess if you add in everything else, Hamlyn's lack of friends and zero social media profile, he comes across as a loner."

"Apart from Laura Brown."

"Indeed. And that's a bit of a mystery. I wonder what she saw in Hamlyn."

"I would say his money and good career prospects, but surely she would meet a lot of successful people and business owners doing her promotion work, so I guess there has to be more to it than that."

"Her background checked out?"

"Preliminary details so far, but she works for a company, Classic Promotions, and they supply models and promotional people for trade events, advertising and the like. She's the director. We can't find out who owns the company, as it is registered to another private company, but we'll keep at it. She rents a flat in Hampstead."

"Okay. And the cash we found at the murder scene?"

"That's why I came to see you. We got access to Hamlyn's financials this morning. The guys are running a full check, but the cash appears to have come from four of his accounts, held at different banks. He took just under £5,000 out of each one. It didn't trigger any suspicious transaction reporting, as he did take out a few grand in cash occasionally."

His response was fast. "Who needs almost £20,000 in cash these days?"

"Someone who is up to no good?"

"Perhaps, certainly someone who doesn't want a record of what they're doing or who they're giving money to."

"Gambling? Or prostitution? Maybe drugs?"

"You'd get a lot of either for £20,000, or a little of the very best." The question was which one was Hamlyn's vice?

Drug use was much more prevalent these days. Prostitution wasn't a big business on the island. They busted the odd small-time pimp every now and again, but the bigger issue was the high-class escorts who shipped in for a few days at a time from the UK. However, they weren't so easy to catch as the deals were high level and sophisticatedly planned. A part of Le Claire thought they ought to just let them get on with it, as long as no one was being harmed or coerced. But if you were an upholder of the law, that meant upholding all laws – not just the ones you thought were valid.

Dewar's voice broke into his thoughts. "I checked out the parents. Charles Hamlyn is an engineering consultant, and Sarah is a housewife. There are no adverse hits against either. She chairs an organisation called MAI, which is short for…"

"Mothers Against Immorality. Sasha told me." She looked slightly affronted that he was aware of this. "Carry on, what else did you find out?"

"She's well respected and seen as a poster girl for clean living, playing by the rules and toeing the line. Last year she was honoured at a posh dinner, which was covered by local TV. Here, have a look."

She picked up her tablet from her desk and pressed the screen. "This came up when I googled her. It's from the TV archives."

The first shot was a wide view of a crowded dining hall; the well-dressed guests looked relaxed and had shifted in their chairs to face a raised dais. The camera panned across the room to a woman standing in front of a microphone. Sarah Hamlyn wore a demure evening dress and was clutching a silver plaque. Her hair was styled and her face made-up. She looked elegant and very pleased with herself. Dewar turned the volume up, and they listened as Sarah Hamlyn addressed the audience. "Our young people live in a very different world to the one we enjoyed. They are constantly connected through social media, sharing intimate details of their lives. They devour the antics of reality TV personalities, whose shameless behaviour is beamed into living rooms, somehow normalising their debauchery. Loose morals, divorce and extra-marital affairs carry little shame, and children are increasingly born out of wedlock. We have a duty to act as role models, to lead by example, teach right from wrong and show, in our own decisions, our very actions, the value and beauty in living a moral life. I am honoured to accept this award and want you to know that I will devote all my energy to furthering our aims. We will bring morality back."

The camera switched to the diners, who were rapturously applauding; some had risen to their feet, and Sarah Hamlyn beamed. Le Claire recognised several politicians and business personalities. This was an influential crowd.

The screen went black as the clip ended. Dewar shook her head. "Well, that was a bit evangelical."

"The words obviously struck a chord, given the reaction of the audience." He had seen the looks on their faces as Sarah Hamlyn spoke. She was a powerful force.

Dewar started sliding toward the ad-hoc kitchen area they'd set up at the back of the room. No doubt she was headed for yet another of her cups of tea. He hated to burst her bubble, he really did. "No time for that, Dewar. We've got someplace to be."

CHAPTER EIGHT

It was a very different-looking Laura Brown who opened the door to Le Claire and Dewar. Her face was makeup free, and an undoubtedly sleepless night had resulted in puffy bags that discoloured the delicate folds beneath her eyes, grief emphasising the tiny laughter lines. The air of fragility did not detract from her attractiveness. "Come on in. What can I do for you?"

Le Claire got straight to the point as they moved into the lounge. "As part of our investigation, we'd like to know more about Scott. To do so, it would be good to start with his private papers, emails, that kind of thing. Is there a study?"

"Sure, it's this way."

Laura opened a heavy oak door and ushered them into a cluttered space, which was in direct contrast to the modern sleekness of the rest of the apartment. There was a strong musty smell, and the windows, which overlooked the inner courtyard, were closed tight, and the heavy heat was palpable in the room. Le Claire glanced at one wall, which was covered in rows of book shelves. However, they weren't filled with eye-catching, colourful dust jackets. The weighty tomes were bound in dark leather and tooled in gold. Built-in drawered units took up the rest of the wall space. A desk sat in the middle of the room. It was covered in a jumble of papers. Neatness and organisation hadn't been Scott Hamlyn's strong point; or at least not in his private study.

"Scott tended to work from home in the evening. He said it gave him something to do when I wasn't here. I guess you'll find work and personal papers jumbled together. It's a bit of a mess, I'm afraid." Her shoulders slumped, as if the weight of grief was a physical presence.

Le Claire could never understand how people allowed their desk spaces to get into such a chaotic state. He'd bet half of them would

48

never be able to tell if they'd been burgled or not. In fact, a burglar would probably leave less mess.

"Thank you. DS Dewar and I will have a look through everything."

He had perhaps been more abrupt than he intended, but there was something about Laura Brown, a vulnerability that was at odds with her usually self-confident air. He didn't want to feel sorry for anyone; his job was to be impartial. He saw her draw back slightly, a perfectly reasonable reaction to his words of dismissal.

"Oh. I'll leave you to it. Can I get you tea or coffee?"

Dewar was too quick for him. His swift refusal was drowned out by her loud acceptance. "Thanks. I'd love a cup of tea."

"Sure. Is a mug okay?"

His heart sank at Dewar's enthusiastic yes; she'd be in and out of the loo all day. He couldn't care less when they were in the office. It drove him crazy when they were on the road. He could recite the whereabouts of the publicly accessible loos in every parish. Not a talent he was proud of.

The door closed behind Laura, and he turned to Dewar. "I'll have a look through all these drawers, and you tackle the desk and the papers on the floor." He tried to keep his voice professionally authoritative with a hint of innocence. Dewar cast him a black look that said she knew when she was being stitched up. They pulled on the thin, transparent plastic gloves that were part of their everyday field kit. Le Claire opened drawers and rummaged through their relatively neat contents. He couldn't see anything of interest – just used notepads with legal scribblings, pens, old photographs and last year's Christmas cards. He looked over his shoulder at Dewar, who was sorting out the papers into neat piles, carefully reading each one.

There didn't appear to be anything of interest in the drawers. "This is a waste of time. You have any luck?"

"I have no idea; there's a load of draft legal documents, some bank statements, nothing more. Although there is something odd."

"What's that?"

She held up an unattached power cord. "There isn't a desk PC, but there is a printer. Where's the laptop?"

Laura's voice came from behind them as she edged into the room, a tray of coffee and tea in her arms. "That is what I was going to ask. Scott pretty much used his laptop as a static device. He didn't take it into work with him; in fact, I've never known him to even unplug it. He just didn't carry anything except a work Blackberry. He wasn't into mobile gadgets. Did he have it with him?"

Le Claire's radar went off on red alert. "So Scott's laptop is missing? Thank you, Laura. We need to get back to the station." He walked to the door and tried to hide his smirk as he saw Dewar walk past Laura, and the untouched tea tray, with a mournful glance.

Several hours later and Ana was glad of the distraction of work. She'd typed up some handwritten notes, made several flight bookings and was finalising her boss's travel schedule for a trip to Switzerland when there was brief knock on the study door and Elizabeth walked in, followed by a young man. He was tall and tanned with thick blond hair that curled over his collar. He carried a huge bouquet of cream and pale pink flowers.

"Ana, this is Ben Travers. He'd like a word."

Ana was puzzled. She had no idea who he was.

"Miss Zielinska, I'm Aidan Gillespie's business manager. Actually, I'm his cousin as well. Aidan asked me to find you and offer his apologies. He sends these flowers with his regret that you had such a distressing experience."

She took the flowers and looked around, trying to work out what to do with them. Elizabeth took them from her. "I'll pop these in a pretty vase for you. They'll look gorgeous on your desk. I'll leave you to have a chat, but shout if you need me."

Ben Travers said, "It must have been a terrible shock for you to find that poor guy."

"It was. He was my cousin."

His mouth dropped open. "Christ, I'm sorry. We had no idea. Did you know he was going to be at the party?"

Ana briefly closed her eyes. "No, it was completely unexpected."

There was an uncomfortable pause in which neither seemed to know what to say next. The quiet was broken by the sonorous chimes of the grandfather clock that dominated the corner of the room. Ana glanced at her watch. "I'm afraid I need to go now. My bus is leaving soon."

"Where are you off to?"

"St Aubin. I better hurry."

Ben held up his hand and shook his car keys. "I'm headed into town. I can drop you off on the way."

She thought of the heavy backpack. "Sure, that would great. Thanks."

Once ensconced in the passenger seat of his low-slung sports car, she sank into the butter-soft leather, inhaling the unmistakable smell of money. As the engine roared to life and they exited onto the lanes, Ana grabbed her hair in one hand to keep it from blowing in the wind.

Ben asked, "You been in Jersey long, Ana?"

"About six months. My mum was a Jersey girl but moved to Poland with my dad."

"I wondered why you don't have a strong accent."

"Mum would speak to me in English and my dad in Polish. I got used to switching between the two."

"You have brothers and sisters?"

"No, I came along just as they'd given up hope. I guess being an only child is why I gravitated to Scott so much."

"I am sorry about your cousin. It is so weird that it was you that found him. What a shock, especially as you weren't expecting to see him at the party."

"Yeah, I mean, he knew I was working there on Saturday. He was teasing me. Said I'd soon be earning as much as him if I kept taking extra jobs."

Suddenly, she realised they were nearly at her aunt's house. He was a bit too easy to talk to. "We're here." She pointed to a narrow turning. "Just drop me there, please."

Ben popped the boot and handed her the heavy rucksack. "Whoa, what have you got in there?"

"It's a long story. Thanks for the lift."

She walked away but stopped when Ben called her name. "Ana, I'm sure this is inappropriate, and the timing isn't great, but could I take you out for a drink sometime?"

She was surprised, and a refusal was on her lips when she held back. It didn't seem to be her speaking as she said, "Sure, okay."

"Great, what's your number?"

She reeled it off, and he keyed it straight into his phone.

"Bye, Ana, see you soon."

She turned and walked down the lane. Looking back, she saw he was leaning against his car, watching her. She waved and carried on to her destination-one she wasn't looking forward to reaching.

# #

Ben watched Ana walk away. His eyes lingered on her figure, neat in her dark dress. He checked his watch. His newest gadget was also connected to his mobile phone. He pressed speed-dial, and the call was answered immediately.

"Well, what happened?" As usual, he was straight to the point.

"I don't think she saw anything. However, it seems Hamlyn was her cousin."

"What? I don't like that at all. It seems too much of a coincidence. You took your time."

"I gave her a lift. She wanted to be dropped off in St Aubin."

"Hamlyn's parents live there. She must be visiting them."

"I'll keep an eye on her."

The snort came through loud and clear. "Yeah, I'm sure that won't be a hardship for you."

As he hung up, Ben rued, not for the first time, the places his work took him.

# #

Ana didn't have far to walk. Her aunt's home was the first in the terraced row, the walls washed in palest shell pink, contrasting with the blue-painted window boxes overflowing with multi-coloured geraniums. She rang the bell and waited. Her stomach twisted at the thought of what awaited her on the other side of the door. She saw a slight movement at one of the downstairs windows as a curtain twitched.

Charles opened the door. Ana neither liked nor disliked her uncle-by-marriage. She simply didn't know him. He was a man of few words, and most of them were put in his mouth by his wife. His eyes were dull, his complexion sallow and, if possible, he seemed to have aged a decade or more since Ana had first met him a bare six months before.

"Charles, I am so sorry about Scott."

"Thank you. You better come in."

He shut the door behind her and, to her surprise, pulled her into a tight bear hug. "I know how fond you were of each other. You were very dear to Scott."

Ana cut to the heart of her visit. "How is she?"

"Ah, not good. Sarah is sleeping at the moment."

A voice shouted down the corridor. "I am not bloody sleeping. I just don't want to speak to anyone. I don't care who it is."

Ana's gaze shot to Charles. Sarah Hamlyn never swore.

He called back. "It's Ana, dear."

She winced as quick footsteps came thundering down the corridor, bare feet slapping against the wooden floor. Sarah was dishevelled and unkempt; her hair an un-brushed mop and her eyes red-rimmed. Her voice was harsh, the words spat out. "What do you want?"

"I've been trying to speak to you on the phone. I came to say I am so sorry about Scott. I want to know if I can help?"

The laugh was derisory. "You? Help me? Doing what?"

Waves of anger radiated through the room, and Ana backed away. "I'm sorry. I didn't mean to make things worse. I shouldn't have come."

"No, you shouldn't. We don't need you. We don't need anyone, just Scott. Oh Christ."

At that, Sarah stumbled and fell, hard and heavy, against the wall. She leaned against it, tears falling as she sobbed.

"Sarah, Aunt Sarah…"

Her aunt's voice was quieter, laced with weariness. "Just go, Ana. I don't want you here. Your mother knew better than to come back. She said she'd teach you that as well, but she failed. You're not needed. Just go." Her aunt's voice ended on a whisper. "Please leave us alone."

Ana didn't say anything. She couldn't. Her throat was burning and her eyes stinging. She hoisted her backpack onto her shoulder and opened the front door. Looking back, she saw Charles standing beside his wife, not touching her, not even looking at her. He just rubbed his hands together in a rhythmic motion, as if trying to work out how to navigate through these unknown waters.

Ana pulled the door tight behind her, but it wasn't enough to blot out the howls of grief that echoed through the door, the windows, even the walls and followed her down the path.

Charles Hamlyn stared at his wife. Her shoulders were shaking, and her breath came in huge, messy gulps. Her skin was blotched and her colour high, but it was her eyes that told everything. They were blank, dead pools. She looked at him but seemed to be staring through him, past him.

He wanted to hold her, give comfort and perhaps even gain a measure of that precious commodity himself; to feel her living body in his arms, to be reminded that the world still turned, even though their place in it was being played out in slow motion.

"Sarah, come here." He reached out, laid his fingers on her arm, but she pulled back as if scalded by his touch. He felt the reaction like a spear to the heart and was surprised that his stomach contracted as if suffering from a blow. Perhaps it was. A rush of anger surfaced, and he couldn't dampen it. "Sarah, I'm suffering too. Can we at least grieve together? He was our son."

Her sobs quietened. She was still slumped against the wall and, using one hand, pushed herself upright and stood before him. "No Charles, he *is* our son, not *was*. He was my life, my joy, my pleasure. He was the reason I felt my life had meaning and now that he is gone, I am broken, absolutely broken. I don't want you or anyone else near me. I need to be alone."

He told himself it was the grief talking. His wife had a way of spitting out her anger that he had long become accustomed to, and so he refused to feel upset or belittled by her words. At least that was what he told himself. "I think you made that abundantly clear to Ana. Why don't you like the girl? Scott was enamoured of her. Surely, that's what matters."

"Scott was too nice for his own good. We didn't ask her into our lives, didn't want her to come here. There is nothing in Jersey for that girl, and the sooner she realises that, the better."

Her bitter words made him ache. Would Sarah ever let him in fully?

"She is family, Sarah. I will be asking Ana to attend the funeral and sit by us." He held up a hand to halt his wife's words of refusal, and when he spoke, he could hear the ice in his voice. "No buts, Sarah. We will do the right thing. After that, you never have to see her again if you don't wish to, but we will behave properly at Scott's funeral."

His wife nodded and turned away from him again.

CHAPTER NINE

Le Claire sat alone in his cramped office, far enough away from the madness of the incident room to try and hear himself think as he read the initial report from the Home Office pathologist. The specialist had arrived in the island by Sunday lunchtime and carried out the autopsy immediately.

No fluid was found in Hamlyn's lungs. It was highly unlikely that he had drowned. The pathologist's finding was that he had died the instant his skull had smashed against the pool tiles.

He returned to the report, skimming some of the more technical details. He was scanning the next page when his attention was arrested. Hamlyn had a black eye, bruising on the ribs and broken skin on his knuckles. He had been in a fight, but the injuries were several days old, certainly earlier than the date of his death.

So Scott Hamlyn had at least one enemy; he just had to find out who. Plus, his laptop was missing. They'd need to check his office work space, but it just seemed odd that a long-term habit changed and Scott decided to take his laptop out of his apartment just before he was killed.

The door to his office burst open, and Dewar breezed in, several sheets of printer paper in hand. "I've got the security checklist from Gillespie's party."

"And…"

"It was a bit much for a private bash, even though the governor was there."

"Define 'a bit much'."

"All the guests were identified on a list, and there were guards on the main gate and the side entrance, described as the tradesman's entrance off Rue du Vert—" Her indelicate snort told him what she thought of that before she continued. "The caterers had to supply names and details of their people coming and going. There was also a random search of those employees. He can't have been at the party as either a guest or staff. So how did Scott Hamlyn get into the grounds?"

Le Claire stood and grabbed his jacket. "Come on, I need to check something out. I'll drive."

Elizabeth had insisted that Ana go home after she visited her aunt. She had spent the afternoon lying on her bed, remote in hand, flicking through the TV channels. Nothing could keep her attention or distract her thoughts. She needed to get away from her own company.

Decision made, she jumped up. She'd go see Daria Baklarzska. There was no point in calling, as she never answered her mobile, but she only lived two streets away. Daria rented two rooms at the top of the house owned by the couple who ran the employment agency where she worked. They had organised the employment for Irena and Ana. She didn't like meeting Daria there because of Daria's landlord and boss, Basil Davies.

The first time she'd gone round there with Irena, he and his wife, Lena, had opened the front door to the girls, his watery, bloodshot eyes lingering over their bodies. His wife had coldly appraised them before shooing them upstairs to Daria's rooms. As they had climbed the stairs, Ana had looked over her shoulder and saw Basil Davies staring at them. He must once have been a handsome man, but his face was red and puffed, and his clothes were starting to strain in testimony to a weight gain. Ana hadn't liked how his hooded eyes had lingered over her, his gaze heavy and his smile slow. Ana had felt uneasy – perhaps even a little fearful. They had run up the stairs, but Ana had looked back as they rounded the corner and had watched in horror as Basil Davies slowly ran his tongue over his lips as his gaze tracked their steps.

Her heart was hammering a little as she rang the doorbell. Please, please don't let Basil Davies be there. As the door swung open, Ana cursed the gods that no one was listening to her. Basil Davies's eyes were bright and seemed unfocussed. He must have been drinking – maybe he had taken something else, something more dangerous.

She found her voice. "I've come to see Daria. May I go up?"

"Come in, my dear, come on in."

He didn't move back, just twisted to the side, and Ana had to squeeze past, holding herself in so that she didn't have to touch him. She smelled his fetid breath as his mouth skimmed her ear as she pushed past him. He also stank of sweat.

The front door slammed shut, and the light in the narrow hallway disappeared. Basil Davies stared at her; a look she didn't like was accompanied by a smile she couldn't ignore. Ana felt ridiculous. Her voice caught as she spoke. "I'll just pop up to Daria."

As she turned, his arm shot out and caught her wrist. "She isn't in. Wait with me. I'm sure she won't be long."

Ana hesitated, but she had no option. She would look like a fool if she made a scene. "Thank you, that is kind."

She followed him into the apartment and felt a compulsion to break the silence. "It will be good to say hello to Mrs Davies."

His smile was lupine. "I'm afraid you've missed her. She has gone to visit a friend."

Ana considered what to do. Say she was ill? That she had forgotten an appointment? A noise broke into her thoughts. Basil Davies had turned and carefully closed the door with a sharp click that echoed in the silence. He leaned against the door, blocking her way, and motioned for her to sit. The moment was lost, and Ana meekly sat down with a burning shame that she could not speak up for herself. But as Basil Davies smiled, a smirk that matched the calculation and triumph in his eyes, Ana felt fear course through her, each nerve-end seemingly aware of her predicament. She had to say something.

"Mr Davies, I better go. I have friends waiting for me."

"Call me Basil, and I don't think your friends will be expecting you for a while. I mean, you came here to see Daria, didn't you? Here, have a drink."

He had moved to the large oak cabinet that sat to the side of the door and poured two large glasses of red wine. The bottle was now empty; he had probably been drinking earlier, as she thought. She took the glass and sipped a little of the wine, then regretted doing so – what if it was drugged? Jesus, her imagination was running away with her.

Basil sat down next to her on the sofa and spread his knees wide, which meant his leg was pressed tight against hers. Ana felt panic rise. A wet, clammy hand landed on her knee, touching the skin beneath her skirt hem, and she almost leapt out of her chair and her skin. Basil leaned forward, his eyes snaring hers. Her mind was a whirl, but one thing was clear. She had to do something. Ana opened her mouth to scream and tensed her body, ready to fight him off, when the apartment door flew open and banged hard against the wall. "Basil, leave the girl alone."

Lena Davies casually entered the room, a mocking smile on her face. Basil shot upright and immediately moved away from Ana. "Darling, I didn't expect you back for ages."

"I can see that." She turned to Ana. "I assume you came to see Daria. Go on up."

"But I thought she was out?"

Lena shot a razor-sharp look at her husband. "Really, Basil? No, dear, Daria is getting ready to go out, but she is definitely upstairs."

Ana placed her wineglass on the table and jumped up and fled out the door. Before it closed behind her, she heard the voice of Lena Davies. "Now what have I told you before? Not in the house! Do what you like elsewhere, but keep your little trysts away from my house, dear. And you stink. At least try and cover it up!"

Ana shot upstairs and banged on Daria's door. When there was no answer, she tried the handle and the door opened. She went in. "Daria, are you here?"

There was a noise to her side, and Daria came through from the bedroom. She had on earphones and was dancing as she walked, her shoulders and hips moving in time with whatever music she was listening to. She stopped still and gasped as she saw Ana and pulled off the headphones. "You shocked me. What are you doing here?"

Ana explained about Scott. "I just didn't want to be on my own."

"That is so awful. I can't believe this. How on earth did he manage to drown in a pool? Was he drinking, maybe?"

Ana shrugged. "It seems crazy, but I guess he could have been tipsy and slipped. But what was he doing there in the first place? And not just at the pool house. What was he doing at the party? He knew I was waitressing there and never said a word. The police say they'll be treating his death as suspicious until they know more. What does that even mean?"

Daria shrugged and disappeared into the kitchen, returning with an opened bottle of wine. As she poured two glasses, she was dismissive of the scene with Basil.

"He is a fool and wouldn't have done you any real harm. You must learn to stand up for yourself, Ana. Men are all bastards, and you need to learn how to control them."

Ana nodded in agreement; she didn't have the strength to disagree with the strong-willed Daria.

"And I am pleased that your job worked out. A good job makes all the difference."

"Do you enjoy yours?"

"For sure. Basil and Lena are not so bad to work for once you know how to deal with them."

"It must make you feel good, helping out so many girls coming to the island."

A quick smile flashed across Daria's face. "Of course, it is a pleasure to help people get settled. You shouldn't be alone all the time. Would you like to join me for supper tomorrow night? "

"Yes, please, thanks." She needed a respite from being left alone with her own thoughts.

"Good, meet me outside here at seven thirty. That way you don't have to see creepy Basil." Daria paused and then asked, "Have you heard from Irena?"

"No. I am disappointed, but what can I say? She can't have thought that much of me."

Daria was sympathetic, and her look softened with understanding. "Never mind; people move on. Jersey is that kind of place."

Ana was overcome with tiredness and said her good-byes and left. She ran down the stairs as softly as she could; she did not want to face either Basil or the sharp-tongued Lena. Once outside, she made a quick decision. Pulling out her mobile, she dialled a number she had recently stored. It was answered after a few short rings. "Hello, Mr Adamson, this is Ana. I am sorry to bother you, but have you heard from Irena?"

She could just hear his barely audible sigh. The impatience in his voice was more apparent. "Ana, you've caught me at a bad time – Stop it! Sorry about that, the kids are playing up merry hell. They miss their mum. As do I. Anyway, that is enough of me. No, I haven't heard anything, and I don't expect to. You'll just have to accept Irena's moved on. Now I'm afraid I have to go."

"Wait, please. I think you should call the police. I am worried, and I don't think she would disappear without telling me. I can call them if you're too busy."

There was a long pause. When he spoke, his voice sounded pitying. "Ana, you seem like a good kid, but Irena, well, I don't think you knew her at all. After she left, I discovered some things were missing – the petty cash we kept in a jar in the kitchen, plus some perfume and clothes that belonged to my wife. She has just run off."

In her heart, she recognised the truth in his words. "Thank you. I am sorry to have bothered you."

"Ana, don't worry. Irena is a survivor. I am sure she's fine."

CHAPTER TEN

Honfleur Manor sat atop a rocky incline, bordered by the sea on one side and countryside on the others.

Dewar let out a gasp of surprise as the car sped past the manor's main gates. "I thought we were going in?"

"We are, I hope."

Before Dewar could satisfy her curiosity, Le Claire turned into a narrow lane. It went straight on for a few minutes, and then, just before it veered off to the right, Le Claire drove off the road and parked on the scrubland that faced the dense woods.

As they exited the car, he pointed at the tree line and said, "Come on, it's just up here if I remember right."

He pushed aside low-hanging branches and pointed to a well-worn dirt path. He knew his smile must look mischievous as he motioned for Dewar to follow. They bent low as they pushed their way through the tangled copse. The undergrowth was trampled, and small insects swarmed around them, filling the air with their humming. Shafts of sunlight speared through the tree branches and cast dappled shadows on the ground. Le Claire could feel dampness oozing from the leaves underfoot; a musty smell assaulted his nostrils, and his mind jumped back twenty years.

"I was ten when I first came here. My friend's big brother had shown him this place, and the next day he'd called for me and we'd cycled here. Our rucksacks were filled with lemonade and sandwiches.

"How sweet, your mum sent you with a picnic."

Le Claire was caught in his memories, and his words were unguarded. "No, that was Martha. She was our housekeeper, and she always made sure us boys were fed."

From the look on Dewar's face, he realised he had given away rather more of his background than he had wanted. Dewar would have heard talk in the station of his being a fancy little rich boy, but he didn't need to corroborate it.

His mind was now firmly in the present with a dim echo of the past. "There it is, and it hasn't been fixed in all these years. In fact, it has just got worse."

Here, at the densest part of the woods, time and the elements had worn away sections, leaving an open area of about two feet across; a handy route for small boys to sneak into the manor's grounds, or anyone else for that matter. He checked the area in front of the gap; the leaves were compacted. Someone had come this way recently.

"Call it in, Dewar. Get the CSI guys. We'll head on in through the undergrowth so we'll skirt the path."

Dewar dutifully called for support, but Le Claire could sense her unease. "What's up?"

"Nothing, sir."

"I thought we'd got over you sir-ing me half to death. Come on, what's the issue?"

"I just don't like insect-ridden creepy, damp, smelly woods," she snapped.

"You'll be fine." She had wrestled a gun-wielding murderer to the ground in one of their recent cases. Now she was freaking out at the thought of a daddy longlegs? "Come on."

He stepped to the right of the path, into the thick foliage. He heard long sighs and heavy steps as Dewar followed close behind. On the worn pathway, the leaves and heavy branches had been naturally thinned after decades of small feet and inquisitive hands beating a path to the manor's back door. Before Gillespie, the manor had been owned by the UK-based heirs of a retired military man. For over thirty years, they had let the place decay until only a man with a fortune as large as Aidan Gillespie's could afford to buy and renovate such a white elephant. With absent owners, the place had become an unofficial public amenity. Families came to picnic, kids to play and teenagers to hang about. Young lovers had often crept this way as well.

Le Claire recalled the last time he had sneaked into the manor's grounds. He hadn't been a ten-year-old then, but an adventurous eighteen-year-old with a fast motorbike and a pretty girlfriend. As he showed her where he had played as a boy, they'd ended up in a game of another sort.

"Le Claire, is something wrong?"

He'd stopped. Dewar was so close behind him he could hear her breathing. The late summer sun couldn't find much passage in the woods, and the air was chilled. He hadn't noticed. His memories must have kept him warm.

"Sorry, I was just wool-gathering. We're here."

Through a gap in the dense tree line, they could see manicured lawns, carefully pruned bushes and symmetrically planted shrubs. The garden was neat, contained and under control. They faced the back of the main house; to their right lay the pool annex. A lone glass door was set into the back wall, and that's where they were headed. The crime scene guys had finished, taken all from the site that they could and handed access back to Gillespie. Le Claire reached out and pressed down on the long metal bar handle, and the door swung open.

"Anyone could have accessed the grounds and pool house this way. We need to spread our net wider."

Laura had spent the day at the apartment; even Sarah Hamlyn hadn't been so hard-hearted as to tell her to book into a hotel. Laura hadn't spoken to her. Scott's mother had left a message that morning asking her not to call but saying that she could stay in the apartment until after the funeral, which would be on Wednesday. If, IF, she wanted to attend the actual funeral, the cold voice had said it would probably be best if she didn't go to the gathering afterwards at a nearby hotel.

She'd gone for a walk. The apartment block had a private beach access. Long, wide steps led to the line of shingled top shore below the sea wall, which slowly faded to soft, creamy sand. She'd strolled from Greve D'Azette to the beach at Green Island, breathing in the tangy sea air, listening to the whooping gulls as they gracefully swept over the bay. Green Island itself was a sheltered suntrap, famous for its preternatural stillness; its rocky seabed, exposed by the fierce tidal movement, was typical of the east of the island. She'd bought a Styrofoam cup of tea and a bacon roll from the kiosk and sat on one of the benches gazing out to sea. A nearby plaque told her that she was on the southernmost part of the British Isles. She'd drunk the tea and thrown away the roll. She'd barely eaten since Scott had died.

She had walked back along the beach to the empty apartment, and had fallen into an exhausted sleep in the afternoon. Now, as the sun sank gracefully past the horizon, she mixed a strong gin and tonic and sat on the balcony. The colour had leached from the day and the sky and a low cloud formation buttressed the horizon like a faraway mountain range. The sun had sunk low, casting an ethereal rosy glow over the sand. From nowhere, fiery crimson streaks lit the sky as the sun began its descent to give way to the night. It was a sunset to watch with someone you loved, but Laura was now on her own, again.

This was a high-end development, and the walls were thick slabs of granite. It was only out here, on the long balcony, that she could hear any neighbourly noise at all. The sliding of a patio door, the clink of glasses, the scratch of cutlery on dinner plates, the murmur of voices. It felt comforting, made her feel less isolated.

Until she met Scott, she hadn't even known what it was like to feel you had someone to rely on, someone to be in your corner. She had opened herself up to him, allowed her defences to drop. She had cared for him so much and wished he hadn't acted so foolishly, for foolish he had been. She felt a rising anger that bubbled away under the surface. He had brought this on himself, and where did that leave her? Waiting for the police to come?

Le Claire sat up in bed, crumpled covers around his waist and a light sheen of sweat covering his body. The dream was already fading, the images mere shadows, but the sensation of being trapped, not being able to breathe, still lingered. He carefully eased himself out of bed so as not to wake the slumbering Sasha, who lay beside him. He rose and, opening the blinds a little, looked out across the garden. The moon was high, casting shadows amongst the shifting trees and bushes; the night belonged to nocturnal animals of every kind, and to those who could not sleep for the demons that chased them.

The soft voice floated across the room. "Jack, what are you doing? Come back to bed."

Sasha was lying on her side, naked to the waist, her dark hair splayed over the stark white pillowcase. She sat up in bed, and he regretted that she automatically pulled the covers up. "It's chilly, come here." She fumbled on the bedside cabinet, found the clock and her sigh was a gentle echo in the room. "It's 3:00 a.m. Come on. You need your sleep."

He complied, lay on his back and pulled Sasha into his arms, her head resting on his chest. Her breath fanned his skin as she spoke.

"This is becoming a habit. We spent last night at my place, and tonight we're at yours. Do you think we're doing the right thing?"

He held her closer, kissed the top of her head. "It feels right."

She burrowed in until it felt like they were sharing the same skin. "Let's play it by ear, then. So what woke you up?"

He hesitated, didn't want to open that can of worms.

She spoke into the silence. Her voice was wary. "Did you dream? Did you?"

"I can't remember."

"Oh, Jack, are the nightmares still as bad?"

"No, it's fine. I'm fine." His voice didn't sound convincing, even to himself.

"You can talk to me, you know that now, I hope."

In the dark, her voice was a comfort and a fear. He hadn't been able to talk to her last time, and that's when it had all gone wrong. Could he guarantee it would be different this time? He held her tight and lay awake long after she had gone back to sleep.

CHAPTER ELEVEN

The incident room team was doing what they did best, sorting through the mundane, cross-checking alibis and digging deep into the clutter and debris of a life, searching for cause, motive, clues – and unfortunately getting nowhere fast.

Le Claire and Dewar sat in front of the main white board at the far end of the incident room – the somewhat sparse whiteboard.

Scott Hamlyn's picture took centre place. It was one borrowed from his apartment. He stood on his balcony, the sunlit sea glistening behind him, champagne glass in hand. Le Claire wondered if Laura Brown had taken the photograph. Connecting lines led to the names of family, friends, persons of interest. All supposition so far, as there wasn't much to go on. Work colleagues described Hamlyn as a loner who had recently blossomed. They thought it was love. The few who had met her couldn't match the beautiful Laura with the very ordinary Scott. But together they had been, and if he'd lived, it looked like they'd have made a match of it. When questioned, no one seemed to have any idea how he had got his bruises. Le Claire rather thought they hadn't cared enough to ask.

It was taking some time to trawl through the statements from the party guests and compile a report, accounting for the attendees and where they were at the time. There was the press to deal with as well. They wanted updates and so did the general public. Social media, especially Facebook, was rife with incorrect information and accusations. People forgot, or just didn't seem to realise, that investigations took time, that every angle had to be researched, analysed. It wasn't all light-bulb moments, flashing lights and car chases. His phone rang. Dewar jerked as if she had been sleeping, probably mesmerised by the banality of what they had to go on so far. He checked the caller ID and mentally straightened up in his chair.

"Sir?"

The chief's voice was brusque.

"There's been an incident. Sir Hugh Mallory has been found dead. It's a suspected suicide. Given who he is, I need you to get to Fairland Fort and do the initial report. I don't assume there is anything urgent pending?"

He took the dig on the chin. He knew they had nothing so far.

"Okay, sir, we're on it, and point taken."

Le Claire quickly updated Dewar and got the expected puzzled look. "Why send you? We don't have any details on cause of death yet."

"Mallory was a jurat. I know you've not been in the island long enough to deal with any criminal matters in court, but we don't conduct trial by a jury. The elected jurats are effectively the judges of facts. They come from all walks of life. This is not a position only taken up by the privileged; it's about those who are respected in the community, who are grounded. It's an honorary post, and those elected are held in high esteem as the height of respectability. The chief will want this dealt with appropriately."

"So what do we know about him?"

"He came to Jersey in his fifties. Made his money in something or other, inherited a baronetcy from his father and became high profile in the island. He and his wife are big patrons of several charities. The news will be shocking. Let's get going."

# #

Fairland Fort was a landmark, jutting above the headland on the northern coast. Once important coastal defence posts, these Martello Towers were built in the Napoleonic wars. This particular one had been redeveloped into a family home. Sir Hugh had bought it several years later and completed its transformation into a showpiece.

The gated entrance opened onto a circular drive, the wide, busy borders crammed with colourful blooms. The main building, the original fort, was long and low and buttressed along one side by the high and rounded Martello tower, its slatted windows remnants of its initial use.

Le Claire beckoned for Dewar to follow. "Come on, this won't be pleasant."

Several police cars, a few other vehicles and an ambulance crowded the space in front of the open front doors. They were met by a uniformed officer.

"Sir, Dr Viera is with the deceased. Lady Mallory is in one of the downstairs rooms with her granddaughter."

"Thanks, I'll go to Viera first." They were directed to the back of the house, where they were shown into a huge space that was strewn with paintings. Brightly coloured canvasses were hanging up, leaning against the walls and laid out on several easels and trestle tables. Open-fronted, ceiling-high cupboards held pots of paint, tubs of brushes and rolls of paper. Viera was bent over a figure lying on the floor when he noticed Le Claire and Dewar. As the doctor stood, Le Claire got a proper look at the body. Sir Hugh lay on his back beside an upturned chair. He looked strangely peaceful, his features soft, as if in the midst of a deep sleep. His striped shirt was unbuttoned, and his chest was a bloodied mess, the gunshot wound a vicious blot on his tanned skin. An elegant pistol lay on the floor beside him.

Le Claire commanded, "Tell me what happened."

"Lady Mallory found Sir Hugh around 10:30 a.m. We'll need to do a post-mortem, but from the discolouring and body temperature, I'd hazard he hadn't died long before that."

He pointed to marks on one hand. "We've got gunpowder residue. From that and the angle of the shot, it looks self-inflicted."

"Any note?"

At Viera's head shake, Le Claire said, "Okay, you carry on, and I'll await the final report."

As they turned to leave, Viera called, "Hey, Dewar, did you have a good time last night?"

"What? Oh, err, yes, thanks."

Dewar had coloured, a fiery blush that stained her cheeks. Le Claire held his tongue until they were back in the main hallway. "What was that all about?"

"It was nothing."

"It didn't look like that. When Viera spoke, you coloured up like a fire engine. You two got a thing?"

Dewar looked embarrassed. "Absolutely not, no way. Nope. We just bumped into each other last night at a bar."

In time-honoured fashion, Le Claire suspected the lady protested far too much. Viera was built like the rugby player he was, and the surreptitious looks thrown his way by the females – and some of the males – at the station made Le Claire think he had more than his fair share of admirers.

"You know what they say. Don't mix business and pleasure. It only ever leads to trouble."

If anything, Dewar was even redder and looked decidedly uncomfortable.

She shook her head. "Nothing to talk about at all."

He thought she sounded a little disappointed, but he didn't have the time or the inclination to think about that right now.

# #

Lady Mallory was typical of women of a certain age and class. Her neatly cut brown hair was held back by a thin velvet band. Her figure was trim and spare, and she was pale beneath her carefully applied makeup.

Dressed in slacks and an open-neck shirt, the only visible sign of her distress were her red-rimmed eyes and the way she sat hunched over on the sofa, clutching the hand of a pretty brunette who looked to be in her early twenties.

Once Le Claire had introduced himself and Dewar, the younger woman gestured for them to sit. "I'm Louise Mallory. Grandma's a bit upset – we both are – but, well, I guess I'm more shocked than anything else. Yes, shocked." Her voice tailed away, and Le Claire saw the bewilderment in her eyes.

He addressed the older woman. "I am very sorry for your loss. Can you tell me what happened?" His voice was gentle. He could see she was in deep shock, and he didn't want to upset her any further.

"Hugh was in the studio. He loves to paint, you know. I usually leave him be in the mornings. I was just popping in to say I'd see him later as I was going to do some shopping in town with Louise. I knocked, but there was no answer, so I just went in, and, oh God, he was just lying there. I didn't know what to do. I can see it was foolish now, but I called his name, asked him what was going on. What a stupid woman I am. I screamed, I guess. Louise was waiting for me in the hall and came in. She dealt with everything."

"Hush, Grandma, there is no need to say anything else." She placed a comforting arm around the older woman, who looked completely worn out. "I called for an ambulance. They arrived and so did the police."

"I know this is indelicate, but do either of you know why Sir Hugh would take his own life? Did he leave a note?"

"No. My grandfather had a good life; he was very well respected in the community. He had no reason, none at all to do this. I can only assume that he many have been ill and thought, in a blind moment, this was his only option. They say, don't they, that suicides often have a split second where everything seems so dark there is no alternative?"

"And was your husband ill, Lady Mallory?"

Before she could speak, Louise Mallory butted in. "My grandfather would not have wanted to distress my grandmother. It would be just like him to try and conceal something like that."

"So you don't know if he was ill? It doesn't matter. We'll be speaking with his doctor. If you're up to it, we'll take down some details."

As they climbed back into the car, Le Claire looked around at the magnificent fort. "A long and distinguished life and all he'll be remembered as is a guy who committed suicide. Have a chat with his doctor, but I think we can close the file on this quickly."

The Hampton Bars was a comfortable pub and diner, popular with the young and also the not-so-youthful. The food was cheap, the drink not overpriced and the surroundings more congenial than the bedsits and shared flats a lot of people lived in.

Daria had commandeered a velvet-covered booth, and they'd eaten steaming plates of mussels with a creamy sauce and sipped ice-cold white wine.

"How long have you been in Jersey, Daria? I don't think you've ever told me how you ended up here."

"Same as a lot of people, I guess. A friend was working here, and I came to join her for a summer season, just over six years ago. I got a job in a hotel, mainly reception work. Once I'd done my five years, I moved from hospitality into the employment agency."

"Did you suggest the agency start bringing in girls from Poland?"

"Sure, and Romania as well and farther across Europe. There are loads of jobs here for au pairs and nannies and even in shops and financial services. If you don't have five years' residence, you can still get a job somewhere that has a spare licence to recruit non-locals. Well, that's how you got the job with Mr Le Claire's business."

"Yeah, I was lucky there. Pity the accommodation can be so crappy for the unqualified. As soon as I get some money saved up for a decent deposit, I'm going to try and find something better."

Daria looked puzzled. "But your mum was born here; doesn't that mean you get your qualifications earlier than ten years?"

"Afraid not. I spoke to Housing, and everyone, even those born in the island, need to do ten years' residence before they are residentially qualified. There are no shortcuts just because Mum was a Jersey girl."

Daria sipped her wine, her eyes shadowed by lowered lids. "I am sorry about your cousin. You were close, weren't you?"

"Yes, I came here thinking I'd have a chance to be part of a family again. Things haven't worked out with my aunt, but Scott was amazing. He welcomed me, and we became close. The funeral is tomorrow, and I'm dreading it."

Daria went to speak and then shut her mouth as she looked straight past Ana, who recognised the flirtatious look in her friend's eye. Ana sighed. No doubt Daria would get chatted up, and she'd be the usual wallflower. The next words told her how wrong she was. "Ana, what a surprise to see you here."

She recognised the voice, and her heart stuttered in her chest. She could feel her cheeks burn as she turned round. "Hi, Ben. Yes, this is a surprise." She wanted to kick herself and mentally rolled her eyes as she berated her gaucheness.

He glanced at Daria before turning back to Ana. "You girls out for a quiet drink?"

"Yes, and a bite to eat. This is my friend, Daria. Daria, this is Ben."

Daria's smile was sly. "Ah, Ben and I go back a bit. I know him well. How is Danny?"

Ana felt Ben stiffen beside her, and his voice had an edge to it. "He's fine. How do you know Ana?"

"Ana and I met through the agency. She is friends with Irena. You remember her, don't you?"

Ana turned to Ben in expectation. How did he know Irena? Then again, this island was pretty incestuous at times, the usual six degrees of separation was more like three in Jersey.

"Vaguely. I'm here with friends and better get back to them." He turned to Ana; his gaze was direct and unwavering, and she held his eyes, didn't back down from the look of admiration that probably matched her own. "Ana, I'll give you that call, huh?"

"Sure, that would be good."

He reached out, and his hand skimmed over hers. The touch was fleeting, but the sensation lingered long afterwards.

# #

Laura had been waiting to be contacted since Sunday morning, but no one had called. Or at least not who she'd been expecting.

The phone had rung once. It was a colleague of Scott's; the office sent their condolences. That had amused Laura. He hadn't been aware of it in himself, but there was an arrogance about Scott, he gave off a sniff of superiority. He was shy and sometimes awkward and countered with an attitude that made him seem distant and mocking. People didn't see though the mask; who had the time to understand a colleague's psyche? Instead, they saw a man, not yet thirty, who acted as if he knew everything and needed no one. But he'd needed Laura. What started out as a casual arrangement had grown into much more. He'd wanted to marry her, look after her, and she'd capitulated. He'd said the past wasn't important.

She'd said they should wait, see what happened, but he'd been impatient, had wanted everything cleared up. He said he needed to know they were safe. That was immaterial now.

The phone call still hadn't come. Tomorrow was Scott's funeral, and she wasn't sure she could stand the not knowing any longer. Her hand hovered over the phone. She pulled it away. Not the landline. Best to be safe. She moved to the bedroom, found her suitcase and rummaged around until she found her phone – her private phone. There were no records of incoming or outgoing calls, no monthly contract where your information could be passed over. She'd got into the habit of using these phones a long time ago and wasn't going to give up now.

She dialled from memory. She hadn't called it in a while, but it was funny how some numbers, seemingly forgotten, tumbled back when you thought of whom they belonged to. She shivered, hoping she was doing the right thing.

The ringtone sounded one, two, three times and was answered on the fourth with a simple "Hello," the voice unmistakable.

Her mouth felt dry. "It's me."

This was answered by a growl of impatience. "Why the hell are you calling me? You better not be on a traceable line."

"I'm not that stupid."

He was apparently mollified, for his tone was less aggressive. "Good, what do you want?"

"Isn't it obvious? I thought someone might have called. Let me know what's going on. What have the police said? Have they spoken to you?"

His voice had regained its usual smoothness. "I assume they've spoken to lots of people."

Impatience rose. She wasn't in the mood for games. "Do they know what happened?"

"What are you talking about?"

"Don't play with me. Do they know?"

His laugh was mocking. "I don't know what the police know. However, I am sure they'll ferret out what is relevant to their case and even perhaps some secrets that aren't."

"You've always been a cocky swine."

His voice was serious. "I'm winding you up. You just keep your mouth shut and don't act guilty. I mean, you've got nothing to worry about. You've never broken the law, have you?"

"Did you threaten him? Is this down to you?"

His laugh was vicious. It was obvious he still bore a grudge. "Just keep quiet and act the grieving girlfriend. And don't call me again."

The line went dead. She threw the phone down beside her and covered her face with her hands. Fat, hot tears fell as she wept, mostly for Scott Hamlyn, and a little for herself.

CHAPTER TWELVE

Le Claire and Dewar stood at the back of the church as Scott Hamlyn was laid to rest. Sarah and Charles Hamlyn occupied the front pew on the left side; an uncomfortable-looking Ana perched next to her uncle as his wife stared straight ahead. Laura Brown sat in isolation on the right side pew. Behind the Hamlyns sat several older couples – relatives or family friends, he supposed. There was a scattering of younger people. Le Claire caught a few of them checking their watches; one even seemed to be reading through phone messages or email. Work colleagues perhaps, with the obligatory showing of face; for some it would be skiving off work for a few hours with an excuse no one could complain about.

Le Claire was drawn from his musings by an elbow being poked into his side. Dewar. She caught his gaze and flicked her eyes to the other side of the room a few pews back. Some of the work colleague types sat there, and Le Claire recognised one immediately: Paul Armstrong. They had met the lawyer on a recent case when his client, and long-term friend, was murdered. That had only been the start of a killing spree built on greed.

As the choir voices faded and the last chords of "Jerusalem" floated on the air, the pallbearers stepped forward, and the coffin of Scott Hamlyn was borne aloft and carried outside in a sombre procession. A private burial was to follow.

Charles and Sarah Hamlyn stood just inside the church doors in a receiving line with Ana and two of the older couples. Laura Brown wasn't present.

Le Claire gently shook Charles Hamlyn's hand and then clasped that of his wife. "Please accept our condolences."

"Thank you for coming." They spoke in unison, their voices robotic and faces unsmiling. Sarah Hamlyn's eyes were slightly unfocussed, and Le Claire could almost hear her scream, *How did this happen? Why?* Le Claire silently promised that he would find out what had happened. Small comfort to Sarah Hamlyn, but he would make sure her son's murderer was caught and punished.

He nodded at Ana and made to move out the doors and then turned back. "I see Miss Brown has gone. Could she not face the receiving line?"

Sarah Hamlyn's face distorted with distaste, her nostrils flared and fire lit her eyes. "My boy would still be alive if it wasn't for that woman. And she isn't in the receiving line because she has no place here."

"Sarah!" Her husband's voice was shocked, but he laid a gentle, consoling hand on her arm.

"Don't," she snapped as she shrugged him away. "Detective, I am sure you are doing what you can to find out who did this. But you need to look at Laura Brown; there is something off about her."

"We are looking at everyone connected to your son, everyone. But what do you mean about Miss Brown?"

Her sigh was audible as her shoulders sank. "Nothing, I meant nothing."

Le Claire realised there was no use pressing her, especially on this of all days. He and Dewar made their way toward the high, arched doors. The thick granite walls of the church made the inside cool, dark and hushed; the only light came from the beams that illuminated the stained-glass windows, sending prisms of light creeping along the stone-flagged floors, undulating over the grooves worn from centuries of penitent feet, or at the least, well-shod Sunday churchgoers.

As they exited, the sun was blinding, and Le Claire raised a hand to shield his eyes. Once he grew accustomed to the light, he saw a lone figure standing by the small alms gate. As he walked up to her, she hastily wiped her eyes with a handkerchief. He couldn't help but think that grief suited Laura Brown. Her eyes were moist, lending her a vulnerable air, but her makeup was intact.

"Are you all right? Could you not face the receiving line?" He didn't reveal that he knew she wouldn't have been welcomed by the Hamlyns. He wanted to know what she thought.

Her laugh was brittle and sharp. "Scott's mother would have had a fit. I'm just waiting for my taxi, and then I'm out of here. I better go. That looks like my cab."

His eyes followed her as she walked up the stone pathway that led to the road. Le Claire was heading to where Dewar waited when a familiar voice rang out, "Miss Brown, wait, please wait."

Paul Armstrong hurried toward Laura Brown, who was about to get into the waiting taxi. Heads bent, they conversed for a few moments. She was shaking her head; Armstrong looked like he was pressing her to come with him. Laura Brown seemed to droop in defeat, and she stepped aside as Armstrong searched through his pockets and, pulling out some notes, paid the taxi driver and led her to his own car. Now what was that about?

# #

Le Claire had been staring at his virtually blank personal case board since they had returned to the station. It contained a picture of Scott Hamlyn, together with a random scattering of names and comments, including Laura Brown, the Hamlyns, Aidan Gillespie, the manor and £20,000 in cash. A copy of the guest list for the party was tacked to one side. With a sigh, he returned to his computer screen. Each of the officers on the team regularly loaded their reports onto the electronic case file. All information, no matter how small or insignificant it may seem.

He was jerked out of his reverie by his phone ringing; it was the emergency operator.

"A call has come in. They asked specifically for you, sir. It's a Paul Armstrong at the Somerset Hotel. There's been an incident. I'll send some uniforms down there."

He sat upright in his chair, all alert. The Somerset was where Scott Hamlyn's wake was being held. "Yes, get someone down there and put the call through to me."

There was a dull tone, a click and then the line was opened. "Mr Armstrong, what can I do for you? I hear there's been an incident?"

The lawyer's voice was tense. "Yes, you could say that. There has been a bit of a rumpus between Sarah Hamlyn and Laura Brown, Scott's girlfriend. I saw you at the church, and Sarah said that you've been asking questions. I know you can't say anything, but if you're involved, I'm assuming that Scott didn't voluntarily end up in that pool. If you are investigating his death, then I think you should get down here."

"Fine, I'm on my way."

Le Claire grabbed his jacket and swung by Dewar's desk to collect her. What the hell was happening?

PC Hunter was standing ramrod straight outside double doors that lay halfway along the long corridor. His stiff shoulders visibly relaxed when he saw Le Claire.

"What's up, Hunter?"

"I think it better if Mr Armstrong explains, sir. He's waiting just inside the door."

Hunter knocked three sharp taps, and the door opened immediately, wide enough for Armstrong to just squeeze through.

He briefly smiled at Le Claire, who didn't bother smiling in return. He assumed there was nothing to smile about; why else would they be here? "Mr Armstrong, tell me what happened."

"Sarah Hamlyn and Laura Brown had an altercation. I guess you'd call it a fight." He removed his glasses and rubbed the bridge of his nose. He was a man who carried a bit more weight than he should, but he must be in his mid-fifties and, with his carefully styled grey hair, had the look of money from his deep yachting tan to his impeccably tailored suits. However, at the moment he was looking a little crumpled. He reached into the inside pocket of his suit and drew out a spotted handkerchief that he used to wipe his brow.

Le Claire and Dewar exchanged glances as Armstrong continued. "All hell broke loose after the will was read. Sarah Hamlyn launched herself at Laura Brown and felled her to the ground. Charles Hamlyn and a few others piled in to separate them. Sarah Hamlyn was going berserk, shouting and screaming. Then she turned on her niece, Ana, sweet girl who looked absolutely shell-shocked. I didn't know what to do. Then I thought of you."

"Thanks. So tell me about the will."

"I was Scott's executor. It's a service we often carry out for our colleagues in the firm. Sarah Hamlyn, as next of kin, was adamant that the reading of the will was to take place during the drinks reception. I tried to stop her, said I didn't think it was a good idea, but she ignored me. Said she wanted everything dealt with today and had booked a small conference room. The plan was that we could withdraw there to read the will and then re-join the reception."

"What caused her to attack Laura Brown?"

"Tempers were getting frayed the second that Mrs Hamlyn realised I had asked Laura to attend the reading. She went ballistic when I revealed that apart from a legacy to his parents the remainder of Scott's estate was left, in its entirety, to Laura Brown. Sarah Hamlyn started screaming about the wages of sin."

Dewar whistled. "And how much would that be?"

"Minus any debt, Scott's main assets, his apartment, investments and cash were worth around £3 million; there was also a £750,000 insurance policy."

"I take it Mother Hamlyn obviously had high expectations herself. And Laura Brown, how did she take the news?"

"She seemed surprised when I insisted that she attend the reading of the will, but she doesn't strike me as someone who wears her heart on her sleeve."

"Not even when she's told she has inherited what must be virtually £4 million when everything is totted up?"

"As I said, she didn't seem to show any emotion, and then Sarah Hamlyn was on her."

Dewar spoke up. "And what was the legacy to the Hamlyns?"

"I don't know that I can divulge that, not unless it's relevant to a criminal investigation." Paul Armstrong's look was sly as a fox.

Le Claire put him out of his misery. "We are treating Scott Hamlyn's death as suspicious. So please answer the question."

"Ah, I knew something was up when you two attended the funeral. The parents were left £100,000 between them."

"Where are they now?"

Hunter moved forward. "Miss Brown is in the conference room, and Mrs Hamlyn has been taken to a small library. The only other family is Mrs Hamlyn's niece, who is in the main reception room."

Le Claire rubbed at his temple. "God knows I don't want to cart Sarah Hamlyn off to the police station on the day she buries her son. Let's talk to Laura Brown first."

Dewar followed Le Claire through the room where the drinks were being held. The mourners had apparently been indulging in the free champagne as testified by bright eyes, flushed faces and laughter. Their quick glances and whispered conversations were proof that the incident was the talk of the room. He saw Ana, standing alone by one of the tall windows.

A second uniform stood blocking the entrance to a corridor that led off the main room. He stood to attention as he recognised Le Claire.

"Where can I find Miss Brown?"

"She is in here, sir." He pointed to the door he was standing next to. "Miss Brown has refused medical treatment and asked to be left alone, sir."

Laura Brown was pale and dishevelled and merely glanced at the door when Le Claire entered followed by Dewar. Her hand shook slightly as she sipped from a plastic water bottle. She turned her face fully toward Le Claire, and he could see a dark bruise forming across one cheek, the purple hues in stark contrast to the rest of her unblemished skin. Her hair was ruffled and unkempt, but none of this distracted from her looks. He was reminded of the old adage that beauty marries up, or in this case, should that be doesn't marry, but ends up with the money anyway?

"Miss Brown, how are you?"

Her smile was weak and rueful. "I've been better, but I am okay. It was just such a shock."

"What was a shock, the attack or the contents of the will?"

Her voice grew cool, and her eyes were devoid of emotion. "Both. The attack was completely unexpected, and I had no idea that Scott had redone his will in my favour…no idea at all."

"About the attack – what would you like us to do? I am sure there will be no lack of supporters if you decide to press charges; it was in full view of the mourners after all."

"No, I don't think I could do that. Sarah Hamlyn couldn't stand me in any event. This was just the final straw, I guess. Scott mentioned to her a few weeks back that he had serious feelings about me. Apparently, his mother went crazy, screaming and shouting that he'd marry me over her dead body."

"And was marriage on the cards?"

"I thought so. We got on very well indeed. Scott and I had been seeing each other for six months. I came to the island virtually every weekend, and we spent a couple of holidays together. I would have been very happy to move to a more permanent stage, but that's not going to happen now, is it?"

She sounded bitter, and Dewar butted in, tensed and combative, before he could stop her.

"No, it isn't, and I hate to be indelicate, but you did get the money anyway."

Laura Brown's voice was cold. "Yes, I did, but I didn't ask for it, and I certainly didn't kill for it."

Le Claire moved in. "We'll get someone to take you back to the apartment. I think it best if you stay away from Mrs Hamlyn for the time being."

"I can assure you that won't be a problem at all."

They headed for the next door along the corridor and what Le Claire assumed would be a very angry Sarah Hamlyn.

On opening the door, Le Claire reminded himself not to make assumptions. Sarah Hamlyn was in a serious state, but it didn't seem to be driven by anger. Her face was tear-ravaged and covered in blotches.

She sat on a low sofa, her husband by her side. She was staring straight ahead, her body rigid; her husband leaned into her, holding one of her hands in both of his. He was running his fingers gently across her flesh, no doubt intended as a soothing rhythm, but Sarah Hamlyn seemed anything but comforted.

She snatched her hand away, an angry look in her eyes as she held herself even tighter. Turning, she hissed at her husband, "Let me be. Just leave me alone."

She turned to Le Claire. "My son left virtually all he possessed, all he had worked for to that girl. He just couldn't see through her. I don't know what came over me. I just wanted to hurt her."

Sarah Hamlyn's eyes were wet with unshed tears, and her pain resonated in the otherwise quiet room.

"Sarah, stop it. We're in enough trouble as it is." Charles Hamlyn smiled weakly at Le Claire as if in apology.

"We? I hardly think so. You'd have kissed her hand instead of giving her the slap she deserved – and got."

Le Claire asked, "You admit to assaulting Miss Brown?"

"Admit it? I'd be a fool not to, not when there is a room full of witnesses. Scott is dead, and Laura Brown is now a rich woman. She'll have a lifetime of living off my son's money."

"You have something to say about Miss Brown?"

"She slept with our son, made him think she cared about him and now that he's dead she walks off with everything. There is no decency anymore. Look at Laura Brown, Inspector. Surely, the money's motive enough? And who is she? Where does she come from?"

"Miss Brown is adamant that Mr Hamlyn did not tell her he had changed his will."

"I am sure she is correct. However, he was not the most organised of men in his personal life. His private papers could be strewn over his study desk for days before he filed them safely away. Let us not forget that woman was often alone in his apartment. I warned him to lock his study, not to allow her access if he was going out. He wouldn't hear a word said against her."

"Miss Brown is not going to press charges. I suggest I organise for her to be taken home, and you and Mr Hamlyn can mourn Scott in peace, but please stay away from Laura Brown."

"Oh, I intend doing that. I won't give her the satisfaction of having an opportunity to press charges; she has everything else."

CHAPTER THIRTEEN

Le Claire had seen Laura Brown taken to what was now her home in a squad car and had released Sarah and Charles Hamlyn to join the other mourners and say good-bye to their only child. He had sent Dewar back to the station, saying he'd walk; he needed some fresh air, needed to think. He headed for the exit and passed the open door of a small lounge, stopping when he heard his name called. "Le Claire, in here a moment."

Paul Armstrong relaxed in a winged armchair, a tray of coffee on the table in front of him, what looked like an empty brandy glass sat beside it. Le Claire swung into the room and wearily sank into the matching armchair. "You didn't re-join the gathering?"

"I've had more than enough drama for one day. Seriously, though, I came to say good-bye to a colleague, and I've done that."

"Some of the team have been to your offices and spoke to Scott's colleagues. I have to say I forgot it was your firm."

"They didn't speak to me. I've been in long meetings for a couple of days. Were my colleagues helpful?"

"They were certainly willing to help, but I don't think we found out very much."

Armstrong sighed. "Scott was a strange egg. He had a wall around him that few ever climbed, far less breached. He didn't have an easy manner, and we all like easy these days, don't we? God forbid we have to expend energy and work at something. He was too difficult for his colleagues to get to know, so they just coexisted on the same plane. His PA would know the name of his doctor and how often he went to the dentist, but she'd never have a clue what he did in his spare time, whether he spent a Saturday night watching reality TV or listened to classical music with a glass of malt whisky. And on that note…" He beckoned for the waitress and ordered another brandy. Le Claire refused a drink.

"He wasn't well liked?"

"They didn't know him well enough to dislike him. The boy had his insecurities, and he kept himself back from people. But when you got him to relax, he had a clever wit and was an interesting chap to talk to."

"No one seemed to know how he came by his recent bruises."

"Ah yes, the fight was quite out of character."

Le Claire snapped to attention. "You know what happened? Who did he have a fight with?"

Armstrong looked apologetic. "I am afraid I only know what happened, not with whom. I asked Scott outright how he got those bruises. He gave me some stuff and nonsense at first, but I kept on at him. That boy was too insular for his own good sometimes. How he got involved with that girl, I will never know. He was undoubtedly punching above his weight there." He must have seen the impatience Le Claire was attempting to keep from his face, so he continued. "He said he'd had one beer too many, had an argument with a friend and traded blows. He was still seething about it, I could tell."

"He didn't say who it was?"

"No, but I can't imagine it would be difficult to find out. I mean, I didn't even know he had a friend. I'd ask his mother if I were you."

Le Claire's response was dry. "Thanks for the tip; I might just do that."

"Sorry."

Le Claire smiled. "You weren't questioned with the rest of your colleagues, so do you mind if I ask some now?" At his easy nod, he continued. "We know Scott was in discord with at least one person, whoever he had the fight with. Do you know of anyone else he was at odds with or who might want to harm him?"

"Afraid not, Scott wasn't forthcoming about his life unless probed."

"So he didn't have any ongoing issues, not even work related."

Paul Armstrong looked contemplative; his posture stilled, he went to speak, hesitated.

"Come on, say whatever it is. You have to let me determine if it's important or not."

A heavy sigh preceded his words. "Scott had taken his eye off the ball a bit. We'd had a chat about it. I was anxious, I hate man-management issues, and he was arrogant, difficult to deal with. Truth is that Scott was wrapped up in his girlfriend and seemed to think of nothing else. He messed up a couple of deals, had a few irate clients."

"Anyone in particular?"

He huffed and rolled his eyes. "The main issue was with Aidan Gillespie."

Le Claire leaned forward in his chair, all ears. "Carry on."

"Aidan Gillespie is a self-made man. Now he is all softened edges and pretty manners, but there is steel beneath the sophisticated veneer. Scott never quite realised that. He messed up in what should have been a straightforward boundary dispute over some land at the edge of the manor. There's a strip of wildflower meadow with a pretty little stream running through it that was originally part of the manor lands. Apparently, the argument was that it had been ceded to the next-door property as a dowry at some point and the title never straightened out. However, there was a subsequent document returning the land to the manor. We had an open-and-closed case, but Scott had just got back from holiday with Laura. He hadn't known her that long and must've been starry-eyed or lost his mind, for he forgot to submit the latest document, and the court ruled against Gillespie's claim."

"I assume Mr Gillespie wasn't too pleased?"

"He was apoplectic. I was there on another case that day. When we all spilled out of court into the Royal Square, Gillespie just went for Scott. Before it turned nasty, the brother pulled Gillespie the Elder off and they went huffing away. A formal complaint was made to the office, and we had to cancel the latest invoice and return the fees already paid. Not good all round."

"Yet Scott Hamlyn somehow gets into Gillespie's party?"

"I wondered what he was doing there. That doesn't make sense."

"Exactly. Anything else to add?"

Armstrong sipped his brandy. "I think I've spilled my guts enough for today, don't you?"

Dewar disconnected the call from Le Claire. He was heading back to the station but wanted her to do two things. The second would be the most challenging, today of all days, so she decided to quickly get the easy call out of the way first as her Scots pragmatism came to the fore.

The telephone number was in the contact sub-folder in the main case file. The landline rang five or six times before it was answered by a male voice. "Danny Gillespie."

"This is DS Dewar, Mr Gillespie. We'd like to have a couple of words with your brother."

"He'll be back tonight. He has been in London and is on the last flight into the island. May I ask what this is about? Can I help?"

"I'm afraid it's a matter we'll need your brother's input on, but thanks for offering." She disconnected the line without waiting for a reply. She knew she shouldn't let personal feelings intrude onto the job, but there was something about Danny Gillespie she just didn't like. She half expected him to ask to speak to Le Claire instead of her, the way he'd looked through her when they last met, as if in a man's world she was invisible; or was that her own insecurities talking? She shook the thought aside and got on with the job.

She checked the computer contact files again and dialled a mobile number. Sarah Hamlyn answered after only a few short rings. Dewar took a deep breath. "Mrs Hamlyn, it's DS Dewar. I am so sorry to bother you. Can you speak now?"

The voice that responded sounded defeated and perhaps a little broken. "Yes. I'm at home. We couldn't stay there any longer. Have you news?"

"No, but there has been a development. Your son had bruising on his face and to his torso."

"Yes, I saw that. Was he beaten before he died?" His voice ended on a whisper.

"No, we don't believe so. The post-mortem results indicate that

87

the bruising was a few days old. A colleague of Scott's has confirmed that he said he had got into a fight with someone."

"That is ridiculous." There was a pause and a less certain voice continued, "Who did that to Scott?"

"I don't know, but he apparently said it was a friend and that they had gone out drinking and it turned into a fight."

"I don't believe this. I mean, he went out for a drink last week with a good friend. But David wouldn't harm him."

"David who?"

"David Adamson, they've been friends since school."

Dewar parked on the road outside the house. It was one of the typical new-build, executive-type homes that seemed to have sprung up everywhere, tucked away in small closes. All cream walls and French-trimmed windows in bright colours, they housed those who had money to spend and wanted people to know it. The front garden, pristine lawn and carefully tended borders were littered with brightly coloured plastic toys. A harassed-looking man opened the front door, his brows rising as he took in Le Claire's badge and Dewar's uniform. "Save us from hysterical young girls. Come on in."

Le Claire exchanged a puzzled glance with Dewar. "I'm DCI Le Claire and this is DS Dewar. Are you Mr David Adamson?"

"Yes, yes come on in." He held a checked tea towel in his hands and threw it over one shoulder as he beckoned them to follow him into a large kitchen diner. To say it currently looked lived in was an understatement. Adamson was apologetic. "Sorry about the mess. I've just fed the kids."

Sounds of childish voices were coming from the next room, interspersed with the odd scream and shout, and Adamson quickly shut the door. "Sorry, they go a bit crazy and have a mad half hour after they've eaten."

"You don't seem surprised to see us. Why is that?"

The man in front of him seemed taken aback by his comment. "Well, no. I mean, I'm surprised you bothered following up. I'm sure the girl was just being overanxious."

Le Claire asked, "What's the problem?"

"Our au pair has done a bunk, got her last wages and took off the next day. I was away doing some work in London. Luckily, my wife was back and took the call from the nursery to say the kids hadn't been picked up. We checked out Irena's room – virtually everything was gone."

Dewar's tone was neutral, but impatience lit her eyes. "Looks like she skipped out on you."

"I know, but she has a friend who has called a few times to see if I had heard anything. She even turned up here on Sunday. She's a sweet little thing and seemed pretty worried. She said she was thinking of calling the police about her friend being missing. Irena probably just didn't tell her she was taking off, but now the poor kid seems really concerned."

"Okay, understood. We aren't here about that, but we'll pass a message to our colleagues.

Adamson looked confused. "Oh, right. Well, how can I help you?"

Dewar's voice was soft. "We don't want to distress you, but we have a few questions to ask about your friendship with the late Scott Hamlyn."

His face sagged. "Ah God, poor Scott. Do you know what happened? Was it an accident?"

"We are investigating a suspicious death."

"Murder? Jesus."

Le Claire was direct. "We didn't say that, it is simply classed as suspicious until we learn more. I understand you had a disagreement with Mr Hamlyn a few days before his death and that it turned physical?"

He held out his hands in supplication. "You've got me bang to rights. I was really upset to hear about what happened to Scott. However, it doesn't erase that we had a nasty argument, and a few punches were thrown."

He lifted up the front of his T-shirt and exposed his lightly tanned stomach, which was covered in several purplish bruises. "Scott caught me a couple of corkers."

"What did you argue about?"

A wry smile accompanied his words. "What do men ever argue about? A woman – my wife, in fact. Look, Scott and I had sunk a few pints. He was talking about his relationship with this girl he was seeing, saying he wanted to marry her. I was only trying to be helpful, said not to rush things. That maybe he should live with her for a while. I mean, he hadn't known her long."

"And he took offence?"

"Yes, but that's not what the fight was about as such. Scott got defensive, said he knew what he was doing. If he'd left it there, we'd have been fine."

"What happened?"

"Scott went nuts, laid into me, saying what did I know about relationships, that I had a part-time marriage, and she stayed away because I was a lousy husband. Then he said she was probably seeing someone else. Only the words weren't so polite. That's when I said maybe we should talk outside. We went into the lane by the back of the pub, and I smacked him. He hit me back; we traded a few ineffectual blows and then went storming off in different directions. I was going to call him once I'd cooled down, but then it was too late. I never got a chance to make it up with him."

"Out of interest, why did he say that about your wife?"

"Beth works abroad. She's a director in a trust business. The money is brilliant, but she works away for three weeks at a time and is then back for a couple, then off again."

Dewar looked at the toys scattered around the kitchen, the childish drawings stuck to the fridge door. "That can't be easy."

"It isn't, but we're doing this for our future. I run a small property management company. It does okay, but it brings in nothing near like what Beth earns. That money tips us into a very comfortable lifestyle. Financially, it's fantastic, but it totally sucks from a personal level."

"Where were you last Saturday evening?"

"What! Are you for real? That's the night Scott died. I wasn't at Gillespie's party, if that is what you're asking."

"Where were you?"

"Here with the kids. I don't have an au pair at the moment, do I?"

"No alibi?"

"Not unless you count a four-year-old and a two-year-old."

Dewar changed the subject. "You'd known Scott Hamlyn for a while?"

"Sure, we hung about at school but lost touch when Scott went to England to go to university. I bumped into him a few years after he was back, and he did some of the legal work in setting up my business."

Le Claire stepped in. "You say you had a property business. What exactly do you do?"

"I've got two lines. One is straightforward sourcing and management of rental properties for local and foreign owners, you know, rent collection and the like. The other side, which is growing, is looking after empty properties. Either those that are up for sale and we make sure they're looking tip-top for viewers, or where the owners are out of the island. We check the properties on a regular basis, make sure they're secure, that the utilities are working and collect the mail. It's just general maintenance and security, really. I've started doing a bit of work in London as well."

Le Claire looked around the room, took in the chaos. "How do you manage without childcare?"

"The kids are usually at nursery for most of the day. Costs a fortune, but it's worth it. Any work trips to London have to wait until my wife is home."

"So you had no more contact with Mr Hamlyn after the night you fought?"

"Yeah, more's the pity."

Dewar asked, "We didn't see you at the funeral. You didn't attend?"

He looked a little shamefaced, and his words were defensive. "I couldn't go, could I? The little one had an upset tummy and had to stay off nursery. I didn't have anyone who could babysit for me."

"Okay, we'll be in touch if we have any more questions. No need to see us out."

They left him standing in his kitchen. As they buckled themselves into the car, Le Claire was pensive. "What do you think?"

"Seems plausible. That was some bruise."

"Yes, but we need to take a further look at him. He was obviously at odds with Hamlyn."

"Yes, looks like they really went for it. I don't know if you can make up that easily with a friend after something like that.

"He'll never know now."

CHAPTER FOURTEEN

Le Claire's feet and hands were bound tight with rough rope. His eyes were uncovered but of no use in the heavy and impenetrable dark. Initial disorientation gave way as his survival instincts took over. He kicked both legs up and came into contact with what sounded like heavy wood; kicking out to the side met the same obstruction. There was no sound, just the heaviness of an unnatural silence, the air was dense and fetid, and that's when Le Claire realised he was trapped. Panic rose and his body bucked as he kicked out, his feet battering against his prison walls. To no avail. The silence grew heavier as he recognised there was no escape. He opened his mouth to scream…

He sat bolt upright, the bed clothes twisted and coiled about him, evidence of his disturbed sleep. Sasha lay on her side, dead to the world. He always swore she could sleep through a hurricane. She certainly hibernated through the vicious storms that often hit the island. To his disgust, he was covered in a fine sweat, physical evidence of his nightmare, the content of which was fading fast. All that remained were tiny wisps flitting through his consciousness, too quick to grab hold of. He'd woken with a jolt and still felt unsettled now that he was wide awake. Probably best he didn't remember what he'd dreamed of.

With surprise, he saw that the clock on the bedside table said 11:50 p.m. They'd gone to bed around an hour ago, made love, lazy and slow, and drifted off to sleep. He drew back the covers and headed for the bathroom. He couldn't sleep and needed to wash away the sweat that clung to him.

After a quick shower, he threw a towelling robe over his nakedness and padded into the kitchen area. He flicked the switch on for the kettle and busied himself getting a mug and the fixings for a cup of milky coffee. He closed the wooden door of the overhead cupboard a little too quickly, and it slammed shut, the noise even louder in the quiet stillness of night. The sound jolted him back into his dream; recollection came fast. "Christ!" He braced his hands on the counter and hung his head, trying to block the images, the thoughts. He'd dreamed he was trapped, buried alive, but that hadn't happened to him. It had happened to April Baines. The very name, whispering through his mind, was enough to open the door to an onslaught of memories.

The kettle beeped and switched itself off as it reached boiling, the noise registering at the very back of his mind. He ignored it and, without thinking, without making a decision, reached into the cupboard for a clean wineglass, sought the opened bottle they hadn't finished earlier and poured the remainder of the red wine into the glass. It was half-full, and he downed it in one, tipping his head back as the blackberry aroma and peppery taste filled his senses. He reached down to the wine rack, chose another bottle at random, opened the screw top and poured a full glass. He greedily drank a long draught whilst he picked the bottle up and moved to the seating area. He thumped down onto the sofa and sat there, glass in one hand, the bottle of wine in the other.

He hadn't thought of April in weeks, and part of him despaired that he could even find a moment's peace after what had happened to her. She'd been a fifteen-year-old from the care system who no one bothered looking for as they branded her just another runaway. But she hadn't run. She'd been taken. Defiled, used, beaten and ultimately murdered. Colin Chapman was rotting in a prison cell awaiting trial for the abduction, rape and murder of several girls, April included.

But Le Claire knew he was the one who had really killed her. His rage, his uncontrolled response to Chapman's taunting as he'd chased the bastard through the half-abandoned industrial zone had put an unconscious Chapman in a hospital bed. Three weeks later, a laughing Chapman had told him about his last victim, the one no one knew about. April Baines. She'd been dead for weeks, buried alive in a wooden packing chest, but she'd been alive the day he caught Colin Chapman. Le Claire felt the bile rise in his throat and chased away his guilt and the sight of what had lain in that makeshift coffin with the rest of the wine in his glass.

"Jack, honey, are you okay?"

Sasha stood in front of him, her eyes heavy with sleep, dark hair mussed. She'd thrown on the denim shirt he'd been wearing earlier in the evening, her long tanned legs uncovered. She held the front of the shirt closed, and he had a glimpse of golden skin. Even in despair, she still drew him in. Her eyes flicked to the bottle of wine, and he saw from the tightening of her lips that her concern was fast fleeing.

"You get out of bed and sit here alone, at gone midnight, drinking? Is that what you've been doing whilst we've been apart?"

"I had a bad dream, couldn't sleep."

"I just knew it. You are having the same dreams. Well, you should've had some hot milk, not half a bottle of bloody Pinot."

"Don't start, Sasha, just don't, okay!" He knew he snapped, he knew he was shouting her down, he knew she didn't deserve it, but he couldn't help himself. She visibly drew back, an expression of hurt on her face. Her eyes looked straight into the very heart of him.

"How much longer, Jack? How much longer will you let this eat away at you? You need to talk to someone. If it can't be me, then you need to see a professional. You went to see someone when it first happened, but you gave it up."

"Yes, because going on and on about it doesn't do me any good. I just need to cope with it, and I do." He looked at the empty wineglass in his hand. "Well, most days I do."

She didn't say anything for a moment, and when she did the words came out as if rehearsed. It seemed as if she had been planning on saying them for some time. "Hiding isn't coping. Blocking isn't coping. Running away from your emotions definitely isn't coping. You've put what happened into a little box in your mind and closed it shut, but every now and again it sneaks out and catches you unawares. I love you, Jack, but living with you became unbearable." She went quiet, simply stared at him. She opened her mouth to speak and then obviously thought better of it as her lips clamped shut. When she eventually spoke, her voice was quiet, but it reverberated with hurt. "We know what happened. You turned to someone else—"

"I told you a million times, nothing happened."

"Maybe you didn't sleep with her, Jack, but you emotionally invested. You talked to her when you wouldn't talk to me. You were with her when you should have been with me."

"We worked together…"

"Stop it. I told myself not to bring it up again. That I should just believe you when you said that you never slept with her, but it hurts. It bloody hurts that you could talk to someone else and not to me."

"Sasha…"

She held her palms up as she backed away. "I'm going to sleep. I can't talk about this now."

He let her go and poured another glass of red. It was all he was fit for tonight.

CHAPTER FIFTEEN

Ana had dumped her backpack in her office and was just about to collect Buster, the Le Claires' dog, for his early morning walk when her mobile rang. It was an unknown number. Her heart flipped when she recognised the voice asking for her. "This is Ana. How are you, Ben?"

"I'm good. You?"

She was sure he'd be able to tell she was grinning as she spoke. "Yes, I am well. Did you want something?"

"Well, I wondered if you would maybe like to meet up tonight, perhaps grab a movie and a pizza or something. But you're probably busy. Are you? Busy, I mean?"

The words rapidly tumbled over one another, and strangely his display of nervousness made Ana grow confident. "Yes, I'm free, and that would be lovely."

"Great, that's brilliant and makes what I have to say next much easier. I thought perhaps I might pop in for a coffee?"

"Oh, I'm sorry; I have to walk the dog. I've got to leave now."

His voice was smooth and flowed like melted chocolate through the line. "Perfect, I'll join you. I'm parked outside."

He was outside? Ana stood and peered into the antique mirror above the fireplace and checked out her reflection. She'd need to brush her hair, maybe some lipstick and a bit more eyeliner. *Be calm.*

Buster – he never would answer to Edward – was waiting for her, peering through the glass kitchen door, barking and running in circles when he saw her. She could barely open the door for him pushing forward to nuzzle her. The little dog had come to know that when Ana was here, one of the first things she liked to do was to walk and then feed him. She figured she was fast becoming one of his favourite humans.

Elizabeth was leaning against one of the cabinets waiting for the whistling kettle to boil. "Good morning, Ana. Edward is ready for his walk. Edward, come and say good-bye to me. Edward? Oh, for the love of God, Buster, come here!" The little dog immediately ran across the kitchen, planting wet, slobbery kisses on the immaculate Elizabeth, who didn't seem to mind at all. "I do wish Jack hadn't starting calling him Buster as a puppy. Edward is such a lovely name."

Within seconds, Ana had his lead on, and an excited Buster was trying to race toward the gates. She saw the car as soon as they exited onto the public lane. Today Ben was driving a mud-splattered Land Rover. He was leaning against the driver's door, watching for her, grinning as he waved them over. "I thought maybe we could drive down to the beach. So who is this?"

"This is Buster." Ana bent down and scratched the head of the little dog, who was bouncing and clamouring for attention. "But won't he get your car dirty?"

"I don't think it could get any dirtier! This is one of the manor cars. I'm using it today to collect some freight we have coming into the airport."

She smiled and carefully settled Buster onto the backseat and climbed into the front.

As the silence lengthened, her mind started thinking of what she could say. Nothing came to mind, zip. She could hear Buster panting as he lay in the backseat. Worryingly, she could also hear the excited little yips he usually made when he chewed on something; she hoped it wasn't the car seat.

Ben saved her from having to be the first to speak. "I checked with our housekeeper – she has a dog – and apparently we'll still be in good time to walk on the beach and let Buster off the leash."

"Oh, that'll be lovely."

The long stretch of beach was one Ana hadn't been to before. She saw it laid out in all its glory as the car wound its way down the steep, curved road. Ben glanced over at her. "St Ouen's Bay. It's got some of the best surfing in Europe. You ever been surfing?"

"Believe it or not, I've not been to this beach before as I don't have any transport. I've definitely not been surfing. I'm not a strong swimmer."

"We can fix that if you like, just takes practice and gaining confidence. And don't worry about where you've yet to see. Jersey may be only nine miles by five, but there are a multitude of hidden bays and small, secret lanes. I've been here a few years now. I oversaw the redevelopment at the manor and got to see a bit of the island on the weekends. I'll be happy to show you around."

Ana felt her pulse quicken at how he spoke; as if they would see each other more, a lot more. But was he just saying it? He was good-looking, sophisticated and, from the looks of his clothes and usual car, reasonably well-off. What did he see in her? She was working but not earning great money; she shared a house and couldn't afford a car. She dressed okay but certainly couldn't run to spending much; if it wasn't for the odd waitressing job she took, she'd barely be making ends meet.

They were now driving parallel to the beach, and Ben carefully turned the large vehicle and parked in a virtually empty car park. "We'd have a job to get parked here in the evening or on weekends. Come on. Good job you've got a jacket on. It's pretty windy."

They reached the seawall, and Ana held tight to Buster's leash. The beach lay far below them. They navigated the narrow, foot-polished stone steps that led to the sand. At the bottom, an excited Buster barked and strained at the leash. Ana let him loose and, taking an old tennis ball from her pocket, launched it across the beach. Buster raced after it, his little body quivering with excitement, as Ana and Ben followed. The fine golden sand was firm beneath their feet, and they stopped for a moment and gazed out to sea. The sky was grey and low, as if the very clouds would press down and crush them. The white-tipped breakers rolled effortlessly to crash against the shifting sand.

"I see what you mean about the surfing; those waves look pretty fierce."

"Yeah, it looks good today. You can see there is someone out there already." Ben put his arm around Ana's shoulder and turned her slightly, using his other arm to point straight ahead. Ana saw a small figure appear on the crest of a wave and then disappear as the swell rose. "Those breakers roll in from the Atlantic. It's spectacular when the surf is up and the place is busy. Some weekends we come down here with a friend's VW camper, park up, and after the surfing is done, we have a barbeque. Hopefully, you can come someday."

Buster came running up and laid the ball at Ben's feet with what could only be termed a hopeful expression on his face. Ben laughed and threw the ball. He linked his arm with hers, and they strolled after a running Buster. Ana wanted to pinch herself. In the time she'd been in Jersey, she'd had a few dates, but the guys weren't looking for anything more than a short-lived fling. She had walked away as soon as she'd sensed this. There was a transient aspect to certain parts of Jersey life. Ben was seeking Ana out, overtly so, and there could be no other reason than that he wanted to be with her. She hugged the thought to herself as Ben spoke.

"I hate to bring this up. Have the police spoken to you? Have they found out any more about Scott's death?"

The light mood disappeared as remembrance came crashing down, and she clasped her arms tight around her. Not to ward off the blustery breeze, but to keep her steady and grounded, to stop the emotions coursing through her from knocking her off-balance. She found her voice. "No. I guess they are still saying it's suspicious until they know more. They wouldn't speak to me in any event. They would talk to my aunt and uncle, and those two aren't going to rush to tell me anything, especially after yesterday."

He looked puzzled. "Yesterday?"

She felt slightly anxious as she remembered her aunt's rage. "It was my cousin's funeral."

"Ah, that must have been difficult."

"My aunt was undoubtedly upset over Scott's death, but it was his will that had her enraged."

"What happened?"

She hesitated, but only for a moment. She knew enough of this island to know that nothing stayed secret for long, and there had been more than enough witnesses to yesterday's incident to set the gossip mill chattering. "My cousin left most of his assets to his girlfriend. My aunt doesn't like her, and she kicked off, physically attacked her and knocked her to the ground. It was shocking. I went to help Laura – that's the girlfriend – and Sarah turned on me. The lawyer who read the will separated them, and the police came. God, it was a nightmare."

"Poor you. The girlfriend must be upset about Scott."

"I would guess. I don't know her that well. She was very quiet at the funeral. It was pretty obvious there was already tension between her and Sarah, and the will was apparently the icing on the cake."

"This Laura is obviously pretty well-off now. Does she live in Jersey?"

"Not usually. She's from London, but I understand she's staying at Scott's flat. It is hers now after all. She won't be able to live there permanently, as she doesn't have her residential qualifications, but I assume she'll be okay to stay there in the short-term."

"Where is his flat?"

"By Greve D'Azette, the big granite block. It's a lovely place, directly on the beach."

"Hopefully, the girl will be comfortable there; at least that will take her mind off her grief."

Ana shivered a little. "For sure. I better head back now. I've got to finish some travel bookings for the Le Claires' next trip."

She called the little dog, who came rushing back, an expectant look in his soulful eyes. She rewarded him for his obedience with a treat, and, leash on, they headed back to the car. Ben's smile was warm as he looked down at Ana. She really was so lucky to have met him.

Le Claire and Dewar had battled their way through the early morning traffic for their first appointment of the day, although appointment might be an exaggeration as they hadn't been invited and hadn't told anyone they were coming. At least they had headed out of town in the opposite direction to the traffic coming into St Helier from the west, which was its usual heavy flow.

Now they waited for Aidan Gillespie in a lavishly decorated lounge. He'd obviously hired some fancy interior designer; for the refurbished manor had a decidedly "done" look in all the rooms he had seen so far. The place was filled with antiques, gleaming mahogany sideboards and occasional tables covered in fancy knickknacks

A massive marble fireplace was topped with a huge lavishly framed mirror that reflected the view from the open doors that led to a terrace. Aidan Gillespie walked in from the gardens, very much the well-to-do gent in his rust-coloured trousers, pale pink shirt and brogues. Le Claire wondered if the setting for the meeting had been chosen to display the wealth and importance of Aidan Gillespie.

Gillespie marched to a side table and poured himself a drink from a glass decanter, an annoyed look on his face. The smell of whisky wafted across to them. "What do you want? I was in the middle of an important conference call but understand from my housekeeper that you demanded to see me immediately."

Le Claire kept his smile to himself. "I simply said that we would wait unless you wanted to come down to the station for a more formal chat."

Gillespie drew him a black look. "Load of bloody nonsense. Now what is this about?"

"You said Scott Hamlyn did some work for you?"

"Yes, routine stuff, the purchase of the manor and some other bits and pieces."

"And you were happy with his services?"

"Yes." The monosyllabic reply was curt.

Dewar piped in. "So you were happy with your lawyer but didn't ask him to your fancy party? Yet I saw from the guest list that you invited your estate agent?"

"Gordon found me this place at a great price. He deserved to be at this party."

"And Scott Hamlyn didn't?"

Le Claire stood back and let Dewar get on with it. She was sharp as a tack and had a sly way about her sometimes. It often worked to their advantage.

"No, he bloody didn't." He downed his whisky in one.

Le Claire's voice was even, calm. "And why was that? We know about your problems with Scott, so you may as well just tell us everything."

"Oh, for Christ's sake. He messed up the boundary dispute. His mind wasn't on it, and because of him I lost access to a nice little spring that runs along the north perimeter."

"You were annoyed with Mr Hamlyn?"

"Of course, but not enough to kill him, if that's what you're thinking. So let's get past that foolish idea."

Gillespie's smile was mocking. He was the king of his castle, with millions in the bank. What did he care, his smirk seemed to say.

"Well, ridiculous as you think it, let's explore the evening of the party. Apparently, no one recalls seeing you around the time of the incident. Where did you say you were again?"

"As I have already told you, I had been speaking to a group of guests. Why, I believe your father was one of them. I excused myself as I had an urgent matter to deal with. I re-joined them as soon I had completed what I had to do. Shortly thereafter, one of your men came in with the shocking news about Hamlyn."

"It was indeed a pretty fancy party, as my colleague said. And, I hesitate to say, an important one for you. Pivotal, one might say, to your future acceptance in Jersey."

"Careful, your background's showing – and a privileged one it is." He sighed. "Yes, it meant a lot to me. I want to be part of this island, and to do so, I need to break into the right circles."

"Yet your urgent matter was more important to you than ingratiating yourself with some of the island's elite?"

"You'd know more about them than me, but yes, there was an urgent business matter I had to deal with, and it couldn't wait."

"And what was this matter?"

"You can ask, but I won't tell you unless compelled to do so. It's a time-sensitive deal where privacy – the buyer's – is paramount."

"Very well, but we both know that I can force you to tell me if I do need to know. And I'll decide if it's relevant or not. We'll be speaking to you again, no doubt."

CHAPTER SIXTEEN

Le Claire had called a progress meeting on the Hamlyn investigation as soon as he got back to the station. At the back of the room, they had slotted a conference table and eight chairs, six of which were now occupied. Dewar sat next to Le Claire; Hunter sat opposite him flanked by Vanguard and Viera. Bryce Masters settled himself at the head of the table, and the remaining members of the incident room team were dotted around the nearest work stations.

"Thanks for coming in." He addressed the crime scene chief and the young doctor. "I just wanted to recap everything we've learned to date and see if we can put fresh eyes, and thoughts, on any aspects. We know that Scott Hamlyn was killed at Honsfleur Manor on the night of Aidan Gillespie's party, but he hadn't been invited. There was some bad blood there due to what Gillespie believed was Hamlyn's incompetency whilst working on a legal case regarding the manor. Hamlyn died sometime between the pool house being routinely checked at 17:00 and the body being found at 22:00. There was a load of cash in the pool, and we now know this was taken from Hamlyn's account. His body had bruising that was several days old, inflicted by his friend David Adamson, after an argument about Adamson's wife. Hamlyn's girlfriend, Laura Brown, arrived in the island the following morning. He'd told her he had a business meeting the night before. She inherited his estate and is apparently surprised to have done so. Apart from the cash withdrawal, Hamlyn's finances seem pretty much in order. Okay, thoughts?"

Masters was first. "I don't like the look of Aidan Gillespie or his brother. Gillespie Senior is a self-made man, but it isn't immediately apparent where his money originally came from."

Le Claire surprised himself by agreeing, a rare occasion with the plastic-looking Masters and his often cavalier approach.

"Okay, look into him further. Anything else?" He addressed the table, and Viera was first to speak. "Cause of death was massive trauma to the head, which was split open on impact with the tiled floor. There is no gender or strength bias in looking at suspects. He could have been pushed by a woman as easily as a man."

"Except that Laura Brown wasn't in Jersey on Saturday night. She'd also, presumably, have had to have known what was in Hamlyn's will. That is if money was the motive."

Vanguard flashed a wry smile. "Seems to me it's usually money or sex that's the root of a lot of the evil we deal with."

Le Claire nodded. "Yep, that's the usual."

Hunter piped up, his face red and his voice breaking a little at his excitement at being part of the team. "Hamlyn was a loner; he racked up hours gaming online. Where did he meet Laura Brown again?"

Dewar commented, tongue in cheek, "Maybe at a gaming convention?"

Le Claire shook his head at the joke as an image of the sophisticated Laura Brown shot to mind. "Very amusing, but it was at a party."

Vanguard looked thoughtful. "There's his work as a lawyer. I've wanted to strangle one or two in the past."

"Point taken. We need to go deeper into Hamlyn's life. I want to know all about him, his work, his social life, finances and his relationship with Laura Brown. We need to know more about her as well. Have the airline records come in to corroborate her timeline?"

Dewar shook her head. "Not yet, I'll chase them up."

"I want any loose ends tied up. Hunter, get right into Hamlyn's finances, look at his expenditure, everything, with a fine tooth comb. Were the cash withdrawals a one-off or has he done this before? Masters, get some detailed reports on the Gillespies. Finally, Vanguard, anything from the back way into the manor?"

"I'm waiting for the results. I'll come and see you when I have anything concrete. We've carted away a fair bit of stuff and running the analytics."

"Great. Let's get on with it."

# #

Several long hours later, Le Claire pushed back from his desk in the incident room, stood and stretched his arms high above his head. He had got through a long day with no real results. He'd talked to people but mainly spent the day hunched over his computer, going over files again, trying to see any leads, but he hadn't got anywhere.

He noticed that some of the team were huddled around Hunter, and their laughter caught his attention as he joined them.

"Hunter, what are you doing?"

The young policeman was rifling through a plastic bag, next to which was a pile of clothing that looked like underwear and socks. Hunter looked at what he held in his hands, a pair of ladies skimpy knickers, and flushed a deep, dark red. Le Claire honestly though the boy would self-combust. Dropping the panties into the plastic bag, he said, "We've had reports of a cat burglar, sir." His words were accompanied by a backdrop of sniggers from his colleagues.

Le Claire was getting impatient. "What's that got to do with a bag of underwear?"

"That's what has been stolen. My auntie brought it in to me. Said she found all this stuff stashed behind her sofa, and then she saw her cat coming in with a sock in its mouth. She was too embarrassed to go round all the houses and ask if anybody was missing anything, so she asked me to help."

Le Claire was lost for words. Not so Dewar, who piped up behind him. "We don't have the time to be dealing with this nonsense."

Hunter looked at Le Claire. "What should I do, sir?"

Le Claire couldn't help his grin. "Get someone to take photographs of the garments and post them on our Facebook page and website with a call to action to contact us if it's their property. Say we've caught the offender and post the culprit's picture. What is the offender called?"

"Tigger."

"Right, get the admin team onto it and say they can collect their stuff from the station and that Tigger has been cautioned not to do it again."

He walked away, the laughter floating after him. Dewar was by his side.

"We're busy. We have others things to do than mess about."

"Everyone is working hard and is under a lot of pressure. There's no harm in a little fun to release tension. It's also community spirit. Plus, Tigger did commit burglary, people lost property and we want to return it."

Dewar rolled her eyes. "I suppose so. I guess I'm just a bit grumpy sometimes."

He didn't say anything as he figured it wouldn't be in his best interests. He looked at his watch and realised it was gone 7:00 p.m.

"I better get off. I'll see you tomorrow."

He headed back to his office to close down for the day. He guessed he wouldn't be seeing Sasha. She'd been gone when he woke up this morning, and she hadn't called him. He figured it was down to her to call as she'd been the shouty, angry one. He grabbed his phone and dialled her mobile before he had time for another thought. The answerphone clicked on. He hung up. Then dialled again. This time he left a message. "Hi, it's me. Just wondered how you were. So…right, then. Give me call when you can. Bye."

He hung up and slid the phone across his desk. The night stretched ahead of him. He'd grab a takeaway on the way home. He turned off his computer and started storing the papers on his desk in his large cupboard. He had just finished when he heard an unmistakable beeping sound. He had a text message. His heart leapt as he saw the sender. Sasha. He read the words, and a wave of disappointment crashed through him. She was going to St Malo for the weekend with some friends, apparently a last minute decision. She'd be in touch when she got back.

Ben was wearing dark jeans and a casual shirt, topped by a leather jacket. Ana had tried on nearly everything she had, which wasn't a lot, and settled for skinny black jeans and a loose grey chiffon top over a strappy vest. She may not have a wardrobe filled with expensive clothes, but Ana's hair was freshly blow-dried, flowing down her back, and she'd applied a light makeup that widened her eyes and emphasised her lips. A pair of black courts and a plain black jacket and she'd been ready. She'd stuffed her phone and some precious cash into her coat pocket.

Instead of heading to the waterfront, and the island's only cinema, Ben advised of a detour. "I'm sorry, but I need to drop some documents to Aidan. I just picked them up for him, and he needs to sign them tonight. That okay?"

Ana nodded in agreement, but she dreaded the thought of going back to the manor.

Tonight the huge house stood in virtual darkness apart from a couple of lit windows on the ground floor. She stayed put as Ben got out of the car. Hopefully, he wouldn't be long. He bent down and looked through the open car window.

"What are you waiting for? Come on, I want to introduce you properly."

Now she really felt nervous. Her heart beat a little faster as she got out of the car and followed Ben through the open front door into the huge entrance space. In any other house, you'd walk into a hallway, but this was so much more than that. Black-and-white checked tiles gleamed and reflected the light from several uplighters and spotlights. A tall urn was filled with a massive display of cream flowers surrounded by dark green foliage. A low table held some carved incense stick holders, and the wisps of smoke dispersed a musky fragrance. The last time she'd been here, the entire ground floor had been crowded with people. Now it was quiet and still.

There was a murmur of voices from a room to the side of the hall. Ben knocked on the door and walked in, and she followed close behind. He placed the envelope with the papers on the desk that dominated the room.

"Ah, Ben, thanks for this." Aidan Gillespie was sitting behind the desk, and he turned and handed the envelope to the man he had been talking to. "There you go, have a look and see what you think of the deal. We've got to get back to them by tomorrow. Ben's already had a good look at it." A brief scowl darkened the younger man's face.

Ben gently clasped her hand and pulled Ana forward. "Aidan, this is Ana, Scott Hamlyn's cousin. Ana, these are my cousins, Aidan and Danny."

The easy smile slid from Aidan Gillespie's face as he rose from behind the desk. "I remember meeting you at Philip Le Claire's office. I am so very sorry that you had to find your cousin like that. It must have been a terrible shock."

"Yes, it was. Thank you for the flowers."

"It was the least I could do. I also sent some to your poor aunt. I was so shocked when Ben told me that Scott was your cousin. Life is indeed strange."

Ana was shy but took Aidan Gillespie's outstretched hand and shook it as she glanced at his brother. "It's a pleasure to meet you both."

Danny Gillespie took Ana's hand from his brother. He was dark and handsome, and Ana figured he knew that only too well. "Hi, Ana. And what are you doing going out with Ben, huh? I'm sure we can find something better for you to do." Ana smiled, unsure what to say, and gently disengaged her hand from Danny's.

Ben draped his arm around Ana's shoulder. "I'm sure you could, Danny, but, foolish girl that she is, Ana is coming to the movies with me. Come on."

They said their good-byes and left. Ana could hear laughter, and she just knew it was coming from Danny Gillespie.

# #

Irena Kobus sat in front of the brightly lit mirror. She loved this room, the long counter with various makeup stations, the retro dressing-table bulbs running along the top of the mirrored wall and the heavy smell of perfume and hairspray. She fluffed her hair, smacked her lips together to make sure her lipstick was in place and ran her hands over her breasts to make sure the scraps of leather held her secure and tight. She stood up and, twisting and turning, admired herself in the mirror on the back of the door. The tiny string bra top clung to her pert breasts; she was bare to the waist, her hips and groin barely covered by a floaty black chiffon skater skirt. She flicked up the back of the skirt to expose the high-cut triangular see-through panties and her tight ass and smiled in appreciation at what she saw. He would love it. If only he was here tonight. But he wasn't. At least she wouldn't have to wear the wig.

Irena was finally on the way up. She was done with looking after other people's snotty, whining children, cooking their meals and cleaning their houses. She had a real man in her life, and he had shown her how to grab what was available. Her boyfriend had given her this opportunity, and she wasn't going to waste it. She just wished he could be here more often.

The door crashed open, and the music and cacophony of voices came banging into the room. The door swung back on its hinges, and the music and noise receded.

Marianne strode in, naked as the day she was born, although her vertiginous heels were still on her feet. Her dark skin was oiled and glistened with a coating of sweat, her large breasts were surgically perfect and her shaven mound on full display. She threw herself into a low armchair and, groaning a little, pulled off her shoes and chucked them into a corner. "Tonight is – what you say – you know, so many people, a crowd."

Irena knew what the other girls said, that Marianne's accent was often more of a turn-on than her perfect body; put together it was an unbeatable package. She was the only French girl in the place; the others were mainly, like Irena, Eastern European.

"So it is busy; that is good for tips."

Marianne's smile was sly. "You are shaking your ass good on the pole, but there are easier ways to earn good money than that."

Irena was shaking her head before the words had finished. "No, I am okay with the dancing; it's no different than what girls do in nightclubs all the time, just with fewer clothes. I am not doing the private booth dances though…"

"I didn't mean that."

"And I am not comfortable with what you do mean. I am not going to open my legs for some stranger."

"How do you think I paid for these?" Marianne lay back in the armchair, spread her legs wide and, licking her fingers, ran them around her nipples. Her eyes challenged Irena.

Irena tried to hide her disgust. She had to work alongside these girls and did not want to alienate them. "It is not for me. I am content with – what did you say? Shaking my ass." Irena bent from the waist and ground her backside in a slow circular tease. As she made to leave the room, she turned back and blew Marianne a kiss before she went to, literally, face the music.

CHAPTER SEVENTEEN

Ana was working in the town office today. Philip Le Claire had been a successful lawyer and Jersey politician and was now investing in a number of different businesses. She was disappearing under a pile of paperwork from her ever-increasing workload.

A call from the reception desk advised her that Mr Le Claire's noon appointment had arrived. He must have booked the meeting himself, for she didn't have it in the diary. She rose, smoothed her dress and knocked on Philip's door before entering. Ana had rarely seen her boss and his son in the same room, but when she did she marvelled at their similarities. The same height, similar builds, although Philip was slightly thickening around the middle and his dark hair was starting to sport a little grey. So much in common and so little. She'd often overheard Philip and his wife as they bemoaned their only child's choice of career, as if being a policeman was something to be ashamed of.

"Your appointment will be up in a moment. Do you want tea and coffee?"

"No, thank you. We're just having a quick meeting, and then they've invited me for lunch."

She smiled and headed to the elevator doors, and when they opened, she was surprised to see Aidan Gillespie walk out, followed by another man.

"Mr Gillespie, this is a surprise. Are you here to see Philip?"

"Yes. Hope you and Ben had a good time last night, and please call me Aidan."

"Thank you." She turned to the man behind him, a smile of welcome on her face, which turned to surprise. "Oh, Mr Adamson. How are you?"

David Adamson was handsome in crumpled chinos, a pale blue shirt and a checked jacket. "Ana, all good with me. Look, could we have a quick word?" He looked apologetically at Aidan Gillespie, who pulled out his phone. "I've got a quick call to make before we meet Philip, so go ahead."

"Ana, I am so sorry. I heard that you were Scott's cousin and you found him. That must have been shocking."

"You knew Scott?"

"Yes, we were old friends. I remember him saying his cousin had turned up. It is such terrible news, and I am so sorry."

She bit back the tears that threatened to fall, took a deep, shuddering breath and kept a smile on her face. "Thank you so much. Now if you'd like to follow me, I'll show you through."

It was only later, when the three men had left for lunch, that Ana realised she hadn't asked if David Adamson or his wife had heard from Irena. Maybe it was time to forget her friend. The only problem was she didn't think she could do that.

# #

They were getting nowhere fast. Le Claire was about to call Dewar and ask where the hell she was when his phone rang. *What did he want?*

"Hello, sir."

The chief's voice was rasped with tiredness. A murder investigation took its toll on everyone. "I need to see you. Come up now."

Le Claire knew there was no point saying he was busy, that he had a murder to solve and was getting nowhere. If the chief called, you ran.

As Le Claire got the nod from the watchdog that sat outside the chief's office, he was momentarily taken aback. Did Margaret just smile at him? The chief might be fierce, but his PA ran a close second.

As he entered the room, he realised that someone else was already there. He was surprised to see that it was Will Blair, one of the undercover drugs guys, and he wasn't looking too sharp.

"Christ, Blair, you're in a bit of a state. What happened?"

Blair's right leg stretched out in front of him as he perched awkwardly on a chair in front of the chief's desk. The leg was completely encased in plaster, and he sported a vivid bruise along one cheek.

"I fell down the stairs."

"Very droll. What happened? Did you get rumbled?"

Le Claire knew that Blair walked a fine line. His identity was only known to a few senior officers, and he rarely worked from the station. His workplace was the bars and clubs and more private places.

Blair tensed and grimaced. "No. My five-year-old left his Thomas the Tank Engine at the top of the stairs. I tripped over it and went arse over tit to the bottom. Pardon my French, sir."

"Don't worry about that, Blair. This is just such bad timing." The chief turned to Le Claire. "Blair has a solid lead. He's been on this case for six months and is getting ever closer to the real power behind the drugs that are coming into the island. There is a private house party tonight. The word is that drugs are being supplied by the heavyweights who've been taking over some of the smaller suppliers. They'll have a bloody monopoly if they carry on."

Le Claire could hear the frustration in the chief's voice. The island was awash with drugs, not that the majority of the population had a clue. Most people lived in their bubble of security, rarely noticing the darker elements that thrived in an island that, for some, was overflowing with disposable cash. In the world's cities, you'd see down-and-outs, their lives ravaged by drugs; here the problem was trust fund kids who used their ridiculously generous pocket money to get legal and increasingly illegal highs. Some of them even had their own bank accounts and cashline cards. At fourteen, that was a joke, and a dangerous one at that. Those kids became adults, adults with nasty habits and the money and connections to feed their addictions.

"You don't know who they are yet? Do you know who owns the house? Surely, that is the first place to start?"

"No, it's all a bit cloak-and-dagger. The invitation says that I'll be met on the road past St Mary's pub."

The chief interjected. "And that brings us to a key point. No one at the party has met Blair before; even if they had a rough idea of what his face looked like, it wouldn't make any difference."

Le Claire was puzzled. "Why not?"

It was Blair who answered. "Invites for these parties are tightly controlled and very sought after. I'm told they can get a bit wild, and anything goes. Everyone has to wear a mask and a coloured wristband, which are delivered with the invitation. I'm not sure what the significance is, but the attached note asks for a confidentiality agreement to be signed and handed in at the door."

Le Claire was starting to feel suspicious. "What does any of this have to do with me?"

"The wife had to wheelchair me in here today. There's no way I can get there tonight. My part in this investigation may be over. I simply can't walk. You need to go to the party, be me."

"I thought no one who knows you is going to be there. Couldn't someone else take your place?" He was thinking of Masters. About time he did some real detective work, and his egotistical colleague would love the idea of being undercover. He'd probably like wearing a mask as well.

The chief's voice cut across them. "The build and hair colouring isn't quite right. We can't guarantee that there won't be someone who even vaguely knows Blair, and we can't run the risk. Tell him the plan."

"I was just going to keep a low profile, find out all I could and try and get some clues as to who the suppliers are. Apparently, these party invites get issued to low-level guys like me as a bit of a reward."

"Reward for what?"

"I believe it's for keeping my mouth shut."

Blair's eyes were blank, and Le Claire felt for him. Undercover work wasn't easy, it was stressful and you had to play a long game. Blair, trained to uphold the law, would need to know when to keep quiet, letting certain crimes go unpunished.

"After tonight, I'll say I got drunk and fell down and busted my leg. If I don't show this evening, if my invitation isn't handed in, then it's going to look suspicious. That was made clear. I've waited too long to let this opportunity pass."

"I'm in the middle of a murder investigation. I can't take my eye off the ball."

"You have a perfectly good team around you. It will be fine."

Le Claire took the words as the chief intended, as an order.

"Okay, tell me what I need to know."

Several hours later and Le Claire was versed in the rudiments of Blair's undercover persona, what he was about and who he knew. Now he just had to get on with it.

CHAPTER EIGHTEEN

Le Claire was driving Blair's car and, as previously directed by his colleague, parked up a narrow dirt track that was a few minutes' walk from the pickup point detailed in the instructions for the party. He navigated his way through the unlit lanes. The invitation had said black tie for the men and long dresses for the ladies. It didn't sound like some drug den, but he'd have to reserve judgment until he got there.

He felt trussed up in his winged-collar shirt and carefully arranged bow tie. He carried a black silk half mask in one hand and wore the silver-coloured plastic wristband that had accompanied the invitation. He didn't know what all this was about, but he'd put up with it for the sake of Blair's investigation.

He saw the dark-coloured BMW parked in a lane along from the pub. Following instructions, he quickly placed the mask over his face and tied the tapes in a tight bow at the back of his head and then headed for his ride.

A burly man waited by the vehicle's open doors, his head covered by a wide-brimmed hat, and he wore dark glasses. It certainly disguised the man's features, but it was dark, and they were in the middle of St Mary, so it did make him look a little conspicuous. Le Claire was the sole passenger, and he settled himself in the backseat. Without a word, the man placed a thick black scarf over the mask, blocking his vision. He hadn't been expecting that, and, caught unawares, it took him a moment to recover. The car turned left and left again. They were going deeper into the lanes, more twists and turns. The car slowed, and he heard the familiar click and whirr of electronic gates opening and closing. The car door opened, and a hand touched his arm, the accompanying voice, female and light, was soothing. "Good evening, sir. Apologies for the inconvenience. However, I understand that this is your first time here, so we can't be too careful. Let's get this off and come inside." He felt a tug, and the scarf covering his eyes was removed, leaving his half mask firmly in place.

The owner of the voice was a slim girl in a tight cocktail dress. She too wore a mask, but her wristband was red. As he exited the car, Le Claire took a moment to stand and fuss with his clothing, straightening cuffs and brushing away imaginary lint, which allowed him to take in his surroundings. A tall wooden fence surrounded the property. He noticed video cameras on top of several posts; the blinking lights showed they were continuously recording. Heavy security for what he assumed was a private home.

"May I have your invitation and confidentiality agreement, please?"

Le Claire handed over the papers, and she scanned them as they walked up the shallow, wide steps that led to the front door. Once they were inside, Le Claire was handed over to a waiting man, again wearing a mask. They were very security conscious.

The woman spoke. "Here is the invitation and agreement. Everything checks out; would you please complete the induction?"

Induction? What the hell was going on here? He found out all too quickly. He was handed a piece of paper filled with instructions, and Le Claire concealed his jolt of shock. Now he knew exactly what kind of party this was.

The list contained do's and don'ts and more information. The silver wristbands were worn by guests, some repeat guests had been upgraded to gold, and apparently the latter had access to certain areas that weren't available to anyone else. The "entertainment" wore green, the serving staff red. It was made clear that the last were out of bounds and were not allowed in the private areas. He wasn't sure of the specifics, but the comment that condoms were compulsory and that anything was okay as long as both, or all, participating parties consented gave him a good idea of what tonight was all about.

A long hallway with a number of closed doors running off it led to a huge modernistic lounge/diner. The room was filled with masked people, the men in sharp dinner suits, and the women in provocative evening wear. Most of the men wore silver or gold on their wrists, and nearly all the women wore green, clearly delineating between guests and the so-called entertainment. All the masks were made of heavy material and left the eyes and lower face exposed. The waiting staff wore black, and each wrist was enclosed by a red wristband. Le Claire supposed that he could at least be thankful that the organisers took pains to protect their staff from the worst excesses of their guests.

Le Claire accepted a glass of sparkly stuff from a passing waiter. He took a small sip. It was champagne and not prosecco. From the way the drinks appeared to be going down, someone was spending serious money on the evening. Why would they do that? He looked around and saw even more money on display. A long trestle table, covered with a crisp white cloth, held plates of canapes and nibbles. In the middle sat a five-tier cake stand, but it wasn't holding any sponge fancies. Piles of multi-coloured pills jostled for space alongside tiny bags of white powder. Greedy hands were popping the pills and washing them down with champagne. He saw a couple giggling as they crouched over a low coffee table, snorting what was undoubtedly cocaine. Christ, the place was awash with a fortune in drugs.

He must have been paying too much attention to his surroundings because a voice behind him said, "First time?" The voice was cultured and matched the man who stood in front of him in a well-cut tuxedo.

"Yes, it is. I wasn't sure what to expect."

"You can get whatever you want. I mean, we pay enough for the privilege."

Blair had said his invitation had been a thank-you; obviously others were willing to pay for whatever was on offer. "Indeed, anything I should know?"

"You'll have seen the rules, but all you need to remember is that the silver bands, like yours, and these," he lifted his wrist and pointed to his gold wristband, "denote guests. We are off-limits to each other unless a reciprocal arrangement is made. Green is for the escorts – they'll do whatever we want, and the red are the waiters and waitresses and the like. The general serving staff don't wear masks. I assume that's because they don't take part in the evening's events. They are out of bounds. They concentrate on dishing out champagne and tiny canapes, ignoring the drug-taking and the shagging. I would imagine they are paid well for their silence. They leave at midnight; we just help ourselves after that – in more ways than one. Carriages are at 4:00 a.m."

Le Claire kept a smile firmly in place, but his mind was racing. He knew that sex parties took place in the island, but they were private, suburban affairs, controlled by confidentiality agreements. The worst that usually happened was when a couple attended and one of them got cold feet, jealous and then abusive. The police were called to calm them down, but there was nothing else they could do. It was consenting adults in private homes. They seemed like tame affairs compared to the bacchanalian orgy that was on the cards for tonight. But the people here were apparently paying for their fun this evening, and that made it something else entirely.

His jovial new friend raised a glass in Le Claire's direction and, exhorting him to enjoy himself, wandered off to talk to a group in the corner of the room. Within moments, Le Claire saw him run his hand, slowly and deliberately, over the silk-covered backside of a tall blonde. Her dress was a slither of metallic silver that dipped low in front and fell to the floor. As she gently moved, a thigh-high slit fell open to reveal long, shapely legs with a glimpse of stocking. She turned and ran a caressing hand down her new friend's arm. Her bracelet was green. All systems were go.

"You're new, aren't you?"

Le Claire wondered if he was wearing a neon sign. The woman who stood facing him wore a black lace mask that covered most of her face apart from her glistening red-lipsticked mouth. Her hair, a black precision-cut bob, was so perfect that he couldn't tell if it was a wig or not.

Her tight red dress wrapped around her body, showing her curves to full advantage. She held the fabric tie that apparently secured her dress and lightly flicked the material against her fingers, which drew Le Claire's eyes. No doubt that was exactly what she intended from the slow smile that curved her mouth, that she paint an image of one tug releasing the covering folds and exposing her to his gaze. Le Claire might be a policeman, but he was only human, so he let the image float through his mind, just for a second. The red bracelet on her wrist shimmered in the light.

"Yes, this is my first time. Does it show?"

Her laugh was a slow, throaty gurgle. "Afraid so, you look like a lost lamb. Are you looking for anything particular this evening? Because if you are, and I could help, I would change this to green in a flash." She shook her wrist and jangled the red staff bracelet. Her tone was flirtatious, her voice husky, and it struck him that it sounded strange, as if she was trying to disguise her natural voice. What he wanted was information, and maybe she'd be the one to give it to him.

He kept his voice a little hesitant, played the flustered newbie. "To be honest, I am pretty overwhelmed. I got my invitation out of the blue."

"Then you have been rewarded, and we must make sure you have an enjoyable evening."

"I would like to thank whoever issued the invitation to me. Is that possible?"

"I am afraid not. Our benefactor prefers to remain behind the scenes. Now let me get you a refill, and we can get better acquainted." She beckoned to a passing waiter, and Le Claire's half-full glass was topped up. As she turned to him with a smile, he saw a hard look flash into her eyes as her gaze was caught by something behind him. "I am sorry, please excuse me. I must deal with something, but I shall return soon."

He sipped from his glass as his eyes followed her across the room. She stopped by a man who stood in the far corner; his posture screamed louche boredom. The woman in red bent and whispered in his ear, her cupped hand covering her mouth. She nodded toward the far corner of the room. A group of guests were chatting as a waitress cleared empty glasses. The young woman was carrying a glass-laden tray as she carefully manoeuvred her way through the throng. He could see how her arms strained as she hefted the heavy weight. Like all the other staff, she was dressed in black, and for her this was a simple black dress, lightly flared at the hips. For the first time, Le Claire realised that although the serving staff were dressed in black, they didn't wear a uniform. Perhaps they didn't all come from the same catering firm? The girl turned as she bent to pick up some more glasses. His heart stuttered in shock. He knew the waitress. It was Ana Zielinska.

CHAPTER NINETEEN

Ana was tired, nervous and on edge. She had agreed to this job weeks ago. Irena had waitressed for the same catering manager before and had come away with a wad of cash and a request to bring a friend next time; a pretty, trusted friend who could keep her mouth shut. Irena had said she would be fine; she just had to smile, do what she was told and not be shocked by anything she saw. She'd said yes, much against her better judgment. In the end, there had been no choice. Ana didn't have the catering manager's telephone number, but the woman had been given Ana's by Irena, together with her full name and address. She'd had no way of cancelling, and in any event, she liked to stand by her word. She had said she would work at the party, so work she would. Even if Irena was nowhere in sight. She wouldn't have been doing much else anyway. Ben had dropped her home after their night out, gave her a chaste kiss on the cheek and said he'd be in touch early the next week. He had to spend the weekend working in London. She'd been disappointed, but at least he had said he'd call – at some point, that was.

She sighed and looked around. She didn't like this atmosphere, it was heavy with the smell of alcohol, and she'd been shocked at the open display of drug-taking. Then there was the undercurrent of what felt like a mass of swirling emotions; the rising sense of anticipation that was given away by excited chatter, heightened colour, dilated eyes and lascivious looks. She saw flirtatious eye contact, hands skimming over flesh and open fondling. It was getting outrageous, and she tried to keep her eyes down and just get on with the job. You wouldn't catch her doing this again; no money was worth being here.

Ever since she had set foot in the place, she'd been itching to leave. Her feet were aching in her high heels; as did her face from all the smiling, but it was more than that. There were bad vibes here. She could see it in their eyes.

Le Claire looked at his watch. It was nearly midnight, and he recalled this was the witching hour for the servers. He had managed to avoid Ana. He didn't think she would have recognised him, the masks certainly did their job, but he hadn't wanted to tempt fate. He'd wait until he knew she was gone, and therefore safe, before he left himself. The events would surely heat up soon, and he wanted to be gone before they did. He assumed that nonparticipation in the night's entertainments was a no-go, so he had to be gone before it became obvious that he wasn't joining in with the fun and games.

At least he knew what kind of parties these were, that payment was being made for the services on offer and that whoever the organiser was, they kept a low profile. This wouldn't be enough for Blair to move forward on, but it was a start, and at least the undercover guy wasn't seen as an ungrateful no-show. He'd done all he could here. He drained his glass of champagne and pretended to stumble a little. His friend from earlier was by his side in a flash, her eyes filled with sympathy and concern. "Are you all right?"

He carefully slurred his words. "Just had a bit too much to drink. Whoa!" He stumbled and grabbed on to the nearest object to steady himself. It was soft and yielding. Red dress smirked as she held his hand closer to her breast.

"I think I better go before I embarrass myself."

She quirked her mouth in what he assumed was a regretful smile. "I understand, really I do." To his shock she ran her hand over the front of his trousers. He resisted the automatic response to pull back and instead gave her a lopsided smile. He hoped he looked drunk and regretfully incapable.

She ran the tip of her tongue over her lips. "Next time I promise you'll be interested in more than alcohol. How will you get home? We usually organise transport for everyone later on, but I can get a car to take you home now. Would you like that?"

No, he wouldn't like that. At all. He had to think quickly. "I could do with some fresh air. I figure it's a fifteen-minute walk to the pub. I'll get there and call a cab."

"Fine, whatever suits you. Take care, and I know I'll see you again."

He walked in a drunken parody, just enough, he hoped, to be convincing. He saw some smirking glances thrown his way, but they were fleeting. People had more to think about than him.

The heavy security had thinned out. He noticed a guy by the front door and figured there might be more of his colleagues outside. He assumed they weren't so bothered about people leaving before midnight, but he did wonder at their laxness. What cards did they hold that kept the details of where the parties were being held secret? All Le Claire had to do was leave and he could pinpoint where this property was. The island was only forty-five square miles after all.

He saw a shadow out the corner of his eye as someone disappeared around the far end of the corridor, away from the front door. From the stealthy movements, they were creeping around. His gut instinct was to find out who it was and what they were up to. He reached the end of the corridor and carefully looked around the corner.

It was the man who Red Dress had spoken to. He was following Ana. Her gait was slow, hindered by a heavy tray, as she made her way in the direction of what was presumably the kitchen. He felt uneasy. The man had deliberately followed her. Had he been put up to this by the woman in the red dress?

He heard a female voice. "Wash those glasses, and be careful you don't break any. We'll wait for you outside. If you're not out of here in five minutes, the driver will be gone. We must be out by midnight or we don't get paid."

He heard a door slam. The man advanced until he was by the side of the kitchen doorway, concealed in the shadows of the dimly lit hall. Le Claire could hear Ana as she cleaned up, water running, hands splashing and the clink of glassware. The sound of haste permeated every move.

The man took a step into the kitchen, and Le Claire crept farther down the corridor until he could see inside. Their footsteps were drowned out by a funky beat coming from the in-room speakers, echoing the sounds that had been playing in the main lounge.

Ana was drying the last of the glasses quickly but carefully. She wiped the water droplets away with paper towels, placing each cleaned glass into waiting cardboard boxes. She did so with care, whether because she was that way by nature or to prevent breakages that would probably come from her pay, Le Claire wasn't sure.

The man advanced toward her and grabbed her shoulder. She swung around, a look of surprise on her face that turned to shock as the champagne flute in her hand tumbled to the floor. The sound of shattering glass was followed by a panicked exclamation. "Oh no, I must clean that up now."

A braying laugh made him jump. Someone was coming down the corridor. He moved farther back into the shadows and pressed tight against the wall, the kitchen now concealed from his view. A man and woman came stumbling round the corner. It was the guest he had spoken to earlier in the evening, and he was with the blond in the slinky dress. He had his arm draped around her shoulders; her top had fallen down and uncovered her breasts. His hand groped her as they staggered along. She didn't seem to mind, but her bracelet was green, and Le Claire assumed she'd be paid for this evening's work. The woman laughed as she opened one of the doors that led off the corridor and made to pull the man inside the room, but he was impatient and pushed her against the wall and started kissing her. Le Claire was on alert as he watched them, willing them to disappear. He needed to get back to Ana. He hadn't liked her follower's stance and didn't trust his intentions.

Ana recoiled as the man tightened his grip. "Don't worry about a broken glass, love. I've got better things for you to do."

Her voice was strained, but she tried to keep it even and calm. *Don't show fear.* "I must go; the catering manager is waiting for me."

The man's laugh was mirthless. "Afraid not. They know the ropes and obey the rules. They have to be gone by midnight. It's five past now."

She glanced at the back door. The rest of the waiting staff had been hanging out by the back, smoking and talking whilst they waited for everyone to finish. The door lay slightly ajar, but now she heard nothing, no laughter, no chat – nothing. Her senses hit the alert button. They'd left her here, just like the catering manager had threatened. What a bitch! She had no idea where she was in the island, no transport and this creep had an edge to him that made her nervous. She doubted anyone in this house would help her, not from what she'd seen of their antics this evening. She was going to have to just act like she was in control. "Look, I have to go, so please take your hands off me."

"We'll get you home eventually, but first you and I are going to have a little party."

He pulled her closer, and she could smell the fetid stench of his breath and stale sweat as he pushed her against the wall. Panic rose; this man was serious. His mask was still firmly in place, which emphasised the predatory look in his eyes and the cruel twist to his mouth. He grabbed both her wrists in one hand and pinned her arms above her head. She twisted and turned, trying to free herself. His other hand roughly pulled at the front of her dress, exposing her serviceable black bra. She was shocked, shamed. His voice was mocking. "Not the most enticing of kit, but don't worry, we'll have it off you soon." She opened her mouth and screamed, "Help!"

He pushed her back against the wall, trapping her with his body as his other hand covered her mouth. "Keep quiet, bitch. Anyone who hears you isn't going to care, and struggling is no good either. You're going to get royally fucked, and I'll be taking a few photos as a memento so you can't cause any trouble later."

She froze, foul bile rising in her throat as her mind raced. How the hell was she going to get out of this?

He'd released his hand from her mouth, and her voice was a hoarse whisper. She had no option but to beg. "I don't know what you mean. I won't say anything. I haven't seen anything to talk about. Please just let me go."

"Don't play me for a fool. The photos will be security. You keep schtum or you'll be all over the net, tits and bits on show. Wonder how many hits you'd get?"

He reached down and slid a hand up her thigh. His skin was rough through her tights, and he pinched her flesh as he spoke, his voice lower and huskier. "Nice and firm, that's what I love about you young ones. Nice and firm. Oh yes."

She struggled, twisting and turning, but his grip was strong. He moved his head, and his teeth nipped at her neck. Ana twisted away, but he held her tight. His aftershave was strong, musky, and it seemed to seep into her pores. It enveloped her, made her gag. She looked up over her attacker's shoulder and saw a masked man, dressed in a dinner suit, silently watching them. Not two of them? Ana knew the shock must have been evident on her face.

Her attacker lifted the front of her skirt and pawed at the waistband of her tights. The man's hands were all over her, but she ignored his touch. She mutely appealed for help; she couldn't move. The man who was watching her moved, slow and careful, out of the shadows and into the room. His fingers reached for his mask, and he slowly pulled it up, enough that she could clearly see his features. Oh thank God – it was Jack Le Claire.

CHAPTER TWENTY

He caught Ana's eyes and saw hope rise. He flicked off the light switch, plunging the room into semidarkness, illuminated only by the moonlight shining through the tall windows and the low-lit lampshade in the hall. He stepped inside and shut the kitchen door behind him, extinguishing the light from the hall. Without breaking stride, he charged across the room and grabbed the attacker by the shoulders. The man reacted instinctively, releasing Ana as he spun to face Le Claire, who held on tight, drew back and punched the man directly in the gut. As the man bent over, clutching his stomach, Le Claire caught him on the side of the jaw with a sharp uppercut. Turning to a petrified-looking Ana, he whispered, "Quick, wait for me by the back door."

She quickly complied. He could hear her trampling over the broken glass in her haste for freedom. The man had fallen to his knees, still clutching his stomach. They needed to get out of here and fast. Le Claire turned to follow Ana. Suddenly, he crashed to the ground. The man had recovered his wits enough to grab Le Claire by the ankles. He fell onto his back, and the shadowed figure was on him in moments. He quickly pushed his hands down as he tried to raise himself up but winced as his palm made contact with broken glass. That damned champagne flute.

The man bore down on Le Claire and lunged forward, his arm outstretched. There was something in his hand. Moonlight glinted off a shard of glass. The man was atop Le Claire, the glass at his throat. He struggled and felt the sharp sting as skin was broken. The smell of blood was sharp and pungent. His hands were around the man's wrist, pushing him back. His attacker had the advantage, his elevated position allowing him to pin Le Claire to the floor.

He twisted and caught his ankles around the man's right calf; using his weight, he scissored his legs and rotated his attacker. Le Claire was on top. There was no time for finesse. He smashed a fist into his opponent's face, grabbed a handful of his jacket, pulled him up and punched him again. The man lay still, unmoving. The only sound was his groaning.

Le Claire ran to Ana. "Come on, let's go. You can tell me later what the hell you're doing here."

Her voice was strained. "I could ask you the same thing. Thank you so much…"

Her voice faltered, and he knew the enormity of the situation she had just escaped, and its possible outcomes, had shaken her. He nodded and inched out the back door, quickly checking the outdoor area. No one was there. A tall brick wall, over six feet, enclosed the garden. Le Claire looked at his shirtfront. It was spotted with blood, and the collar had been ripped in the fight. They couldn't double back and go out the front. Who knew who'd be waiting there, even if only to say good night to the guests? Searching in his pocket, he pulled out his multi-tool and, with a flick, switched on a torch, which illuminated the garden with its sharp beam. He ran the light around the perimeter, stopping with relief when he saw an arched wooden gate set into the wall.

"We're going to have to hurry and be very quiet. Can you run in those?" He eyed her high-heeled shoes with suspicion.

"I'll be okay. I can always take them off later if needed."

"Let's go. Stay close behind me."

The wooden gate was a simple latch affair. "We'll go straight across the fields. I have a car perhaps fifteen minutes away. Come on."

They were just a fraction too late.

The kitchen lights flashed on as two men rushed out. Le Claire pushed Ana through the gate. "Run. Head for the trees. I'll follow as soon as I can."

All the while, Le Claire was searching for his next move. He'd happily take on either one of them, but he'd struggle with both, and he had Ana to think of. He moved farther into the shadows. He rocked gently on the balls of his feet, readying himself.

The taller of the two asked, "Who the hell are you?"

Le Claire didn't speak, just leapt forward and caught the shorter of the two, who was still nearly six feet, with a quick jab. It glanced off the man's jaw but startled him enough to buy some time. The taller man circled around and caught Le Claire a blow from behind. Winded, he bent over, and as he did he kicked his leg back and caught the man direct on the kneecap. The groan of pain was unmistakable. Without missing a beat, Le Claire spun around and punched him in the stomach and threw a side kick at the second man, who had recovered enough to join the fray. Both went down, but that wouldn't last for long.

Le Claire quickly covered the ground to the open gate. Ana had gone through it but no farther. She stood trembling, tensed against the wall. Le Claire grabbed her hand and commanded, "Keep low."

He started to pull her across the fields that backed onto the property. Heavy with corn, the swaying crop gave them a modicum of protection. They were crouched low, but he knew a decent beam would easily track them. He scanned the area in front of them. There was a copse of trees to the far left corner of the fields, and he headed in that direction, a stumbling Ana following. He could hear a commotion behind them, from the direction of the house. Raised voices, many of them, car engines revving. Were people being taken home? He guessed he'd ruined their evening's fun.

The shouts were getting louder, closer. Le Claire could hear Ana's rasping breath and figured her heart would be madly pumping adrenalin through her body, the same way it raced through his.

"Wait. Stop." Ana's voice was hoarse, and she pulled on Le Claire's arm to release her.

He stopped, didn't hide the impatience in his voice. "We have to keep going."

"Just wait a second, please?" She leaned on him for support as she removed both her shoes. Holding them in one hand, she said. "Come on, then, I'm ready."

"Fast as you can, we're heading for the trees."

They ran side by side, no longer hidden, as an undoubtedly later crop of corn only reached to their waists. They ran fast, hearts pounding; even then Le Claire could hear the thundering steps behind them. Two men, maybe more. He heard a wheezed shout, looked back and saw one man stop, hands on thighs as he bent over. His voice was hoarse but still carried across the air to Le Claire. "Keep after them."

They needed to reach the car. Le Claire kept going but ran a hand across his chest as he did so. The small bump in his inside pocket confirmed that the car key was safe. Ana was keeping up with him. Once they reached the camouflage of the trees, he figured they'd veer right, hug the tree line and come out on the lane parallel to the one where he'd left the car. Not for the first time he was thankful that he knew this island so well. He regretted that he didn't have a phone with him. The instructions had said no mobiles, and he hadn't wanted to take the risk of being searched. Their pounding feet were rhythmic as they beat a path through the corn, their pursuers close behind. Le Claire increased his speed and ran slightly ahead of Ana. She followed. He ran into the tree line and turned to the right. The mass of foliage would give them some protection, although it was a more difficult passage and wasn't a straight run.

There was a chance their followers might run straight through the woods, following the clear path. Le Claire glanced back. No such luck. One man had run directly ahead, but another was following, even as he called for his friend. Le Claire heard a muffled oath. Ana had stumbled, stopped and was rubbing a stocking-clad foot. "You okay?"

"Yes, yes, fine."

She looked behind her, and when she turned back to Le Claire, there was a look of determination on her face. She started to run, wincing a little, and then her features settled into a taut, tight look. "I can do it."

She was masking her fear well. She'd just been assaulted, and now she was running through the woods from a couple of maniacs. He kept his voice calm, even though he knew he was getting slightly out of breath. "Good girl."

It must have come from somewhere deep within them, but they increased their pace, driven by the threat behind them, closing in. The trees were thinning out in front of them. "Look, through there. There's an opening onto the lane. I'm parked not far from here."

Or at least he hoped he was. It was pitch-dark, he was disorientated and he couldn't be entirely certain of his directions, but he had to be positive or they were both doomed.

They ran on, ducking down to avoid low branches, and he noticed the trees were growing sparser, which accounted for the thick shafts of moonlight that illuminated their path. Suddenly, the trees ended and they were in open space. In front of them lay a low bank that dropped to the lane. Le Claire looked around, thankfully got his bearings. "This way, that's the church spire. Get in front of me."

Their feet pounded on the tarmac. He had to give Ana credit as her soles would be ripped to shreds. Hopefully, that would be the only casualty of tonight. The few houses they raced past were mostly in darkness. The moon cast a preternatural glow. He'd have preferred it be hidden by cloud.

He could hear their followers. Above the pounding of his heart, which echoed in his ears, he could hear their own footsteps and Ana's gasps. He had to push their pursuers to the back of his mind and focus on the road ahead. He had to keep going. They were almost at the end of the lane. There were streetlights ahead, and he could see the odd car passing the intersecting road. Nearly there. He reached into his jacket and took out the keys, held them tight.

The men were getting closer. He looked at Ana. She was starting to weary, and her steps were getting slower. "Come on, Ana – not long now."

They reached the end of the lane – they'd made it. He couldn't see the men chasing them once they were on the main road. Too many lights, still a few cars and even late-night revellers walking home.

Ana turned round, her face clearly illuminated. Her eyes widened in fear, and Le Claire saw the moment, as if in slow motion, as she stumbled and collapsed to the ground with a scream. The men kept coming. He bent, picked her up in his arms and ran into the road. He saw lights ahead, a car crawling along as if looking for something, as if patrolling. A police car. They revved the engine, and he knew they'd seen him. He looked behind him; their pursuers had seen the car as well. They stopped, and he saw one pull out a phone, make a call and both turned tail and ran.

He gently placed Ana on the pavement and carefully checked for injuries. He sat back on his haunches in relief. Nothing looked serious.

The driver of the police car was Hunter. At any other time, the look of relief on the young PC's face would have been comical. But there was no place for that tonight. "There was a tracker on Blair's car, standard MO for undercover. When you didn't report in at midnight, the chief sent me to do a patrol around the area where the car was parked."

Le Claire simply nodded. "Head for the hospital and then call it in and get a car out here. The house we're looking for backs onto the cornfields at the side of the old woods. Tell them to call me when they're by the fields. They can talk me through what they can see. We'll find that place tonight."

Le Claire gently laid Ana on the backseat of the car. Her eyes flickered open. Her voice was hoarse. "What happened?"

"You fell. You'll be fine, but I want someone to take a look at your ankle and give you something for your feet."

He hesitated, unsure of how to broach what he knew was a necessity. He didn't know Ana that well, but he had always thought she was an honest and trustworthy girl. In the time she'd worked for his father, he had never seen anything to contradict that impression. "I have a favour to ask of you, Ana. I can't tell you why I was at that party, but it is vital that nobody knows that I, or any police officer, was there tonight. I would like you not to lie exactly, but just to say that a man in a mask came to your rescue. I'll come and have a proper chat with you tomorrow, but can you do this for me?"

Her eyes were wide, pupils dilated and face flushed. She would soon come down from the adrenalin burst that would have rushed through her system, and she'd want to sleep, heavily. He wanted to be sure she understood before that happened.

"Yes, of course. I get it. A man in a mask saved me." Her smile was disarming. "It's the truth, isn't it?"

He climbed into the front seat, and they headed for town. His head was throbbing with what had to be done. Finding the exact house was first and foremost, searching it was next and after that he'd turn his mind to what was behind Ana's attack.

CHAPTER TWENTY-ONE

After leaving Ana at the hospital, Le Claire headed to the station. He had to pass the incident room, and as he glanced in, he saw a couple of uniforms hunched over their desks. The overhead lights were off, and the room was cloaked in inky darkness apart from the two occupied workstations. Each unit was spotlit by a solitary desk lamp that cast a pool of yellow light across keyboards and piles of paper. "Fernandez, Peterson, how's it going?" Both men looked up, their wary looks giving way to recognition. Fernandez's grin was cheeky as he made a mock show of eyeing up Le Claire's bedraggled dinner suit and checked his watch. "Fine, sir. You on the late shift?"

Le Claire smiled. It must be 3:00 a.m. by now. "I guess. Keep on at it. Good night."

He headed to his office and closed the door behind him, grimacing as a twinge of pain shot across his back and into his shoulder. Ana's attacker had got a couple of good punches in. He'd been surprised by the first one, which caught him on his undefended side. Was the guy left-handed? He'd remember that when he came across him next time. He eased off his jacket and threw it over the back of the desk chair. His trousers came next. They'd be headed for the dry cleaners once the CSI team was done with them. His shirt was ripped and bloodstained. Some was definitely his. At the thought, his tongue darted out, and he tentatively licked the corner of his mouth. It stung like mad, and he gagged in reflex at the strong taste of bitter blood. He rummaged in his filing cabinet and pulled out the spare jeans and T-shirt he kept there. He eased the shirt over his aching shoulders and grabbed a leather jacket hanging behind the door. He only had his dress shoes, but they'd have to do.

He was soon back in the incident room, where he saw Hunter and Cobb hanging about by the hot drinks machine. "Come on, guys, you're with me. I'll meet you downstairs. You drive, Hunter."

He wasn't going to risk getting stopped for drunk driving. He didn't think the fact he had only drunk the champagne in the line of duty would go down too well.

He checked the time. Damn. It was gone 03:30 a.m. He shrugged and dialled the number. He had no choice.

One ring, two, three, four – please don't say he was in a deep sleep. That would be another black mark against him. The call was answered with a gruff, "Yes?"

"Sir, it's Le Claire. There has been a situation."

The next time the chief spoke, any vestige of sleep had fled his voice. "I'm moving into my study. I take it you know what time it is? Just start telling me what the position is."

Le Claire quickly brought him up-to-date. There was heavy silence. He couldn't help the wave of apprehension that swept through him, as if waiting for the headmaster to tell him off. The situation wasn't without its parallels.

"Christ. What a cock-up."

The criticism stung, and Le Claire was about to try and defend himself when his boss carried on. "There was nothing else you could do. You couldn't leave the girl. I may not want Blair's position compromised, but that girl could have been raped if you hadn't stepped in. Mind you, did you have to let it evolve into a full-on chase across St Mary? If anyone saw that, the phones won't stop ringing, and the conspiracy theorists will be on full alert."

"Sorry, sir, but we had to get away, and I didn't exactly have many options." And there was an understatement.

"Don't get uppity. You did what you had to. What now?"

"I've got men stationed near the party house. I want to go back there and see what we can find, talk to anyone who is still there."

"By the sounds of it, they'll have scarpered, or they will if they've any sense. This mask thing makes me think that there would be some well-known faces who attended that party." His long-drawn sigh was replaced with acquiescence. "I'll organise a search warrant. I'm up now, so I may as well ruin someone else's sleep as well.

Make the search about the attack. Not the drugs, nor the heavy-handed bully boys. I don't want Blair's investigation jeopardised, but neither do I want the slimeball who attacked the girl to get away with it."

# #

The house was easy enough to find once you were in the area running off the woods. The property lay in a leafy lane, and the front perimeter was protected by the same high wall that ran around the back. They drove past it and parked several metres away. As they backtracked along the narrow lane, Le Claire could see the top windows of the house. They were in darkness. He motioned for Hunter and Cobb to stop and listened carefully. There was no noise coming from the property. He looked on top of the wall and saw with surprise that the security cameras were gone. Had the party's organisers installed their own cameras, all the better to film the arriving and departing guests? His gaze shifted, and he saw that the tall wooden entrance gates were slightly ajar. He pushed them open and motioned for the waiting uniforms who made up the advance team to follow him in.

The courtyard was empty of parked cars and the front door closed. The entire house lay in darkness, no lights and no sign of occupation. He took his cue from the unlatched gate they'd walked through and tried the front-door handle. It gave way with ease. Even as they walked into the hallway, Le Claire sensed what they would find. Nothing. The house was silent, and Le Claire opened his mouth to speak when he stopped. His throat was burning with a fierceness that made him choke. His eyes had started to stream, and he rapidly blinked, trying to clear them. "Christ, what the hell is this?" The distinctive smell made him rear back. Bleach, and massively strong stuff at that.

He pointed to the advance team. "You two search the place; let's do it by the book." Hunter was next. "Right, get Vanguard on the phone. Tell him to get his team down here. I want this place gone over with a fine pair of tweezers." As he spoke the words, he already knew it probably wouldn't do any good; these people were professionals. They'd cleared the place, cleaned it, they'd even disinfected. It smacked of experience. They had done this time and time again.

CHAPTER TWENTY-TWO

Le Claire had gone home and grabbed a couple of hours of sleep. After a hurried bowl of cereal, he went to deal with what would no doubt be his most challenging task of the day.

"Morning, Mum."

She sat at the scrubbed wooden kitchen table, its scarred top at odds with the rest of the room's pristine décor, but it had belonged to his grandparents, so he assumed his mother must have at least one sentimental bone. He'd checked the time just before he'd left his flat above the garage. It was 7:30 a.m., yet his mother was already smartly dressed in pressed jeans and an open-neck shirt.

"Good gracious, Jack. What do you want at this hour?" Her hands hovered over the open magazine on the table.

"I just wanted to let you know that Ana has had a bit of an upset."

"Delayed shock, I expect, after finding her cousin like that. Ghastly."

"Last night Ana was…"

His mother's look was suspicious, her voice sharp. "How do you know what Ana was doing last night? Oh, Jack, have you been making a nuisance of yourself?"

"Mum, stop it! Why would you even think that?"

Her look was malicious. "Oh, I think we both know why I'd think that, Jack. It wouldn't be the first time you'd been a bloody idiot where a woman was concerned."

He flushed but wouldn't rise to her bait. "Ana was attacked last night and injured. It happened when she was waitressing at a private party. Luckily, one of the guests managed to intervene. She had to stay in the hospital for observation."

His mother paled, but she didn't say anything, just looked at him. "Mum, did you hear me? Ana has been attacked; she's in hospital."

"I'll have to go and see her, won't I? Make sure she gets home okay."

"I'm sure we can arrange for Ana to be taken to her place."

"No, no, I'll go." It may have been the light, but he thought her eyes softened for a moment. "Jack, she's okay, isn't she? She wasn't, I mean, was she…"

"She'll be fine. She got away before anything too bad happened. She'll probably be pretty shocked though."

"Thank you, Jack. Well, off you go, my morning's disrupted enough as it is."

He shook his head. Who'd have thought it? His mother must have a soft spot for the girl. Maybe she was mellowing in her old age. Her voice called after him. "Jack, I was talking to your father last night. I do hope you aren't going to keep annoying Aidan Gillespie over that boy's death. You must know he's got nothing to do with it. Your father has been having some interesting chats with Aidan, and they may have an opportunity to do a little business together."

That was all he needed. Le Claire simply ignored his mother.

A shocked Ana was settled in Elizabeth's plush car, being driven home. The older woman had swept into the hospital, demanded she be told all about it, barked at a few doctors and the paperwork was signed for Ana's release. Ana had been told that she had a sprained ankle that would need to be rested for a couple of days; some antiseptic salve had soothed her feet and soon any pain would disappear. It would take longer to get the image of the attack out of her mind, to remove the vivid pictures that thrust to the fore every time she closed her eyes. Her employer's cultured voice broke the silence.

"It is lucky that chap got you away from that disgusting lecher. Odd that they were wearing masks though. Makes it all the more difficult to catch him."

She shivered as an icy chill of fear took hold. It would be nigh on impossible to recognise her attacker. She could walk past him, be standing next to him, and would never know. The car slowed, and she realised the short journey was at an end. She pointed to a three-storey terraced house. "I'm in there. Thank you so much."

Before Ana could unbuckle her seat belt, Elizabeth was parked up and out of the car, holding the door open for her. "Come on, I'm not just dumping you on the pavement. I'll see you inside."

Ana's heart sank. She didn't want anyone, especially this woman, to see how she lived. The house was owned by a middle-aged divorcee who rented out rooms to single girls. She currently had three other lodgers in addition to Ana, who had been there the longest. There was a never-ending troop of new faces as the girls either found somewhere better to live or moved back to wherever they came from. The place was clean but the decor dated, and, for a reason she couldn't fathom, Ana was ashamed for anyone to see how she lived. The front door would be far enough. She hobbled up the path and, key in hand, turned to say good-bye to Elizabeth, who reached out, took the key and ushered an astonished Ana through her own front door.

"Right. Where's your room?" The voice brooked no nonsense, and a defeated Ana simply gestured for her to come upstairs. She held on to the unpolished banister, putting the weight on her good ankle as she limped upstairs. She stopped at the first door in the long, dark corridor and pushed it open. She kept her voice light and cheerful to hide the dismissal. "Thank you, I appreciate the ride home."

The older woman wasn't listening. "Come on, let's get you settled. You need to rest."

Ana had no option, and she held back a sigh as she reluctantly let Elizabeth follow her into the room. She quickly glanced around, grateful she had made the bed and tidied up before she had gone to work the evening before. She saw Elizabeth's eyes scan the room, and the blinkers of familiarity fell off; Ana wondered what she saw. A small single bed pushed against the wall beneath the room's one window. A cheap wooden wardrobe, chest of drawers, low bedside cabinet and a lone armchair took up the rest of the space. Ana spied the strap of her backpack peeking out from under the bed.

She quickly bent down and pulled it free, opening the top zipper and rummaging inside. Everything was still there – passport, money fold and the plastic wallet with her important papers.

"Ana, are you okay? You looked a little panicked for a moment."

"Yes, I'm good. My door doesn't have a lock, so I was just making sure that my stuff was okay."

"Ah, I wondered why you carried your backpack with you all the time."

There was a silence then, which Ana didn't know how to break. She knew she shouldn't be ashamed of where she lived, but it was all she could afford whilst she saved up a deposit for something better. Scott had offered to loan her money, but she'd refused. Her parents hadn't left her much. Academics weren't exactly renowned for high salaries, but the little she had in the bank was there for an emergency, not to pay rent.

A voice at the door had them turn around. "Morning, Ana. Your week's rent was due yesterday. Did you forget?"

The words were pleasant enough, as was the tone, but her landlady's face, with its sharp features and habitual pinched expression, rendered the words a challenge.

"Oh, I am so sorry. Yes, I forgot. I'll get it now."

"Good, because you know I've a waiting list for girls who'd love this room. I could rent it to someone else in a snap." Her eyes rested on Elizabeth, and her landlady's next words made Ana cringe. "I don't know who you are, but you'll have to leave. I don't allow anyone in the girls' rooms."

Ana momentarily closed her eyes as she saw Elizabeth raise one perfectly arched brow. There was going to be trouble.

#

Le Claire had run through the night's events to an increasingly incredulous Dewar. Any minute now her jaw was going to drop open.

"I can't believe it. Is Ana okay?"

He shrugged. "I hope so. What she went through wasn't pleasant, but it could have been a great deal worse. The guy was a real piece of work, and he was making his intentions clear. I dread to think what could have happened if I hadn't been there."

"How did she end up working at the party?"

"She was in no state to be pressed last night. I'm going to go and see her now to find out. You should come with me. At least I know she won't be going anywhere. My mother was collecting her from the hospital and will have taken her straight to her home." Out of familial loyalty, Le Claire didn't mention that his mother didn't usually take no for an answer, so she would have taken Ana home and probably barred her from leaving.

"Have we found out who owns the property?"

"I got Peterson to do a run on the title records. The owners are a Geoff and Tina Black. The place doesn't look habitually occupied, the fridge and freezer were empty and turned off, little things like that. I've sent Hunter up there to see what he can find out." He glanced at his watch. "I'll call my mother and make sure she dropped Ana off okay."

The shrill tone of his phone butted in. He looked at the caller ID. "Speak of the devil." He answered the call with a "Hello, Mum."

It took a minute for the words his mother spoke to sink in. Then he thought he must be hallucinating. She couldn't have said what he thought. His "Why did you do that?" was met with a rejoinder that he mind his own business. He found himself saying yes to his mother's last request just before she disconnected the call.

Dewar must have guessed something was up from his tone, stance and expression. "You okay? You look a bit shocked."

"It's my mum. Apparently, she took Ana to her place, didn't like the look of it, so she packed Ana's stuff up and she's taken her home with her."

"Ana has moved into your spare room? Your mum must have a good heart."

He didn't know where to begin with the comment about his mother. Best not to respond. As to the one about the spare room, he didn't want to go there. "I'm going to have to drive back to my place and interview Ana. There's no need for you to come."

Le Claire felt uncomfortable. As soon as he heard what his mother had done, he had every intention of sloping off home to see Ana – alone. He didn't want Dewar to accompany him and see where he lived, stupid as that was. She would have heard the talk about his background, but seeing was an entirely different thing.

"My mother is refusing to have Ana interrogated – her word, not mine – until she is rested up. I was thinking I'd head up there in an hour or so, but I thought you had a meeting scheduled with the financial guys around then?"

Dewar beamed. "I do, but they're flexible time-wise, so I can probably catch up with them when we get back. Now I can go with you."

Le Claire's smile was automatic, but inside he was grimacing. He just hoped his mother was in a good mood and on her best behaviour.

Le Claire felt himself tense as he flicked the indicator at the turn into their private lane. "Right, nearly there."

Using his zapper to open the gates, he navigated up the drive and parked in front of the house. Dewar's eyes were like saucers, but she said nothing. He hurried out of the car. "Come on, let's get this over with."

The front door was unlocked, as usual, and he walked straight in, Dewar following. "Mum said they'd be in the kitchen. I can hear them." There was a low rumbling of voices from the end of the hallway, and they entered the spacious kitchen, finding his mother and Ana seated around the table. "Ana, Mum, this is DS Dewar." Ana looked pale and tired but unharmed. "How are you?"

"I am fine, honestly, just a bit bruised from where I fell, and my feet are sore. I dread to think what might have happened…" Her voice tailed off and she shivered.

Before he could speak, his mother jumped in. "I can't believe the poor girl had to run in her stockinged feet. Have you arrested the vile beast who attacked her?"

"Afraid not, we're here to find out a bit more."

"Well, we can't have people like that running about the island. It's just not on."

"Mum, perhaps you could let me interview Ana and get on with my job."

She huffed, pursing her lips, but eventually stood. "Very well, I'll be in the study. Ana, don't let him bully you. Dewar, it's nice to meet a colleague of Jack's. You'll have to come for afternoon tea sometime."

Dewar looked taken aback and slightly horrified. "Err, sure, thank you." Her face said, *Oh please, no.*

Le Claire waited until he heard the study door open and close. He sat down opposite Ana; Dewar slipped into the seat beside him. "Ana, we went back to the house last night, but there was no one there, and it had been given a thorough cleaning. The place stank of disinfectant and bleach, so it looks like they were trying to get rid of anything that could identify anyone. Can you tell me what you know? Who employed you and what you know about them?"

"Not much, I'm afraid. My friend set the job up for me weeks ago. Just said I was to wait at Liberation Square and a minibus would pick me up and to look smart and wear black. That I was to be discreet and ignore anything I saw. I needed the extra money. She said I'd be paid, and very well, at the end of the night." Her smile was wan as she joked, "All that hassle and I didn't even get my wages."

"Okay, fine. Can we have your friend's details? We'll need to ask her what she knows."

"I can give you her mobile number, but she is not answering. She's left Jersey, and I haven't heard from her. Her name is Irena."

Ana recited the details to Dewar.

Le Claire said, "So you didn't recognise anyone there. Did you speak to any of the other staff?"

"There was no time. When I got on the coach, the manager – she said to call her Betty – said we were to make sure the glasses were filled and hand round food. She was very strict that we had to be gone by midnight. The rest of the time she just instructed us what to do." Ana shook her head. "I can't believe she just left me there."

"The man who attacked you, did you recognise him at all?"

"No. His mask covered most of his face, and it all happened so fast."

Le Claire didn't reveal that it was the woman in the red dress that had sent the man after Ana. "Did you recognise anyone at the party?"

"No, I was just serving the drinks, so I didn't look at anyone. In any event, everyone except the serving staff were masked. I didn't like it there and didn't want to draw attention to myself." She shivered, a look of disbelief on her face. "But that didn't work out too well. I am so grateful to you. I mean, if you hadn't come…"

Dewar reached out and patted Ana's hand. "You're safe now, and, luckily, the worst didn't happen. Would you like to speak to someone about this? We can arrange that."

Ana shook her head. "No, thank you. I just want to forget it. The only thing that freaks me out is that I don't know what he looks like. I mean, maybe I do know him? I could meet him again and I wouldn't even recognise him."

Le Claire stood. "I'm sure it was a one-off, an opportunist taking advantage of the situation, but be vigilant. Call us if you see anything or anyone you're uncomfortable about."

Dewar handed out her card, and the two moved to the door. "Mr Le Claire? I mean, Detective," Ana looked at the table, played with the card in her hand, "I am sorry about this, about me being here." She waved her hand around the room. "Your mum had a bit of an altercation with my landlady. Said it was a disgrace and she wouldn't let the dog live there. She insisted I move in here, said it would be handy on the days I wasn't in the town office. She made me give my notice to the landlady, and next thing I knew my things were in the car, and here I am." She shook her head, and he recognised the look of bewilderment. His face had often worn the same expression until he'd grown to manhood and was more able to handle his mother's controlling tendencies, or at least ignore them.

His voice was gentle. "Ana, this is my mother's home. She does what she wishes, and I don't have any objection to you being here, none at all."

She smiled, and her furrowed brow relaxed. Trust his mother to bully and push, even as she was doing a remarkably kind thing. He pushed open the kitchen door, stopped and turned back to Ana. "Your friend, Irena. Where was she working?"

"For a Mr and Mrs Adamson. She was the au pair."
He aimed a look at Dewar. This island got smaller by the day.

CHAPTER TWENTY-THREE

Le Claire and Dewar arrived back at the station; he excused himself and withdrew to his office. The small space suited him. Here he could close the door, shutting out his colleagues, his partner and any other distractions. The whole force was getting ready to move to a brand new purpose-built police headquarters at the other side of town. They were promised all mod-cons and plenty of space. He just wished for a small, quiet room, tucked away in a corner. Just like he had right now.

He checked his watch. Blair was due in soon, and they had a meeting scheduled with the chief to run through the events of the night before. That gave him time to focus on what they'd learned so far about the Hamlyn case, which, admittedly, wasn't much. His door opened, the noise jarring in the Saturday quiet. Why couldn't people just leave him alone for five minutes?

Before impatience could take hold, he smelled the distinctive aroma of roasted coffee beans. Someone had come bearing gifts. Or at least he hoped they had. The door was shouldered wide open, and John Vanguard, the head of the CSI unit, clumsily entered holding a cardboard coffee cup in each hand, grande size, a paper bag clutched between his teeth and a plastic file folder tucked under his arm. He kicked the door shut behind him, handed Le Claire a coffee, placed his own on the desk and liberated the bag from his mouth. He placed this on the desk and opened it. The aroma of fresh-baked pastries turned his office into a fancy French patisserie. Breakfast was a distant memory, and he hadn't eaten lunch.

Vanguard smiled. "By that look, I take it that you're famished. Help yourself."

Le Claire selected what he hoped was a chocolate croissant, bit into it, savoured the gooey chocolate, sipped his coffee and said, "What brings you here? It must be something special to drag you out of the lab."

"It could be. You may have been right about access to the property being through the lanes at the back of the estate. Our search threw up some odd findings."

Le Claire sat upright, croissant and coffee discarded. "What have you got?"

Vanguard opened the file folder and pulled out some pieces of paper. There were photographs as well. "There has definitely been movement through that area recently. We searched the surroundings and took samples on Monday. Scott Hamlyn died on Saturday night. We have to remember that it rained heavily that morning. It would have dried out a bit by the evening but still be damp. Therefore, anything before Saturday morning could have been wiped clear by the rain. We found several prints and have discounted those from you and Dewar. It was smart of you to retrace your steps back in your own footprints and to get Dewar to follow you in the same way. People often discount footprints as being too unreliable, but remember the role of CSI is to prove that someone could, or could not, have been present at a crime scene."

He spread out his papers on the desk and pointed to five A4-sized photographs. "We took casts of these prints. They were fairly well preserved, having been laid down in mud and then dried out before we picked them up. We have two distinct sets of footwear. One is a UK size eleven. This one here." He pointed to a smooth print. "If I had to hazard a guess, I'd say it was some sort of man's dress shoe."

"Does it match Hamlyn's shoes?"

"From what we can tell, there's a high probability that Scott Hamlyn left that print."

"And the other one?"

"Much smaller. Here, have a look." He flicked through the photographs and pulled out two that displayed a distinctly different, petite shape. "These are probably some form of plimsoll or Converse shoe. See the ridges on the sole?"

Le Claire eyed the photo. "Definitely smaller and narrower."

"Yes, probably a boy or youth."

Le Claire considered the photo. "Or a woman?"

"Indeed, that is possible."

"Anything else?"

"There were some other partial prints, but they were too indistinct to tell us anything, plus some random debris, which could have fallen from anyone's pocket. But we've bagged and tagged what was there." He pulled another group of photographs from the pile. They were a mishmash of items. Some sweet wrappers, what looked like a faded bus ticket, a ragged scrap from what could have been a flight boarding pass, a button and some fragments of material. "Not a lot to go on, but the boarding pass is dated the fifteenth. The month can't be read though. Saturday was the fifteenth. To be frank, that boarding pass could be weeks or months old."

"Okay, we'll see what we can do and run a check on passengers who flew into the island on Saturday. At least it's something to do. Anything else about the shoes?"

"It isn't much, but the smaller print shows an obstruction in one of the ridges, like a small stone. If you ever find the shoe, it may still be there. People conceal their faces, they wear gloves, but, invariably, they forget that their shoes can be a powerful silent witness."

The call he'd been waiting for came in the early afternoon. His stomach rolled, but he answered with a resigned air and then headed to the chief's office with a sinking heart. Chief Officer Wilson was not in a particularly good mood. Le Claire could tell by his set features and unsmiling welcome. "Le Claire, take a seat. Blair has just arrived. I haven't updated him as I thought it best that you report to us both. All I know is that last night was apparently a bloody debacle. Do enlighten us."

Le Claire immediately turned to Blair. "The first thing you need to know is that your cover is intact. I interacted with only a few people on more than a superficial level, and, to be perfectly frank, most were only interested in their own pleasures. If they remember anything, it will be that the man in the plain black mask got hopelessly drunk and left early."

Blair's face sagged, and relief was evident in his voice. "I can't afford to lose any ground here. Go on, what happened?"

Le Claire quickly outlined the evening's events. The chief's face grew stonier by the minute. "Is this how people get their kicks? Sex on tap, drugs and attacks on young girls. What is bloody going on? I hear the girl works for you?"

He felt himself bristle inside. The usual reaction whenever his family was mentioned. "Not me, my parents. Ana is my father's PA and helps my mother as well." That didn't sound odd, did it? How many people had personal assistants to deal with their private affairs?

"Well, the girl is safe now. Any leads?"

"I took a few men back to the house. It was deserted but smelled like a team of cleaners had been in with industrial-strength bleach. The place was immaculate. It's obviously not permanently occupied, and we're trying to track down the owners."

"Okay, I'll get someone onto it. You've got enough on your plate with the Hamlyn case. Any news there?"

"No, nothing solid enough to take us in any particular direction."

"What about Sir Hugh Mallory? Is that investigation firmly closed?"

"Yes, no note was left but all indications point to suicide.

"Damn shame. Okay, get on with it."

Taking the dismissal as intended, Le Claire made to exit the room. The chief's voice stopped him. "I've had a call. The national press are sniffing around, and apparently their take is that we're incompetent buffoons who couldn't manage a candy thief, let alone a murder enquiry. I don't need any negative exposure on this. Get it cleared up, quickly."

He said, "Yes sir," and left. There wasn't anything else to say. He was disgruntled and fed up and felt like baring his teeth when he found an overly buoyant Dewar waiting for him in his office.

She brandished a bundle of paper. "I've got the background report on Laura Brown and the airline passenger confirmations. I think we need to speak to her."

# #

Laura Brown was wearing tight workout clothes when she opened the door. The short leggings and midriff-baring top showed an expanse of lightly tanned flesh. Le Claire buried any flash of attraction. Her smile was wide and her eyes inquisitive. He didn't know if she was a murderer. He did know she was a liar. Her voice was soft. "Come in. This is a surprise. Hold on while I turn this off."

She aimed a remote at the huge flat-screen TV that dominated one wall; with a click, the digital yoga class was frozen in time, the instructor bent over in an impossible pose. Laura Brown sank into one of the sofas and gestured for Le Claire and Dewar to settle into its twin. "Have you any news? Have you caught the person who did this?"

In her casual attire, her hair pulled back in a high ponytail, she looked young and innocent, although her eyes were red-rimmed and shadowed.

Le Claire took the lead. "Not yet, Miss Brown. We've come to clear up an inconsistency."

"Please call me Laura; I hate to be formal. So what is this inconsistency?" She glanced between Le Claire and Dewar. He wanted to keep an eye on her, so he motioned for Dewar to proceed.

"There appears to be a discrepancy in your statement of your whereabouts when Scott Hamlyn was killed."

"And what would that be?" Her voice was even, but her shoulders had tensed.

Dewar continued. "You said you arrived into the island on Sunday morning; however, the airline records show you arriving on Saturday afternoon. You were already in the island when Mr Hamlyn was killed."

There was a long pause whilst she just stared at them, her face a cool mask.

"I've been debating whether to call you or not. I did arrive on Saturday and booked into a hotel. When you arrived here, I told you what I was going to tell Scott. I didn't know he was dead then."

"So you admit lying to us?"

"Yes, but it doesn't matter." She shook her head from side to side, a look of exasperation on her face. "It's no big deal. I had to tell you that as that was exactly what I was going to say to Scott when I saw him. Of course, I never did."

"Why were you deceiving him?"

"I occasionally come over the night before I see Scott. I just need my space sometimes. I relax at the hotel, take a long bath, read, and have a glass of wine. It's a simple separation from the working week to the relaxation of a few days with Scott. I didn't tell him as he would have wanted to see me."

Le Claire took over. "Do you have an alibi for Saturday?"

She raised an eyebrow. "Not as such, I didn't think I'd need one. I drove my hired car to the hotel, went out for a walk, came back, and had my bath and some late dinner. It was room service, and there will be a record of the order delivery."

"What time did you get back from your walk?"

"I can't recall. I wasn't keeping a check on the time."

"Okay, we'll need exact details of your whereabouts. Now, onto another matter. How did say you met Scott Hamlyn?"

She arched one brow. "At a party. Why is this relevant?"

He didn't answer, smiled, let it linger. "When was this?"

She looked impatient; her eyes narrowed, and he could see the moment suspicion crept into her expression. "About six months ago. Again, I ask you, what relevance does this have?"

"Did you meet Scott Hamlyn through your profession?"

A slight twitch was her only reaction. "Not exactly, I had been working at a trade show, organising the team, and the organisers asked me to their party. Scott was there, we met and that was that."

Dewar spoke. "I don't think the DCI meant that profession. I think he meant the one you were arrested for five years ago. The crime was suspected prostitution, but there was insufficient evidence to charge you."

She paled and her features tightened; when she spoke, her voice reverberated with controlled anger. "How dare you bring that up? I was in the wrong place at the decidedly wrong time, with a crowd I soon dropped. This is bullshit, complete bullshit." Her voice had risen and her face reddened.

"So you are saying that you were no longer a prostitute when you met Mr Hamlyn?"

Her nostrils flared, and she held her arms tight across her body. "That is correct. However, I am not, and never have been a prostitute. You have insulted me and all to hide your incompetence that you cannot find who killed Scott. I would like you to leave now."

Le Claire nodded and rose, beckoning for Dewar to follow. "Of course. However, before we go, we'd like to know if you have any trainers or Converse-type shoes with you?"

She shook her head in apparent confusion. "Yes. Look, what on earth is this about now?"

"Just a routine check regarding the crime scene to exclude you from further enquiries. If you are innocent, you have nothing to worry about."

She shook her head in an impatient huff. "Hold on."

Laura Brown came back into the room with a plastic bag in hand, which she handed to Le Claire. "Here you are, one pair of sneakers. I assume I get a receipt?"

Dewar pulled out her notebook and quickly scribbled something. "Here you are. We should be finished with them in a day or so, and we'll give you a call."

CHAPTER TWENTY-FOUR

Le Claire was dog-tired, and his head was buzzing. He'd left Dewar in the incident room and headed for his office. Usually, the quiet helped him think. Unfortunately, his thoughts couldn't fight past the noise in his head.

The smell of strong coffee preceded Dewar into his office. "I nipped out to that place you like, thought you could use one of these." She placed a brightly coloured cardboard cup in front of him. Steam and the unmistakable aroma of quality coffee wafted through the drinking hole in the plastic lid.

"Oh yes, I do indeed need this. Did you get yourself one of those teas you can stand a spoon in?"

"Of course!" She put her own cup on the desk and unhooked the handles of a paper bag from around her wrist. "I got you a choc-chip cookie as well."

She must think he was in a bad way. "Thanks. So what do you think?" He waved his hand, which held the cookie, toward the small whiteboard affixed to the wall.

She turned and faced the board, chewing her bottom lip as she stared at the images and marker pen scribblings. Scott Hamlyn's photo had been printed from his parents' digital album. It wasn't strictly necessary to have the photo on the board, but Le Claire wanted a visual reminder of what they stood for, of whom they were acting for. Yes, it was for the law, for the justice of the land, but more than that, the badge stood for the vulnerable, the disadvantaged, the injured and, of course, the dead.

"There's David Adamson. We know he got into a fight with Hamlyn days before he died."

"Indeed, but what was his motive? Was the argument fierce enough to take that irrevocable step, and days later at that?"

"Yeah, we don't have a lot there."

She moved farther back from the board, considered the other names he'd written in the thick marker. "Aidan Gillespie? Scott Hamlyn cost him land that should have rightfully been his. Add in that Hamlyn was killed at Gillespie's estate."

"Stupid of Gillespie to bring death to his own door, or maybe he just couldn't help himself?"

Then, hands on hips, she shook her head. "No. The girlfriend is our best line so far. She's inherited Hamlyn's estate. She lied to us about not arriving in the island until Sunday morning."

He played devil's advocate. "I guess her explanation could ring true in that she didn't know Scott was dead when she first spoke to us and was simply trying to tell the same story she'd spin to him."

"Meaningless lies, perhaps, but if that was the case, why not tell us the truth later, even if it did put her in a bad light? She must have known we'd check the airline records."

"I agree. We now know she had the opportunity, the inheritance gave her a motive and her past added another dimension. Laura Brown is our only real person of interest at the moment."

He suddenly realised he'd hijacked the conversation. "I'm grateful for the coffee, but did you come in for anything specific?"

"Yes, sorry. Hunter called me when I was at the coffee shop. Can you give him a ring?"

Le Claire smelled a problem. So that's why she got him a coffee. He exhaled loudly. "Okay, I'll give him a call. Catch you later."

She just stared at him. He sighed. "Fine, I'll be gentle with him."

Hunter answered immediately. He must have been clutching his mobile.

"Dewar said I was to call you. What have you found out about the owners?"

"There are two properties which back onto either side of it. I tried the one on the right first. An elderly lady lives there, and she said the couple who live in the house, the Blacks, go away a lot. She'd heard some noise the night before and figured they were back for a bit. She didn't know much more but said that she knew they were friendly with the people at The Meadows, which is about four houses down on the left. Apparently, they all take it in turns to have drinks on Christmas morning, and they have known each other for years."

"Did you see these people?"

"Yes, they know the Blacks very well. He was in finance, and they retired a few years ago. They have a villa in Greece and spend a lot of time there. That's where they are at the moment. I explained that we needed to speak to them about potential trespassing, and they passed on Mr Black's mobile number. Greece is two hours ahead, so I called them from the car. There was a recorded message saying they were on some remote island tour and wouldn't be contactable until tomorrow."

A black slash of disappointment darkened his mood. "Damn, the trail will be cold before we get anywhere on that bloody house."

"Sorry, sir. The couple I spoke to said someone was looking after the house, but they didn't know what the arrangements were."

"Okay. Call them tomorrow and inform me as soon as you know anything." He disconnected the call and replaced the handset with a heavy-handed thud. What now?

The man had deliberately gone after Ana, but why? He had then told Ana that she had to keep her mouth shut, but she didn't know anyone at the party. Was that right? Or had she simply not recognised them?

He checked his watch and saw it was nearly 2:00 p.m. A grumble from his stomach was a reminder that breakfast had been a long time ago, and the cookie had barely dented his appetite. He grabbed his jacket and wallet, his mouth already watering at the thought of the toasted cheese and ham panini that he invariably ordered from his usual lunch haunt. He'd have another coffee as well.

His eyes swept the room as he neared the front door, his mind firmly on his lunch. A middle-aged woman was standing by the front desk, her voice getting louder, her words clear.

"It's a crime, a financial one, and so I want to speak to the Financial Crimes Unit. What is so difficult to understand? That lot are always bragging in the paper about how they prevent the island

157

being used for dodgy deals and money laundering, so the least they can do is show some interest and get down here and talk to me. We've been defrauded out of tens of thousands of pounds, and I want someone to do something about it."

He recognised her and mentally bade farewell to lunch. "Lady Mallory, may I help you?"

She turned, frowning for a moment as she tried to place him. Then recognition lit her eyes. "Oh, it's you. Tell this man I need help."

Le Claire complied. "Sergeant, I'll take this. Is Interview One free?"

At the desk sergeant's nod, Le Claire took Lady Mallory's arm. "Let's go somewhere we can speak properly." As they walked, he slowed his pace to match hers. For all her bravado, she seemed a little bewildered and looked on the verge of tears. The interview room wasn't the most comfortable of spaces, but it was private. Lady Mallory seemed even paler in the dismal grey of the room.

He'd filched a bottle of water and some glasses as they'd passed the refreshment stand, and he poured a glass for each of them. She gratefully took a sip. "Thank you, sorry if I was a bit loud out there. It's all been too much recently. The funeral's next week. We had to delay it as some important bods are away at the moment. Bloody ridiculous if you ask me, but the newly anointed Sir John Mallory doesn't want to do anything that would draw censure. He's a bit of toad."

John Mallory had inherited his father's title and was seemingly relishing his position rather too much for his mother's liking.

"Lady Mallory, why have you come here today? You mentioned fraud?"

"Yes, I did. To keep my mind occupied, I decided to make a start on some of the mundane tasks one has to deal with when someone passes. Cancelling standing orders and the like. I contacted the bank and dropped Hugh's death certificate to them. They reviewed the account, and we ran through some memberships and things that would need to be cancelled, you know, the RAC and suchlike. There was a rather large payment that went out each month to a charity. I remember Hugh mentioning it once. It's one of those organisations that has a general donation policy and benefits all sorts of causes. The bank said it was a little odd as it wasn't a standing order for a set monthly sum but a direct debit. So basically the recipients could take as much each month as they wanted, and boy were they doing that! Over the last few months, the figure has increased substantially." She took a shaky breath and sipped at her water. "The last few payments were for £25,000 each."

He kept his face impassive, but it wasn't easy. "That is a hefty sum."

"I can't believe Hugh was so stupid. He tried very hard to be a charitable soul, but this was ridiculous. He didn't keep any paperwork on them. I looked everywhere. Just a name, the Phoenix Foundation, and a Panama PO Box address. We're very well-off, but this amount of money is astronomical. He can't have been in his right mind. They've taken advantage of him, and I want something done about this. I probably shouldn't have come here, but I didn't know who to turn to."

Le Claire knew he should say some soothing words, send her on her way and ask the FCU if this warranted their looking into. It was nothing to do with him, and he shouldn't get involved. She looked old and worn out. "Okay, leave it with me. One of my guys is a whizz at ferreting out stuff online. I'll get him to have a look at it, and then I'll chat to the FCU guys."

Relief lit her face and took away some of the worry lines. "Thank you, I do appreciate it."

Le Claire saw her out of the building, realised it was too late for lunch and headed back to the incident room. He needed to pass this investigation off to someone, forget about it and get on with his most urgent priority, finding out who killed Scott Hamlyn.

# #

Ana was settled in her new home and wanted to pinch herself, hard, to make sure this wasn't a dream. When Le Claire and Dewar left, she had dutifully risen from the table and followed Elizabeth and a yapping Buster outside, and they'd carried on around the side of the house to a small paved courtyard. A yellow-painted door was set into the pink granite wall; wooden tubs overflowing with masses of geraniums flanked the entrance.

The doorway opened straight onto a sitting room, kitchen and dining area. It was large and airy and filled with soft, colourful furnishings and shiny appliances. An archway led into a large bedroom with plenty of wardrobes and its own en-suite bathroom. Elizabeth had pointed to a closed door at the far end of the kitchen area. It was a connecting door into the house, kept locked, but Elizabeth had explained that made the property available for occupation by people without full residential qualifications. Ana couldn't have cared less. This was paradise.

Scott would have been so pleased for her. Ana had come to know that her cousin was shy, cripplingly so, and that his armour was an arrogant attitude that kept most people at arm's length. She felt a pang of pain at his loss, which, coupled with the events of the previous night, caused a wave of self-pity to cloak her as she felt a momentary despair. When her parents' had died and the opportunity arose to travel to Jersey, she had jumped at the chance. Not for adventure, not to better herself – the main driving factor had been to connect with her mother's family, *her* family, and build a relationship with them. From a tentative start, she and Scott had been well on the way to building a friendship that would last the years, but that had been taken away by Scott's death. Now she was only left with an aunt who wanted nothing to do with her.

Sarah Hamlyn wasn't an easy woman to know but Ana had held a glimmer of hope that the woman would soften in time. She had to accept that this might no longer be an option, not when her aunt had lost her son. If anything, Sarah's bitterness would probably increase, leaving no place for Ana. They were tied by blood, but sometimes that just wasn't enough. She huffed out a heavy exhalation as she rose from the chair and walked to the small kitchen area. There were only tiny pinpricks of muted pain when she put pressure on the soles of her feet, and she was hopeful she'd be back to normal in a few days.

But the worst injuries weren't always physical. She shuddered as she thought of that man, touching her, doing what he wanted, and then she thought how lucky she had been – for how much worse would it have been and, disturbingly, how would the night have ended if Le Claire hadn't been there? Her stomach lurched, and, leaning against the kitchen counter, she sipped from her water glass to combat the waves of nausea.

Her mobile buzzed on the worktop. She'd put it on vibrate earlier, and looking at the caller ID, she smiled and felt some of the day's heaviness lift.

"Ben, hi. How's it going?"

"All good. What have you been up to?"

Ana didn't know how to respond. So much had happened, and most of it wasn't something she felt comfortable speaking about on the phone, so she answered the only way she could. "Yeah, everything is fine. How is London?"

"I just got back. For a change, we got everything agreed in one meeting, and there didn't seem any point in staying over. Look, the reason I called is that I am pretty tied up tomorrow, but I wondered if you fancied meeting up on Monday? Maybe go for a drink somewhere? Or I could make you something to eat at my place?"

"Either sounds good, but I am a little tired; there's been a lot going on, so dinner at yours would be lovely."

She could hear the smile in his voice. "Great. I'll give you a call Monday, and we can finalise the times."

"Okay, thanks. Bye."

"Bye, Ana. I've missed you." The line disconnected whilst she was still wondering if she had heard correctly. She went to sleep in her new bedroom with a lightened heart and a smile on her face.

CHAPTER TWENTY-FIVE

Laura felt sick to the pit of her stomach. A hollow tension had taken hold and wouldn't let go. If the police did their research, if they looked in the right places, they'd see she had been a fixture in certain circles for a number of years. Laura counted millionaires, powerful businessmen and minor aristocracy in her past. She'd been wined and dined by them, but she was no society fixture. The men she'd accompanied, whether for a night, a week or a month, had paid well for her company. No matter what way you coloured it, no matter how she tried to justify it, Laura had been selling sex for years.

She'd often thought hers was the classic story. Small-town girl in search of big-city lights. She'd found the sparkle, the gloss, and then, when she'd been burnt by the ferocity of the bright lights, it had been too late to go home, too late to stop, so she'd carried on. It all started so innocently. In with the right crowd, catch someone's eye, get asked on a date. Then an offer – to buy a dress, shoes; just so you feel comfortable going to a posh party. You say yes, why not? Only they don't take you shopping, they just hand you cash – and you take it. That's how easy it had been.

If it hadn't been for an old acquaintance throwing her a lifeline, she'd still be in, what was in reality, the escort trade. She figured he felt partially responsible, and maybe he was. She exhaled and her heart-heavy sigh filled the room, echoing in the silence.

She gulped the last of her gin and tonic. It was her second, and she'd been heavy-handed in pouring the measure and gone light on the mixer. She was contemplating having a third, was in fact reaching for the bottle, when there was a knock at the door. Damn, some of the tenants had the habit of nipping out to the nearby shops and leaving the main entrance unlatched. So much for expensive security. She certainly wasn't expecting anyone, so she cautiously looked through the peephole in the solid oak front door. What the hell did he want? She contemplated pretending to be out, but she had never been a coward. Pasting a bright smile on her face, she opened the door. "This is a surprise. What can I do for you?"

She didn't invite him in, but he pushed past her anyway. "Just a quiet word, that's all."

She didn't have any choice and closed the door, shrugging. "Sure."

He walked around the lounge and stood in the centre of the room, gazing out to sea. "I've always thought this was a fabulous view. How are you?"

"Getting by. To be honest, I'm still in shock."

"Yeah, I can imagine. Scott was a one-way ticket to easy street for you."

"You know it wasn't like that. I was doing okay on my own."

"What? A monthly salary? Granted, I'm sure it was a generous one, but not quite enough for you to live up to the standard you used to enjoy. Scott had money in the bank and was making more every year. And he had something you could never achieve without him. Respectability. Otherwise why go with someone like him? You had other choices."

Her laugh was harsh and mirthless. "Not marriage options, and not with someone I cared about. I don't think I realised how much I loved Scott." Her voice broke, and she took a deep breath. "I may have made mistakes in my life, but I had one chance to be on the right road, to gain the path I used to be on. Scott knew of my past, and he still wanted me. How many other men would, or even could, do that?"

"I could."

She was unsure of what to say. The silence lengthened. It was not comfortable, and its growing weight was palpable. She could hear his breathing, knew the moment it changed. He turned and looked straight at her. Then she heard his words, and it took a moment for what he said to sink in. "I've waited long enough, Laura. I want another taste of you."

163

She was horrified, even though a tiny, cynical part of her thought that she'd had, and done, worse before. Like the last time they'd been together. He'd called out for every vile perversion he fancied that night. "No, that's never been part of the deal."

"There is no deal. Scott's dead, and I'm sure fingers are pointing your way. I could help that along, or I could send the police in another direction. Whatever you want."

"No, you keep out of my business. I don't trust you."

"You may not trust me, but you need me. Your benefactor paid a good sum to keep your past quiet, and now that he's gone you'll need to get your money from somewhere. I only want to help you."

The way he looked at her, hunger vying with possessiveness, made her regret how flimsy her skirt was and how her top hugged her bra-less breasts. She wasn't dressed for company. She crossed her hands in front of her chest, a reflexive and defensive action. He moved toward her.

"Laura, you know how I've always felt about you. I can't get that night out of my mind."

"Don't romanticise it, for I've no intention of having a repeat run. You just wanted a piece of the pie. I wouldn't sleep with you now even if you paid."

"Payment? Is that what you're after? I'll pay you. Come on, Laura."

The way he said her name, the vulgar caress of the word, made her shiver. She was suddenly conscious of how vulnerable she was at this moment. "I want you to go. Didn't you hear? Scott left me everything, so I don't need you or your money." She walked past him, careful to keep distance between them. She cracked the door open, drew back to open it wide, but before she could react, or even think, a hand slammed against the door, forcing it closed.

She was pinned against the door, facing it as his body pressed tight against her own, his hands planked on either side of her head. He whispered in her ear, his breath warm on her cheek.

"I'm not going anywhere. Not until we've been properly reacquainted."

Laura was trying to make sense of the words and gasped as his hand roughly grabbed her breast and pinched the soft flesh between his fingers. His breathing grew heavier, hitching and rasping. She could feel his erection pressing against her though their layers of clothing. Laura knew how to distance herself from physicality, was an expert in closing down her real self and concealing her very essence as she playacted whatever role her "date" expected or demanded. She could feel the practised tug, urging her to act normal, to tuck herself away, deep down inside, and just let him get on with it. But he wasn't a client, and she no longer felt like an escort. He was just yet another in a long line of men who thought they owned her. She wasn't putting up with that. Not anymore.

She arched her back and pushed away from the door, driving her ass into his groin. His moan of pleasure sickened her, but his distraction was her ultimate objective. She allowed a low sigh to escape, and it floated in the air between them. He relaxed his position, and that's when she acted. She kicked out her left foot and caught him sharply on the shin. His yell of pain gave her a momentary chance; she ducked under his arm and ran across the room toward the sliding doors. All she had to do was get out onto the balcony and scream and scream. At this time of night, neighbours would be in their kitchens or lounges, doors wide open to let in the sea air, or sitting, sipping wine as the sun went down. They would hear her, that was for sure.

She had the lock undone and grasped the long handle, ready to slide the door open, when she turned at his roar of rage as he came running across the room. In one seamless movement, he lashed out, and his blow landed hard against her cheek. She stumbled, and he was on her. "You fucking whore. You dare to treat me like this. You're a piece of meat. You'll shut up and do what I say, and you'll enjoy it, bitch. It's been a while since you've had a real man." He shoved her to the ground and forced her legs apart with his knee. One hand held her throat, squeezing her windpipe until all she could manage were rasping breaths. He pushed her skirt to her waist, ripped her knickers aside and forced his fingers inside her. She jerked at the pain, screaming silently at the violation. He removed his hand and rubbed his body against hers, grinding into her. The buckle of his jeans pressed into her flesh, and a remote part of her wondered if it would leave an imprint. She, who had known more men than most, who had made a living pandering to their whims, suddenly understood the brutality of sexual assault, of rape rendering you powerless and giving the attacker control – marking you a victim. This bastard didn't want to have sex with her right now. He wanted to humiliate her, to control her, to subjugate her in the most unimaginable ways possible. That wasn't going to happen.

She jerked and struggled, kicking, twisting and turning. She managed to dislodge him, pushing him aside; the building rage within her gave a burst of strength. She kicked, she hissed, she would not have this happen.

"Fucking slut."

The first punch was brutal. The next he inflicted was devastating. Her thoughts stuttered; all she could feel, all she could think about was the seering pain. From somewhere, she found her words. "You won't get away with this. I'll get you done. This is serious."

His laugh filled the air, reverberating through the room. "You stupid bitch, this is nothing, you are nothing. No one else decent is going to be willing to take on an aging call girl. You'd have hated being a prissy little corporate wife, dinner parties and screwing the husband on a Saturday night, keeping a smile on your face. You'd still have been a prostitute. He'd have kept you, paid for your services in respectability, conformity and a share of his pension. You didn't love him, so that's still prostitution. You could have had me. Now you've ruined it, RUINED IT."

His raised his arm, his fist clenched, ready to strike, and as the punch landed on her jaw and bones broke, the last she saw was his face, reddened with rage, before her eyes closed in welcome oblivion.

CHAPTER TWENTY-SIX

Le Claire drove along the Esplanade, the sun was shining, and even at this time, just gone 8:30 a.m., the Sunday cyclists and joggers were already out. The roads were pretty clear, and in no time he was walking into the station. His mobile rang, and when he answered it, Hunter's breathless voice poured into his ear.

"Sir, I spoke to the property owners."

"Good work; that was quick. I'm on my way in, and I'll see you in the incident room."

Hunter jumped up to greet him, and Le Claire remembered himself at the same age. He couldn't believe he had ever been so untouched or innocent, but he must have been once. "Come on, tell me what you know."

"I spoke to Mr Black. I said we thought the place may have been broken into, but no apparent damage was done. They were pretty shocked and told us to get in touch with the property company that looks after the place. I've got the details here."

"Okay, you better give them a call. Who are they?"

"An EDA Properties. Here are the details."

Hunter passed across a piece of paper, and Le Claire read the address and smiled. It certainly was a small world. He had a visit to make.

# #

The door was opened by a woman he hadn't seen before. Of medium height, she had an olive complexion and dark hair caught up in an unruly, loose bun. She lifted a brow as Le Claire flashed his badge. "I'm DCI Le Claire. I'd like to talk to someone associated with EDA Properties."

She shrugged, but her eyes sharpened. "Sure, come on in."

He followed her through the house to a small back room that was set out as a study with a smoked-glass desk, fancy office chair and boxes and boxes of papers. A man was at the desk. "Darling, this policeman wants a word. I'll be in the kitchen if you need me."

David Adamson, reading glasses perched on his nose, looked up and blinked in surprise. "Detective, how can I help you? Is it about Irena?"

"No. I believe your company manages a property in St Mary called Fairways?"

"Yes, that is correct. It's the Blacks' place. They're in Greece at the moment. Is something wrong?"

"The property has apparently been broken into."

"Oh Christ, are there damages? Is it a mess?"

Le Claire remembered the pungent smell of disinfectant that permeated the very air at Fairways. "I think you'll find it's probably cleaner than the last time you saw it."

Adamson looked puzzled. "Sorry, I don't follow."

"Never mind. When do you check the place?"

"Every Wednesday." He took off his glasses and dropped them on the cluttered desk. He rubbed his hand across his forehead. "Oh my God, the Blacks will go mad. I better call them."

"We've already done that."

His mouth dropped open. "Oh no, were they angry?"

"We couldn't comment on their feelings. So you don't know of anyone who had access to the premises apart from you?"

"Access? I thought it was a break-in?"

"We're just covering all angles."

The door opened, and the woman came back in. "Everything okay?"

"Yes, yes. Sorry, this is my wife, Beth. Honey, this is DCI Le Claire."

She nodded and turned back to her husband. "What's happening?"

"Fairways, the Blacks' place, it's been broken into, and they know."

She rolled her eyes. "When did you last go there?"

Le Claire clearly heard the wifely criticism, sharp and accusing in the way only a spouse could get away with. Adamson's mouth took on a sullen edge as he glared at his wife. "It's been a tough time. I've got no childcare, remember? And you're usually halfway round the bloody world."

Le Claire was swift to pick up the omission. "You didn't answer your wife's question, so I'll ask it again. When were you last at Fairways?"

His eyes didn't meet Le Claire's. "Over a week ago. The Wednesday before last. Everything was fine, as usual. I've been busy, and the au pair's gone, and I just didn't have time to do everything, so I thought I'd skip a week. I'll have to call the Blacks. I mean, you said it wasn't damaged, so no harm done."

Le Claire knew how Jersey worked. Nothing was ever kept secret, and it would eventually get out that the house had been broken into, a party held and an orgy had been on the cards. Add in that there had been an attack on a girl – for that wouldn't stay quiet either – and EDA Properties weren't going to last long in the field of looking after empty houses for absent owners.

"Before you do that, could you tell me where you were on Friday night?"

Adamson looked puzzled. "Friday night? Don't know what that has to do with anything, but I was here with the kids."

Le Claire turned to Beth Adamson. "I understand you work away? When did you get back to Jersey?"

"I got back this morning, on the first flight. I'm here for two weeks." She said this as if it was a lifetime, and Le Claire felt sorry for David Adamson, and even more so for his children.

# #

His office door swung open. It was Vanguard. His thin face was, as usual, impassive and unyielding, but his eyes were lit by excitement.

"Come on in. What have you got for me? I know it's something."

Vanguard threw two photographs on the table. Each one a foot imprint with a ridged sole. "Look at them. Just look at them."

Le Claire did so and immediately recognised the beauty of what lay in front of them. "They match?"

"They are identical. The one on the left was taken from the print at the manor; the one on the right was taken from the Converse trainers you gave us. Laura Brown, or to be more accurate, her shoes were at the back entrance to the manor at some point after last Saturday morning."

Le Claire barely had time to thank Vanguard as he grabbed his jacket and ran out to his car, mobile in hand as he called Dewar.

Calls to Laura Brown's mobile had gone unanswered. Le Claire had tried several times, but no joy. He had therefore decided just to go and see her and arranged to meet Dewar there. He was impatiently waiting in front of the apartment building when Dewar's car drove in. At last! He schooled his features as she hurried toward him. Instead of her usual buttoned-up uniform, Dewar was wearing casual workout clothes, the type Sasha wore at yoga, loose pants and a tight top. She was pulling on a hooded zip-up. As he got out of the car, her apologies started. "So sorry. I was at my Pilates class when you called and didn't have time to go home and change."

"Don't worry; let's just see what she has to say."

"So the shoe was a match?"

"Absolutely. It puts her at the scene of the crime, sneaking into the manor by a hidden entrance, and add in that she lied to us and arrived the night before she said she did, and don't forget her unsavoury past – well, if I was betting, I'd put money on Laura Brown being involved somehow. Come on. Let's do this."

The main door to the apartments was open yet again, the same piece of smooth wood used as a stopper to jam the door accessible. Dewar sighed. "I simply do not believe people who do this. And then they complain when someone breaks in."

"I know, don't worry about it. We've got more to think about."

They reached Laura Brown's apartment, and after several rings on the buzzer aided by a few sharp raps, the door remained unopened. Le Claire looked at Dewar, who had bent her knees and was peering through the letter box. He recognised the moment her shoulders tensed, and her words confirmed the action. "Oh God, the place is a mess; tables and chairs are overturned."

She looked at Le Claire, and his tone was decisive. "We're in fear of the occupier's well-being, so move back." That covered any need for a warrant.

Dewar moved to the side, and Le Claire took a step back. He braced and threw himself against the door, hitting it full force. "Ah, that hurts." He slid to the floor, clutching his shoulder. He used his uninjured arm to get to his feet just as the next door along the corridor opened and an elderly gentleman came out. His voice was brusque. "What is going on here? I had enough of the racket last night."

"Sorry, sir, DCI Le Claire and DS Dewar. We're concerned for Miss Brown and need to access the property." Le Claire had taken out his badge, which the septuagenarian took from him, carefully reading the words. Apparently satisfied, he handed it back and said, "I'm Edward Farrar. I'll call the caretaker. He has keys to all the apartments." He disappeared for a moment, and his muffled voice could be heard through the open door. He returned almost immediately. "He is on his way. I got him on his mobile. He is in this building, so he won't be long."

Dewar asked, "You said there were noises that bothered you last night? What were they?"

Edward Farrar shook his head. "I don't know, but I had to shut my patio doors to block out the noise. I never had that problem when young Hamlyn was there on his own."

"Morning." A short man with a balding head and a cheerful smile walked toward them. He wore casual trousers and an open-neck short. A tool belt around his middle made clear his identity. "Carl, this is the police. They need access to Scott Hamlyn's place; well, it's that girl's now, I hear." He turned to Le Claire. "On you go, show him your ID. You too?"

Farrar looked at Dewar, and he didn't seem entirely convinced she was a policewoman. Dewar didn't rise to the question in his voice but simply complied. Le Claire couldn't blame the man for being dubious. She looked younger and softer in her workout gear. He made a note to himself that she should always wear her uniform.

Carl, happy with their identity, complied and took out a huge bunch of keys and opened the apartment door. Le Claire entered first, Dewar close behind him. He heard her speak. "Gentlemen, thank you, but we can take it from here. Please remain outside the apartment."

As he moved along the hallway, he could see into the lounge. A table was overturned, and a glass lamp lay smashed on the floor. The panoramic window was uncovered, and bright sunshine streamed into the room, making it difficult to see. After a moment, his eyes adjusted, and Le Claire saw her. Laura Brown lay on her back; she was still, and her face was a bloodied mess. Her top had been ripped open, revealing the dark bruising that covered her chest. He bent to his knees, checked for a pulse and called, "Dewar, get an ambulance. She's still alive."

# #

Viera had arrived with the ambulance and carried out a quick check on the unconscious Laura. "She's taken a beating. If it's this bad on the outside, we can only guess at what damage has been done internally. We need to get her to hospital. You won't be able to talk to her for a while – if she regains consciousness, that is. Right now, she comes first." Within minutes, Laura Brown had been stretchered out, the ambulance rushing her to hospital.

Vanguard's team had arrived and were painstakingly investigating the physical scene. Le Claire was quiet for a moment, reflecting on the situation, when the voices around him brought him back to the present.

"Oh, hi, Dewar, err, I almost didn't recognise you there."

Dewar scowled at Viera, and Le Claire thought she did look different, but he would never tell her that. Knowing Dewar, she'd take it as an insult.

"Why, is something wrong with the way I look?"

Le Claire was treated to the unlikely sight of the strapping young doctor blushing as he stumbled through a response. "No, you just look different, you know, nice. I mean, you always look nice…I think I better be off, then. I want to brief whoever is on duty at Emergency about my initial findings, just in case any of it can be helpful. See you both later." The medic rushed out, taking his medical bag and his blushes with him.

Le Claire waited a beat until he was sure Viera was gone. "You've made an impression there. Must've been the yoga pants."

"Very funny. I could never go out with someone like him."

"Why not? I guess women find him good-looking, he's a nice guy, good prospects and all that." His words were true, but he was joking, a release of the earlier tension, and he knew she could tell.

"Can't you just imagine people asking us how we met? I mean, I'd have to tell the truth and say I first met David Viera over a dead body."

They laughed, but he could see that Dewar's eyes were still sombre, and he knew his own would tell the same story.

Dewar had gone to have a quick shower and get changed. She'd said she might as well do some work whilst she was here. The incident room was quiet when he walked in. Not that it wasn't occupied. There were several officers on duty today, and others had come in to finish up some of their work. Murder was a serious business, and they all knew they were up against the clock. Le Claire glanced around the room and stopped when his eyes rested on Masters. Le Claire was getting on better with him now; maybe Masters wasn't so bad after all. Perhaps he had to accept that he just had a personal dislike and that Masters was perfectly capable of doing his job. Decision made, he walked across the room.

"Bryce, how are you?"

The megawatt smile that greeted Le Claire made his skin itch, but he let it go – manfully, he thought.

"Yeah, all good here. We're data-mining deep into the financials and have finally finished the interviews with the party guests."

"The reports so far haven't thrown anything up?"

"No, everyone checks out okay, and there were only superficial connections with Hamlyn."

Le Claire was about to walk away, changed his mind, decided to be pleasant. "Okay, thanks for your work. I guess you're having to spend time on your normal caseload? Hope it's not too hectic."

Masters flashed white, perfectly even teeth. "No, it's fine. The usual nonsense we get sometimes."

Le Claire kept the conversation going. He had to try and make an effort. "What's been happening?"

Masters laughed. "There was one yesterday. Boy, did I save you from a freak show."

"A freak show? Now you've got me intrigued. What do you mean?"

"This society woman turned up, all posh highlights, stretched face and beige outfit. She was dragging some misfit with her. The man hardly looked like he was top drawer, more like a European migrant. She was asking for you, but I took some details and sent her on her way."

Le Claire mentally closed his ears to the inappropriate comments but picked up on the most salient point. "She asked for me by name?"

The smile was sly. "Yeah, I thought she was maybe one of your society pals, and we can't have them breaking rank, can we?"

Le Claire held his temper. "Who was she, and what did she want?"

"Let me check." He tapped his computer keyboard. "A Mrs Caro Armstrong. She was with a Boris Tchensen. Seems his daughter, Armstrong's au pair, has run off, and they're asking what we can do about it. I mean, that's not our problem."

"Why come to us if she has run off?"

"Yeah, I know. Mind you, they said she was missing."

Le Claire had a flash of memory. His mother had introduced him to Caro Armstrong at Gillespie's party, but she'd said her au pair had skipped out. What had made her change her opinion?

"Thanks, Masters. If anyone else asks for me again, don't speak for me. Just make sure I know about it."

Le Claire ignored the affronted-looking Masters and headed to his office.

CHAPTER TWENTY-SEVEN

Dewar was back in less than fifteen minutes. Her dark trousers, plain shirt and casual blazer hit the right tone. From how she held herself as she walked, Le Claire had a suspicion that she had her eye on getting out of uniform. If she kept up this work, he'd certainly help her get there.

Le Claire was leaning against her desk and, pushing himself to his feet, said, "Don't get comfy. We've got somewhere to be."

As she jumped into the passenger seat and buckled up, he checked the address. "Caro Armstrong lives in St Brelade, so we'll have to battle along the Esplanade." The dual carriage way was the main connector between the east and west of the island and the St Helier capital that lay in the south.

"That's all we need on a Sunday. It's the busiest road in the island."

She was quiet for a moment as Le Claire navigated out of the station and crept through the slow traffic until he was passing the hospital and heading for the coast and the Esplanade. "Why are we going to see this Mrs Armstrong?"

"I spoke to her at Aidan Gillespie's party. She's a friend of my mother, and she mentioned her au pair had walked out on her. She was dismissive about it at the time. Apparently, she recently called in asking for me. Masters spoke to her, but decided not to pass the message on." Careful, he warned himself. Even he could hear the peevish tone in his voice. There was no need for him to show his feelings about Masters. He kept his voice professional, even though he saw Dewar roll her eyes dismissively. "The girl's father turned up. He's worried about her. I thought I may as well check it out."

Dewar pulled a face. "Since when is it our job to track down missing persons?"

He simply shrugged. The last case he had dealt with at the London Met involved a serial abductor, rapist and murderer. The last victim had been a product of the care-home system. A fifteen-year-old girl whose disappearance got lost between the cracks in a flawed system. He wasn't going to ignore a direct appeal for help.

Caro Armstrong lived as he had assumed she would. Her father had been big in pharmaceuticals, and she'd been his only child. She'd moved to the island with a husband, third or fourth, several years ago. She'd ditched the marriage and stayed on in the island with their twins. The estate, for there was no other word for it, was one of the largest on the island. They were summoned through smooth electronic gates and directed to the main house, a four-storey Georgian manor that was painted a blinding white, and the dark green shutters lay half-closed against the late afternoon sun. A dog barked somewhere in the distance, the only noise that broke the expensive quiet.

Dewar whistled. "You know, it's easy to forget how much money some people have. I mean, we see some nice places, but a lot of the time they're owned by ordinary people who've worked hard. This, well, this is something different."

"Let's try to keep our tongues in our heads, okay?"

Dewar took the gentle rebuke with a smile. "Tongue held firmly in check."

The door buzzer was answered by a uniformed maid who was obviously expecting them. "This way, please. Mrs Armstrong is waiting in the garden room for you."

They followed the stiff-backed woman through a spacious hallway and down a wide corridor. The place had obviously been remodelled as it was light and airy with good proportions. The decor was something else. Huge tapestries and paintings of well-fed aristocratic-looking types lined the walls, every tabletop, every nook and cranny was stuffed with objets d'art and curiosities and heavy, ornate, overstuffed chairs and chaise longues were scattered about the place. The same with the garden room. Louis XV spindly legged chairs battled for supremacy with wing-backed armchairs and, surprisingly, some old wicker barrel chairs that were occupied by two people. Caro Armstrong stood and greeted them. "Do come in, Jack, and who is this?"

"My colleague, DS Dewar."

He looked pointedly at the other occupant of the room. The man was probably in his early fifties; he wore casual clothes that slightly hung off his thin frame, his shock of wild black curls adding to his dishevelled look. Caro Armstrong waved a hand in the man's direction. "This is Boris Tchensen, Katrina's father."

"How do you do, Mr Tchensen. I am DCI Le Claire." After refusing a seat, as nothing looked in the slightest bit comfortable, he asked, "Mrs Armstrong, could you tell me what the issue is, please?"

Caro Armstrong nodded her smoothly coiffed head and complied. "Boris came to see me a few days ago. He hasn't heard from his daughter in a couple of months. I said she'd skipped out without any notice, and Boris said…" She turned to her guest. "Boris, you may as well explain."

His voice was accented, but his English was excellent. "Thank you. Katrina came to Jersey to better her English. She has a business administration degree and, with excellent English skills gained from living the language, she can get a very good job back home. She was happy here. It is such a beautiful place to be and two lovely children to look after. Her weekly calls were full of how lucky she was."

Dewar interrupted. "But she left?"

"Yes, she told me she had met someone and was going to visit London with them for a short break. She always called me on Sundays, but said that they'd be busy. Said if she couldn't call, she'd be in touch when she was back in Jersey. She never called me again and doesn't answer her phone. That is not like my daughter. I have waited and waited and decided to come and see for myself."

Caro Armstrong was quick to speak, the words tumbling out in a rush. "And when poor Mr Tchensen called me a few days ago, I was pretty dismissive. And then I asked what I should do with Katrina's things, and he got worried when I explained what they were."

Le Claire recalled her ire at the party that she had to go to the bother of getting rid of her au pair's belongings.

"My wife died many years ago. Katrina is our only daughter, and I gifted her with her mother's jewellery when she turned eighteen. We are not rich people, so the actual value is small, but the sentimental value is huge. Katrina always wore her mother's emerald engagement ring, which is now so tight she cannot remove it, but never the wedding ring. She said she would be too scared to lose it. The wedding ring was left in her room. She would not simply discard her mother's memory like casual rubbish. Even if she wanted to have a new life, to disappear, she would not have left that ring behind. Not if she had a choice."

Le Claire considered the man's impassioned words. "Do you have any idea what happened to Katrina?"

The strength seemed to seep from the man as he sank deeper into the chair. His eyes were pained. "Something bad. She would not leave me to worry; she would get word to me somehow. My Katrina has been gone for nearly three months. I have not known where to turn. I am not a rich man and a cousin helped me with the airfare."

"Right, we'll take down some details. Perhaps you have a photo of Katrina, and you could let us know any distinguishing marks, what the ring she wears looks like and on what finger."

He could feel Dewar's eyes boring into him, no doubt wondering why he was further involving himself with a missing person case. He wasn't going to make the same mistake twice.

Le Claire had sent Dewar home; it was her day off after all, although it was now edging toward evening. He'd head home himself soon, but he had a quick phone call to make first. He perched on the end of his desk, one leg swinging, as he listened to the ring tone. The call was swiftly answered.

"Paul Armstrong, how may I help you?"

"Paul, it's Jack Le Claire. I hope I'm not disturbing you, but I have some bad news." He knew from past experience it was best to just dive in. "Laura Brown is in hospital, and her condition is serious. She was attacked at her apartment last night."

He could hear the shocked inhalation. "What? I can't get my head around this. That poor girl. Have you got who did it?"

"No, but we're working on it. I have a quick question for you. If Laura were to die, who inherits Scott Hamlyn's estate?"

"That has to be the wrong tree you're sniffing around."

"Probably, but just answer the question."

"Fine. I don't even need to look it up. We just put in a fairly standard clause that if Laura didn't survive Scott by more than thirty days, then his parent's would inherit everything."

"You say that's standard. What is it trying to achieve?"

"It is mainly meant to cover situations where people are involved in an accident and one survives the other by a matter of days. If the clause wasn't there, then the assets would form part of Laura Brown's estate. Scott, like most people, wanted to choose who his assets went to."

"Okay, I get it. Thanks."

"Wait, can I go and see Laura?"

His voice was gentle. "I wouldn't think so. She is unconscious, and we haven't had any proper feedback on her condition yet."

He hung up, grabbed his jacket and was out the door in a flash. He'd speak to the Hamlyns on the way home.

He swung past the incident room and was about go in when he heard his name mentioned. He couldn't tell who was speaking.

"Right, so we've got nine people for the Million Pound Lottery. We need one more. Maybe Le Claire would join the syndicate."

"I doubt it. What does he need with a one-tenth share of a million? That's peanuts to his family. Little rich boys don't need to do the lottery like us normal muppets."

The voice, with its sneering, condescending undertone, was unmistakable. Bryce Masters.

"Are they really that rich? He just seems normal." The speaker was Cobb.

"Don't let him fool you. Not only is his family loaded, his dad is majorly connected. I mean, don't you think it's strange that Le Claire, after years working at the Met, suddenly moves back to Jersey and gets taken on as a full DCI?"

"I guess so."

"And I've done a bit of digging. The last case he dealt with was that Colin Chapman. He was a creep who ended up killing several young girls, raping them as well. Why would golden boy suddenly leave the Met and come home when he's just bagged the catch of a career? Unless he came back with his tail between his legs." The accompanying laughter was harsh and derisory.

Le Claire carefully eased back from the door and carried on his way out the building. It was true. Eavesdroppers never did hear anything good about themselves. His father had never helped him in his career – the opposite, in fact, but he had left London under a shadow. He didn't need it to taint his future as well.

# #

Sarah Hamlyn ushered him into the kitchen, where her husband was reading the Sunday papers. "Have you caught who did this?"

"I'm sorry. I've some other news to discuss." He watched their faces with care. "Laura Brown was brutally attacked at her apartment last night and is now in intensive care at the hospital."

Charles Hamlyn's mouth dropped, and he reared back. "That is shocking. Was it a burglary?"

Before Le Claire could speak, Sarah Hamlyn said, "Was anything stolen? Scott has personal items that shouldn't go to that woman. I was going to ask Paul Armstrong to get them for us."

"It doesn't appear to have been a burglary. If you don't mind me saying so, you don't seem that bothered about Miss Brown's welfare."

"I am sorry for anyone's misfortune, but Laura Brown is nothing to do with us."

"May I ask your whereabouts last night?"

Charles Hamlyn stiffened. "Now look here…"

His wife's voice cut across him as she glared at Le Claire. "You think one of us went round there and beat up that girl? I can't stand her, but I wasn't going to attack her."

His eyes were fixed on her. "You did after the funeral."

She fired back, "That was in the heat of the moment." Her shoulders sagged, and she briefly closed her eyes. When she opened them again, the ferocity was gone. "I don't like Laura Brown. To be truthful, I don't know her, but I didn't want her to ruin my son's life. We didn't hurt her. Charles and I were at home together, alone. So no, I'm afraid we don't have a convenient alibi."

There was nothing more to say, so he took his leave and headed home to his empty apartment, a microwave pizza and a lonely beer. His wife still wasn't returning his calls.

#

He stood in the darkest corner of her bedroom, his back tight against the wall. A sliver of moonlight crept through the narrow gap in the closed curtains, its fine beam cast toward the bed. Her face was tucked beneath the duvet; all he could see was the top of her head and one delicate hand that held the bed cover close. It had been so easy getting in. He held back his laugh, brought on by nervous energy. The key had been in the back of the door. Fools. All he had to do was insert the fine blade of his utility tool into the keyhole and wiggle and move it until the key came free and fell to the floor. The other bit of luck had been the unlocked cat flap. It wasn't a kitty, but his hand that reached through and filched the key.

He crept across the carpeted floor and stood over her. His shadow blocked even the modest light, and with mounting excitement, his hands fumbled across the cool cotton duvet cover until he came to the living, breathing body beneath. With the lightest of touches, he traced a line across her hips, over the ribcage and up toward her head until, with one savage movement, he viciously yanked a handful of her hair, his other hand clamped tight against her mouth to prevent a sound escaping.

She struggled, a reflexive action that simply compelled him to tighten his grasp, almost pulling her hair out by its roots.

He bent down, pushed his mouth against her ear. "I've a message for you. Keep quiet, or you'll regret it. No telling tales."

He moved back, released her hair and pulled the duvet down to her waist. She wore a thin nightgown, and he could see the outline of her high, full breasts.

Her eyes opened wide, and she stared at him over the hand that held her silent. He saw her emotions jostle for supremacy; confusion overtaken by realisation, and then fear took precedence. To his horror, he saw something else. It was the wrong girl.

He stepped back, paralysed by panic, and then, as her shrill scream shattered the night air, he ran from the room, the house and his mistake.

CHAPTER TWENTY-EIGHT

Le Claire had been at his desk for hours, and the clock hadn't struck 8:00 a.m. yet. He'd placed a call to the hospital and left a message for Dr Foster, who had yet to ring back. They'd known each other for years, and so Le Claire felt no compunction in hounding him. He dialled the saved number, and after two short rings, he recognised the unmistakably terse voice. "Well! What are you after, as if I didn't know?"

"Brian, don't be like that. I am calling to see how Laura Brown is? She was brought in yesterday and—"

"I know. I was on duty in Emergency. The girl's in a bad way. She went straight into surgery yesterday to try and halt what was massive internal bleeding. The team has done their best, but she is still unconscious, and we don't know the prognosis yet. I can't tell you anything, Jack, because I don't know yet whether she'll make it or not. What I can tell you is that some bastard worked her over. Her body is covered in bruises, and there may even be some organ damage. That could be a best-case scenario, for there is a very real chance she may never come round."

Le Claire ran a hand through his hair, and his eyes momentarily closed. A muscle ticked at the corner of his mouth, and the rage bubbled away, deep inside. There were many atrocities that he had seen in his job, and he would no doubt experience many more. However, the one thing that he would never get used to, never become inured to, was violence against the weak and vulnerable, which was usually – not always, but usually – women and children.

"Right. Thanks. Let me know if anything changes." As he hung up, he winced at the coldness in his own voice, but it wasn't for

Laura. It was aimed at the heartless coward who had kicked and punched a girl within inches of death – and she wasn't yet out of danger.

"That's a pensive look. Share those thoughts for a penny?" Vanguard was standing in his doorway, clutching a thick file.

"Nothing worth talking about. You? Anything from the Laura Brown scene?"

"That's exactly why I'm here. I tagged Dewar on the way through and asked her to join us. Hope that's okay, but there are some areas you'll need to get checked out, and I thought it easier to brief you both at the same time."

"Sure, come on in. Here's Dewar now."

She came rushing in, and there was a slightly guilty look on her face as she apologised for being late. She'd probably hung back, sending Vanguard ahead so she could finish her habitually full large mug of tea. He was getting wise to her. Some people disappeared to have a sneaky ciggie; it just so happened that Dewar's drug of choice was a builder's brew.

Le Claire gestured at the file in Vanguard's hands. "Right, give us what you've got."

The CSI chief perched on the edge of Le Claire's desk as he motioned for Dewar to take the only seat. "Okay. In time-honoured tradition, let's do the bad news first. No apparent forced entry, so we can assume that Laura Brown let her attacker in. The buzzer at the main front door to the apartments is connected to a video system. As soon as the buzzer is pressed, the recording starts. However, the video wasn't activated at all over the weekend. We spoke to the caretaker, who said the tenants have a habit of jamming the main door open, and often it can be left that way for days at a time."

Le Claire and Dewar exchanged a quick glance. Damn. The door had been jammed open the first time they had gone to the apartment. With a whisper of regret, he wished they'd spoken to the caretaker, made a fuss. If they had, maybe there would be a video image of the attacker instead of absolutely nothing. "Is there any good news?"

A grin spread across Vanguard's narrow face. "There could be. The answerphone at Hamlyn's place was filled with old messages, in excess of twenty. He obviously only deleted them every now and again. There were some from his parents, customs about deliveries that duty was payable on – the usual, mundane day-to-day stuff. There was one from a David, who said he'd meet Hamlyn at the latter's place before they went out. A friend, I guess."

Le Claire confirmed the assumption. "Yes, that would have been David Adamson. We've spoken to him already."

"Fine. However, the most interesting message, which is certainly intriguing, is from an Ian Jennings." He checked the file. "He asked if Hamlyn had any questions on the report he had sent by email. He then said he had posted a hard copy as well and that he had returned the photograph. He was also at pains to say that the balance of his account was now due."

Le Claire had listened carefully, but it sounded like some sort of business matter apart from the photograph bit, but that could be about anything. What they needed was a solid lead, not more of the same. His thoughts were wandering as he tried to piece together what could have got Scott Hamlyn killed and Laura Brown beaten within an inch of her life. If indeed the two incidents were even connected. He knew better than to jump to conclusions. He zoned back into Vanguard's words.

"…it's the last comment that made me wonder. I mean, he said that Hamlyn should just let him know if he needed any more investigative work carried out and also to be reassured of his discretion. He said his business was digging up secrets for those who employed him, not general tittle-tattle."

Le Claire's attention was firmly back on Vanguard. "What the hell does that mean? What kind of investigator is he?"

Vanguard raised his palms in supplication. "Afraid that's down to you guys. I just give you the facts. It's up to you to determine what they mean."

Le Claire scowled. He knew Vanguard was right, but now all they had was more open questions. "Is that everything?"

"There were some strange calls on the day after Hamlyn died. A few where the answerphone clicked in, but the caller didn't say anything, just silence."

Dewar rolled her eyes. "Like a heavy-breathing call?"

"No, but there was a palpable sense that the person calling was waiting for someone to pick the call up. The recording also picked up Laura Brown. She said…" He looked through the file, pulled out a transcript and recited, "Her exact words were *Hello…hello, is someone there? Jesus, don't torment me. If that's you, Danny, just quit this, you hear me?* And then she slammed the phone down. There was another call about ten minutes later; again the answerphone went on, and after about thirty seconds of silence, the caller hung up."

Dewar spoke a millisecond before Le Claire's own words had formed. "Danny? Could that be Danny Gillespie?"

Le Claire grabbed his jacket. "Thanks, you guys did a great job there. Go through Hamlyn's papers and see if there is anything from this Ian Jennings, and then turn that place upside down and find Hamlyn's bloody laptop. Dewar, you're coming with me, but before that, get one of the guys onto the phone numbers and track these callers down."

Vanguard interrupted. "We've also got the video recordings from the underground garage camera, going back to the night of Hamlyn's death. May be worth someone checking the car licence plates."

Dewar nodded. "Right, I'll get someone on it."

Aidan Gillespie did not look at all pleased to see Le Claire and Dewar waiting in his study. Le Claire wasn't too happy to see him either. "We asked to see your brother."

"This is my house detective. My staff knows to keep me informed of what is going on. My brother is finishing a meeting. He'll join us in a moment. Can I ask what this is about?"

"That is something for me to discuss with your brother."

Le Claire turned as a cool voice came from the open doorway.

"I want Aidan to hear anything you have to say to me, so please go ahead." Danny Gillespie sauntered into the room, a mocking expression on his face. "What's the matter? Not caught Hamlyn's killer yet, so you're back to hound us?"

Le Claire let the comment roll over him. He took the direct route. "Tell me, how well do you know Laura Brown?"

The only indication that the question bothered him was a slight widening of his eyes. "Laura Brown? You mean Scott Hamlyn's girlfriend?"

"That's exactly who I mean, and please don't mess with me. I know you knew her." Le Claire hoped his gambit would work. He was simply guessing that he was the Danny who Laura thought had called her.

There was a pause, then a heavy sigh. "Look, Laura and I had a fling years ago when we both lived in London. It wasn't exclusive, and it wasn't long before she'd moved on to someone else. That girl always fancied a champagne lifestyle on someone else's money. There's nothing more to say." His shrug apparently declared the matter closed.

Dewar quickly asked, "Did Scott Hamlyn know you'd had a relationship with Laura? Was he jealous?"

"What bullshit is this? I don't know if Laura ever told him. Why would she?"

Le Claire took over. "Perhaps it's you who was jealous. Laura is a beautiful woman. Maybe you wanted her back, and Hamlyn was in your way."

Aidan Gillespie butted in. "Enough of this bullshit."

Danny was emboldened by his brother's support. "Yeah. Why don't you go and ask Laura? She'll tell it like I did."

Le Claire was unsmiling. "Where were you last night? Can you account for your whereabouts?"

Danny tightened his mouth and narrowed his eyes. "What the hell is this all about?"

"Laura Brown is in hospital. She was savagely beaten and is in a critical condition. This 'bullshit', as you put it, is about attempted murder. So I ask you again – where were you last night?"

Gillespie's voice slashed across their conversation. "I can vouch for my brother. We had a quiet night at home. Stop playing with words. Either charge my brother with something, or get out of my house."

"We're going, but I can guarantee we'll be looking at you very closely – both of you."

#

Le Claire was quietly ensconced in his office, checking some case reports, when an excited Hunter came rushing in. It was the young PC's day off, and he was dressed in jeans and a T-shirt with a skull and crossbones. He looked even younger than usual.

"Working overtime?" He did have a budget to stick to, as did everyone these days, and the young policeman was currently running data checks. Not exactly top of his priority list on how to spend money.

Hunter blushed, and Le Claire wondered when he would outgrow his gaucheness. Then he noticed the excitement evident in the young man's face.

"Yes, sir. No, sir, I'm not on official duty, but I wanted to see something through. I think I've found a connection between Scott Hamlyn and Sir Hugh Mallory."

Le Claire was taken aback. "I didn't know we were looking for one. I just wanted you to look into the foundation Sir Hugh was donating to and see if it all appeared above board or if we should involve the financial crime team. Tell me what you've found."

"Do you recall that Hamlyn was paying a sizable amount to charity on a monthly basis?"

"Yes, go on."

"Sir Hugh was contributing to the same foundation."

He leaned forward, intrigued. "That is a coincidence. Mind you, Jersey is a small island. It's perfectly possible that they just happened to like the ethos of a particular charity. I'm not saying there may not be a deeper connection, but don't get too excited yet. Try and get some more details first."

He realised that Hunter was hopping from leg to leg, excitement radiating from every pore. "That's why I came in, sir. I wanted to dig about. Then I remembered the Panama Papers."

"Wasn't that some leak of financial info? Remind me."

"Yes. Millions of records, a deluge of financial data, were reportedly stolen from a law firm and services provider in Panama. They ran entities – you know, trusts, companies and foundations. The list of connected parties was published online, so I googled it and had a look. There wasn't anything there, but there was mention of some other leaks from smaller firms. I checked them out."

Le Claire could feel a buzz of excitement. "What did you find? I'm assuming it's interesting?"

"The foundation was listed on a whistle-blower's page. The foundation council members are a Jose Alverez, Patricia Roman, Elizabeth Edwards and Madeline Davies. I searched for the foundation on the Internet, and there is nothing about its charitable activities, which seemed odd. I mean, they usually want to have some sort of web presence to attract donors. So I googled the council members – they control what goes on – and one of them lives locally."

"Right, give me the address." He checked the paper Hunter passed him and noted there was a home and office address. "Perhaps Hamlyn and Sir Hugh got to know the charity through this person; maybe they were a mutual acquaintance? Then again, maybe it is something else entirely. I've never liked coincidences."

CHAPTER TWENTY-NINE

The offices of Madeleine Davies were in town and a short walk from the police station. Le Claire had retrieved Dewar, who was sifting through Laura Brown's life, especially her past. It was a sunny day, but the sea breeze was biting. St Helier's main street was busy with shoppers and tourists, even some groups of French schoolchildren on a day trip, chattering away as they crocodiled through King Street.

They found the correct address on a narrow side street off the main pedestrian precinct. The half-glass door opened to the sound of a tinkling bell. A pretty girl sat behind a wooden reception desk; her face was heavily made-up, and her hair, swathes of reddish-blonde, curled around her shoulders. She beamed a smile as they entered, seeming to sit straighter as she took in Dewar's uniform. He never knew if it was the police blues or Dewar's uncompromising stance that had the biggest impact.

He flashed his badge. "DCI Le Claire and DS Dewar to see Madeleine Davies, please."

"Of course, I won't be a moment."

She knocked on a closed door and, in response to the voice inside, opened the door a slice and slipped into the room. A few seconds later, she came back out and beckoned them to enter. A woman came out from behind a glass desk that held a flash computer monitor and several neat piles of paper. She greeted them with a wide smile. "Thank you, Daria. I'm Madeleine Davies, Lena for short. How may I help you?"

Lena Davies was slim but curved in the right places; she wore a red-and-blue patterned tea dress in a 1940s style; her blond hair was cut short, and spiky tendrils framed her face. Her makeup was subtle apart from bright red lipstick, the same shade as her high-heeled shoes.

"We have a few questions that we believe you may be able to help us with."

She motioned for them to sit on the chairs that faced her desk. "Of course, however, I do have to leave soon. There is a charity tea party at Government House, and I mustn't be late."

"Of course. I'm interested in knowing some more about the Phoenix Foundation. I believe you're associated with it? Can you tell me what it is about?"

She cocked her head to one side. "The foundation? Yes, I am a council member. It's a vehicle created for wide charitable purposes."

"Like what?"

"Education, health, general social issues – it has a broad remit."

"Why is it registered in Panama? We have a perfectly good finance industry in Jersey."

"At the time it was created, I believe there were constraints under Jersey's charity laws. Panama had longstanding foundation legislation and allowed the wider definition of charity."

"Who are your donors?"

She looked uncertain, biting her lower lip as she thought. "I don't think I can say. To be honest, I don't know a lot of them. I am more involved in helping find worthwhile causes. I believe we often get cold-call approaches from people who've heard of the good works we do from their friends and want to contribute themselves. I don't really have any ongoing dealings with the other council members."

"Do you know a Scott Hamlyn or Sir Hugh Mallory?"

"The first is the young man who died recently, murder, wasn't it? And I have heard of Sir Hugh but never had the chance to meet him. He had a terrible accident, I believe."

"That's correct."

At that, the door opened, and the receptionist popped her head around the door. Her look was apologetic. "I am sorry to disturb, but your taxi is here, Lena."

Lena Davies stood, as did Le Claire and Dewar. She turned to the wooden console next to her desk and picked up a wide-brimmed straw hat in a deep dark blue that was almost black. Placing it on her head, she bent to pick up the matching handbag. As she did so, the top half of her face was hidden, and Le Claire saw it, really saw it and her. The hat acted like a mask, the dark material whitening her skin and deepening the colour of her lips. Christ! She was the lady in red from the party.

"Mrs Davies, I think we're going to need a longer chat. Dewar, call for a car. Mrs Davies is coming to visit us at the station."

Lena Davies shone like a firefly in the drab room. She'd been vocal, protesting and displaying outraged innocence as she'd been brought in. Le Claire was relishing having a long chat with her. He'd carefully listened to her voice and could hear the husky undertone, now all too reminiscent of the red-dressed temptress from the party.

Dewar entered the interview room behind him, and Lena Davies was on the attack as soon as they had opened the door.

"There you are, what do you mean by this outrage? And some buffoon read me my rights. I demand to know what this is about."

"A girl was attacked at a party recently. It was a party with distinctive characteristics. Where were you last Friday night?"

"At home with my husband. Why?"

She sat with her legs crossed, one arm resting on the table. Her head was tilted and her gaze direct. She appeared cool and completely unruffled, but Le Claire hadn't missed the slight widening of her eyes when he mentioned the party.

"So you weren't at a party in St Mary?"

"I just said where I was."

"You weren't one of the organisers of that party? And you didn't encourage a man to attack one of the waitresses?"

She laughed, a deep, throaty sound. "I don't know what you're talking about. How very dramatic. I'm very sorry something happened to the poor girl, but I really can't help you."

"What if someone saw you there? Recognised you?"

"I can categorically state that no one could have recognised me from any party on Friday. There isn't anything else for me to say."

Perhaps she was telling the truth. In her mind, she no doubt figured the wig and mask concealed her so much that no one could tell it was her. Perhaps she set up the attack on Ana as an insurance policy. He would never have seen the resemblance if her upper face hadn't been shaded by her wide-brimmed hat. He knew it was her, he just knew it. From her rigid stance, her uplifted, determined chin and mocking look, Le Claire knew they weren't going to get any more out of her. He also had to be careful. Blair's cover couldn't be blown. The chief had made that plain enough.

"We're going to have to carry out some investigations, and in the meantime I'd like to keep you under observation. Nice and safe, so we know where you are." And where she couldn't head home and destroy anything, like tight red dresses and a black feathered mask.

Her voice was cool. "Very well. You're making a huge mistake. You'll see that. I would like to make a phone call."

#

The hospital was a short walk from the police station, and Le Claire, realising he had to eat lunch sometimes, had grabbed his jacket and decided to head out into the fresh air, get a sandwich and pop to the hospital and see what was happening with Laura Brown.

He was now hanging about the ward where Laura was. He'd hoped Brian Foster was on duty, and, for once, his luck was in. Apparently, according to the duty nurse, Dr Foster was doing his rounds and would be able to see him shortly. He doubted Foster would be happy to be forced into speaking to him but had happily settled down to wait for him. It wasn't long before the familiar figure come loping along the corridor; his long legs seemed to eat the ground in front of him, and not for the first time Le Claire marvelled that someone who looked so ungainly, all lumbering bulk, could yet be such a fine and precise medical practitioner. Brian Foster was a few years older than Le Claire, but they had known each other for a while, and he had dated the doctor's younger sister many moons ago.

"Jack, I won't have you haunting my wards. Go away." The words were direct, but the tone was relatively amiable, and he knew he would be fine. Dr Foster seemed in an okay mood today.

"Brian, you know why I'm here. Any news on Laura Brown?"

The doctor shook his head, and some wayward strands from his shaggy mop of hair fell into his eyes. He brushed it out of his way and sighed. "Miss Brown is in a critical condition. She certainly can't speak to anyone."

"How bad is she?"

"Very. The bastard beat her badly, smashed her face and left her for dead. It's the internal bleeding I'm worried about." He ran a hand through his hair. "It's touch and go, Jack. I don't know if she'll make it."

"Okay, I know you'll keep us posted, but we'll keep chasing in any event."

"Well, thank you so much." The doctor's sarcastic response followed him down the hall and out of the ward.

Le Claire headed back to the office. He needed a strong coffee and time to think. He also needed to know more about Laura Blair, and he'd hassle Dewar for the background report. He'd see how she was doing on the search warrant as well. He didn't have much to go on, and he had to be careful in relation to Blair's investigation, but every instinct told him Lena Davies was involved in the attack on Ana. He just had to prove it.

Elizabeth had driven Ana into town to collect some files that Philip Le Claire needed for a meeting that evening.

"Why don't you meet me in an hour outside Revitalize? I'll be finished with my manicure by then, and you can help me carry my parcels to the car."

"Of course. It won't take me long to get the files, so I can check my emails while I wait."

"Good girl, excellent idea. Off you go."

As they made their way out of the car park, Elizabeth suddenly stopped. "Oh, damn it. Jack popped in to say hello this morning and left his mobile. I meant to drop it to him, but I don't have time now."

"Don't worry. I'll take it. It's not a problem."

"Oh, bless you." Elizabeth rummaged in her bag and handed over the sleek mobile. "Just leave it at the reception desk for him. Okay, I'll see you in an hour."

#

Le Claire couldn't find his damned phone. He must've left it in his office. He felt offended that the absence of his mobile made him feel slightly bereft, maybe even a bit vulnerable and naked. What the hell! He didn't want to be one of those people who needed to be connected all the time.

He headed straight for the incident room. Dewar was hunched over her computer screen. She turned as he walked up beside her; she looked glassy-eyed. "Oh, sorry, didn't see you there."

"No problem. How is Mrs Davies?"

"Still protesting her innocence. We've given her a cuppa, and she's made a phone call to her husband. She's spitting blood and vowing to bring many evils down on our heads."

"Let her stew. We've got more important business to deal with right now. I need to know Laura Brown's background—"

Her interruption was swift. "That's what I'm doing at the moment. Hunter has gone through the Police National Database and compiled a report, and I've followed up with a few phone calls."

"Go on."

"Okay, so we know that Laura Brown was arrested for solicitation. She was at a party, pretty posh by the looks of it, and she and some other girls were supposedly touting their wares. There was an off-duty policeman at the event, and unfortunately for one of the girls, that was who she approached. Laura Brown was with her, was a friend of hers, but there was insufficient evidence, so Laura wasn't charged."

"Nothing else on record?"

"Not after that. We got our hands on some tax filings, and she made a pretty good income from the promotional business she ran."

"So it could have been a case of wrong place, wrong time?"

"Yes, but her background leads me to think there was perhaps some issue in the past. She comes from Manchester, not that you'd know it from that accent she has now, and drops off the school register at fifteen. The parents said she ran off to London. Their details don't show anything out of the ordinary. They split up after Laura left home. Both are dead now. There is nothing more on her until the arrest."

"What do you mean nothing?"

"What I said, just zip. No tax return, no claiming of benefit, no address on the electoral register. It's as if she disappeared for a few years."

"That is very strange. What are you thinking?" He knew he was putting Dewar on the spot, but he wanted her to have the courage to speak her mind; it was the only way to grow as a detective.

"She is a beautiful woman. She would have been a very pretty girl. I think Laura Brown may have started her trade early on, maybe even had a protector that she lived with, maybe even worked for."

"That background is particularly unsavoury for the wife of an upcoming lawyer, especially in a community like Jersey."

"So, she has, potentially, criminal contacts. Perhaps they didn't want her to marry Scott Hamlyn? And so he was got rid of."

"Good thinking; as they say, cherchez la femme. I'm sure Laura Brown has more to do with this than we know."

"Perhaps it's even more than she knows."

Ana was waiting by the front desk as they tried to track down Le Claire. She hadn't liked to just leave his phone with the desk sergeant and wanted to hand it over in person. She fiddled with her own phone while she waited. She ignored the comings and goings around her. People had good reasons, usually not very nice ones, to be in police stations, and she didn't want to be seen to be nosey. A steady stream of people had approached the front desk and been sent off in different directions. Whoever was there at the moment was not at all happy. Their voice was raised to such a level that you could not help but listen in.

"I don't give a damn what you say. I demand to see my wife. This is a bloody outrage, so it is. I want to see her and see her now."

The desk sergeant's response was measured but firm. "Sir, I have explained that it is not possible for me to give you any information. If you wait in the seating area, I will get someone to come and see you."

"And I've told you that isn't bloody good enough."

Ana kept her head down. This looked like it was going to get explosive.

"Sir, if you carry on like this, I am going to have to ask you to leave."

"You can ask, but I won't go. I want to see Lena Davies, and I want to see her NOW!"

The voice ended on a roar, and Ana's head snapped up, only to see a familiar face. Basil Davies. He looked distraught, and there was obviously something wrong with Lena. He was an absolute toad, but he was going to be in serious trouble if he carried on like this. She turned, laid a hand on his arm.

"Mr Davies, Basil, are you all right?"

He stilled as he looked at her, and his eyes widened in surprise. He nodded and shifted his gaze to the desk sergeant. "I think I will wait over there. In fact, why don't I leave my number, and if someone calls me, I'll come back later." He handed over a card and headed to the door.

As he walked past Ana, her eyes widened in shock as a sharp slug of memory hit deep in her gut. The smell, cloying and sickening, made her gag – the aftershave. It was him. It was Basil Davies that had attacked her. Ana opened her mouth and screamed.

CHAPTER THIRTY

Le Claire had searched the incident room, his office and was on the way to his locker when the call came through from the front desk. There was someone in reception to see him. They had his phone. With a relieved heart and a spring in his step, he'd jogged down the stairs to reception. As he opened the security door to the public area, he heard a woman's scream, loud and anguished. He ran into chaos; the scene played out before his eyes in seeming slow motion.

Ana was there and she was shouting. "It's him, it's him. He tried to rape me."

She stood to the side of the front desk, a shocked-looking man in front of her. The desk sergeant was running toward them, and the few other people in the area seemed immobilised. The man in front of Ana turned and ran for the door. Le Claire chased after him. As the man neared the exit, Le Claire leaped forward and landed on his back, sending them both crashing to the ground. They fell in a tangled heap, and the man immediately struggled and bucked, trying to dislodge Le Claire. It was no good. Within moments, they were surrounded by police and the man restrained by two burly officers.

Le Claire rushed over to a white-faced and trembling Ana and, putting his arm around her, led her to a seat. She sank into it. "I am sorry to scream, sorry."

"Are you sure he's the man, Ana, the one from the party?"

"Oh yes, I know it is him. His aftershave brought the whole thing back. He is Basil Davies. I overheard him; he was here to see his wife, Lena."

Le Claire sat back and looked over at the struggling man. Now that was interesting. He could feel his nerves start to hum.

#

He'd called his mother, who had rushed to the station, manicure half-finished, and collected a shaken Ana. She hadn't shown him such care and tenderness in a long time, and he felt a momentary pang as she led a shaking Ana outside. They would need to talk to the girl again, but that could be dealt with later. Basil Davies had been read his rights and dumped in an interview room two doors along from the one where his wife was being held.

It was a belligerent-looking Davies that awaited Le Claire and Dewar. His puffed and red-veined face betrayed his dissolution. He looked to be a man of appetites – drink, food, maybe drugs. And perhaps girls as well.

He said nothing as they sat across the table from him, just stared. Le Claire took the lead. "Mr Davies, that was quite a scene downstairs. Would you like to explain it?"

"I'd like to, but I can't, I'm afraid. I don't know what the girl was going on about. I just came to see my wife – and by the way, I'd appreciate a full update on what is happening there – when the girl went crazy. Screaming and shouting nonsense." He'd lost the attitude, and Le Claire could see some remnants of a latent charm. Basil Davies would have been handsome once, but the smooth words were at odds with the ravages to his face.

"Where were you last Friday?" Dewar's voice was curt and to the point.

Davies blinked. "At home with my wife. Why?"

"I'm asking the questions. So no alibi, I assume?"

"Why would I need one for a quiet night in front of the TV? I certainly didn't expect today to end up with me sitting here and my wife being held elsewhere. What is supposed to have happened on Friday?"

His voice was cool, and Le Claire couldn't read him. He needed him to say something, to trip up, for the smell of aftershave wasn't going to be enough to keep him for long. "The girl in reception was attacked at a party. A stranger came to her aid, and she got away, but the attacker was intent on rape and, surprisingly, blackmail. The girl knew you by name. Where do you know her from?"

"Our employment agency helped bring her over and get her settled, helped her find a job. I don't know anything else about her."

"Well, she knows you, and she says you attacked her. What do you have to say about that?"

Davies's gaze was direct and unwavering. "Look, she must have got confused. I didn't attack her at any party. I may have got a little fruity with her in the past. She came to visit her friend who lodges with us, and, you know, she's a pretty girl. I thought maybe a kiss and cuddle would be in order. I mean, I never touched her, but she may have thought I implied something when I didn't. My wife came home, and it was all fine, honest."

"So you think she is making it up?"

"I can't comment on that, but I do think she is confusing two different events. All I can say is that I wasn't at a party, and I didn't attack the girl. Now I want to see my wife."

Le Claire stood. "Afraid that won't be possible. We'll see you in a while. Dewar, with me."

Just as he reached the door, he stopped and gestured to a plastic bottle of water on the table. "Help yourself to some water."

Le Claire watched carefully. Basil Davies didn't say anything. He picked the bottle up in his left hand and twisted the cap off with his right.

He closed the door to the interview room firmly behind them and spoke to Dewar, "Get a search warrant. I want to see if they've got anything at their place that links them to the sex parties. We find something, and it potentially puts Davies there on Friday night and in the frame as Ana's attacker. Get the warrant as quick as you can; we can only hold them twenty-four hours."

"Okay, I assume the reasoning is that the purpose of the search would be seriously prejudiced if Mr and Mrs Davies were aware of it and out of custody?"

"Absolutely, I'm betting any links to the parties would be the first thing they'd discard."

CHAPTER THIRTY-ONE

A sharp rap on her door made Ana jump, and she almost spilled the glass of wine she'd just poured. She opened the door to a puzzled-looking Ben.

"When you said to meet you here, I thought you were working late and wanted a lift home. But Mrs Le Claire said you live here now?"

"Yeah, I moved in at the weekend."

"I didn't realise that was an option."

Her voice was dry. "Nor did I."

"So what's been happening?"

Ana quickly brought Ben up-to-date. She skirted over the actual attack. She was uncomfortable enough without going into too many details to someone who might be virtually a stranger but to whom she was hugely attracted.

His face grew darker as she spoke, his eyes were ice-cold, and the easy smile she was becoming accustomed to was nowhere to be seen.

"And then I recognised him at the police station. To think I know him? Christ, it was awful."

His eyes didn't leave her face. "Are you telling me the truth? Was that it, or did that bastard really hurt you?"

"It's as I told you, Ben. Honest."

He sighed as the tension seemed to flow out of him. "I'm sorry I wasn't there for you. I'd have beaten him to a pulp."

Ben's voice was even, his tone unremarkable, and that made it all the more frightening. She knew he would have been capable of that. She reached out and laid a hand on his arm. "I know you'd have protected me."

"I'd have done more than that. I'd have taught that swine to deal with someone his own size." She could feel the waves of anger radiating from him.

"Let me make you something to eat. It won't be much, but I picked up some salad and stuff."

He smiled. His lazy, sexy smile that crinkled the corners of his eyes. "No. I'll do it. You relax on the sofa. I'll get us both some more wine, and I'll attempt to make you something edible."

She complied with a laugh and bent forward as he piled cushions behind her head. Within moments, he had rummaged in the fridge and cupboards and was fixing a salad and cold meat. He sipped his wine, looked at her over his glass.

"Ana, I have a question for you. I need to go to London for a couple of days. I stay in one of Aiden's flats. It has two bedrooms, and well, would you like to come with me? The flight would be my treat. Please don't say no."

"It is too much for you to do."

"Ana, please? I would just like to get to know you a bit better, spend some time with you. I'll have some work to do, but it isn't onerous, so we'll have time together, and I promise that I'm not trying to move things along too fast. Separate bedrooms, remember. What do you say?"

Ana wanted to say yes but was scared of doing so. She hardly knew him, and the thought of spending two days alone with him was a mixture of delicious pleasure and absolute dread. She had left home, had come to Jersey to find new opportunities, to be different, to experience new things. And that was never going to happen if she said no, especially to something – or someone – she was beginning to think she wanted to know a lot better.

"Yes, Ben, I would love to come with you. What are the plans?"

"I was thinking we could go over on Thursday night, have some nice meals, mooch about and come back on Sunday night. Do you think it will be okay for you to get Friday off?"

"Yes, I've got loads of leave to take, and I don't have anything urgent on."

He beamed. "Great. Now let's have our salad, finish the wine and I'm going to leave you to get some rest."

#

Le Claire was exhausted. He consoled himself with the thought that no matter how rubbish he felt, Lena and Basil Davies were bound to have worse nights in their separate cells. No doubt their lawyers would come screeching in the morning, but that was another day.

Dewar popped her head round his office door. One look at her face, and he knew they were on to something. Her eyes were fizzing with excitement, and twin spots of colour rode high on her cheekbones.

"Come on, then, out with it." The air crackled with tension.

"The guys have finished the checks on the data from Laura Brown's place. We have the details of those who called Hamlyn's number over the last few weeks and have matched to the answerphone messages where relevant."

He waited with growing impatience. She loved to drag out the drama.

"Get on with it."

"The day after Hamlyn's death, two calls were made to the landline, as Vanguard mentioned. On one, no message was left, but Laura was recorded asking if it was a Danny who was calling. Around twenty minutes later, another call comes from the same number. This time the call wasn't picked up, and, again, they didn't leave a message. Just silence, as if they were waiting for the caller to answer. Perhaps they were checking if someone was home. Five minutes after that second call, the same individual's car appears on the CCTV from the garage."

He could hear the growl in his voice. "Who? Who was it?"

"Sarah Hamlyn."

He was at the door in a second. "Come on, the lady has some explaining to do."

# #

Sarah Hamlyn opened the door. Her hair was pulled back tight and fastened at the base of her neck. Her face was pale and makeup free. Her eyes wore a battered look; presumably from grief and a pain that would never go away. That is what you'd assume, but he wasn't making any snap judgments at the moment. There was always more going on with someone than appeared on the surface, and it was his job to find out what lay beneath. She had opened the door with an obligatory smile, slight though it was, but her face became set when she saw who was on the doorstep.

"Oh, it's you two again. You better come in."

Le Claire, with Dewar close behind, dutifully followed her into the kitchen and a small sitting area. She motioned for them to be seated with a slight wave of her hand. "Thank you. Is Mr Hamlyn at home?"

"He's in the greenhouse. I can call him in."

"No, that's fine. It's you we came to speak to."

She cocked her head to one side as she sank into an overstuffed armchair. "I sincerely hope you've come to say you've found my Scott's killer. Have you?"

"I'm afraid not. It is regarding another matter. When did you last visit your son's apartment?"

"What? I don't know, maybe two weeks ago. What is this about?"

Dewar pulled a piece of paper from her notebook, passed it to Sarah Hamlyn and asked, "Is this your mobile number?"

She squinted at the scrap of paper and brought it closer to her face. Her eyes widened. "Yes, this is my number. Why do you ask?"

Dewar looked at him. He stayed quiet and briefly glanced at the floor. She got the message and carried on.

"The day after your son died, two calls were made from this number to the landline in his flat. Why did you call to speak to Laura Brown?"

She immediately shook her head. "That's ridiculous. I didn't call her. Why would I?"

Le Claire pitched in. "We traced this number, your number. Tell me something else – you say it's been weeks since you went to Scott's apartment. If that is the case, what was your car doing there minutes after the last call that came from your phone?"

"I don't have a clue what you're talking about. You saw what my relationship was with Laura Brown. I had no desire to see or speak to her."

"What exactly is it that you so dislike about Laura Brown?"

She laughed, a broken sound that echoed in the quiet kitchen. "She was openly staying with my Scott when she visited the island;

living in his apartment like man and wife but without the sacrament of marriage vows. Do you know how badly that reflected on me? She had worked as some sort of promotions girl. Using her looks to persuade people to buy goods they probably neither needed nor wanted. I don't dislike her." She paused, exhaled a deep breath. "I despise her."

"Is that why you went to the apartment the day after Scott died? To have it out with Laura Brown? She never mentioned it to us. Was she out? Did you miss her? I assume you still have the keys to Scott's place. You could have just walked right in the door." He paused, went in for the kill. "Is that what you did on Saturday night? Did you go back in again? Argue? Did you attack her? Just like you did at the funeral, only this time there was no one to stop you. Not only had she tried to take your son away from you, now she had his money. Was that why you attacked her? Left her for dead?"

"Don't try and pin this on me. You're utterly incompetent. You can't catch whoever killed my son, and now you don't have a clue who attacked that girl. Don't you dare drag me into Laura Brown's problems."

Dewar moved to stand beside her, rested a hand lightly on Sarah Hamlyn's sleeve. "I think it best if you come to the station with us, and we can cool down and have a chat there."

Sarah Hamlyn pulled her arm away from Dewar and opened her mouth to speak. Before the words could come out, a loud voice came from the doorway. "Stop this! She's done nothing wrong. It was me. I called Laura from Sarah's phone. I don't have a mobile, and I drove my wife's car the day after Scott died. It's me you should be talking to, but I didn't go near the place on Saturday night."

Charles Hamlyn stood by the open doorway wearing dishevelled gardening clothes, his hair rumpled and his expression unreadable as he held his hands out in surrender and supplication.

There was a stunned silence. Sarah Hamlyn recovered quickest as she moved to her husband's side. "Charles, don't be stupid. They didn't really think I attacked Laura, they were just baiting me. You don't need to rush in and save me. Stop being a fool and tell them you just said it to take the focus from me. Go on."

His eyes were soft as he looked at his wife. "I'm sorry, Sarah, but I did call the apartment from your phone, and I did drive your car there."

She deflated before their eyes. Her voice quivered as she spoke. "I don't understand. Why did you do that?"

Le Claire had gathered his wits. "Yes, Mr Hamlyn, why did you do that? Are you sure you didn't go back there last Saturday? Was it you who attacked Laura Brown?"

Charles Hamlyn was shaking his head. "You've got it all wrong. I have never been at the apartment when Laura's been there. I drove there the day after Scott died, just after we got back from the morgue."

Sarah Hamlyn's voice was a whisper. "You said you needed some air. Why did you go there, why?"

"I needed to get something of Scott's. I parked on the road by the apartments and called the landline. Laura answered. I didn't know what to say, so I hung up. A few minutes later, I saw someone leave and take the path to the beach. It looked like Laura from a distance, so I called the apartment again. There was no answer. I drove into the car park, let myself in and was back out in five minutes. There was no one there."

Le Claire asked, "What did you need to get from the apartment?"

Hamlyn took a moment to answer. "I can't tell you that."

CHAPTER THIRTY-TWO

Le Claire parked outside the garage block, ready for a quick bite to eat, an hour of numbing TV and then sleep. Charles Hamlyn had been taken to the station and interviewed for well over an hour. He was refusing to say what he had taken from his son's apartment, just kept repeating it was something he needed. He had no real alibi for the Saturday night when Laura was attacked. He reiterated that he'd been at home with his wife, and no one else could corroborate that. There was nothing to do for the moment. Le Claire had reluctantly sent him home. They'd be digging further into Charles Hamlyn's life, but Le Claire had nothing to hold him at the moment.

The only other active case he was concerned with was Ana's attack. Hopefully, the search warrant would come in overnight, and they could get the team into the Davies's place at first light. Vanguard had his people on call, ready and waiting.

He wearily climbed the wooden stairs to his apartment, stifling the urge to laugh at himself. At least he didn't live in the main house with his parents, which would have been a bitter pill to swallow. This one-bedroom flat above his folks' garage had been his home when he was back from university. He had never been sure if his mother had decorated and furnished it for him out maternal love or if she hadn't relished the idea of her eighteen-year-old haunting the house and making the place look untidy in front of their influential friends. He had hoped it was the former and feared it was the latter.

He put his key in the door and realised it was unlatched. His mother never came in here unasked. She sent her cleaning lady over to do a couple of hours on a Friday morning, but no one else ever ventured in here. He tensed, carefully pushed the door ajar and entered, scanning the kitchen and lounge area. What he saw made his heart jump and a feeling of peace, one he hadn't known he was missing, settled over him. Sasha was by the cooker, her back to him, stirring a pot of what smelled like her spicy Bolognese, which was one of his favourites. She wore tight jeans and a lace camisole top, the creamy colour a perfect contrast to her tanned skin. Her glossy, dark hair was pulled back in a messy knot, and he could almost feel the smooth skin of her neck as she bent over the sauce pot.

He walked toward her, taking off his suit jacket and throwing it over the arm of the sofa. "This is a surprise."

She turned around in one quick movement, a delighted smile on her face. "Oh, Jack, you gave me a shock. I hope it's a welcome surprise."

"Very much so. How did you know I would be home in time to eat?"

"Ah, don't be mad, but I called Emily; she said you were leaving in about half an hour or so. I got round here straightaway."

Emily? His blank look just made her laugh more and shake her head. "Dewar. Emily is her first name. You are hopeless."

So now he knew that Dewar was Emily; he must have known this before but hadn't retained it as something he immediately needed to know. He also now figured his DS was a romantic, keeping quiet about Sasha's call so as not to spoil her surprise.

"Here, let me get you a drink."

She walked to the small dining table, that he saw was set for two, and poured two glasses of red from an open bottle, handing one to him and holding the other in a mock toast. "I know it's only Monday, but what the hell."

He took a sip of the wine as Sasha picked his jacket up from where he had slung it over the sofa. "I'll hang this up. If you want to go and have a shower, I can have dinner ready in half an hour. I hope pasta is okay?"

He was showered, changed and sitting at the table in just under the allotted time. Sasha laid bowls of steaming hot penne Bolognese in front of them, the rich beef-and-tomato ragu topped with shaved parmesan and basil leaves. It certainly beat the tuna sandwich he'd planned to have.

"This is gorgeous. Thank you."

"It's my pleasure. How is everything going with the case?"

He sighed. "We have a few lines to follow, but no leads. The fact it happened at the party gives us so many potential suspects or simply people to cross off the list."

"I know! I was interviewed by a very dashing policeman."

Le Claire kept the growl in his throat. Masters had been in charge of getting statements from the party guests.

Sasha spoke again. "Shall I answer your unspoken question now?"

He toyed with the stem of his wineglass, buying time, for he didn't want to spoil the evening with an argument. "What question?"

"Why I'm here? Am I still mad at you?"

"Ah, yes, that question."

"Yes. I'm sorry, Jack. I shouldn't have kicked off like that. It just scares me that you drift a bit farther away from me every time you have one of these episodes. I just wish you could…"

"What? Get over it, forget it? Don't you think I wish that too? I do, very much, but I just don't know what to do. And don't say I should talk to someone. The truth is that I'm not ready to face up to what happened. Not yet."

She sipped her wine, eyes downcast. When she looked at him, he was overwhelmed by the sympathy, compassion and, he hoped, love that radiated from her.

"Come on. Let's forget it for tonight. I want to finish this meal, snuggle on the sofa watching trashy TV and then go to bed – early."

His grin displayed his agreement. "Sounds like a plan, but why don't we skip the TV part?"

CHAPTER THIRTY-THREE

The persistent ringtone of Le Claire's mobile blasted through the room. He glanced at the other side of the bed and was taken aback when he saw it was empty. All Sasha had left behind was the barest of imprints of her head on the pillow. He recalled she'd mentioned an early yoga class as he reached out and answered the call with a mumbled, "Le Claire".

"Jack, don't hang up. It's Gareth Lewis. I hope I'm not disturbing you."

He hadn't needed to hear the name. He had instantly recognised the smooth voice of his old boss, redolent with vestiges of the valleys he'd long left behind and the joking reference to the long-ago faux pas when a much younger Le Claire had cut off Gareth Lewis when he was trying to bring him into an important conference call.

"It's fine. How are you?"

"I'm well, Jack. Still missing one of the best I've ever had work for me. How is small-town life?"

Le Claire laughed. Gareth Lewis had lived in London all his adult life. Anywhere outside its boundaries was Hicksville to him. "Small island maybe, but we do have a population of 100,000, plus a stream of seasonal workers and visitors each year. It's enough to keep me busy."

"Good, good. Look, Jack, God knows I don't want to bring up the past…"

Then don't. The words screamed through Le Claire's mind. He wasn't prepared for this; not at all.

"…fact is, he wants to see you."

He didn't need to ask who; the chill was already slowly engulfing him.

"What does Chapman want with me?"

"He says he needs to talk to you. The thing is, Jack, he has pleaded not guilty all along. His side is being closemouthed, but we believe they're going to announce a plea change. If he pleads guilty, it will all be over so much sooner, much better for the families of the girls involved."

His mind was a mass of jumbled thoughts, of razor-sharp images that once again threatened to send him over the edge. Images that drew him back to a place buried deep inside, a place usually kept in the shadows that was moving closer to the light. He did as usual and tried to push the thoughts away.

"What could he possibly have to say to me?"

"I don't know. Maybe he wants to tell you about the plea change?"

"I don't want to see him. I can't see it doing any good."

"Jack, I don't want to jeopardise a guilty verdict. You know that an open court on this is going to be a challenge for us, given the circumstances."

"You mean given what I did."

The sigh was heavy. "Look, we both know that we've been dreading any hint of police brutality. You weren't the only one there that day. All the other officers have sworn that you had no option; you had to stop him."

"I stopped him a bit too permanently though, didn't I?" He rubbed at his eyes, considered what he was hearing. "Okay, when do you want me to see him?"

"Can you come soon? We don't want to be blindsided by a plea change. Could you see him tomorrow?"

"What? I'm in the middle of a murder enquiry."

"Yeah, I know. I just got off the phone with Chief Wilson. He says you've got a great team around you with a particularly diligent DS. He's okayed you to come to London, but only if you want to."

Le Claire knew he had no option. He just hoped he could survive another meeting with Colin Chapman.

The search warrant had been issued in the early hours of that morning by a somewhat grumpy jurat. That had been the text message sent by Dewar, who had also said that John Vanguard and his team had been at the site since 6:30 a.m. Le Claire had showered and dressed; the call with Gareth Lewis had cost him time, and he had missed his morning coffee. He now stood in the Davies's ground-floor apartment. Apparently, they owned the house but had a tenant on the second floor. He'd donned protective clothing and slipped plastic covers over his shoes. Who knew what they'd find. They couldn't be too careful.

The place was filled with similarly clothed scene investigators who were methodically taking the place apart. Their remit was to look for anything of interest and specifically for a red dress, masks and anything that tied them to private, organised parties. It hadn't taken long. John Vanguard shouted down the stairs, "Le Claire, get up here."

Le Claire took the steps two at a time. He could hear the low rumble of suppressed excitement in the CSI chief's voice. "Apart from the studio that is rented out, all the other doors were left open except this one. A bit of deft lock picking courtesy of a misspent youth and we easily gained access. Look at this."

The room was decorated like a parody of a French bordello. Heavy velvets and shiny satins were the order of the day. The walls were painted a deep dark red, the four-poster bed was draped in diaphanous scarlet, the mattress was covered with a black satin throw and more red was displayed in the mound of cushions that acted in place of pillows.

An elegant white-painted, spindle-legged dressing table was topped with a three-panelled looking glass and covered with paints and powders. A lidless lipstick had been carelessly discarded. It was vibrant red. The open doors of a huge freestanding wardrobe held a treasure trove of dresses; reds and blacks, silver and white, silk and satin and chiffon. The side of the wardrobe held a vertical row of shelving. Le Claire smiled. One compartment held a pile of masks, the ones beneath froths of lingerie. "And the piece de resistance." Vanguard pointed to a sideboard that was partially concealed by the open door to what was presumably an en-suite bathroom. On it's top, and displayed like ornaments, was a row of Styrofoam mannequin heads. Each of the five displayed a wig, one of which was black, bobbed and sleek.

Le Claire moved to the wardrobe and started flicking through the gowns, his hands protected in their plastic gloves. He concentrated on the red. "This is it." He pulled out a slither of red that looked much less alluring than when it had been clinging to Lena Davies's body. "Right, get this dress, the masks and the wigs secured and analysed. We need to prove that they were worn by Lena Davies."

"Sir, over here."

A young investigator, who looked like she should still be at school, was kneeling in front of an open suitcase. "This was under the bed sir."

Vanguard reached it before Le Claire. "Looks like some kind of RSVP card or something."

Le Claire knew exactly what it was. For hadn't Blair handed him the exact invitation as his entry to the party? He had them now.

Le Claire headed straight for the incident room. It was still early, but most of the desks were already occupied. The distinctive aromas of buttery breakfast pastries vied with strong coffee for supremacy. The coffee was winning, and his noise twitched and his mouth watered. Reluctantly, he conceded that he didn't have time to stop. As he had expected, Dewar was already at her temporary desk.

"Dewar, with me. Let's have a chat with Basil Davies. Get him brought to the interview room."

She looked up from the papers she'd been reviewing. Her eyes were wide, and they glittered with excitement. He recognised that look. He stood still, and his heart was beating a little faster. She waved the papers in her hand.

"I've heard from Ian Jennings. He's the guy who left the voicemail for Hamlyn. He's just returned my call. He's a private investigator all right, ex-force, so he knew the score. He sent over a copy of the report he prepared. You better have a read of it. I think you're going to want to see someone else first."

Puzzled, he took the papers from her and started skimming. Then he stopped and read through from the start, slowly. The contents were explosive. He looked at Dewar. "Let's go and pay a call to Mr and Mrs Hamlyn."

# #

Sarah Hamlyn sat next to her husband, close together on the sofa in their neat lounge. Both were pale-faced with dark shadows and heavy bags under red-rimmed eyes, and Le Claire wondered if Hamlyn had been interrogated by his wife after he'd got home from the police station. He'd debated how to broach the subject on the way here. Decided to dive in. "Mr Hamlyn, I need to ask again what you took from your son's home?"

Sarah Hamlyn jumped in. "Charles has told you again and again. He isn't saying any more; he just needed something, and it has nothing to do with Scott's death or Laura Brown's attack. He won't even tell me what it was for."

Charles Hamlyn laid a hand on his wife's. A subtle, soothing gesture. "Detective, it's a nonsensical, personal matter, nothing to do with anyone else."

"I'm afraid it's for me to decide what is relevant to my investigation." He hesitated; they gave him no choice. He had to raise the issue that could ruin their lives.

"Did you know your son had engaged the services of a private detective?"

Sarah Hamlyn looked relieved. "He was having Laura investigated, wasn't he? I just knew he wouldn't be taken in by her forever."

Dewar replied. "No, that wasn't it. Was there any issue between you and Scott?"

Sarah Hamlyn was still. "Issue? Of course not. What are you getting at?"

Dewar glanced at Le Claire; she was chewing her underlip and he took pity on her, took over. "Scott hired an investigator to look into the past. His past and yours."

She didn't so much as blink, yet her shoulders tensed and her clasped hands worried away at each other. Her eyes flicked to her husband. "Charles, darling, go and put the kettle on. I'm parched. Coffee all round?"

Hamlyn shook his head. "Let's just get on with this Sarah."

Her look beseeched. "Please? I really am desperate for some caffeine."

With a sigh, Hamlyn pressed his hands against the sofa and boosted himself to his feet. He shuffled through the doorway with Dewar's request for a tea floating after him.

When Sarah Hamlyn looked at Le Claire, her gaze was direct and unflinching. "Get on with it and be quick, please."

"The report details the time you spent in London when Scott was three. I understand you had split from Mr Hamlyn and were living with your elder sister and her husband. You think of all the millions of people who travel through London every year, multiply that by over twenty-five years, and you'd think there'd be no memories of a young Jersey girl and her small son." A tic worked away at the side of her mouth. He continued. "A teenage girl lived with her parents, just two doors away from your sister and her Polish husband. When her parents died, she inherited the house, and now she lives there with her own family. Apparently, babysitting Scott was her first job, and she'd been so proud to be trusted. Even more so when the baby, Ana, arrived, and she sometimes sat with her for an hour or so. She remembers you well."

Sarah Hamlyn's face was closed, but he could sense the fear that had gripped her. Her tongue darted out from between tight lips, and she briefly looked to the left of him, not meeting his eyes. Her words were rushed. "I don't know where this is going, but I think it would be better if I came to the station with you. You can talk to me there."

Charles Hamlyn's voice, strong and certain, came from the open doorway and cut off Le Claire's reply. "There's no need. I know, Sarah. I know it all."

Le Claire would bet that he'd never got as far as the kitchen, but that he'd been listening, waiting for his moment.

She was ashen; the blood had leeched from her lips and her eyes locked on her husband's. "It's not true, Charles. Whatever they say, it isn't true." There was a panicked edge to her voice.

The air was heavy, pregnant with the tension that radiated between the married couple. Hamlyn's sigh filled the room as he walked over to his wife. "Yes, it is, Sarah. It is so simple and yet explains so much. You're Ana's real mother."

CHAPTER THIRTY-FOUR

Ana's day had been busy, deliberately so, as she tried to distract her mind from the confrontation with Basil Davies. The snake! She'd called Daria, who hadn't been surprised and had said, with a dark undertone, that she wouldn't put anything past that man and his wife.

She was working from Philip Le Claire's town office today. Her in-box was flooded with emails, and she was currently drafting a schedule for some high-level meetings. She couldn't afford to mess up and had to give the task her full concentration.

The shrill sound of her mobile broke the silence. She checked the caller ID, and her heart flipped. She quickly answered. "Ben, this is a surprise. How are you?"

"I'm well, but something has come up." He sounded stressed. "I'm in London already, got here this morning."

Her shoulders slumped, and a rush of disappointment enveloped her. She kept her voice light. "Oh, that is a shame. Maybe we can go away together another time?"

"No, we're still going to have our break. The only difference is that you will need to travel here on your own. I'll email you the e-ticket number, okay?"

Excitement bubbled. Her emotions were on a roller-coaster these days. "That's great. Thank you."

"And I'll meet you at Victoria Station." There was the briefest of pauses, and when he spoke his voice was a butterfly of a caress. "I can't wait to see you."

This was the most direct he had ever been about feelings, so she didn't think, just spoke and leapt off the cliff with him. "Me too. I'll count the days."

"That's what I like to hear. Look, I'm going to be crazy busy, so I won't be able to call you. I'll see you at Victoria Station on

Thursday. Send me a text when you're on the Gatwick Express. Take care."

She hung up and basked in the memory of his words, hugging them to her like a warm embrace. She just had to make sure she didn't mess it up, for she could see this maybe going somewhere. For the first time since Irena had left and Scott had died, she was feeling happy and confident and, surprisingly, at home.

Le Claire had sent Dewar to put the kettle on, telling her he had a quick call to make; anything to get out of the room and allow the situation to calm. He had stepped into the hall just as Sarah Hamlyn burst into hysterical, messy tears, her hitching sobs echoing in the otherwise silent room. She was now huddled in the corner of the sofa, rocking back and forth her arms wrapped tight around herself. She was staring straight ahead, eyes fixed, and he figured it had been best to give her time to gather her wits. Charles Hamlyn was tense and silent, his back to the room, as he stared out the window that overlooked their well-tended garden.

A rattle of china heralded Dewar's return, and she carefully settled the tray on a low table. Coffees all round and a tea for her. No one reached for a cup, not even Dewar.

Le Claire broke the silence. "Mr Hamlyn, when did you find out that your wife was Ana's mother?" The secret was out, and it wasn't going back in the box.

"About ten days ago. I overheard Scott talking to Ana. I was at his apartment, helping with some odd jobs. Ana had come round for coffee. She was shy when she saw me. Sarah's attitude has made her wary of us both, I guess. He was being a bit bossy, telling her he had never liked her friend – Irena, I think she is called – and that Ana better not get a boyfriend unless he okay'd him. The two of them were laughing their heads off. Ana put on a mock-pout, said he could keep his opinions to himself, it wasn't like he was her brother."

He ran a shaking hand across his brow. "I was watching from the hallway. Scott stopped laughing. Said nothing would make him prouder than to be her big brother. It was the way he said it. I knew something wasn't right." He reached out, picked up a cup of coffee and gulped half of it down.

Le Claire waited a moment and then urged him on. "What happened next?"

"Ana left. I asked Scott what he meant about being Ana's brother. He wouldn't say, but I knew he was holding back. We argued. I asked him when he found out, and he realised I had suspected something. He told me about the private detective, said he knew everything. I begged him not to speak to his mother, to let it be. He wouldn't listen. He did promise he wouldn't say anything to Sarah until he and I had spoken again. We never had a chance to do that."

"How did Scott find out in the first place?"

"We never told Scott that we had split up, and we thought he didn't remember London. Sarah had told him that his aunt had gone to live in Poland and had a child and the sisters had lost touch over the years. However, he did have some memories, and they were coming back stronger. I think Ana's arrival may have been the trigger. He remembered a little baby and a big house set on a square with a garden in the middle. Then Ana told him she'd been born in London and not Poland. He said he wanted his mind at rest, so he hired the investigator."

Le Claire asked, "What made you think that your wife was Ana's mother?"

"I knew something wasn't right when Sarah came back to me. I couldn't understand why she said we were over and then, months later, wanted to come home. She was changed – physically and mentally – in little ways that I could easily dismiss as the years went by. But I guess they have always stayed in my mind. And then Ana arrived, and Sarah's reaction to her was so extreme. It all started falling into place."

A keening moan escaped from his wife.

Le Claire was quick as a whip. "Did you kill your son, Mr Hamlyn?"

His head jerked up. "No, of course I didn't. I loved him."

"I'm afraid that's not mutually exclusive."

"Charles couldn't have killed Scott." Sarah Hamlyn's voice was a ghost of a whisper. "Why would he? Would a man who'd kill his son for knowing a secret leave his wife unharmed when she was the guilty party, the wrongdoer?"

Dewar faced Charles Hamlyn. "But you took his laptop, didn't you? And the letter from the investigator. That's why you called the apartment. You wanted to make sure that Laura was out. Did you see her leave? Then you parked in the car park, let yourself in, searched for and took the letter and also your son's laptop for good measure. That right?"

"Yes. I had to get the letter, for my wife's sake. I took the laptop in case there were any emails about the report, but I did not kill my son."

"I hear you, but the proverbial jury is out on that at the moment."

He moved in front of Sarah Hamlyn. She lifted her head and looked at him; her eyes were red-rimmed and slightly unfocussed. "For the record, and to be clear, are you Ana Zielinska's mother?"

"What do you mean, for the record? This is no one's business but mine. You can't tell anyone."

"If this has nothing to do with Scott's death, then I can assure you that it will go no further. In the meantime, we'll put any notes under the highest security access. However, if this is related to your son's death, then we can't keep it quiet."

She pursed her lips and looked to the side, seemed to think for a moment and then conceded. "Fine. Yes, I gave birth to Ana, but her mother was my sister. I wanted nothing to do with the child."

"Can you tell us what happened?"

Her eyes pleaded with him. "My husband doesn't need to hear this. This is ancient history. It has nothing to do with Scott's death."

Charles Hamlyn's voice was weary. "I read the report. I think I deserve to know after all these years, don't you?"

She was looking at Le Claire, but he knew she was really speaking to the man sitting next to her, her husband of thirty years.

"Charles and I weren't getting on. We'd been arguing nonstop since Scott was born, and he was nearly three by that time.

Nowadays people would say I had postnatal depression; at the time I just seemed like a bitch. After a particularly vicious row, I took Scott, packed our bags and caught a flight to my sister's in London. I didn't mean to be gone long. I just wanted to teach Charles a lesson. In the end, it was a year before we went home."

Le Claire prompted her. "Tell us about Ana. May I ask who her father is?

Her voice was husky as she let go the weight of her secret, now released after all these years. "Her father was, is and will always be Pieter Zielinska, my sister's husband. The man I had an affair with was just the catalyst; he never even knew about the child. A stupid, drunken fling that lasted a few days. I was an immoral little slut. He was a Polish colleague of Pieter's on a sabbatical. I had already ended it before he was due to return home. I'd realised that I loved Charles and wanted to come back and try again."

"But you didn't?"

"Charles was working as an engineer then and was on an assignment abroad. That was what we mostly argued about. He was travelling, and I was left at home with a small child. The contract had weeks to run. We planned that he'd come and see me after that. By then it was too late. I was pregnant. I had to tell Charles I'd made my mind up and we were over. I couldn't terminate the pregnancy. That's against all I believe in. I made arrangements with my sister, Alison, that she would take the child, and my secret, to Poland. We'd break contact. Ali would have a child, something she longed for, and I could forget my mistake and get on with my life. When the child was a few weeks old, I went to Charles, cap in hand, and he took me back." She reached out, fumbling, and grabbed hold of her husband's hand. "Charles was wonderful."

Le Claire knew they'd get nothing else of use today. The emotions were running high, and they all felt wrung out – he certainly did! "There's nothing more for us to say at the moment, but we will be talking to you again. Can you get me the laptop and the letter, please?"

Hamlyn went to do his bidding as Sarah Hamlyn walked them toward the front door. They waited in an uncomfortable silence. Le Claire was relieved when his phone rang and answered immediately. He listened, a growing anticipation in his gut. He ended the call. "Dewar, go and hurry Hamlyn along. We've got to get to the hospital. Laura Brown has woken up and is asking for me."

# #

Laura Brown was a mess. Her face was swollen into a round ball, and huge swathes of multi-coloured bruises covered every inch of flesh. Her eyelids were puffed and yellowed, the entire eye area battered and bruised. A nurse sat by the bed and rose as she saw Le Claire and Dewar. Her disapproving look disappeared as she realised Dr Foster accompanied them. The doctor's face was tense as he asked, "Any further improvement?"

"No, she is coming in and out of awareness and is virtually incoherent when she is conscious. I can't make out what she is saying except she asks for a Le Claire."

He looked at the nurse. "That's me. Can I try and speak to her?"

It was Foster who replied. "Go ahead. I wouldn't normally let a patient in this condition be approached by anyone except the medical staff, but when she is awake, she is anxious and gets upset when we say you aren't here."

The nurse moved away from the bed, and he saw Foster motion for her to leave the room. He sat in the chair and gazed at Laura Brown. The room had a closed-off, claustrophobic feel; the slatted blinds were down but slightly open, and strips of sunlight lay across the bed. Laura Brown's breath was shallow, and she lay flat on her back, her arms atop the covers. Multiple drip lines were connected to an intravenous feeder. The intermittent soft beep of the machine was strangely hypnotic.

Foster stepped forward, took Laura's hand in his and, bending down, leaned close to her ear and spoke gently. "Laura, we've done what you wanted. We have the police. DCI Le Claire is here. Laura?"

There was silence in the room, only broken by the rhythmic noise from the machine. Le Claire kept his voice low. "Laura, it's Jack Le Claire. You wanted me. I'm here." He abstractly ran his fingers over her hand. It was cold to the touch, and there was no response. Her eyelids flickered, just a fraction. "Come on, Laura. What is it? Who did you go to meet the night Scott died? Who did this to you?"

Her eyes were slits, and he could tell from the taut, swollen flesh that she couldn't open them any farther.

Her lips parted. Twice she tried to speak, and each time her bone-dry voice faltered. Foster gave her a drink of water, carefully holding the back of her head in position to allow her to take small sips. She choked a little, and the words came in a rasping whisper. "I went to see him. The night Scott died. I begged him for help, wanted the past forgotten. Said he couldn't help.

"Who, Laura, who?"

"Gillespie…" She broke into a coughing fit, the raw sound causing more than one of them in the room to wince. And with that, she closed her eyes, and her head fell to the side.

Le Claire spoke quickly, "Did Gillespie hurt you? Which one? Laura!"

His voice had risen, and Foster shoved him aside. Le Claire saw the moment the doctor visibly relaxed.

"She's still alive, thank God. You two," he looked at Le Claire and Dewar, "get out of here. This is a very ill girl."

CHAPTER THIRTY-FIVE

Le Claire was making his way to interview Lena Davies when a voice called out. "Sir, wait, please."

A puffing Hunter was hurrying toward him. "What is it?"

"You need to know before you go in, sir. A girl was attacked on Sunday might. Someone broke into her bedroom. Groped her a little but mainly scared her witless."

He tapped his foot. "Why is this important for me to know right now?"

"Because the landlady said she had only just moved in that day. The previous occupant left the day before. It was Ana Zielinska."

Le Claire stilled. "How is the girl?"

"Fine, the attacker apparently ran off in a panic as soon he looked at her face."

"Thanks for letting me know. It appears that Basil Davies's depravity knows no bounds."

Lena Davies's face was set and her chin lifted in a stubborn tilt when Le Claire opened the door to the interview room. "I told you yesterday that I don't know what you're talking about. My husband and I are sexually adventurous. Big deal. You've gone behind our backs and searched our house, so what if you've found some masks? We like to dress up, don't you?" Her smile was flirtatious. She wasn't looking her best today. Her makeup-free face was blotchy, which accentuated the dark circles under her eyes. Without the glossy lipstick, her mouth looked small and mean.

"Lena, we know all about it." For a moment, what looked like fear crossed her face, then she lifted her chin higher, and he saw defiance in her eyes and a smirk that said it all. Prove it.

"We found the stock of invitations. The same invitations that were issued for a party where a young girl was molested. Now I think I could make a damned good case that you organise these parties, lure young and innocent girls to them and let them be used by lecherous swine like your husband."

He looked at Dewar. "What do you think?"

"I think that is exactly what happened."

"Yes, and that will carry a much higher charge than molestation alone. You're going to jail, Lena, and if you don't mind me saying so, I don't think that's going to be complimentary to your looks."

"Stop, don't be ridiculous. You can't prove anything."

"We have the invitations, the masks, the dress and wig you wore at the last party."

"That little bitch, she did recognise me."

He couldn't believe she had organised all this on her own. "I assume Basil was in it with you. I can just see it, the two of you getting your kicks, lining up people to pay to get into your parties. Did you blackmail them later? Basil said he was going to take pictures of Ana. Is that what happened? You photographed people and blackmailed them?"

"I don't know what you're talking about, I don't." She looked frantic as she glanced from one to the other. "All I did was help with the arrangements. I don't know anything about blackmail, I don't! Basil and I just needed to keep that girl quiet. She could easily have recognised us."

"But she didn't. Basil was going to rape her. You think that was okay? He's going down for that and for breaking into Ana's old place and attacking the girl who moved in there. He's got a nice long stretch coming up for that. You'll be down as an accessory at the very least."

"He wasn't supposed to do any of that. I just told him to frighten her. Make sure she kept her mouth shut."

"You're my only suspect for the parties, Lena."

"There's nothing against holding private parties."

His voice was dry. "No, but it does get tricky if you use someone else's house without permission. Then there's tagging people as entertainment. Are they paid for that? People certainly pay for the pleasure of attending the parties. What's the going rate for free access to drugs, sex and perversions?"

"Everyone is consenting adults."

"Ana wasn't consenting." He paused, spoke carefully, making sure she took in every word. "I have no one else in the frame, Lena. Basil will be charged with the attacks, but I think he's too lazy and stupid to be the organiser, to be the brains behind these parties. Everything I have right now points to you."

Fear clouded her gaze, and he saw the exact moment realisation hit of exactly how much trouble she was in.

"It wasn't me. I just did what I was told. It wasn't me." Her voice ended on a hitching sob, her breath coming in hard, sharp gasps.

"Then who was it?"

"Danny. Danny Gillespie."

Le Claire tensed, and for a split second his breathing was suspended. "What did Danny do? You need to give me something. Tell me what happened."

Tiny beads of sweat glistened on her upper lip; her pupils were dilated and her eyes unfocused.

"Come on, Lena. Don't make it harder on yourself. You think Danny Gillespie would keep quiet for you?"

She gnawed on the side of her lip; her shoulders slumped as she leaned forward and cradled her head in her hands. Her words were a murmur. "How the hell did this happen?"

Dewar snorted. "You tell us, Lena." He had to admire how well she naturally fell into the bad-cop routine.

"It was just fun. Basil and I are, well, I told you, we're adventurous. We started having parties for like-minded people. We just wanted a safe place for people to express their sexuality. We used to hold events at various houses. They were just private, suburban parties, but they got more popular. We had to start charging an entry fee to cover drinks, toys and condoms."

Le Claire kept a straight face. "How did Danny Gillespie get involved?"

"We met him socially, and I got on very well with him." The innuendo hung in the air. "I invited him to come along, said he didn't have to participate fully. He could just be with me. Afterwards, he said the parties were too tame, not private enough, that confidentiality was a problem. He suggested the masks and started supplying the venues. The entry fee went up, as did the class of the clientele. The *Jersey Evening Post* would have enough material for a year if the guests' details got out. We've entertained senators, local businesspeople and even an occasional honorary policeman."

"Whose idea was it to bring professional escorts in?"

She jerked her head back. "How the hell do you know so much?"

He smiled. "Never mind, just answer the question."

"Danny organised them. Well, he gave me details of a guy in the UK, and we flew them over. Sometimes one of the girls we met through the agency would be up for a little extra pocket money." Her eyes flicked to his face. "No one was forced into anything. I mean, I paid them well."

Dewar's voice was dry. "So it was you who organised for multiple persons to have sex with people for money?"

Lena's eyes widened. "No! I mean, yes, but it was Danny, not me, it was Danny."

Le Claire stood. "Yes, he's culpable, but you're caught in the coils, Lena. There's no way out for you."

# #

Dewar had made the call immediately. The manor's housekeeper informed her that both Gillespies were in London and wouldn't be back for at least a week.

Le Claire had gone straight to Chief Wilson.

"The Gillespie name is popping up too many times to be ignored. They are both in London, so I'd like to go over there, and I can deal with the Chapman situation at the same time."

"The timing is perfect. I know Gareth Lewis wants you to meet Chapman. I don't think it is necessarily a good idea, but you must do as you think best. I'll be supportive of whatever you decide. However, this Gillespie situation puts a new perspective on things. I'll call Lewis and tell him our investigation has spilled onto his patch and ask him to provide whatever resources you will need."

"Thanks. I've got some bits to tie up here, but I'll get myself booked on the first flight in the morning."

He headed back to his office. Dewar was still at her desk. "Come on in and bring the Gillespie reports."

She grabbed a pile of papers and rushed in behind him. "Did the chief okay you going to London?"

"Yes." He quickly checked his watch. "It's late, so I'll go online and book the flight myself. First, give me what we know about Aidan and Danny Gillespie."

She sat before his desk and spread her papers in front of her. "We know Aidan Gillespie is very rich. We don't know how rich because Income Tax wouldn't give us any info as we don't have enough cause for them to go through the palaver of getting the approvals to release tax returns. We do know he initially made his money from private clubs in the UK."

Her pinched lips let him know the kind of clubs Adrian Gillespie was involved in.

"He basically made a packet and started investing in other areas." She flicked through the papers in front of her. "We've got transport, long-distance lorries and the like, restaurants, mainly fast-food chains, and latterly he got into real estate, buying up brownfield site land and rendering it fit for residential use."

"And neither brother has any record?"

"Their names pop up here and there, but nothing has ever stuck. Danny runs the clubs now and is based at one in London. They don't call them gentlemen's clubs any longer; they are now just private clubs, and open to both men and women. From the reports, everything is apparently above board and well run. No real trouble with the local force."

He leaned back in his chair, rolled his shoulders and stretched his arms above his head. It was late, and he still had to book flights and get ready for what tomorrow would bring. "Okay. I'll report back tomorrow on what I find."

# #

Irena could barely contain her excitement. She had the night off, and her lover would be here soon. She was primped, shaved, made-up and ready for him. She knew how he liked to find her and had followed his instructions to the letter – almost, that is. She ran into the bedroom to finish her preparations. When he had shown her this apartment, said it was for her, she had wanted to weep. It wasn't fancy, and he said maybe the area wasn't so great, yet it had seemed like a palace to her. The flat downstairs wasn't even rented out, so she had the building to herself and could play her music as loud as she wanted. It was certainly a change from living in someone else's house, relegated to one room. That she didn't miss about Jersey. She missed Ana though. A stray thought, one she had often had, flickered through her mind. Ana wouldn't understand her life right now, and she doubted her friend would approve of the decisions she had made. She had been his from the second she'd seen him and would do anything to keep him, anything at all.

He'd said the place was well stocked, and it was. She took a see-through ziplock packet out of the bedside drawer, opened it and chose two small pills. She washed them down with a glass of vodka she'd poured earlier. They'd start working soon, as they did every night. He'd shown her this, taught her how the calming, floating feeling would help her rise above anything, anything at all. She should have taken the pills earlier; he liked her to be calm and fully relaxed when he arrived. She hoped they'd start working very soon. Later, he'd give her a little something special. They'd share the white powder and let the night, and the drugs, take over.

The metallic click of the key in the door heralded the start of her evening, and her pulse quickened. She rushed into the lounge as he came striding in through the door. He held his arms open wide, and she ran into them. He held her close, and she knew all was right in her world.

When he spoke, she marvelled at how the timbre of his voice made each nerve-end tingle. "Irena, I've missed you. Come on, let me look at you."

He held her at arm's length, and the searing look in his eyes set her afire. She tried to move closer, but he kept her at bay. "Take it easy; let me take it in."

He ran his hand over her hair. She knew the long honey-blonde wig, with its caramel highlights, looked sleek, shiny and expensive. He'd bought it for her, along with a whole new wardrobe of clothes, when he had moved her to London. He'd shown her how he liked her makeup. Expensive foundation that made her skin look soft and peachy, dark eyes with a flick of liner and a pale pink pout. It was so different from how she normally looked, but if this was what made him happy, then she was okay with it. She pushed the thought away that there was something not quite right about being made to look like another person. She often wondered if that woman existed but brushed the thought aside.

She tilted her head to one side and coquettishly asked, "What's the verdict? You like?"

She knew she looked good. The skin-tight bandage dress was a deep red that matched her high-heeled sandals. She couldn't walk far in them, but she'd be spending most of the night on her back so wasn't bothered.

His grin was long and slow and very sexy. "Oh yes, however, I think you'd look even better without anything on."

She smirked. She knew exactly what he wanted. "Sit down, lover, this one's on the house." She pushed him backward, and he sank down onto the sofa, placed his hands behind his head and stretched his long legs in front of him.

She ramped up the volume of the music that had been playing in the background, placed her hands on her hips and began a sensuous dance, grinding and thrusting toward him, never close enough for his outstretched hand to reach. She'd learned a lot over the past few weeks, and her erotic dance quickly got a reaction from him. He pounced, grabbing her and dragging her down to the floor. He was on her immediately, pushing her skirt around her waist, thrusting his hand inside her flimsy, see-through pants. He was rough, and she tried to say something, she really did, but her limbs were heavy, and she was rooted to the spot. She tried to speak, but the words couldn't escape past her dry throat. She closed her eyes, and a kaleidoscope of pulsating, spiralling colours continuously flashed. She tried to open her lids, but they were leaden. The wonderful, soothing numbness started to creep through her limbs, trapping her mind and coalescing her thoughts into one throbbing sensation. *Him.* Her heart was beating faster, a rhythmic, pill-induced tattoo that thundered through her head, devouring anything that took her focus from him, from the moment. He brutalised her body with savage thrusts, and all she could do was lie there and freely give all that he took.

CHAPTER THIRTY-SIX

Le Claire had wondered what he would feel walking into the Met again and was surprised that the answer was not much at all. The devil on his shoulder asked him if that was because he genuinely wasn't concerned or if he was just masking feelings he preferred not to acknowledge.

He sat in the modern reception, dreading the Chapman meet, wanting it over and done with so he could get on the trail of whoever killed Scott Hamlyn.

"Jack! I didn't know you were back in town."

He looked up and couldn't stop his unbidden smile of welcome. DI Penny Powers was neat and trim in her black skirt suit, her dark, glossy hair was trimmed just short of her shoulders. She was a very attractive woman with satin skin, a generous mouth and sparkling eyes framed by long, thick lashes.

"Pen, good to see you. What a surprise. I'm just here on a last-minute flying visit, so I didn't have an opportunity to tell anyone I was coming over."

Their last meeting had been tense and awkward. He hadn't thought he would ever see her again. He'd certainly promised Sasha that would be the case.

She held his gaze for just a fraction too long. "And how are you, Jack? How is the wife?" There was an edge to her voice, which he knew he didn't deserve. He had done nothing wrong. He chose his words with care. She couldn't have known that he and Sasha had been on the verge of divorce.

"She's fine." He didn't want to talk about Sasha with her. He was uncomfortable and felt a disloyalty he hadn't experienced in his previous encounters with Penny. The silence between them grew, and it made a mockery of the close friendship they had once shared. A friendship born of working in the same job, sharing the same ethics. One night had destroyed all of that.

"I better be off, then. Bye, Jack." Her voice was cool. He watched her walk away and thought how, on paper, the diligent Penny, a career policewoman, was a better match for him than pretty, spoiled Sasha, with her fierce temper and independent spirit. The loud voice booming in his direction shook him from his musings.

"Le Claire, there you are." He noticed that Gareth Lewis had retorted to the more formal use of his surname. Then again, this was a formal situation.

"Good to see you, sir."

"And you. Now come on. You'll want to get this over with. We had Chapman driven up here last night. It seemed easier than you going to the prison, especially as you've got a case to look into here."

"Thanks, how is he?"

"Charming." Gareth Lewis grimaced. "You know how he has the ability to appear the opposite of his psychotic inner self."

Le Claire knew indeed. His head was aching, and his nerves were tight, senses on full alert. He didn't trust Chapman.

They zigzagged their way through a labyrinth of corridors until they reached a heavy metal door, bolted from the outside and flanked by two uniforms. Gareth Lewis motioned toward the security measures. "I don't trust him either. You go on in. I'll be in the viewing area to keep an eye on proceedings."

The door opened, and he saw Chapman. He was a seated on a plastic chair behind a matching table, and both were made from one-piece moulds. They weren't taking any chances that he could break off something and try and harm someone, even himself. A woman in a tailored suit sat next to him. She was an attractive forty-something, and Le Claire figured this was one of their ploys to make Chapman look more likeable. Give him female representation; show him with women by his side. Play to the crowds and let them ask if she could really countenance defending the vile monster the prosecution would paint him to be. He had lost weight, was even looking gaunt. Le Claire wondered if it was another cynical move to make him appear vulnerable and ill able to cope with a long jail term.

The woman spoke first. "I'm Abigail Larsen, Mr Chapman's lawyer. I take it you are DCI Jack Le Claire?"

He pulled out a chair and sat on the opposite side of the table. He wasn't quite able to make eye contact with Chapman yet, couldn't bear to see that self-satisfied, smug grin that had been on his face last time they had met. "Yes. What is this all about?"

"Mr Chapman wished to speak to you. We have argued against it, but for the sake of his mental health, we have reluctantly agreed." Her soft look at Chapman turned Le Claire's stomach. He glanced at the viewing window, where Gareth Lewis would be observing. Mental health? What the hell was Chapman up to?

Chapman's eyes were downcast as he stared at his handcuffed hands, which rested on the table. His voice was quiet. "DCI Le Claire, thank you for agreeing to meet me. I am very grateful."

The tone was conciliatory, pleasant almost. The hairs stood up on the back of Le Claire's neck. Something wasn't right. His voice was harsh. "You asked to see me. What do you want, Chapman?"

He raised his eyes, looked straight at Le Claire. "Why did you do it? Why lie? You said I told you about that girl, but I didn't."

Le Claire exploded. "What utter bullshit is this? What are you trying to pull?"

Chapman's voice was shaking, his eyes pleading. "I didn't do any of the terrible things you accused me of. I never said I hurt that girl, that April Baines. My lawyers are on the case, but I had to ask you, had to look into your face and ask how you could do this. Please tell the truth. Please."

Le Claire stood. He wasn't being a party to whatever game was being played by Chapman and his lawyer. "I've had enough of this. I've no idea what you're up to, but I'm not going to be your stooge."

Le Claire left the room. Gareth Lewis was waiting for him, his face a hard mask of granite. "What the hell was that all about?"

"I have no idea, but what I do know is that he is playing us. Chapman never does anything without a good reason."

# #

Dewar ruffled her hair with one hand as she flicked through the notes she had made. Notes on a killer. Were Scott Hamlyn's death and Laura Brown's attack the work of the same person? Or was Laura simply the victim of a random crime gone wrong? The odds seemed remote. And if the same person was to blame, then what was the connection and the motive. Why?

A loud cough dragged her attention away from the files. Hunter stood beside her, hovering by her shoulder. She looked at him; he looked back at her. He didn't say anything. She knew he felt intimidated by her, God knew why. The exasperation rose, and her voice was sharp. "Yes, what is it? Can't you see I'm busy?"

His downcast eyes and fiery blush shamed her. "Okay, sorry. Let's start again. We've got an unsolved murder, the boss is in London and I'm at my wit's end. So what are you after?"

"Sorry, but there's a Lady Mallory in reception asking for the DCI. The desk sergeant told her he is away for a few days, but she won't take no for an answer, nor will she say why she is here."

She answered the unspoken plea in his eyes and, with a heartfelt sigh, pushed her papers to one side and locked her computer monitor.

"Okay, tell them to put her in an interview room, and it better be a nice one."

Dewar headed for the lift as Hunter called the front desk. She sniggered to herself as she heard him ask for a "nice" interview room. The desk sergeant would rip into him, but they'd all laugh about it later. Her mission in life was to toughen up Hunter. He had a good mind and a solid heart. He just needed to add some grit.

She left thoughts of the young PC behind as she reached the ground floor and headed to the desk. The duty officer directed her to interview four. She hid a smile, for it was the better of the clinical interview rooms. Two women were waiting for her. Lady Mallory was accompanied by her granddaughter. The younger woman had obviously been crying; her face was blotchy and her eyes swollen and puffed. Grief lingered and came out at unexpected times. Dewar felt an ache of sympathy. She'd suffered loss herself, and that was why she'd ended up in Jersey.

"Lady Mallory, how do you do, and Miss Mallory."

Lady Mallory was blunt. "Call me Eleanor, if you like; we're not standing on ceremony, certainly not today." There was an edge to her voice that triggered Dewar's senses. Lady Mallory – she couldn't think of her as Eleanor – sounded weary and on the verge of tears.

She felt slightly out of her depth. She'd grown up in a council house, and meeting any posh people dragged her out of her comfort zone. She took a breath, shelved her inadequacies and retreated behind the wall of her uniform. "Thank you. How may I help you?"

The two women, decades apart, shared a look that Dewar immediately recognised. Complicity. Whatever was the matter, they both knew about it. She tried to keep her voice gentle. "Ladies, how may I help you?"

Lady Mallory looked at her granddaughter, direct and sharp. "Louise has something she wants to say, or rather, needs to say."

Louise Mallory was silent. She looked at her grandmother and whispered, her tone beseeching, "Grandma, I can't…"

Lady Mallory's face contorted, and Dewar saw steel mixed with anger as she volleyed. "Yes, you can. We are not liars in this family or concealers of truths."

"But Dad won't like it."

Lady Mallory's voice was like a whiplash. "I don't care what he thinks. I want justice."

Dewar was looking from one to the other and had no idea what was going on. "I hate to rush you, but I'm not sure why you are here; perhaps you should explain?"

Louise Mallory held herself tight, hugging her fancy handbag in front of her like a shield. "Sorry. Please give me a moment." Her voice was shaking, and Dewar was intrigued. What the hell was going on?

Trembling, she withdrew a white envelope from her bag. It was made of heavy, expensive vellum. She handed it to Dewar. "I'm sorry, but we couldn't let it be like this."

Dewar looked at Lady Mallory, who nodded toward the envelope. "Go ahead and open it. I've seen the contents, and, unpalatable though they may be, they do need to be investigated."

The envelope was addressed to Eleanor. Intrigued, Dewar pulled a folded piece of paper from the envelope. She was trying to make out the words when Louise Mallory pulled it from her grasp. "No, don't."

The girl's voice shook, and Dewar held herself still. She didn't want to exacerbate the situation.

Lady Mallory's voice was a lash that cut the air. "Louise, don't be a bloody fool. Read it out and explain what you did. Get on with it."

Louise Mallory flashed a glance at Dewar, and her words tumbled out. "I couldn't let this be his legacy. My dad agreed…"

"Your father might be my son, but he is a total prat. So let us not use him as the barometer of what is right or wrong." Lady Mallory's words were snapped, her diction precise. "Just read it."

The girl's eyes teared up, and she fumbled as she unfolded the piece of paper. "Whilst Grandma was kneeling by Grandpa, I saw this on the table. I didn't think. I just put it in my pocket. Then it seemed too late to tell Grandma, and, well, Dad said I shouldn't."

Eleanor's eyes flashed. "My son decided that he wouldn't like anyone to know why his father saw fit to take his own life. He didn't consider that I might want the closure. I needed to know." The air seemed to leave her, and she visibly deflated, reducing in stature, in vibrancy. She grabbed the letter from her granddaughter and passed it to Dewar. When she spoke, her voice was lower, less strident. "Read it, please. There is something nasty going on here."

Dewar took the letter and read aloud.

Eleanor,

I am sorry about all of this, what I've done and what you will undoubtedly have to suffer. There is no other way out. Whilst I am alive, they will bleed us dry. It was the old problem, I'm afraid. There wasn't anyone special this time. I kept my promise. But there were distractions, and I paid dearly for them. I thought if it was a business transaction it wouldn't be like real adultery, and it wasn't. It was worse, for I kept having to pay more and more, and you're going to find out soon.

This is the only way of stopping this madness. Forgive me.

Hugh

Dewar looked at Lady Mallory. "I hesitate to ask, but – the old problem?"

The older women's face was set, unsmiling. "Affairs. For years, he always had someone on the go."

Louise Mallory gasped, and her grandmother leaned across and patted her hand. "Sorry, darling, but he was an unfaithful beast. It started as soon as we married. I didn't let on I knew for the longest time. We rubbed along well together and, to be brutally frank, he gave me a very nice lifestyle. We had a massive row a few years ago, and I threatened to leave him. He broke down; it was quite touching. He said he would never have another relationship with anyone else again, and I guess he didn't. I am assuming he just used prostitutes, and someone was blackmailing him or charging extortionate amounts."

"Lady Mallory, my hat is off to you for how well you are taking this. May I ask why you decided to bring the letter to us now and not before?"

"I only realised it existed this morning. Explain, please, Louise."

The shamefaced girl looked reluctant to say anything, but as the silence grew, she reddened and spoke, her voice a little hoarse. "I showed my dad the letter. He said best to keep quiet about it as it would only upset Grandma and be a terrible slur on Grandpa's memory."

"What made you change your mind?"

She glanced at her grandmother. "I went to see Grandma today. She was upset and well…"

Lady Mallory took up where she left off. "My husband's funeral was yesterday. I was in a reflective mood this morning. Poor Louise got the worst of it, I'm afraid. I was trying to make sense of what happened, asking why Hugh would have done this, why he would have taken such a staggering step."

"And I couldn't bear to see Grandma so upset, questioning why Grandpa would have taken his own life, how he could have left her like that. I didn't want her to blame herself, so I showed her the letter."

"I was furious. How dare my son encourage her to keep something like that from me? Then I realised how important it was. Someone was blackmailing my husband. That led to his death, therefore they as good as put that bloody gun in his hand, and I want them punished."

Cogs started connecting in Dewar's mind, and another piece of the jigsaw fell into place. She needed to get back to the station.

# #

Le Claire had gone outside for fresh air and strong coffee. He wanted to blow the remnants of Chapman from his mind before he got on with chasing down the Gillespies. They had Danny in the frame for organising the sex parties and potentially bringing the drugs in, plus Laura Brown had a connection to one of them. She'd been Danny's lover, but was it him or Aidan Gillespie that she had gone to visit at the manor the night of Scott's death? The ringing of his telephone cut short his musings. He saw it was Dewar.

"Hi, what's up?"

"Lady Mallory came in looking for you. The granddaughter concealed a suicide letter from Sir Hugh. By the looks of it, he was paying for sex. He was worried about escalating demands for money, so I'm thinking the payments to the foundation may have something to do with this."

"And Scott Hamlyn was also a donor."

"Yes, should we try and make direct contact with the people in Panama?"

"No, I don't want to scare them off. Look, I need the team to run deep searches on the Gillespies and get me a full brief on business interests, etc. In the meantime, how quickly can you get to London?"

"What?"

He just knew that she would hate it that she squeaked. "I need you over here. We'll need to work alongside the Met, so I need someone else firmly in my corner. I don't give a damn who gets the glory as long as we get our man, whoever the hell he is."

"Okay, I can see if I can get across tonight; if not, it'll be first thing tomorrow."

"Fine, keep me posted."

As he disconnected the call, he realised that he was already back outside the Met. Gareth Lewis had said there was a pass left for him at reception which would give him fairly wide access, and there would just be some papers to sign on the usual disclaimers and authorisation rights. The desk clerk had him sign in triplicate and then handed across his pass. "Here you are. I understand you'll be working alongside DI Powers. I'll give her a call."

CHAPTER THIRTY-SEVEN

Penny Powers was a good policewoman with a fine mind and tenacious attitude. However, the trait Le Claire currently valued most was that she wasn't openly displaying a grudge against him. At least not in front of her team. Whatever the reason, he was grateful they could at least work together. He'd found a desk and logged into the secure system via remote access. Dewar had updated all the files, and he spent some time bringing himself up-to-date.

Penny clapped her hands together and called out, "Can you lot gather round, please? As I mentioned this morning, DCI Le Claire has an ongoing murder enquiry and a related sex-for-sale case where one of the suspects overlaps. They, and another person of interest, have London connections and so the chief wants us to cooperate. Okay?" She glanced around and, apparently satisfied that there were no dissenting faces, gestured toward Le Claire. "The floor's all yours, Jack."

He saw the sharp glances at her familiar use of his Christian name. He didn't recognise many of the team, and of those he did, previous contact had only been on a superficial level.

He moved to the centre of the room. "Thanks. You'll have seen the briefing notes my DS sent across. There are various people we're interested in with regard to the death of Scott Hamlyn. We are led to believe that two of them are in London at the moment. They are an Aidan Gillespie and his brother, Danny. They are now Jersey residents but lived in London until a year or so ago. Danny also had a past relationship with Hamlyn's girlfriend, who is currently in intensive care. She was badly beaten a week after Hamlyn was killed."

Graves was well named, a sombre man in his late forties with a quiet, authoritive way of speaking. "I don't know much about Gillespie the Younger, but I've run across Aidan Gillespie, the elder brother, a few times."

Le Claire was all ears. "There wasn't anything in the records."

"We never pinned anything on him. If you ask me, Aidan Gillespie has sailed close to the wind, may even have ventured onto the illegal side here and there, but I don't see him as being an out-and-out no-gooder. He is a man who came from nothing, and it's rare to do that without cutting a corner here and there."

Penny interrupted. "Cutting corners and sailing close is one thing. The question here is whether Danny Gillespie is responsible for these Jersey crimes and whether his brother is involved, even at an awareness level."

Le Claire agreed. "There are too many connections to ignore. But we have to prove it. Don't we?"

Penny smiled. "Exactly, Jack – sorry, Le Claire." Graves shot her a look, an interested what-is-going-on look that she ignored. "So what's your plan?"

"Danny Gillespie runs a private club here in London. The word is that it is clean, well run and regulated."

Graves butted in. "From what I've seen, Gillespie's clubs stick to the rules and don't appear to be up to any of the tricks you get from the lower-class places."

Le Claire was interested. He hadn't had cause to investigate any of the so-called lap-dancing clubs whilst he was in London, and Jersey certainly didn't allow that sort of thing. People like his mother would be apoplectic and march on the Royal Square. No doubt joined by the likes of Sarah Hamlyn. He shuddered at the thought. "What tricks?"

Barnes, who was Graves's younger sidekick, laughed. "You name it. The obvious one is obeying the rules in the club but having a setup nearby where the girls can offer extras. Drugs are big news. The worst are the forced situations."

Le Claire frowned. "What, you mean like people trafficking?"

"It happens all the time. Girls are brought in from all over the place. What pisses me off is that you have these decent girls who they get hooked on some nasty stuff and have them working all hours, doing God only knows what to feed their habit. They end up with no money, no passport and no liberty. They basically become non-people. And it's all over the place, not just the big clubs."

"I don't know everything Danny Gillespie has been up to, but for me to get a result here I need to handle this properly. My DS is going to be here tomorrow, and the cross-force formalities should have been dealt with by then. I'd like us all to get together and get a plan in place. Danny Gillespie needs to be taken in. It may not be murder, but he is definitely guilty of something."

#

Le Claire sipped his ice-cold beer as he gazed around. The hotel didn't have a restaurant, but this busy bar served pub-style food. He'd polished off a steak pie and chips and was now thinking about ordering dessert. A shadow fell across his table, and he looked up to see an unexpected face.

"Penny, this is a surprise. What are you doing here?"

She pulled out a chair and plonked herself down opposite him. "You didn't say good night, so I thought I'd come and see you. Graves mentioned that you were staying here."

"Can I get you a drink?"

"No thanks, I ordered a glass of wine as soon as I saw you. They'll bring it to the table."

Now that was being presumptuous, but he guessed he owed her some time. "How are you?"

"Fine. How have you settled back into Jersey?"

"It's good. There have been challenging moments after being so used to working at the Met, but we've got some great professional teams in Jersey."

There was a tiny pause before she spoke. "And how is Sasha? Still a yoga bunny?"

"Yes, she's great."

A waitress arrived with Penny's wine. She maintained eye contact as she took a long draught of the pale liquid. She placed her glass on the table with a determined air. "I didn't think I'd have the guts to say anything, but let's get the elephant out of the room, shall we? Were you just leading me on? Did you ever have feelings for me?"

"I'm sorry. I thought we were friends. I didn't mean you to think it was anything else."

She stared at him for a moment and shook her head. "Friends? You confided in me. Nights when you should have been at home, you sat in bars like this with me. What was I supposed to think?" Her voice had lowered to an angry hiss. "How do you think I felt when Sasha walked in on us? I was humiliated. You just left me sitting there and ran after her. Next thing I know, I'm persona non grata, and you've resigned from the Met and gone back home to Jersey."

Dread washed over him. "I'm sorry, but there has never been an 'us'." He had to speak frankly. "You just leaned over and kissed me, Pen. I was shocked, didn't know what to do. I guess I'd just have tried to laugh it off, pretend you were joking. Then I saw Sasha. She's my wife. I had to go after her. Try and make her understand."

That hadn't been easy. Sasha had gone looking for him because she was sick of his distance and what she'd seen as his emotional withdrawal from their marriage. He'd tried to let her know that there was nothing between him and Penny. She'd fired back that he was talking to another woman, confiding in her, and that was too much to take. She'd moved back to Jersey a week later, and he'd chased her like a puppy dog.

"You obviously managed to persuade her that she had nothing to worry about."

"Not entirely. I was overwhelmed by what had happened with Chapman. There was so much I couldn't talk about with her, confidential police stuff. We split up for a while and were headed for divorce. We've only just got back together."

She looked sympathetic. "I am sorry, Jack." She downed the rest of her wine and carefully set the glass down. "I better go before I do – or say – something I'll regret, again. Sleep tight, Jack."

He watched her walk away. He cared for Penny but had always known that it was as a fellow detective, a kindred spirit. Sasha was his love, his life, and he had to make sure she never had any further cause to doubt him.

# #

Le Claire had risen with the sun and been at his desk before anyone else. He needed to speak with Penny as soon as she came in. He wanted to make sure everything was okay between them. They had a job to do, and no personal issues could intrude. Team members had come and gone, but there was still no Penny. He checked his watch. It was past 10:00 a.m., which meant that Dewar should arrive soon.

The door banged open, and Penny rushed into the room. "Morning. Damn rail strikes. I waited ages for my train, and then it was on a total go-slow. Christ, I need a coffee."

She headed to the narrow kitchen area at the back of the room, and Le Claire followed her. She leaned against the counter as the kettle boiled, and her mouth lifted in a slight smile as she saw him. He took a deep breath. "Morning, Pen. Look, about last night. I want to make sure we'll be okay. You know, to work together."

She busied herself making coffee and didn't meet his eyes. "I know the score. You've made that clear. We're friends and always professionals. There's nothing else to say."

"I am sorry."

She held a hand up as if to ward off any further comment from him. "Let's just leave it, huh?"

He went to speak when his phone buzzed with a text. He quickly checked it. "I'll be back in a minute. My DS has arrived."

Le Claire didn't recognise Dewar when he saw her in the reception area. She wore a black fitted dress that showed off surprisingly long, slender legs. He didn't think he had seen Dewar's legs before, ever. Her mop of hair was neat and combed, and he could swear she even had some makeup on. A well-cut blazer kept the chill away and looked extremely professional. His surprise must have shown on his face.

Her words came out in a rush. "I didn't think it was appropriate to wear uniform and, well, I didn't want these London cops thinking we're all country hicks in Jersey. So I went shopping yesterday. Don't worry, I won't let you down." She looked so earnest he didn't have the heart to say anything. This wasn't a fashion show. Then he thought of Penny, even Graves and Barnes; there was a flashiness to all their dress, and he was glad that Dewar would at least feel that she fitted in.

His phone rang. It was Penny. He still had her number saved, and he idly wondered if that was a good thing or not. She was abrupt and to the point.

"We've got a case. A body has come in. Young girl, looks like an overdose. She's covered in track marks. The ID apparently matches that of a girl reported missing in Jersey. Meet us in the morgue."

Penny was waiting for them. The attendant led them into the coldly familiar area, where a body was laid out on one of the long metal worktables. The attendant moved forward and drew back the concealing sheet. She was pale, dark bruising vivid over the delicate facial area. Penny's voice was as ice-cold as the room.

"We have multiple bruise sites of varying ages. She's had a hard time recently." Penny shook her head. "She was found in a squat. The other residents didn't know much about her, but the body tells its own story. There are signs of frequent and recent sexual activity; she was used roughly. Track marks on the arms are recent. She was probably forced or coerced into using over a matter of months. Addiction grows quickly."

Her cropped, dyed blonde hair emphasised her fine features. He recognised her, had seen her photo only recently. He turned away in disgust.

#

Le Claire and Dewar were elbow deep in reports and computer printouts. Le Claire sighed and pushed back in his chair. "I can't get the Hamlyns out of my mind. Sarah Hamlyn would have been ruined if it came out that she'd had a kid from an affair. I don't think the crowd she runs with would approve at all."

"What if Scott was going to tell Ana? That would have caused a family rift and social uproar."

She was right, and they couldn't discount the Hamlyns from being party to Scott's death, either of them. His phone rang. He knew it was his from the ringtone. He'd been playing with his settings earlier and had accidentally changed the caller notification to "Duelling Banjos", the theme from the seventies movie *Deliverance*. He hadn't had the time to work out how to change it back.

His phone was in his jacket pocket, which was hanging by the door. Several pairs of eyes looked at him, and impatience battled with embarrassment. "Would someone mind getting that please?"

Penny snapped close the files she was reading. "I'll get it and say you're unavailable."

She picked up the phone, glanced at it quickly and answered. "DCI Le Claire's phone. Can I help you?"

She listened to the caller and then responded. "It's DI Penny Powers. I'm afraid the detective is busy. Who is this? Okay, I'll tell him."

She hung up. Looked defiant. "That was Sasha."

He momentarily closed his eyes. Shit. If anything was going to set his wife off, it was having his phone cosily answered by Penny. Why couldn't someone else have picked up the call? It took him a moment to realise that when Penny had looked at the screen, she would have seen the caller ID.

CHAPTER THIRTY-EIGHT

Ben was true to his word. He'd been waiting for Ana at Victoria Station with a hug and a kiss that made her burn.

The apartment he took her to was small, but it had two bedrooms, a comfortable lounge, a galley kitchen and a neat bathroom. He'd been apologetic about the size. "I usually just stay here on my own, and it's fine for one, but I guess it's small, and there is only one bathroom. I didn't think that through. I should have seen if Aidan had another one of his places that was empty. Sorry."

Ana burst out laughing. "Until last week, I was living in one room in someone's house. So no more apologies."

He shrugged. "Okay, okay. Guess I'm a little nervous. I like you, Ana, I really do." His eyes were locked on her face. He carried on before she could think what to say, and the moment was gone. "Come on. Let's dump your bags, freshen up and go get some dinner."

He'd suggested some fancy French place, but Ana had been adamant. "No, I can't afford that, Ben." She'd held a hand up to stop him protesting. "You paid last time we went out, so please let me pay for this. You bought our flights and train tickets and heaven knows what else, so please let me pay my way by getting dinner tonight?"

He'd reluctantly capitulated, and so they'd found a table at a small Italian place a few doors down from the flat. Plain wooden tables were topped with glowing candles, shiny cutlery and the obligatory red-and-white-checked napkins.

They'd eaten pasta, carbonara for Ben and ravioli for Ana, with a fresh green salad and plum tomatoes oozing with flavour. They'd debated over ordering garlic bread and decided it would be okay as long as they both ate it. Ben offered the almost-empty plate to Ana.

"You want the last piece?"

"No, thank you. I've had three slices already. I must stink of garlic!"

His laugh reached his eyes, crinkling the corners. He smiled easily and often, and Ana liked that – very much.

"It doesn't matter, does it? I mean, I'll be the only one close enough to you to notice. We'll just have to share garlic kisses."

Ana could feel her face heat at the suggestion that they'd be intimate later. She certainly hoped they would be.

Ben leaned across the table, and his hand brushed a stray lock of hair off her face. He opened his mouth to speak just as his phone rang. He pulled a mock grimace and shrugged his shoulders as he pulled his mobile from his pocket, checked the caller ID and said, "I better take this. Hello, Aidan. Yeah, we're having a great time."

Ben was quiet as he listened to the caller. Ana self-consciously looked around the room, trying to give him a little privacy. When she glanced back, the smile had gone from his face. His voice was resigned. "Okay, sure, I understand. We'll finish up here, and I'll head over." He disconnected the call. "Sorry. That was Aidan. He needs me to pick up some paperwork from one of his clubs that we'll need for the meeting tomorrow."

"No problem, let me settle up and we can go." She signalled for the bill.

"Thanks, Ana." Ben started to look a little uncomfortable. "I think I better go on my own. You can stay at the flat until I get back. The Beaumont isn't the type of club you'd like."

"What do you mean?"

If anything, he looked embarrassed. "It's what you'd call a gentlemen's club, although you do get women going there. It's a bit saucy, there are girls dancing and, well, as the night goes on, they're not wearing much, if anything at all."

Ana was open-minded, but she was surprised. "I wouldn't have imagined Aidan in that type of business."

"He's trying to get out. His UK clubs have made him a lot of money, but he's been selling them off. They don't fit in with how he wants to live his life now. He's only got the London ones left, and the meeting this weekend is to finalise their sale." He grimaced. "Mind you, don't mention that to Danny. He doesn't know yet."

Ana made up her mind. She'd never seen the inside of one of those places. "I'm coming with you. You don't think I'm letting you near a load of half-naked girls on your own, do you?" They were still laughing as Ana paid up and they left the restaurant.

#

The taxi stopped in front of an elegant Georgian building. The front steps were roped off, and two men manned the doors; both were well built and immaculately dressed. Ben greeted the men by name, and one of them promptly moved the rope to the side to allow them to enter.

As they went in, there was a coat-check area to one side and a woman in a low-cut halter-neck dress was checking the membership cards of the group who had arrived before them. Apparently, all was in order as she waved the men through with a smile. She turned, and her eyes lit when she saw Ben. "I wasn't expecting you this evening. What can I do for you?" Her voice was husky, and there was definite flirtation in her tone. Whether that was for Ben or just anyone who came in, Ana had no idea.

"Hi, Becca, I'm just on an errand. Is Danny around?"

"Sure, he's in the office. He knew you were coming and said to give him fifteen minutes and he'll be free."

Her eyes flicked toward Ana in a cool stare. She felt self-conscious, wishing she had worn something other than her jeans and plain top. At least she was wearing heels and had twisted and coiled her hair into an updo, which made her look less casual.

Ben introduced her. "Sorry, this is Ana. Ana, this is Becca, who basically runs the place."

Distant hellos were exchanged. Ana sensed that Becca wasn't a woman's woman. She dismissed her from her mind as she followed Ben down a long, narrow hall with mirrored walls. Black velvet curtains swagged around a closed door at the end. Ben opened it, and Ana reeled back as her senses were assaulted by pounding music and flashing lights. The club was set on different levels with an empty round stage dominating the centre. A pathway ran off it, like a catwalk, and this was no doubt where the girls came out front. There was a main bar on the ground level and several smaller ones on the tiers. Tables for two and four were scattered around the place. Ana's eyes were wide, and she took it all in as Ben held her hand and led her to the bar. He ordered a beer for himself and a white wine for Ana. He looked around. "Cheers, Ana. Come a bit closer, love. Don't want anyone bumping into you." There was a crowd at the bar, and Ben's arm rested possessively across her shoulder, their backs to the stage. She looked to the side and spotted a row of intimately lit alcoves, a voile-like fabric rendering the occupants into faint, shifting shadows. "What's in there? Or shouldn't I ask?"

Ben shook his head. "Ah, that's the lap-dance area. I guess that's to make it feel private when, in reality, anyone can see in."

Ana could see that several people stood outside each booth as they watched the dancers gyrate for their paying customers. She turned away. A dance tune had filled the air, and Ana could see the stage reflected in the mirror behind the bar. The crowd surged forward, and judging from the shouts and catcalls, the dancer was putting on a good show. The girl had long honey-blonde hair with subtle caramel streaks. She wore a tiny fringed string bikini, and waved a chiffon wrap in the air, drawing it over and around her body as she danced and posed, bending over and stretching. Ana thought it looked more like posturing than dancing, and maybe that's what it was. The girl had a great body, and the customers had paid to see it. She raised her arms, reached behind her neck and untied her bikini top. She held the loosened material to her full breasts for a heartbeat and then tossed it aside. Ana could feel her face burn and looked away from the mirror. There was a strange freedom in the girl's actions, and for a moment Ana didn't know who was being exploited – the woman who was reduced to nothing more than her looks and her body or the men who paid to watch but not touch. Ben was looking at her.

"I'm sorry. I shouldn't have brought you here. Look, drink up and we'll go and wait in the back for Danny to finish whatever he's doing."

She finished her wine but drank it a little too quickly. She could feel her head buzz immediately. Ben gently propelled her forward, his hand on her back as he navigated past the stage. Ana glanced up.

The girl was dancing, twisting and turning in an energetic frenzy. She raised her hands, thrust out her chest and shook her shoulders from side to side, her breasts, free from any restraints, jiggling and swaying. Suddenly, she spread her legs, bent forward and placed her palms on the ground, grinding her hips in a sexual parody. Still bent over, she brought her hands to her hips, pulled at the string ties and in one smooth movement stood up, threw back her head and ripped off her bikini bottoms. She stood tall, her hair back from her face, seemingly proud and confident in her nakedness. Her eyes were slightly unfocussed, and then her glance rested on Ana. Her eyes widened and her mouth dropped open as she took a step backward, and then stopped, as if rooted to the spot, a look of horror on her face.

In a moment of shocking clarity, Ana saw past the glamorous wig and heavy makeup. Irena! She advanced, her hand outstretched, as Irena ran off the stage, her nakedness displayed for all to see. Cheering men threw notes in her wake, twenty pounds here, and a fifty there.

Ana froze, and her stomach roiled and twisted as sour bile rose in her throat. She thrust a trembling hand against her mouth, closed her eyes and shakenly accepted that what she had seen was real. She turned to Ben in disbelief. "Ben, that's Irena, my friend. I need to go find her."

"We can try, but from the look on her face when she recognised you, she may not want to be found."

Ana was distraught. She had thought it awkward enough to be in a bar where women took their clothes off, but for it be Irena was mind-shattering. "I am so relieved to see her, but I'm just so shocked that she is stripping. That is not the Irena I know. Why would she do this?"

Ben looked at her as if measuring his response. "I think that perhaps you shouldn't judge your friend. She definitely won't want to see you if you belittle what she does."

"Belittle? I hardly think that I am wrong to criticise such an extreme move. I am surprised that you seem to think it's okay."

"I might be his cousin, but I work for Aidan. It isn't up to me to moralise on how he made his money. He is moving away from these businesses, and I want to be right by his side as he invests in other areas. I'm employed as his business manager – if Danny ever lets me get past him, that is. So it doesn't matter what I think about your friend's job. I think what matters is what she thinks, and maybe that is what you need to ask her."

Ana's eyes stung at the implied criticism, but she was also taken aback at this reminder that she didn't know Ben at all. She scanned the room and shuddered as she took in the glassy eyes and lustful looks. There were only a few women in the audience, and she recoiled as she realised some of the lascivious stares were directed at herself. Ben must have noticed as well, for his brows lowered, and his easy smile disappeared. "Come on, Ana, I need to get the papers, and then we'll see what we can do about your friend."

He moved easily through the club, obviously very familiar with the place. They walked to the opposite end of the room from the main bar. A stony-faced man leaned against the wall by the side of a closed door.

"Hi, Mike, I've got business in the back. Danny's expecting me."

"Okay, go on through. Mind you look after your little friend." His look was more like a leer, and Ana instinctively drew closer to Ben as she followed him through the doorway.

The deafening sounds from the bar were reduced to a subdued murmur as the heavy door closed behind them. "It's down here." Ben turned to the right and walked past several doors; one was open, and Ana could see a man and a woman sitting at a long table, counting money. Ben stopped outside a door near the end and entered after a perfunctory knock. "Hey, Danny, you ready for me?"

"I'm always ready for you, Ben. Come in. Ah, the lovely Ana is with you. Want a drink?"

Danny Gillespie sat behind a large smoked-glass desk in a big important-looking chair.

"No thanks, I'll just take the papers Aidan wanted and we'll be on our way."

Danny picked up a manila envelope and passed it to Ben. "Here you go. Any idea why he wants these figures?"

"Sorry, mate, he just called and asked me to pick up the envelope. I've to drop them round to him tomorrow. I think he just wants to check something."

Danny looked at Ben, a long, slow stare. "Well – you'd know, wouldn't you?"

Ben grabbed Ana's hand. "Come on, let's go."

Ana didn't move. She placed a hand on Ben's arm and spoke quietly, "Could we maybe ask Danny about Irena?"

Ben looked as if he was going to refuse, but the plea in her eyes must have softened his attitude. "You don't give up, do you?"

He asked Danny, "Look, tell me if this is awkward, but Ana just spotted a friend of hers. She was, well, I guess you could say she was dancing – on the stage, that is. Ana would like to speak with her."

Danny's eyes locked with hers, and his voice was gentle. "Ah, but will she want to speak to you? Not everyone would appreciate being recognised here. The Beaumont Club can get a little naughty."

Ana could have used other, more choice, words to describe what she had just witnessed outside, but she let it be. "Irena did run off the stage, but she is my friend, and I only want to know she is okay."

Danny pursed his lips, looked as if he was considering her words. "Tell you what, leave me your phone number, and I'll tell her you want her to call. Okay?"

She wanted to say more, to ask that he let her go to wherever the girls hung out when they weren't performing, but she figured she'd best take what was being offered. "Yes, that is fine, thank you."

CHAPTER THIRTY-NINE

The team had wanted to take Le Claire and Dewar for dinner. He had refused for both of them. They planned to pick up Danny Gillespie the next night and bring him in for questioning if all the relevant cross-jurisdictional formalities were in place. Their chief officer had written to the Met's equivalent asking for cooperation and assistance. They were now just waiting for the official reply. They were in a pizza place next to the hotel. The food was ordered, he was having what he thought was a well-deserved beer and Dewar was sipping at a robust red wine whilst they checked their emails. He'd called and texted Sasha, but it was no use. She wasn't answering her calls and hadn't replied to his texts. He'd have to sort everything out when he got back. Right now he needed to focus on his work. He looked up as Dewar puffed out a heavy sigh.

"Masters went to see Boris Tchensen and advised that we believe we've found Katrina's body. He was obviously devastated."

"The too-tight ring was a giveaway. It matched Tchensen's description of his late wife's engagement band. I don't think there is any doubt that it's her. Poor girl."

"I know. She was only trying to make a better life. What kind of bastard does this, just uses someone, gets them hooked on shit and then discards them, like they are nothing? It's horrifying."

"You ran through the report with Graves. How could this happen?"

"A story as old as time. Katrina's arms were riddled with needle marks and bruising from continued drug use. She was found inside a flophouse by the people she'd hooked up with. They'd known her for a couple of months. She said she'd come to London with her boyfriend for the weekend. Before she knew it, he had persuaded her to stay and got her a job in a club. Then he got tired of her or sick of how she'd turned to drugs. She was dumped and on the street with nowhere to go."

"Does anybody know anything about the boyfriend?"

Dewar shook her head. "Not yet, the case has been assigned to another team, and they're going to interview Mrs Armstrong. See if she knew who Katrina was hanging around with. It could be someone from Jersey or perhaps a bloke from London she met when he was in the island."

"It's heart-breaking, but we need to get back to our investigation. I'm sure that the Gillespies are connected to Scott Hamlyn in more ways than they've let on so far. Talk me through where we are."

"Okay. Lena Davies is apparently sticking to her story that she is just a fixer and that Danny Gillespie runs the whole show. He controls the drugs, the sex parties, everything."

"And therefore the blackmail."

"And Scott Hamlyn's dead body was found surrounded by cash, and he'd been paying into a charity about which we can't obtain any official details. Lena Davies is playing dumb and says she knows nothing as she was just one of several council members who sat at the top level of the foundation. She maintains her appointment was a nominee one and she left the running of the charity to the Panamanian resident members."

"Yes, the more I think about it, the more I am convinced that Danny is connected to all of this and had a good little earner going there. Apparently, he is at the club every night, so, warrants willing, we'll pick him up tomorrow."

Their food arrived, and they started to eat. A mechanical process that was more about fuelling the system than enjoyment. They had no time for that right now.

"What about the charity? Any update on getting financial data?"

"Absolutely nothing. Panama is surrounded by a wall of silence that you can't get through. The latest before I left was that we've gone higher, and there might be a government-to-government approach, but we need more cause for an order."

"Okay. Let's finish up and get some rest. We'll have a long day tomorrow."

Dewar's phone was on the table beside her plate. There was a buzz as a message came through.

"Sorry."

She picked it up and checked the text. Her eyebrows rose, and he could swear her eyes sparkled. "Everything okay?"

"Yeah, yeah, I mean, yes, sure."

She seemed a little distracted as they left the table and headed to their respective rooms.

Ana was shaken and subdued as she followed Ben into the apartment. She'd barely said a word during the taxi ride from the club. He walked straight to the kitchen, calling over his shoulder, "Go and get comfy in the lounge. I think we need a drink."

She kicked off her sandals and sank into the corner of the couch. Moments later, he was back with two large glasses of ruby-coloured wine. She took the proffered glass, sipped and her taste buds exploded.

"This is gorgeous." Her voice hitched a little, and she closed her eyes.

She felt the sofa cushions give as Ben sat down next to her.

"One of the good things about staying at one of Aidan's places is that he always has it stocked with decent wine. Cheers."

Before she opened her eyes, her body sensed how close he was. He turned toward her, and she saw the compassion in his eyes. "I'm sorry you had to see your friend like that. You okay?"

She shook her head. "I can't make sense of it. I mean, I've got over the initial shock, and I know it's up to Irena to do whatever she thinks is right…" She paused. "I guess I just feel so hurt. Why wouldn't she tell me she was okay? I can't count the number of messages I've left on her phone."

"Maybe she was embarrassed about what she was doing?"

"I can buy that, sure, but why couldn't she send a text? Anything, just to let me know she was still alive." She banged her hand against the armrest and rolled her shoulders to ease the tension that seeped through her body.

Ben moved forward. "Turn round." He indicated that she face away from him, and, setting down her glass, she did as he bade. Strong hands rested on her shoulders as he gently stroked, his fingers massaging deep into her muscles. "Oh, that's good, ouch!" The sweet release was a perfect blend of pleasure and pain.

"Sorry, you're wound up and knotted. You need to relax. Let me help."

His fingers stroked up her back in a feathery trail, caressing her shoulders and the nape of her neck. She closed her eyes and relaxed into the moment. How could the lightest of touches cause the deepest of sensations? She wasn't concerned about her tense muscles anymore; her focus was on the heat that was building deep within her.

"Ana, come here." His voice was gravelled, and when she faced him, she could see the desire burning in his eyes. He leaned closer until there was only a breath of air between them. His mouth covered hers, and she fell into the kiss. He pushed her back against the cushions until she was laying the length of the sofa, his mouth still nipping and teasing at hers. His stubbled chin rasped against her, but it wasn't unpleasant, and her body acted of its own accord as she arched and pressed closer to him, telling him in actions what she couldn't in words. His hands caressed as she held him close to her. His breath was heavy, and as he pushed up her top, his fingers stroked bare skin and a jolt of desire exploded within her. His hand travelled south, his fingers settling over the button of her jeans, which he opened with a flick and then pulled on the zipper.

Her eyes opened wide and stared into his, which were hooded and clouded. Reality hit. She laid a hand on his, gently pushed it to the side. "I'm sorry; this is just going too fast."

He stared at her for a long moment, and she wondered what was going through his head. He nodded, drew a slightly shaky breath and rolled over so he was lying next to her. He drew her zipper back up and her top down and held her close, her head resting on his chest. "I'd apologise, but I'm not sorry. I've been thinking about touching you ever since we met. I don't want to rush what's between us. Let's chill for a minute and then go to bed. You've had a long day."

She stiffened and then immediately relaxed at his rumble of laughter. "Separately, of course." He kissed the top of her head, and she burrowed into his side, hugging a smile deep inside her.

# #

Irena awoke with a start and sat up in bed, groggy and disorientated. The covers fell to her waist, and a chill raised the hairs on her arms, but it wasn't caused by the cool night air. There had been a noise – someone was in the apartment. She threw the duvet aside and crept out of the bed, squinting as she sought a weapon in the dark room. It had rained the day before, and she'd left her umbrella in the en-suite bathroom to dry. She tiptoed across the room, found the long-handled umbrella and wielded it in front of her as she slowly slipped through the open doorway, pausing for a moment to listen.

She knew someone was behind her before she heard the creak of a floorboard. She spun round, raised her weapon and felt like a fool as she realised who was in her apartment. The hunter's moon cast a wide beam through the lounge window, and the light pooled in the hallway, illuminating his familiar features.

"Oh, thank God it's you." She shrugged and gestured to the umbrella as she laid it against the wall. "See, I was prepared to battle intruders."

She could hear the laughter in his voice, and her heart flipped, as usual. "I've a mind to do battle of some sorts with you, but I had something more intimate in mind."

She reached up, draped her arms around his neck and drew him tight against her. "I've missed you. How was the dinner?"

"How these events always are. Boring. Sorry I'm so very late. It couldn't be helped."

"I wasn't expecting you, so I'm just happy that you're here."

He shrugged off his jacket, grabbed her hand and pulled her toward the bedroom. "I've got something for you."

She giggled, a high, girlish laugh full of anticipation. "I bet you have!"

"Down, girl. Wait and see what I've got."

He drew her onto the bed and pulled a plastic packet from his pocket. The pills were delicate white ovals, and her senses thrummed at what they might be. The pills she'd taken earlier were wearing off, and there was a jarring edge to her nerves that wanted soothing.

"Wait here."

He was back in a moment with two tumblers of clear liquid. She took the glass and the two pills he held out.

"Come on. Get these down you and you'll be nice and calm. You'll be a good girl."

She held the pills in her hand – she wasn't ready for numbness yet – and simply took a swig of the vodka, grimacing as the fiery liquid burnt a trail down her throat. "I had a bit of an upset tonight. I saw my friend Ana at the club."

He stiffened, and his glance was sharp. "Did you now? Who was she with?"

"I don't know. I couldn't see. I panicked when I saw her and ran off the stage. Then I got to wondering what reason she would have to be there. She wasn't expecting to see me. I could tell by her face. Ana couldn't do what I do. The money is great, and I know you like watching me, but Ana, she's too naive for all this."

She chewed the side of her finger, worrying away at a jagged nail. Ana would never cope in this world. Perhaps her being there was just a coincidence. She pushed the thoughts away. She couldn't do anything about them, for she wasn't going to call Ana and speak to her.

He ran a finger over her shoulder, pushing down the thin strap of her nightgown; the top loosened and exposed one high breast, which filled his groping hand. "How did it feel? To have her look at you? Were you naked?"

"God, yes, I was. It was awful."

His hand kneaded her breast. "Irena, we've been together a little while now, and it's time we moved to the next level."

Her stomach flipped, and she took a deep breath, waiting for his next words. Would he live with her permanently?

"You know I love to see you on the stage, being looked at by other men, even by the women. The power you hold over them turns me on so much, knowing that it's me you'll be fucking later."

His crude choice of words left a jarring note, but the talk still excited Irena, and she leaned closer, the pills falling from her palm. He looked at her short cap of hair, and something reminiscent of disappointment crossed his face. Was he bothered that she wasn't wearing the wig? Surely not, for it was she he wanted, wasn't it?

He continued in his soothing, seductive whisper, "You know what I'd love? There's a party next week, a very private affair. It'll be just me, you and a few like-minded others."

She frowned. "I don't know what you mean by that."

He smirked. "Oh, come on, don't play coy. Just a few friends indulging their senses, enjoying what – and who – they want. You'll love it. I want you on your knees, another man behind you, but you're looking at me, right at me as he does as he pleases."

"Christ, you're insane." She jumped off the bed and stood in front of him. "That is sick. I am not going to be doing anything like that, and I am disgusted that you could even suggest it. You repulse me. Get out."

His face darkened as he stood and slapped her. She reeled back, stumbling against the wall. "You little bitch. Don't ever talk back to me – ever. You hear me?"

She held a hand to her throbbing face in disbelief that he had hit her. His face was red and his eyes hard. She didn't recognise him like this. The devil on her shoulder whispered that she'd rarely been drug-free in her dealings with him over the last weeks, and she'd simply done as he directed. Well, screw him. No one hit her and got away with it.

"That's it. I'm leaving. I'm going to phone Ana. She'll help me. You touch me again and I'll have you done."

He laughed. Such a simple action, yet it chilled her.

"You're going nowhere, nor will you be speaking to Ana. You'll do as you're told and stop this defiance. You're my woman, and I own you. Get on the bed." He unbuttoned his shirt and started to undo his trousers.

She cowered into the corner and glanced at the open bedroom door. If she ran, she could maybe get out onto the street. It must be 3:00 a.m., perhaps later, but London cabs ran beneath her window all night long. Surely, someone would stop for her.

"Don't even think about." He kicked the bedroom door shut and locked it, placing the key on the dresser. He turned back to her, holding the wig in his hands. "I'll tell you what we're going to do. You're going to wear this and do exactly as I want."

He threw the wig at her, and it landed by her feet. Her mind settled on and discarded options till she was left with none. She bent her head and, with fumbling fingers, put the wig on, tugging the long caramel locks until they framed her face.

His smile was a lupine leer. "Come on, Laura, come to me."

She had no choice. She rose to her feet and crossed to the bed, but all she could think was, *Who the hell is Laura?*

CHAPTER FORTY

Ana was already showered and dressed as the sun began its golden ascent over the rooftops of London. She'd lain awake for an age last night as she replayed in her mind every look, every word, every touch that had passed between them, marvelling that this man appeared to have real feelings for her. She had hugged the thought to her like a comforter as she drifted off to sleep. A noise had briefly awoken her at some point. It sounded like a door creaking open and then being carefully closed. Sleep had overtaken her in seconds, and she'd next awoken just as the dawn was flirting with the horizon.

There was a small balcony that ran off the galley kitchen with just enough room for a bistro-style table and two chairs, and it was here that Ben found her as he stepped, bleary-eyed, onto the balcony. He eyed the pot of coffee and said in a voice heavy with sleep, "I thought I smelled something delicious."

Ana poured him a mug of the steaming brew, and he briefly closed his eyes in appreciation as he sipped. "Okay, starting to feel human now. Did you sleep well?"

"Yes, except I did wake in the night. I thought I heard a door closing."

He looked shamefaced. "Sorry, that was me. I got a call from Aidan at gone 2:00 a.m. He couldn't wait for the figures I picked up from Danny, and he needed me to get them round to him."

"At that time?"

"Yeah, he was talking to his lawyer in the States on Skype, and they wanted to redo the sale terms for the contract we'll be discussing today." He checked the clock on the wall. "I better get moving. The meeting starts at nine thirty, and Aidan will want us to have a debrief first. Are you sure you'll be okay on your own?"

"Absolutely. I am going to take a walk through Leicester Square and maybe have some lunch at Covent Garden."

"Great. I'll be finished up by mid-afternoon, so I'll give you a call. We can maybe sit somewhere nice and have a drink before we come back and get ready for dinner. I'll call you."

"Sure." Ben went off to get showered and dressed for business, and Ana helped herself to another cup of coffee. Thoughts of Scott crowded her mind as she gazed out at the Georgian buildings that lined the leafy square, which was a verdant oasis in a sea of concrete and tarmac. She knew her cousin could be withdrawn and difficult with some people, but that wasn't enough reason to kill a man. She had called her aunt before she flew to London but had to leave a message on the answerphone. Sarah Hamlyn wasn't picking up, or at least not for Ana.

With Scott gone, her reason for coming to Jersey had disappeared. She had wanted to be part of a family again, searching for connections to fill the gaping hole created by her parents' deaths. Admittedly there was Ben now; however, he seemed to spend a lot of time in London. Maybe she should become a big-city girl instead of a small-island one? She might even visit some recruitment agencies today. See what London had to offer a girl like her. Irena was here, and perhaps, over time, she would let Ana back into her life. Her mind made up, she finished her coffee and went to enjoy the day ahead.

Le Claire had been at the Met for hours. He'd had an early breakfast and texted Dewar to say he'd meet her at Penny's offices whenever she was ready. He used a secure remote access to pull up his files in Jersey via HOLMES 2. The IT system was a far-advanced mechanism to collate all data related to a crime, such as witness statements, evidence logs and situation and update reports. He could see that the team, led by Masters, had been chipping away at Lena and Basil Davies. Lena protested her innocence, but it was her name that was on everything. She couldn't say how they sourced the properties, and was at pains to explain how they never caused even a smidgen of damage and left the places cleaner than they'd found them. She figured the owners never even knew. Le Claire didn't doubt that. He winced whenever he recalled the stench of ammonia at the Blacks' place, and his eyes virtually watered at the memory.

A shadow fell across his desk, and he looked up to see a sombre-faced Gareth Lewis.

"Hi, Jack, can you spare me five minutes? Let's go get a coffee."

"Sure." He grabbed his jacket and followed Gareth, who stopped by the industrial-style coffee machine in the corridor. Le Claire's heart sank. "You wouldn't know a decent cup of coffee if it introduced itself to you."

Gareth snorted. "I'm not paying over two pounds for a hot drink made by some trendy barista. It's 50 pence a pop here and perfectly okay. My treat."

"Thanks." What else could he say? As soon as possible, he was heading to the coffee shop at the end of the street. He could wait, he could.

Gareth collected the tiny plastic beakers from the machine and nodded at a door across from them. "Be a good lad and open that up. We can chat in there."

Le Claire followed his old boss's orders, and they entered the meeting room. Gareth placed the cups on the wooden table and flicked a row of switches, bathing the room in an electronic glow. Le Claire sniffed. The coffee didn't smell too bad. He sipped and cringed; it was foul.

Gareth took a long draught and drank half his coffee. He set the cup down, smacking his lips in unmistakable appreciation. "Right, bad news, so I'll just spit it out."

Le Claire tensed. "Go on."

"We've had word that Chapman is claiming intimidation and police brutality."

He exploded out of his chair. "This has to be a joke. We've been down this road already, and I was cleared of any wrongdoing."

Gareth's voice was calm, aimed at soothing. "I know, but the context is different this time. No one doubted that you had to use extreme force to get him to stop. He also had at least one knife on him that he wasn't afraid to use. He slashed your arm up pretty good."

Le Claire touched his left arm in an automatic motion. The visible scars had healed fine. He sighed. "So what's being said now?"

There was a pause, infinitesimal, but enough for him to know he was not going to like whatever came out Gareth's mouth next.

"His defence team is saying that he's terrified of you. That you had it in for him and just wanted to pin the blame on someone so you didn't look like you couldn't do your job. They're citing the speed with which you've moved up the ranks and saying that you couldn't afford to fail. That you had to get someone charged for these crimes. All young girls, emotive stuff."

"Bullshit! He told me where he'd left April Baines. Let's not forget the bastard buried her alive."

Gareth rubbed at his temples. "I know, I know. Fact is, you were alone in that hospital room with Chapman apart from a nurse who is now saying she couldn't exactly overhear what you both said. His lawyers are claiming that you found out about April from other sources and that you came to Chapman before searching for her to make it look like he was the one who told you where she was. Chapman is saying he never told you anything, that he never confessed, and he's been too scared until now to speak up."

Le Claire picked up the inference. "So that's what the scene on Wednesday was about. This is utter nonsense."

"I know. But it keeps Chapman on remand and out of a courtroom, giving his team more time to spin their fabrications and throw mud at you."

"What should I do?" He felt like a probationer again, looking to his mentor for guidance.

"For the moment? Nothing at all. The prosecution will work with us to get this sorted out."

His stomach was knotted, and his head was starting to pound. He didn't need this, not today.

Irena awoke slowly, and it took a moment for the foggy cloud of sleep to clear enough for her to remember. She lay flat on her back and willed the shadowed, jumbled memories to become clearer. After her dance. She had, oh God, she had seen Ana, beautiful innocent Ana, and run away, her shame racing after her. How could she ever look at her now? Especially after what had happened later.

She had cried herself to sleep after he had gone. The man who professed to love her had rummaged in her bag and taken her mobile and tablet before leaving her, alone in the dark, without a word. She'd heard the unmistakable click of the lock turning and had rushed to the door, banging on it for the bastard to let her out. She had winced and rested a hand against the door frame to steady herself.

He had been rough, and she could feel a dull ache between her legs. Her head ached too, and she regretted not taking the beautiful pills. Why did she have to remember? Why couldn't she stay in oblivion? Why?

She lay back down on the bed, unseeing eyes staring at the ceiling. The air was heavy, and dust motes floated in the light beams. Christ only knew what time it was. She rolled over onto her side and froze when she heard a noise.

The door opened, and there he was.

She tried to keep her voice strong and hated that it wobbled. "I don't understand? I thought we were going to be together now? I've done everything you wanted. If that isn't enough, can't you just let me go, please?"

"Afraid not. You don't leave until I kick you out, and I'm not ready to do that yet." He tossed a paper bag onto the bed. It bounced, and the contents – a croissant, small sandwich and a bottle of water – spilled out onto the cover. "That should see you through most of the day. Oh, don't go anywhere, will you?"

His mocking laugh filled the air but didn't mask the locking of the door as he left. She looked around her prison and silently screamed.

CHAPTER FORTY-ONE

Le Claire chewed on a slice of spicy pepperoni pizza as he mentally reviewed their plans. He sighed at the thought of what Sasha would say if she knew he'd had pizza two nights in a row. Then he remembered she wasn't talking to him. She certainly wasn't answering his calls. He drew his mind back to the investigation. Everything was in order; the cooperation paperwork was in place. Le Claire and Dewar would accompany Penny and Graves to the club. Barnes and a uniform would provide backup support in case matters got out of hand. Danny was going to be picked up for questioning in relation to procurement and solicitation of prostitution, the attack on Laura Brown and, for good measure, the blackmail of Sir Hugh Mallory.

He filched another slice from the open cardboard delivery boxes that were littered over the meeting table. The team was having some sustenance and ironing out any last-minute issues. He thought that at another time it would be good to sit with this crowd of people and talk shop and simply relax. His eyes flicked across the table to Penny. Maybe not with her though. He was sure she'd pulled a fast one and that she'd clocked the ID and seen it was Sasha calling before she answered his phone. He didn't want to analyse that too deeply; didn't want to wonder if he had led Penny on, even if he hadn't realised it.

He brushed away any thoughts of his personal life. He suddenly realised that Sasha was right; there were times, like this, when his job did take precedence over their relationship. He was a husband, but he was also a policeman, and when conflicts arose, he couldn't run home to pacify his wife. He had a job to do. The knot of worry that maybe this time Sasha was done for good wouldn't go away though, so he'd bury it deeper until all this was over.

Dewar was thinking. He could see it on her face, the way she stared at one spot on the table, unblinking. "The money Scott was paying to the foundation. What if it wasn't blackmail to keep quiet about Laura's past, but about Ana's beginnings?"

He gave her his full attention. "Now that would narrow the field. I'm sure more people knew about Laura than ever had a thought that the moral-crusader Sarah Hamlyn had an affair that resulted in a child. But why would the blackmailer kill Scott? He was their cash cow. Look at the money floating in the pool; he was happy to pay and pay, by the looks of it."

She sighed, and her shoulders slumped. "Yeah, you're right."

"Maybe, maybe not. But if Danny Gillespie is our blackmailer, we'll be asking him these questions later tonight."

Ana was having the best of days. She'd mooched through London, peered in the windows of some job agencies and lunched alfresco at Covent Garden, people-watching and staring, enthralled, at the street entertainers. She'd pushed Irena from her mind. She didn't know where her friend was, and her calls weren't being picked up.

Ben had phoned, and they'd met by the Embankment and sipped chilled rosé as they watched the river boats and cruisers glide past on the Thames. They'd meandered through the London streets, talking and laughing until they reached the apartment. Dinner was a quiet affair at a Thai restaurant. And now they were back at the club.

Ben was apologetic. "I need to have a chat with Aidan about today's meeting. He stayed on to have a drink with the buyer, and I just hope he didn't scupper the deal. He can get feisty."

"No problem. Maybe I could try and find Irena whilst we're here. I just want to speak to her."

He gave her a long, intense look. "I'm not sure what you'll find. Sometimes people just want to be lost."

"I know, but I need to try."

"Come on, then."

She followed Ben through to the back of the club. Away from the gloss and glitter of the front, backstage was functional and business like. Ben stopped in front of a closed door. There was a froth of laughter floating through the wood, and cheap perfume scented the air. He gave her a sheepish half smile and pushed the door open. The noise increased, and Ana drew back, suddenly unsure of what lay ahead. Half a dozen girls, all in various stages of undress, were putting on makeup, teasing their hair and applying fake tan; the pungency of the latter made Ana gag slightly.

Ben strode into the middle of the room, and Ana saw a light blush cover his face in response to the catcalls from the girls. A statuesque brunette with gleaming, dark skin turned away from the mirror and faced them. "Ben, what are you doing here? Not your usual haunt." She peered behind him at Ana. "I see you brought your own entertainment. Nice." There was a bubble of laughter in her voice mingled with sultry French accent, and Ana couldn't take offence.

"Marianne, this is Ana. She's looking for her friend Irena, who's working here."

Marianne looked her up and down. "She isn't here tonight. I guess she is off. Sorry." With that, she turned back to the mirror.

"She's left." The voice came from a bored-looking blonde who was perched on the dressing table counter, one leg bent as she applied shiny red polish to her toenails.

Ben asked, "I don't think we've met before. Who are you?"

"Misty Bennett, who are you?" Her bored look had disappeared, her head was tilted flirtatiously and Ana thought the woman was going to lick her lips. Ben was a good-looking guy, but Ana had a feeling the likes of Misty Bennett were more interested in his expensive-looking clothes and the watch on his wrist. Ana decided to break up Misty's daydream. "What do you mean Irena has left? Where has she gone?"

Misty rolled her eyes. "I'm not her keeper, how would I know? I just got a call to say I had to work tonight 'cos Irena wasn't coming back."

Ben addressed the room in general. "And no one knows any more?"

He was met by blank looks and silence. "Right, thanks." He took Ana's hand and led her from the room. Now she had no idea where Irena was. Did her friend want to avoid her so much that she had given up her job? Ana didn't know where to turn next.

# #

Ana was still waiting for Ben. He'd told her to stay at the end of the bar, next to Mike, the leering bouncer. She'd lasted five minutes before she'd sidled to the bar and ordered a drink. Then she'd wished she had stayed where she was. The glances aimed in her direction were direct and calculating. She self-consciously pulled at the front of her top to make sure it hadn't dipped too low. She wished she had worn different clothes, but she had wanted to look her best for Ben. Her tight jeans and high heels were topped by a silky top with tiny straps that fully exposed her smooth shoulders. Her hair, soft and shining, cascaded down her back.

The thunderous music and flashing lights from the stage disorientated her. The crush of people, mainly men, gave a threatening tinge to an atmosphere that already seemed heavy with menace.

"Hey, sweetheart, join me for a drink." She turned and faced the speaker, a middle-aged man of average height with a florid face and a shirt that strained to contain his stomach. It was the predatory look in his eyes that was the worst. His hand held tight to her bare arm, and Ana winced as his fingers dug into her skin.

She looked around, vainly, in the hope of getting some help. No one was looking. They were all too intent on their own pleasures and vices.

She found her voice, kept it firm. "No thanks, I'm with someone."

"But he's not here, sweetheart, and I am. So come and be nice to me."

He pulled her toward him just as a dark-clad arm snaked out and removed the hand that was restraining her. "There you are. Come along, darling."

Ana turned with relief and registered surprise as she looked into Danny Gillespie's handsome face. He turned to the man. "Sorry, I'll have to steal this lovely away from you." With a flick of his fingers, he summoned the bartender. "A bottle of champagne for the gentleman, please, on the house."

The man lost his belligerent expression and smiled. "Thanks," he turned to Ana and winked, "when he's done with you, feel free to come back and look for me, if I'm not otherwise occupied, that is." And he laughed.

Ana shivered as she felt Danny tense. His voice was icy, and from the expression on the other man's face, his features no doubt looked as cold as he sounded.

"She's with me, okay?"

The man nodded, looking a little pale. "I didn't mean any offence, sorry."

Danny turned to Ana and steered her toward the door to the offices. "Come on; let's get you out of here. Where's Ben?"

She gratefully followed him. "He had to speak to your brother. Ben told me to stay where I was and not move but…"

He flashed a smile. "You moved, huh?"

She could feel the blush spreading across her face. "Yes."

"Don't worry. You can wait in my office. Come on in."

Without asking, he poured her a generous glass of red wine from a nearly empty bottle that sat on his desk. He picked up the desk phone and dialled a number. "Hi, it's me. If you see Ben, can you send him into my office? Tell him Ana is waiting for him here."

He gestured for her to sit, and she sank into a leather armchair. Danny rested on the edge of the desk, his legs stretched out in front of him. "So, Ana, did you ever speak to your friend – what was she called again?"

"Irena, and no. She didn't call me. I came here with Ben tonight in the hope I would see her, but she is not here. One of the girls says she has left. I think maybe I frightened her away."

He looked a little disinterested. "Girls come and go here. They earn a little money and then move on; sometimes they find someone to look after them. Someone who will keep them around on a more permanent basis."

While he was speaking, he had opened another bottle of wine and poured himself a huge glass; he drained half of it. Ana realised that although Danny seemed okay, his eyes were glassy and a little unfocussed. He looked like he'd been drinking a lot, and suddenly she didn't feel comfortable. She'd go and wait back in the bar near the door to the offices; surely, Ben wouldn't be that long, and he'd soon come to collect her.

She stood up. "I think I should go now. Thank you for the drink, but I don't want to take up any more of your time."

Ana had to pass Danny to get to the door. She gasped as he reached out, grabbed her arm and pulled her back. He trapped her against him and smirked. "Not so fast. Stay for a bit. Then we'll see what happens."

She pushed her upper body as far away from him as possible. His arms had snaked around her waist and held tight. "Ben will be here soon." She realised there was a warning in her voice, and she hoped it was justified. Ben relied on the Gillespies for a living. Would he stand up for her?

"No, he won't, love I didn't switch the handset on, so I didn't tell anyone to let him know where you are. No one's coming."

As Danny bent his head to kiss her, Ana struggled, and as she did so, a bubbling rage coursed through her. She was sick of being vulnerable, of people – mainly men – trying to take advantage, but most of all she was sick of herself for her timidity. Ana realised she only had herself to rely on.

"Leave me alone, I mean it."

His mirthless laugh echoed through the room. She took a deep breath, eyed the distance to the door and, raising her leg as fast as she could, kneed Danny Gillespie directly in the balls.

"Arghhh, you bitch."

He released her and, bending over, cupped himself. Ana ran for the door. She stumbled and went down on one knee. Her bag fell to the ground, the contents spilling out. She quickly stuffed everything back inside, tucked the bag under her arm and ran toward the door.

His voice hollered after her. "You don't know who you're dealing with, what I can do to girls like you. I'll make you sorry." His voice trailed away and finished on a groan.

Ana wrenched open the door and sped down the hallway. The entrance to the bar was unguarded on this side. She slowed, opened the door and sailed past the goon standing outside.

The man barely glanced at her before he went back to scanning his mobile. Ana looked around. The place was heaving, and the sleaze factor had edged up a notch or two. A topless dancer was gyrating on the stage; the way she was suggestively fingering the ties of her string bikini bottoms had the crowd screaming, their obscenities seeming to egg her on. Ana had no doubt that the girl would be completely naked in a moment, and she didn't want to be around when that happened.

She headed toward the exit with not a little trepidation. She didn't know what was worse, staying inside this club where she was now sure the few females present offered more than a dance or a cocktail, or to go and hang about outside in the dark. She'd take her chances with the night.

CHAPTER FORTY-TWO

Le Claire was ready. He was with Dewar, Penny and Graves. There was no doubt in his mind that Danny Gillespie was guilty. Guilty of many things, not all that had been proven yet. Intel said he was in the building, and they were going to bring him in for questioning. The woman at the front had been challenging, to say the least. It was only when he had threatened to call the entire Met into the building that she had relented.

They'd followed her through the club, thick with smells of booze and sex and anticipation. She led them through a door, past a growling bouncer, and stopped and indicated to her left. "In there."

She entered the room first. "Danny, I'm sorry. It's the police."

Danny Gillespie stood as they came in. His eyebrows rose as he welcomed Le Claire. "This is a surprise, Detective; you've come all the way from Jersey to see me, and with your redoubtable sidekick." His gaze flicked past Dewar and rested on Penny. "Now who is this lovely? Let me see your pretty smile."

Penny's smile was non-existent.

Le Claire ignored his comments. "We'd like you to come into the station for a chat."

"This is bullshit. You have nothing on me, and," his smile was sly, "you certainly don't have any jurisdiction outside your little island. So I think we'll leave it at that, don't you?"

Penny smiled. "I'm DI Powers of the Met, and this is DI Graves, and we have more than enough authority, so yes, you're coming in with us."

"Look, if this is about Laura, I didn't touch her. I haven't even seen her in ages."

Le Claire said, "We've been talking to another friend of yours."

"Who is that, then?"

"Lena Davies. Quite a talker when she gets going."
The easy smile slid off Danny's face.

Ana collected her coat as she left the club. She was ignored by the bouncers, who seemed more concerned with who wanted to come in than who was leaving. She quickly scanned her surroundings. She didn't know London, didn't have a clue what kind of neighbourhood this was but thought maybe it wasn't the worst. Across the road were a couple of small restaurants, and there were some bars with tables spilling onto the pavement. The night was cool, but patio heaters lit and warmed the small seating areas. There was a late-night coffee shop directly across the road. She would sit by one of the windows and keep an eye on the door of the club; that way she could see Ben as soon as he left. It would all be fine.

She reached into her bag and was rummaging for her phone when what she saw completely surprised her.

David Adamson was just leaving the club. He looked as taken aback to see her as she was to see him. "What on earth are you doing here, Ana?"

Her smile was brief. "I'm waiting for my boyfriend. He had some business here."

"Are you okay? You look a bit on edge."

"I'm fine. I had a little incident, and someone upset me."

"You should wait inside. Not in that main area, but I'm sure Danny Gillespie – he runs the place – would find somewhere quiet for you to wait. Come on, I'll take you to him, show you the way."

"NO! I mean, no, thank you – not Danny Gillespie. Look, I have something to tell you. I've seen Irena. She's been working here."

"This place? Have you spoken to her?"

"No. Then tonight I hear that she has left and isn't coming back. It just strikes me as odd. I don't care if I look like a fool. My boss's son is a policeman, and he used to work in London. I'm going to ask him if he can help. I've already mentioned Irena to him, and now I can tell him where I last saw her."

"Look, we're on the same mission. I thought I saw Irena with

Aiden Gillespie yesterday. I came back here to see if I could find anything out, but he isn't in."

Ana was tense. "Surely, she'll be okay if she is with Aidan."

"Aidan Gillespie isn't the man a lot of people think he is. There are stories, rumours, about him. I think he's capable of anything. I brokered a real-estate deal for him a few months back. He's moving into development, and the property is lying empty. I thought maybe he'd taken her there. I thought I'd go and have a look and just satisfy myself she is okay."

"I'm coming with you." She had to; there was no way she would leave Irena in trouble.

He looked taken aback and was shaking his head before she had finished speaking. "No, stay here. There isn't any need."

"I'll just follow you, David. We are wasting time arguing. If Irena is hurt, I can help her whilst you deal with Aidan Gillespie. Come on."

He looked resigned. "Fine, this way. I borrowed a car from one of the guys, said I needed to check out something for Aiden."

She fumbled around in her bag. "Let me leave a quick message for Ben." Her hand came out empty. "Damn. I must've left my phone at the apartment. Can I borrow yours?"

David Adamson looked impatient. "You can call him when we find Irena. Come on, we should hurry. She might be in danger."

#

Danny was standing behind his desk with a defiant look. He was refusing to speak until he'd spoken to his lawyer. Le Claire was about to ask Penny if they could take him into the station when a young man ran into the room, stopping as he saw the restrained Danny. Le Claire recognised him straightaway. It was the Gillespies' cousin, Ben.

"Ben. We've met before. I'm DCI Le Claire."

He looked confused. "Le Claire? From Jersey? What's going on?"

"We're just having a word with your cousin. You came in here fast enough. Anything wrong?"

"I'm looking for my girlfriend." He addressed his next comment to Le Claire. "I've been seeing Ana Zielinska. She's joined me for the weekend."

Le Claire kept his face impassive. Getting hooked up with the Gillespies wasn't for the faint-hearted. Ana seemed to attract trouble, or maybe it was her that found it?

Ben continued speaking, "I wondered if she was in here."

Danny Gillespie was immediately on the defensive. "Oh, for Christ's sake. I only kissed her."

"You did? What the hell is going on, Danny?"

"I'm being questioned by PC Plod here, so I'm not too bothered about your missing girl at the moment."

"Where did she say she was going? I went to see Aidan, but he wasn't there. I've spent the last half hour hanging about on the off-chance he'd come in. Ana wasn't where I left her."

Dewar asked the obvious, "Did she call you, maybe leave a message – or did you call her?"

"I don't have any missed calls, and I thought she'd be by the bar. You can't hear a phone ring in there; it's so damned loud. I'll call her now."

He pulled out his phone, dialled, pressed it to his ear and listened. The silence of the room was broken by a musical ringtone. Ben looked horrified. "That's Ana's phone. Where is it?"

"Here." Penny bent down and retrieved the phone from under the sofa.

Ben growled at Danny, "How the hell did Ana's phone get left here?"

Danny held his hands up in mock-defence. "I don't know. I think she dropped her bag when she ran out. She must've left the phone behind."

"Ran out? You're a piece of work." Ben lunged at Danny and, drawing back his arm, threw a punch that knocked his cousin back on his heels. He landed in his chair with a thud and an astonished look.

Le Claire laid a restraining hand on Ben's arm. "He's not worth it. I'll let you away with that one because he deserved it. Keep calm."

#

They had parked the car on the road outside the building. David Adamson had beckoned her to follow him up to the front door of the partially boarded-up building. "This is it. I'm going to feel an utter prat if the place is empty."

Ana whispered. "I just want to know she is okay."

He nodded and carefully unlocked the front door and went in first. A narrow hall ran through the building with a set of bare, wooden stairs leading to the next level. Their footsteps echoed on the bare floorboards. Silence. Nothing but the muted sound of outside life, cars driving by and the odd beep of a horn.

She whispered, "Are you sure this is the place? There doesn't seem to be anyone here."

Just at that, she heard the faintest scuffle, a scraping against wood, then the voice, faint, yes, but a voice all the same. It was coming from upstairs. She looked at David. He pressed a finger to his lips and beckoned her to stay behind him as he climbed the stairs. There was a door at the end of the corridor. David reached into his pocket, fumbled with a bunch of keys and, selecting one, unlocked the door. He slowly opened the door wide and crept in. Ana's heart was hammering, and she had a passing thought that they should maybe have called the police.

They were in a surprisingly neat and tidy apartment. The doors along the hallway lay open; the one farthest from them was firmly closed. There was a key in the lock. Her eyes sought David's. He nodded, turned the key and eased the door open.

It was a pretty bedroom, and Ana's eyes were immediately drawn to the shape on the bed. Irena lay in a foetal position, her face to the wall. David placed a guiding hand in the small of Ana's back and gently propelled her into the room. Irena jerked round, and after a moment of confusion, her eyes lit with joy. "Oh, Ana, thank God, thank God. How did you get here? The bastard locked me in. You need to help me."

She looked past Ana at David Adamson. Her eyes widened in shock, and she shrank back against the wall. "Oh, Ana, you fool, what have you done?"

#

"What the hell is going on here?"

Le Claire looked to the open door. Aidan Gillespie strode in. "What's the problem, Le Claire?"

"Gillespie, this is DI Powers and DI Graves. We need to talk to your brother about his suspected involvement in various crimes, including prostitution, blackmail and murder."

Gillespie's face reddened. Le Claire tensed, ready for a fight. Gillespie surprised him by turning to his brother. "You little shit. I gave you everything, everything, and this is how you repay me?"

"Aidan, it's crap. You know me."

"Yes, I do, and I've ignored the truth for years. I knew you were skimming from the business, stealing from me, but prostitution? Christ."

Le Claire went in for the hammer blow. "And the drugs. We think Danny has been bringing drugs into the island, and he is a person of interest regarding the vicious attack on Laura Brown."

"You bloody fool. Laura came to see me the night of the party. Said you'd been phoning her. I can just hear you, all sly remarks and crude innuendo. Christ, Danny, why?"

"Because I'm sick of it being about you. I can be a businessman too, you know."

Danny Gillespie had a whining edge to his voice, and Le Claire wanted to tie this up. "Why did you kill Scott Hamlyn? What was he to you, Danny? A disgruntled customer?"

He saw genuine surprise on Danny's face that took him aback. "I don't know what you're talking about. Why would I kill Hamlyn?"

"He came to see you at the party. Brought you cash. Was it blackmail money? Weren't the monthly payments enough?"

Danny shook his head. "No idea what you're talking about. His death stopped the payments. Why would I do that? I never dealt with that side of things. That was David."

A sick awareness was taking hold of Le Claire. "David who?"

Danny sighed. "I'm no snitch, but I'm not getting hammered with all this shit." He had the resigned look of a man who was going down, but not alone. "David Adamson. It was his idea. We used the empty properties he looked after to throw some pretty good parties. Anything-goes affairs. People have hearty appetites in the island and plenty of spare cash. We were raking it in. He even set up a foundation to make it look like they were paying into a charity. Sometimes we'd make a bit extra when they really had something to hide. He was seeing this Irena. He brought girls over every now and again from Jersey. They never seemed to stay with him long."

The shrill ring of the desk phone captured their attention. It rang several times, stopped, and started to ring again.

Le Claire said, "Graves, put that on speaker. Danny, get rid of them."

The ringing stopped and was replaced with a gruff baritone. "Danny, it's Sam. Is Ben with you?"

Danny glanced at his cousin. "Yes, what's up?"

"He was looking for his girl. George just came back on the door, said he saw her heading off earlier. She was with a bloke."

Ben was at the desk in a second. Leaning over the phone, he demanded, "Sam, who was Ana with?"

"That estate agent guy. David something."

Ben's voice cut across the room. "He's got Ana! Where would he take her?"

Danny shook his head. "He stays at my place when he's here. I can't imagine he'd go there."

Le Claire asked, "Is there anywhere he would keep whoever he was seeing?"

Aidan Gillespie spoke into the silence. "He bought a building for me a few months ago. We're awaiting planning consent to convert it back to one dwelling. It's split into flats at the moment."

Le Claire turned to Penny. "Dewar and I will search there. We'll need some of your men."

"Graves can tidy up here. I'm with you, and we'll gather some of the guys from outside."

Ana huddled on the bed with Irena, trying to make sense of what was happening. Irena was incredulous. "I don't know what has come over him. I know I've been a bit lippy lately, but he's gone nuts. He wanted me to get involved with his dirty little orgies. Well, I told him what I thought of that."

"Like the party you got me the waitressing job at?"

"Oh, did you still go to that? Yeah, I mean I knew he helped organise them, but he never took part. Well, I didn't think so."

Ana looked at her friend. They had so much to talk about, but most of that would have to wait until they got out of here.

"Why didn't you let me know where you'd gone? I was so worried."

Irena's eyes beseeched. "I'm sorry, but we had to keep quiet in case his bitch of a wife found out."

Ana drew back. Did she know Irena at all? "What possessed you to get involved with a married man?"

Irena shrugged. "She's never there. Leaves him all alone to handle the kids. All she cares about is jet-setting around the place, meeting her bigwig clients and living the high life. I lived there; saw how she speaks to him. Like she's his boss, just ordering him around. When she's there, he's tense, the kids are nightmares. Then she goes to her other life, and everything settles down. A few weeks later, she is back and the tension ramps up again."

Ana looked down at the colourful, flower-patterned duvet cover. She traced the outline of a lush poppy with her finger, thought of what words to use and decided just to let it out. "How did you end up at that club?"

She sensed Irena stiffen beside her, saw her go to speak and then close her mouth as if she was considering her words.

There was a creak from the hallway. He was walking about. Ana drew closer to Irena.

CHAPTER FORTY-THREE

The two unmarked cars parked in a street adjacent to the target property. Aidan Gillespie had insisted on accompanying them. As he had said, it was his property, his employee and he had been working with his brother. Le Claire had agreed on the strict understanding that he was there to show them the correct building. Gillespie had also had the idea of calling Adamson. "He is a money-grabbing swine. If I call him, he will answer. He always does."

Le Claire and Dewar were at the front of the building. Penny and two of her men had gone round the back. Gillespie was to stay with the driver of one of the cars and make the call. Le Claire and Dewar crouched by the solid front door. They glanced at each other as they heard the tell-tale ring of a mobile from inside the building. The plan was for Gillespie to tell Adamson he had an opportunity to make a killing on some apartments, but he needed to act quickly. If Adamson would come to him in the morning, there would be a big bonus in it for him.

Le Claire spoke into his radio in a whisper. "He's downstairs at the moment. Let's take it on three."

On the count of three, Le Claire opened the front door with the key given to him by Gillespie; at the same time, he heard a crash from the back of the house. Penny and her colleagues had broken in that way.

David Adamson came running out of a downstairs room. "What the…" He stopped when he saw Le Claire. One of the officers had pulled his Taser and aimed it at Adamson, who threw the phone he was holding at the officer's hand, causing just enough of a distraction for the Taser shot to go wide. Adamson was blocked in the hallway, but he ran up the stairs, two at a time, Le Claire and Dewar hard on his heels. By the time they reached the room at the end, he had Ana in an arm lock, a flick knife pressed against her throat. "Don't come closer. All you need to do is back off, and she lives."

Le Claire tried to communicate with his eyes that all would be well, silently telling Ana not to struggle.

"Careful, Adamson. Don't harm her. I won't hurt you."

"You're dead right about that. I'm in control, and no one takes what is mine. Right now, that's these two. So get yourself, and the others, out of here before I slash this one." He tightened his hold on Ana and kicked a leg toward Irena, catching her low in the stomach. She howled as she doubled over. He looked at her with contempt. "Her usefulness was coming to an end, but I think she just got a reprieve. I'll tell you what we'll do. You sod off out of here, and I'll let these two go. I've no real use for either."

Le Claire was amazed at Adamson's stupidity. Did he think he was going to get out of this? Out of the corner of his eye, he saw a brief movement. Irena lifted her head from the floor and looked at Adamson with loathing.

"You discard women easily."

"Only the worthless ones. There are some I'd have gone to the ends of the earth for." His voice shook. "But then they don't want you. They want their boring little, respectable lives."

Le Claire took the opening. "Was that what Laura did?"

"I would have done anything for her. I got rid of that fool, Scott. I had the perfect plan. All he had to do was dump Laura and I'd keep quiet about his precious mother."

He looked down at Ana and laughed. Ran the knife across her throat, not breaking skin, but he was threatening, menacing. Ana's eyes were wide, but she stayed still. Good. He didn't need any sudden movements to incite Adamson into something stupid. "He thought he could have her for good. She was too much of a woman for him. I had to put up with a ball-busting wife and poor imitations like this…" He threw his arm to the side and indicated Irena.

Le Claire edged closer. "And what about Katrina? She's dead, you know. Her body was found in a squat."

Adamson's voice was defensive and chillingly dismissive. "That's nothing to do with me. Stupid girl liked the pretty pills a bit too much. Some of the girls at the club got her onto harder stuff. She was useless to me when she was continually zoned out. So I told her she was on her own."

"And you got Irena to take her place?"

"Look, I gave her a home, a good job and a man by her side. I did nothing wrong"

"But she wasn't enough? Nor was your wife?"

"I wanted the real deal, and Laura would have turned to me if Scott didn't want her. I know her type. She can't live without a man to look after her and pull the shots."

And he kicked out at Irena again. Only this time she threw herself forward and, with a primeval howl that made Le Claire's hair stand on head, clamped her jaws around Adamson's leg, sinking her teeth into his calf.

He screeched in pain and loosened his hold enough for Ana to pull herself from his grasp. Le Claire pounced and dealt Adamson a vicious blow to the head. He went down, still screaming as Irena held his leg in a feral grip.

Ana and Irena were in hospital. Ana was suffering from shock. Irena's wounds, physical and mental, would run much deeper. Adamson was in holding, but Le Claire had something urgent to do before he went to see him.

He dialled the mobile number Ana had given him. The phone was quickly answered.

"Mrs Hamlyn, its DCI Le Claire."

"If you're calling at this time of night, I hope you've something good to tell me?"

"I'm in London at the moment, and we've apprehended Scott's killer. It was David Adamson."

"David! No, he was Scott's friend. I can't take this in. Why would he do that? Why?"

Her voice trailed off in an anguished sob. He could hear her talking to someone in the background. Her husband, no doubt.

"I'm afraid Adamson knew about you and Ana. From what I can gather, he was using the threat of discovery to force Scott to split up with Laura Brown."

Silence. Sarah Hamlyn was quiet, but he could hear her breathing. He was about to speak when she said, "And he wouldn't give her up. The bloody fool. I assume he was trying to pay David off. Oh sweet Jesus, the sins of the fathers and mothers."

"There's something else. Adamson held Ana captive tonight with her friend Irena. Both girls are in hospital now. Ana is unhurt but she has had a terrible shock and probably won't be released until tomorrow at the earliest. She asked if I could let you know she's at St Thomas' Hospital. I mean, you are her next of kin. As her aunt, I mean."

"Thank you for letting me know." Her voice was distant and cold.

He sighed, knew he had to warn her. "You won't be able to keep the past hidden. I'm afraid this will all come out."

"Oh, I've got myself accustomed to that over the last few days. Never fear."

CHAPTER FORTY-FOUR

Le Claire and Dewar had caught the morning flight back to Jersey. Adamson was locked up in London, and Penny and Gareth Lewis would sort through the minefield of paperwork and jurisdiction, for Adamson had committed serious crimes in both Jersey and London. Both went straight to work. There were matters that had to be dealt with.

Le Claire had just left a debriefing with the chief when Dewar came thundering in, bursting with excitement.

She had gone to inform Beth Adamson that her husband was under arrest and had received an unusual response.

"She is bouncing with rage. Apparently, the firm she works for in Panama runs the foundation. She uses her maiden name, Elizabeth Edwards, for work, and is one of the foundation council members. She thought it was for Aidan Gillespie to do charitable works through. Adamson must've set the whole thing up, forged signatures and everything. She had thought it was a bit suspicious with money coming in from all over the place and was going to talk to Adamson about it. He had blocked her from meeting Aidan Gillespie before, and she wanted to know why. I said there would need to be a full investigation of the foundation, and she said she's sure her boss will cooperate."

"She sounds very accommodating to our case. I wonder why?"

"Ah, seems she had to take the kids to the doctor. They weren't sleeping well and kept asking for their tonic."

"Tonic?"

"Yeah, Adamson must've been drugging them so they'd sleep through the night and he could get out and about to do whatever he needed. What a charmer."

"And cue the wife's rage. Good work."

"What now?"

286

"Now we try and build a case against Danny Gillespie for running paid sex parties, prostitution and, probably, drug dealing. For Adamson, we'll add in the murder of Scott Hamlyn, beating up Laura Brown, the kidnapping of Irena and Ana and being the bastard who led Katrina to her death, for at the very least he got her hooked on drugs."

"Can I go home and get changed first?" The cheeky quip had him laughing. Dewar joined in, and the tension of the last few days finally disappeared.

"Tell you what. Why don't you take the rest of the day off? I'm going to do the same. I've got something I need to do."

"So have I. See you later." Dewar left, and he sat alone, building up courage for his next task.

#

Laura turned toward the opening door and gave a weak smile as she recognised DS Dewar. She pressed her palms against the mattress as she slid up the bed and, exhausted from the slight effort, leaned back against the headboard. "Hello, this is a surprise, Detective Sergeant."

"Call me Dewar. Everybody does. How are you?"

"Okay, I guess. I came round properly last night, and Dr Foster says I should be out of here in a week, hopefully. I think they're being a bit protective."

"I've been told I've got five minutes and then they're chucking me out."

She laughed, wincing as a sharp pain lanced across her jaw. She tentatively touched the aching area.

"I guess you'll be sore for a while?"

"Yeah, and I won't be looking too pretty either. It's better than the alternative though. Dr Foster says you got the bastard."

"David Adamson? Oh yes, he's being held in London whilst his list of crimes is totted up. How did you know him?"

"Through Danny. I met Danny when I was fifteen and moved in with him the next day. A couple of years later and he'd introduced me to the finer things in life and a long line of men who were happy to look after me for a night, a week, maybe even a month. A few years after Danny and I split up, I bumped into Aidan. He never accepted what a shit Danny could be, but he saw the people I was with – a pretty fast set – and asked me to meet him for dinner the next night." A coughing fit overtook her and Dewar poured a glass of water from the bottle on the bedside unit. She wasn't using to talking so much. "I thought he wanted to be my protector for a little while. I turned up for dinner in a killer dress with a flirtatious attitude. Aidan swiftly put me right."

"He wasn't interested?"

"Not in the slightest." She laughed. If she was honest with herself, she'd been offended at how horrified he'd been when he realised what she thought he was after. "Instead, he offered me a lifeline."

"Your job?"

"Yes. It took me a few days to accept, but then I realised that this was one of those rare opportunities that could reshape my life. So I said yes and went to work for his promotions company."

"We wondered about that. The company was owned by another non-UK company, and the trail stopped there."

"Aidan doesn't like people to know his business."

"Where does Adamson come into the picture?"

"Danny slowly came back into my life. Not how it was before. He'd just turn up at work sometimes, teasing, but with an edge. I hadn't considered that working for Aidan would bring him back into my life. He said he was having a party and wanted to know if I would come. It was an organised orgy. He holds these parties, gets people to pay for the privilege of attending, and then blackmails the shit out of them." She let her eyes close. Funny, it didn't make the shame go away. "He paid me to attend. I guess old habits die hard."

"Is that where you met Scott?"

"That was later. I met David Adamson. To my shame, I took drugs again. I know it doesn't excuse my actions, but I was numbed; everything was blurred. I went with David that night. It was brutal, and I've kept away from him ever since."

Compassion was shining out of Dewar's eyes. It made Laura feel even more ashamed at the woman she'd been for so long. "And Scott? How did that happen?"

"I wouldn't go to any more parties. Danny begged me, just one more time. Said I wouldn't have to do anything. Just be there and look pretty. I agreed, and that's where I met Scott."

Dewar's mouth fell open. "You met him at one of the sex parties?"

"Yeah, funny, I know. David had invited him. Poor Scott was like a fish out of water. He'd gone along to please his friend and been horrified by what he saw. It was a casual thing to begin with between us. I didn't know it until much later, but Danny was making Scott pay a 'monthly fee' for me. I was raging. I wasn't his to sell. Scott carried on paying once we were properly together. Said it was so they'd keep their mouths shut and wouldn't have a hold over me. I had pretty much told him everything."

"But Adamson wouldn't let it be?"

Her skin chilled as she thought of the lengths he had gone to secure her. "He suddenly got even friendlier with Scott. Popping in for a drink, usually when I was there. His eyes would undress me, and he'd make lewd remarks whenever Scott was out of the room. I ignored him, thought he was a harmless fool."

"Why did you go and see Aidan Gillespie the night of the party?"

"Danny was playing up again. He kept phoning me all the time about doing some work. I knew Aidan could keep him in order. I just wanted to be left in peace."

"And now?"

Laura shook her head. "I don't know. Paul Armstrong has been to see me. When I'm out of here, he'll help me with the finances part. You know, selling the apartment and everything."

"Will you keep your job at the promotions agency?"

"No, I can't work for Aidan anymore. It's unhealthy to be around any of the Gillespies. I think I might travel for a bit. Work out what I want to do." And who she needed to be. She had spent a lifetime being what other people wanted. Now it was down to her.

Dewar stood. "We'll send someone to take a proper statement when you're feeling up to it. Good luck, Laura."

As the door closed, Laura sank back into the mattress. There was a stabbing pain in her jaw, her right eye wouldn't yet open properly and every single part of her ached. But she was alive, and she was going to make that count in future. She lay down and daydreamed of second chances and new beginnings, only it wasn't a dream, it was her reality.

Dewar headed for the exit and was almost at the main doors when she heard her name called. She turned and saw David Viera making his way toward her, his long legs covering the distance between them with ease.

"I didn't realise you were back. I was at the station this morning, and Vanguard said that you guys had closed the Hamlyn case."

She ran a hand through her hair, smoothing it a little. Quite irrationally, she wondered if she had put on mascara this morning. "Yeah. We need to get everything tied up, but we've got David Adamson for Scott Hamlyn's death. Adamson is also in cahoots with Danny Gillespie for just about everything else."

There was a brief silence. Viera looked down at her through the thick lashes that surrounded his chocolate eyes. He maintained contact far longer than was appropriate, then cleared his throat. "Did you get my text?"

She kept her voice even. "Yes, I did. Sorry, I didn't have a chance to reply. I was just busy."

She hadn't known how to respond. Viera's text message had been innocuous enough; just hoping that all was going well in London. However, Viera had never contacted her before, and she didn't even know how he'd got her number. She certainly didn't know why he had reached out to her.

He ran his hands through his hair and the silky locks stood on end. He glanced to the side and then those soft eyes locked on hers. "Look, I've been thinking. Well, wondering actually. Would you like to…"

A high-pitched female voice cut across his words. "David, there you are. We're late for the meeting. Hurry up; Dr Wells will be spitting blood, not analysing it, if we aren't there on time."

A pretty red-head, dressed in a tight, fitted dress and matching jacket, hooked her arm through Viera's and started to pull him away. She nodded at Dewar. "Sorry to break up your chat but we'll get a tongue-lashing if we don't get a move on."

"Sure, no problem. See you around, Viera." Dewar shrugged and turned to the exit. She smiled to herself as Viera's deep voice floated behind her.

"Take care of yourself. I'll be in touch."

#

Ana awoke after a restless night. She had lain awake for hours as she tried to piece together what had happened and understand the last few weeks.

She threw a hospital-issue robe on, which matched the plain cotton nightdress, and tiptoed out of her room. The ward reception desk was manned by a sweet-faced nurse who beamed at her. "How are you today?"

"I feel okay. I mean, I'm not hurt."

"Not that can be seen, but we needed to check for delayed shock. What can I do for you?"

"I need to know if my friend is okay, Irena Kobus."

The nurse quickly checked the notes. "She's in the private room at the end and has just had some breakfast. Why don't you go and find out how she is for yourself?"

Irena was sitting up in bed, remote in hand as she flicked through the TV channels. She grinned when she saw Ana and then immediately held a hand to her face. "Ow, that hurts. The swine kicked me right on the jawbone. Pig!"

Ana laughed. "I see you're as feisty as ever. I'm glad."

"Yeah, well, what else can I do? It's heart-wrenching to know you've been used as a substitute for someone else. I bet the wig he made me wear was just like that woman's hair. Laura, they called her."

Ana didn't know what to say to that. She figured that out of anything that had happened, this betrayal was what hurt Irena the most. "David Adamson is a piece of work. No one saw through him. The only person who knew how despicable he was is Danny Gillespie, and he obviously had reasons to keep quiet."

Irena spoke, her eyes downcast. "I don't know what to say about my behaviour. The drugs gave me a warped sense of reality. Things I would never have done before suddenly seemed exciting, and I just wanted to please him. What kind of fool am I?"

Ana couldn't answer. It was down to Irena to work through and accept her past behaviour in all its tawdriness before moving on. "What are you going to do now?"

Irena snorted. "I'm not staying in London, that's for sure. I think I might go home, you know. Lick my wounds and decide what's next. How about you?"

"I don't know. I went to Jersey to find my family, and with Scott gone, there seems little to keep me there."

A deep voice broke in from the doorway. "And here's me thinking I'd made an impression on you."

Ana spun round. Ben was leaning against the doorjamb, two huge bouquets of flowers in his arms. He handed one to Ana and placed the other on the table by the side of Irena's bed. "I got these in the hospital shop. Hope they're okay."

Irena smiled. "These are lovely. Thanks." She looked a little closer at Ben. "Haven't I seen you somewhere before?"

"I think we met in one of the bars in St Helier. You were with Daria; she had a fling with Danny once." He turned to Ana. "I wonder what'll happen to her now. I mean, will the agency close if the Davies' get imprisoned?"

Ana saw Irena's puzzled look and quickly interjected. "I'll tell you all about that later."

Irena lay back on her pillows. "There's more? I'm exhausted as it is."

"Then we better leave you alone. Come on, Ben."

Ben dutifully followed Ana back to her room.

There was a sink in the corner, and she busied herself carefully placing the flowers in water.

"Ana, I can't say how sorry I am about Scott and that he died at the hands of a supposed friend. As for Danny, I'm ashamed to be related to him. Aidan is in pieces, but I think the blinkers have finally fallen off. He said he'll pay for a good defence lawyer, but after that he doesn't want anything to do with Danny for a long time."

She plucked at the dressing gown tie. "It just feels pretty weird that you're connected to all this, even peripherally. I've been thinking maybe I should move somewhere else. There's not much in Jersey for me."

He was right next to her before she'd even finished speaking. "There is. Look, Aidan's deal went through. He's sold the clubs and is out of that business entirely. I'll be living full-time in Jersey, with just the occasional business trip. Aidan had nothing to do with any of this, and nor did I. Give me a chance. Spend time with me; let me show you what life can be like."

"But I only came to Jersey to be with my mother's family, and the only one of them who gave a damn about me is dead."

"Maybe I can be your family in time." He ran his fingers through his hair, leaving a rumpled mess. She wanted to reach out and smooth it but didn't.

"What do you say? Will you be my girlfriend?" The look on his face was like that of an anxious five-year-old.

"I thought I already was!" She reached up, wrapped her arms around his neck and pulled him down until his mouth touched hers. She whispered against his lips, "Why don't you show me how you treat your girlfriend?"

His eyes darkened, he crushed her to him as his mouth caught hers and he deepened the kiss until Ana couldn't think.

It took a moment for her to realise that there was a voice speaking, a familiar voice. She pulled away from Ben and turned round. Charles and Sarah Hamlyn stood in the open doorway. Her aunt was uncharacteristically quiet as Charles spoke. "Sorry to barge in on you. Le Claire let us know what happened, and we got the first flight from Jersey this morning."

Ana was confused. Why on earth were they here? "Have you heard that they've caught Scott's killer?"

"Yes." He looked at Ben. "From that display, I assume you're Ana's boyfriend, or you better be. Come with me, son." He backed out the door, followed by a puzzled Ben. "Sarah has something to say to you, Ana. It may take a while, so call us when you're finished."

CHAPTER FORTY-FIVE

Le Claire parked his car in the covered space outside his wife's house. Her delighted father had bought it for Sasha when she'd left London – and her husband – behind. It had turned chillier, and he could hear the waves crashing against the seawall. Only the best locations for his father-in-law.

Sasha opened the door before he could ring the bell. "You got my text, then? Come on in."

He'd sent her a message in the early hours saying he'd be back in the island in the morning. She replied that he should come and see her. They needed to talk. He'd smiled at the dreaded words. He couldn't wait to speak with her, to make her understand.

He followed her through to the open-plan kitchen and watched as she poured him coffee. His mouth was dry and his throat tight. He swallowed. "Sasha, let me explain."

She held up a hand and shushed him. "Jack, you're a bloody fool. You wouldn't recognise a predatory female if she bit you on the bum. And that's what bloody Penny Powers is. That cow knew it was me when she answered your phone. Well, I've been thinking, and I'm not giving her the satisfaction."

Hope fluttered. "What do you mean?"

"I mean that I'm sick of us dancing around each other. We're either together or not." She paused, and he held his breath. "And I'm for us being together, Jack. I want you to move in here. Don't say a word – we can move later if you hate living in a house my dad gave me. I don't care. I just want us back to normal. I want to wake up with you in the morning and sleep with you at night. I even want to feel peeved when you miss dinner because you're on a case. I want our life back."

The fierceness left her. She looked away. "Well, what do you think?"

He held her to him, raining butterfly kisses over her hair, her face. "I think I'll go and pack my stuff straightaway and then come back here and live with my wife."

He knew he had to be completely honest with her. "However, we might be facing a rocky time. I've heard from Lewis. Chapman is claiming innocence, police brutality and coercion. All aimed at me."

Sasha grabbed his hands, held them tight. "That's ridiculous, Jack, and no one will believe that maniac. But we can weather whatever he throws at us."

He kissed her, long and slow. "I better go get my stuff. I'll be staying here tonight."

"I'll come with you and help." She made to pull away, but he held her tight.

He smiled. "I'm sure you will, Sasha, but first let me see if I fit my new bed." He pulled her after him as he moved toward the stairs. "You better come with me. The testing might take a while."

THE END

<<<<>>>>

About the Author

Kelly Clayton lives in Jersey with her husband and several cats. An avid storyteller, Kelly has been writing for over twenty years but was driven to finish her first novel, *Blood In The Sand*, for a dear friend. Once finished Kelly realised she couldn't stop and several more novels are in production.

If you have enjoyed *Blood Ties,* please leave a review on Amazon. Kelly would be immensely grateful for your taking the time to do so.

Please also visit www.kellyclaytonbooks.com for updates on Kelly's books and for posts on starting, writing and finishing your own novel.

Acknowledgements

"Write with the door closed, re-write with the door open."
Stephen King

I would like to thank the many people who have helped me with this novel and been so incredibly supportive.

Jennifer Quinlan (Jenny Q of Historical Editorial) is my first set of "eyes" and her keen sense of story development keeps me firmly on track and opens up new possibilities. Jenny is also a fabulous copy-editor and always goes the extra mile in everything she does.

Thank you to Christine Wasilewski, Murray and Anna Norton and Paul and Gosia Watson for suggesting the surnames for three of my characters. Very much appreciated.

To Claire, Ann, Elaine, Pam and Suzie – my amazing beta readers. Thank you for taking the time to read, to comment and to help me shape and improve Blood Ties.

Heartfelt thanks to Simon Crowcroft for casting his eye over the "almost" finished book, and for providing such valuable feedback.

Much gratitude to Wendy Leedham for helping with my research at such short notice, and to Andy Daghorn for Misty's name.

Many thanks also to Chief Officer Mike Bowron and Karl Chapman of the States of Jersey Police who helped me with my usual list of what I am sure are quite stupid questions! Any mistakes are mine and mine alone.

I am hugely grateful to Kit Foster Design for yet again designing my amazing cover and Dean Fetzer of GunBoss Books for beautiful, stress-free formatting and layouts.

Many thanks to the wonderful readers of my first book, Blood In The Sand, whose feedback encouraged me write more about Jack Le Claire.

Finally, to my husband Grant, who is my number one fan and supporter. I simply could not do this without your understanding and patience. I love you.

Printed in Great Britain
by Amazon